Also by Kim Redford

Smokin' Hot Cowboys
A Cowboy Firefighter for Christmas
Blazing Hot Cowboy
A Very Cowboy Christmas
Hot for a Cowboy

D0029261

COWBOY FIREFIGHTER

CHRISTMAS

Kiss

WITHDRAWN

KIM REDFORD

sourcebooks
casablanca

Published by Sourcebooks Casablanca, an imprint of Sourcebooks
P.O. Box 4410, Naperville, Illinois 60567-4410
(630) 961-3900
sourcebooks.com

Printed and bound in the United States of America.
OPM 10 9 8 7 6 5 4 3 2 1

Chapter 1

"THERE'S NEVER A DULL MOMENT IN LIFE, NOT WITH sister Fern stirring it up," Ivy Bryant said to the silent walls of one of the oldest dance halls in Texas. She did a little twirl on the scuffed, slat-wood floor as if she had a dance partner. Wildcat Hall might not be as famous as Gruene Hall in the Hill Country, but her honky-tonk had a sterling reputation in Wildcat Bluff County.

"And Fern promised she'd stay put this time." Ivy thrust out her arms to both sides and twirled harder in the center of the large room that had rows of long, narrow, handmade wooden tables with matching benches placed on each side of the dance floor. "Famous last words of a rolling stone. Do I really believe her, or do I just want to believe her?"

She stopped, let her arms fall to her sides, and looked with a kind of wonder toward a recessed, raised stage and hand-painted backdrop. "In Houston, I'd be designing websites by day and enjoying my friends at night. Here, I'm still designing websites by day but running a honky-tonk at night."

She chuckled, still feeling surprised at the turn her life had taken. She was here to manage Wildcat Hall Park, dance hall and cowboy cabins, but she hardly believed it, because what did she know about running the place? It was now all hers—or at least the 51 percent her sister didn't own, but Fern was away on a gig for who knew how long, putting the ball in Ivy's court while she was gone.

She put her fists on her hips as she glanced from the stage to the other end of the dance floor at the long bar that served munchies, beer, and wine. Two open windows allowed bartenders to service customers on the dance hall side and on the front bar side at the same time. It seemed to her that it was a practical setup, although she was certainly no expert.

She walked into the front bar through an open doorway. For her, this room was the heart and soul of Wildcat Hall, and she relished the cozy, old-fashioned ambience that had nurtured folks for well over a hundred years.

Decor was minimal. Rusty metal beer advertisement signs had been tacked around the walls, along with sepia-toned photographs of cowboys on horseback and country music legends. A framed Lone Star State flag hung in back of the bar while a rack of deer antlers loomed above the double front doors.

Ivy glanced at the tattered cardboard box of Christmas decorations that she'd found in a storeroom. Businesses were already putting up holiday decor, so she didn't want the Hall to be left behind. She pulled out a long string of red tinsel, walked over to the antlers, and tossed the strand upward. It fell back down. She needed a ladder, but she hadn't found one yet. She picked up the tinsel and tossed again. No luck.

As she gazed at the antlers with a skeptical eye, she heard a truck pull up outside. By now, folks should've heard the honky-tonk was closed for a week while she figured out how to manage it. Even if the front door was unlocked, since she'd been running in and out, there was a big sign with bright red letters on the door that read CLOSED. No need for folks even to get out of their pickups.

She looped the tinsel around her neck, picked up a straight-back chair from under a table, and set the chair under the antlers. Now she was getting somewhere. She stood on the seat, adjusting her stance to keep her balance while the chair wobbled on uneven legs. She lifted the strand as high as she could manage, but she still couldn't drape it around the antlers. The Hall's high ceilings made for good airflow, along with an impressive historical statement. Not as big a statement as fancy honky-tonks like Billy Bob's Texas in the Fort Worth stockyards, with 127,000 square feet of boot-scooting space or the famous Longhorn Ballroom in Dallas with 20,000 square feet. But Wildcat Hall was plenty spacious with 4,000 square feet inside and room for more in a large beer garden with picnic tables outside.

She just wished the Hall had the tourist draw of those two famous places, but a major destination attraction and music venue could be built with the right promotion and entertainment. Still, she was getting ahead of herself. For the moment, she just needed to put up a few decorations to add Christmas cheer to the place.

As she stood on her tiptoes with arms raised again, she heard the side door that led to the beer garden open and boots hit the floor with a determined stride.

"We're closed!" she hollered, not bothering to look over her shoulder. "Come back next week."

"You look like you could use a little help."

She froze with her hands in the air as she felt the deep male voice with that melodic, slow cadence of a born-and-bred Texan strike her body and go deep, as if she'd been pierced by a flaming arrow. Talk about red-hot. She tried to shrug off the heat, but the chair shifted under her, making her sway.

"Easy does it," he said. "Chairs have a way of pretending they're bulls sometimes."

"Bulls?" She didn't know whether to laugh at the joke or appreciate he'd tried to make her feel better about almost toppling to the floor. Still and all, if she'd known she was going to have company, she'd have put on something besides formfitting yoga pants and top in hot pink with black trim. He was getting an eyeful.

"In my case, I always tried to pretend bulls were chairs."

"How'd that work out?" She eyed the antlers, mind half on her next throw and half on the amusing man behind her.

"About like you can imagine." He sighed, as if life had been unfair. "I finally had to give up bulls for chairs."

"I bet the bulls were grateful." She definitely wanted to see the face that went with the voice, but she wanted to finish her task more.

"Yeah...but I've broken a few chairs."

"Maybe even my chair."

"Looks like it's keeping an uneasy peace with the floor."

"That's one way of putting it." She rose to her tiptoes again, trying one last time to get the tinsel to disobey the laws of gravity.

"Let me help." He spanned her waist with large hands and lifted her so she could easily reach the antlers.

She caught her breath in surprise at his strength—and his boldness. But she wasn't looking a gift horse in the mouth. She quickly twined the antlers with red tinsel until they looked festive for the holidays.

"Pretty," he said.

She shivered in response. What had gotten into her? She should be struggling to get away. Instead, he was revving her up with his hot hands.

"Got any more tinsel to put up?" he asked in a deep voice gone husky. "I could hold you all day and into next week."

"I suggest you put me down before you get into trouble."

"If you're the one handing out trouble, I'd wait in line to get it."

She couldn't help but chuckle because he was laying it on thick in that teasing way Texas men had when they were getting themselves out of trouble with women. "Better put me down before your arms give out."

"Not a chance. You're light as a feather."

She laughed harder. "Guess some women would fall for that one. What are you selling?"

"As a matter of fact, I'm here to help you, but you might consider it selling to you, too." He gently set her down so her feet were steady on the floor, and then he stepped back.

She turned to face him—and felt her breath catch in her throat at the tall hunk of a cowboy.

He wore pressed Wranglers that accentuated his long legs and narrow hips, with a wide leather belt sporting a huge rodeo belt buckle. His blue-and-white-striped, pearl-snap shirt tucked neatly into the waistband of his jeans emphasized the width of his shoulders and breadth of his chest. Blond-haired. Blue-eyed. Square-jawed. Full-lipped. He looked as if he'd been made to dazzle—and she was suddenly and breathtakingly susceptible to every single one of his charms.

"Whatever you're selling, I think I'm buying." She spoke the words with a teasing lilt in her voice and a mischievous smile on her face. Still, she meant it. And he probably knew it because he was definitely heartbreaker material. How many women had already fallen to his charms and been left in the dust? She didn't intend to be a notch on his belt, but if she'd known leaving the city for the country paid off so well in eye candy, she might've followed her sister sooner.

He chuckled at her words and held out his hand with a thick, muscular wrist that came from controlling thousand-pound-plus beasts. "Slade Steele. If you haven't heard of me, maybe you're aware of the Chuckwagon Café and Steele Trap Ranch. Family businesses. I'm not just any guy off the street."

"You're definitely not just any guy." She slipped her hand into his big one and felt him gently enclose her fingers.

"And you're definitely good for my ego," he said with a smile as he let his gaze drop all the way down the length of her and back up to her face. "I thought your sister was lovely and bright and talented, but you leave her in the shade."

"Smart guy to throw a few compliments my way. Guess you're more than a pretty face." She tried to keep the teasing going, so their interaction stayed on a light note, but he was still holding her hand and she wasn't pulling away and his eyes were heating up to a blazing blue fire.

"Nothing but the truth."

"Fern is the star." She tried to tug her hand away, but he held on another long moment, nodding—as if he were deciding or accepting something—before finally letting go.

He grinned with a gleam in his eyes, revealing teeth white against the tan of his skin. "Yeah, she is that...but you make the earth move."

"Oh my." She returned his grin while fanning her face with

one hand in that old Southern way, as if he was too hot to handle. "You really do want to sell me something, don't you?"

"How am I doing?"

"Not bad." She pivoted and walked away from him, intentionally putting the heat they were generating behind her. She wasn't in Wildcat Bluff for a guy. She was here to salvage her financial investment. She had to keep that fact firmly in mind because she was city, not country, and she was here only as long as it took to take care of business. A good-looking, fast-talking cowboy wasn't anywhere on her agenda, particularly one who might slow down her getaway.

"How is Fern?"

"My sister is always okay." She leaned her elbows on top of the bar and resisted a long sigh because she'd been here before—one too many times. She heard Slade approach, noticing for the first time the unevenness of his step, as if he limped from an injury. She wondered how he'd been hurt, thinking how he'd mentioned bulls, but knew it'd be rude to ask. She glanced over at him, deciding to get the explaining over as quickly as possible.

"She left without a word," he said quietly but intently, almost accusingly.

"That's Fern." She turned around and leaned back against the edge of the bar and propped a heel on the long runner. "I suppose she left broken hearts and broken dreams behind her."

"Something like that."

"If it helps, it's not personal. She's a singer, so she's a rolling stone." Ivy took a closer look at him, feeling a sudden tightness in her chest. "I hope you aren't one of the—"

"Not me. But there is a guy. Craig Thorne. Singing

cowboy. They performed together on the Hall's stage. He thought they had something special."

"Guys always do, bless their hearts." She glanced over as Slade leaned his elbows on the bar. "She must've liked this Craig more than a little if she picked up and ran that hard that fast."

"I doubt he'd agree, but she did leave things in a muddle."

"That's where I come in." Ivy turned toward him. "My parents named us well. I'm the ivy that holds everything together, while she's the fern that spreads up and out."

He nodded, glanced around at the room, then back. "So, what do you plan to do here?"

"I'm considering my options."

"Folks are wondering about Fern…about the sister who showed up to take her place…and about Wildcat Hall."

"Fern ought to be back at some point."

"Will she?"

"That's the plan, but you never know about the timing. Right now, she's entertaining on a cruise ship."

"We all thought she was dedicated to preserving and expanding Wildcat Hall."

"Y'all aren't the only ones. It's always been her dream to own a venue where she could nurture country musicians."

"Heard that. Plus, Bill and Ida Murphy hooked up with her on a genealogy website and discovered they were long-lost cousins. The Hall always belonged to somebody in their family. Otherwise, they'd never have sold to an out-sider. Lots of folks in our county would've stepped up for Wildcat Hall to preserve it because it's been the center of community life here from the get-go."

"Guess y'all were surprised when strangers took over.

I helped finance her dream, but I'd intended to be a silent partner. Now—"

"I got it. But if you're anything like your sister—"

"Not so much."

He nodded again, considering her with watchful, blue eyes.

"I'd appreciate it if you'd let folks know I'm here to take care of Wildcat Hall."

"Will do." He cleared his throat. "I came over because... well, it'd be good to generate more interest in the Hall."

"I agree." She smiled, cocking her head to let him know she was listening even as she decided he took up way too much physical space and created way too much heat for her to be easy in his presence. She didn't need a too-hot cowboy disturbing her already disturbed thoughts. She needed to think straight so she could get a handle on what she was going to do with the honky-tonk.

"Good." He rapped the top of the bar with his knuckles, glanced around, and refocused on her. "Place is still good but stale. Christmas is coming up. It'll take more than a few prayers to put Wildcat Hall on the map again."

"Maybe a sound marketing strategy?"

"That, too." He smiled with a teasing glint in his blue eyes. "If you'll let me, I'll be glad to help out. I have a few ideas."

She returned his smile, feeling his magnetism tug at her, stoking fires she'd thought long gone. She could see how he'd be the perfect answer to a lonely lady's prayers, but she needed something else from him. "Do tell."

Chapter 2

SLADE STEELE TRIED TO THINK PAST HIS LUST. IVY BRYANT was dynamite. He'd lit her fuse and got scorched clear to the bone. Now she watched him expectantly with slightly slanted eyes that reminded him of a cat waiting for cream. He'd better give her something good or chance losing her—something he wasn't willing to contemplate. But how was he supposed to think past a fantasy of feather pillows, satin sheets, and her spread out before him like a feast for the senses?

He didn't want to talk. He wanted to let down her thick, auburn hair so he could run his fingers through the silky strands. He'd caress every single curve of her body before he stripped away all her clothes to reveal peaches-and-cream skin.

"Did you change your mind about what you wanted to tell me?" Ivy asked with a hint of impatience in her husky voice.

He felt his fantasy disintegrate like morning mist over a lake. He was reluctant to let his vision go, but he had to set it aside till later. Right now, he needed to persuade her to work with him—not only for his own marketing benefit, but so he could keep an eye on how she handled Wildcat Hall. He'd been all business when he'd opened the door, but it had turned personal the moment he'd laid eyes on her.

"You have ideas for Wildcat Hall?" She leaned toward him as she focused her attention on his face. "Maybe you discussed something with Fern."

"Right." He shook his head to clear it. "I suppose you haven't been in town long enough to learn much about local businesses."

"Fern told me a little about the community." She eyed him with interest. "Wait a minute. She mentioned adding to the snack foods. Are you that award-winning pie baker?"

He nodded at the moniker, comparing it to how he'd once been known on the rodeo circuit as the bull rider to beat. No more. Not since he got busted up. But that was in the past and so was all the glory—and the cowgirls—that went with it. Now he stayed busy with one project piled on top of another to keep the memories at bay, but sometimes in the middle of the night, he'd remember what it'd been like to be in prime condition and on top of the world. That was when he'd have swaggered into the life of a red-hot gal like Ivy without a second thought, expecting her to fall quick and hard for him. No more. He'd be lucky if he could bribe her with pies even to talk to him while he imagined so much more in his fantasies.

"Do you want to serve pie here? Is that your idea?"

At her words, he fell back to reality hard—like coming off the back of a bull. "It's one idea. Right now, the Hall has packaged snacks and drinks. That's it."

"Fern mentioned she was thinking of expanding the food line, but I'm concerned it'll add more problems than benefits."

"Not if it's done right."

"How so?"

"What do you see?" He gestured around the room filled with tables and chairs.

"Simple and stark furnishings."

"That's the way it's always been, and that's the way people like it. Wildcat Hall looks a lot like the simplicity of Gruene Hall, and nobody complains about that standout honky-tonk."

"Gruene is in a class all its own."

"So is the Hall. Here's my point. The dance hall opens out into the beer garden. Folks like beer, water, or a glass of wine there. Snacks are good, too, like the prepackaged dried sausage, chips, and nuts that you already serve."

She nodded in agreement, watching him with interest.

"This front area has been a community gathering place since 1884 when it was first built. Folks get together after work, after events, and even after fighting fires to let off a little steam and catch up on local news. The Hall can also be rented for special events like weddings and reunions."

"You're thinking we could offer more options?"

"You probably wouldn't want to change what you serve in the dance hall, but in here, why not add to the menu?"

"It'd generate more income, wouldn't it?" She glanced behind the bar. "But there aren't any cooking facilities inside, are there?"

"Right. Fern and I discussed it and decided it wouldn't be worth putting in a kitchen. At least not right away."

"I'd prefer not to sink any more money here than necessary."

"The Hall's pretty solidly built. I don't think that's an issue. Those rental cowboy cabins might be another story. Have you seen them?"

"I moved into the main cabin Fern was living in, but I haven't checked anything beyond what I saw when we bought the place."

"Cabins might need some work but probably not much." He took a deep breath, organizing his thoughts again because he kept getting distracted by her green eyes, peach-tinted lips, and single dimple in her left cheek.

"I plan to focus on the Hall first."

"Good. Bottom line, I could prepare food at the Chuckwagon Café and deliver it here."

"That'd be convenient. It's an interesting idea if we could come to terms so we both make a profit." She leaned toward him, thoughtfully tracing the bar top with her fingertips.

"I'm sure we could work out something. I'm thinking you could offer coffee and pie." He looked at those long fingers of hers, thought about them touching his skin—and the fire he'd banked down to embers suddenly seared him. He pulled his collar away from his neck, trying to get some relief from the heat.

"I like the idea." She cast him a slow smile. "But do you have time?"

"I'll make time. What about cookies?"

"Those sounds good, too."

"I'm thinking something simple like Texas tea cakes and cowboy cookies."

"What are those?"

"Texas tea cakes are the old Southern type of sugar cookies. To make cowboy cookies, I might add extra ingredients to the recipe and whiskey to the dough."

She chuckled, smiling in delight. "Those would go well with coffee, too. For the holidays, I'd like to see the cookies decorated in Christmas colors."

"Sounds good. What about one night a week, or more often, you serve chili or stew or something else that goes well with cornbread but is still simple and easy to serve as well as clean up?"

"I like it, but I'm concerned it'll require servers. Cookies and pieces of pie could be picked up at the bar along with drinks."

"Fern and I discussed letting folks serve themselves from a big vat of chili kept warm on a sideboard."

"That might work."

"Glad you think so." He was encouraged that she liked his ideas. He hadn't known what kind of person he'd find when he got here, but Ivy was way ahead of his expectations in more ways than one.

"Let me give it some thought."

"Okay...speaking of Fern." He wished she'd just waltz in the front door even though he knew she couldn't do it. "I still can't believe she just up and left with so many plans and so many people she'd gotten involved to help put Wildcat Hall on the map as a destination honky-tonk."

"You aren't the first one to feel that way." She pointed at her chest. "Take a number and get behind me. I'm always first in line. Not that I don't love every little bit of my sister, but music comes first in her life and always will. She simply received an offer for a gig she couldn't refuse, and off she went."

"Well, there's a long line of folks behind you now." He looked at her, wondering if she had what it took to pull off what had come so easily to her sister. "Are you up for dealing with this community?"

"Excellent question." She leaned forward, then tugged her hair out of a ponytail holder, stretched the hot pink band around one wrist, and let down her thick mane, which fell past her neck to settle like a curtain just below her shoulder blades.

He felt lightheaded at the sight as he caught the scent of lavender that wafted from her hair and enveloped him like a springtime field of delicate flowers. He fisted his hands to keep from snatching her up against him and burying his face in her hair and cuddling her so close there was nothing between them.

She leaned forward, massaged her scalp with both hands, and then tossed her hair back as she raised her head and stared into the distance.

"I could help you with that massage."

She gave a low groan as she slowly turned to look at him. "Thanks for the offer, but I think I'll pass."

"It's always open."

"Good to know." She gave him a little negative shake of her head with a wry smile, sending tendrils of hair across her face.

He reached out—couldn't stop himself—and gently clasped those loose strands and slowly tucked them behind her ear. Feeling the softness of her skin against the back of his knuckles hit him hard. If he didn't back off, he was going to make a move that'd get him banned from Wildcat Hall for all eternity. He was already skating on thin ice. For the life of him, he couldn't remember ever being struck so fast, so hard, like a bolt of lightning, by any other woman. And wouldn't you just know it'd come when he was past his prime and she was in her prime?

"I'm not outgoing like Fern. I'm used to spending my days in front of my computer, designing websites and doing most of my communication through emails. This is all going to be one-on-one, isn't it?"

"Pretty much."

She lowered her face into her hands, moaning in frustration.

On second thought, maybe he had a chance. Maybe she could get what she needed—from him. And who knew where the situation might lead? "I'll help you. I know everybody. They're good people."

She raised her head and looked at him with hope in her pale green eyes. "Will you? I mean, you're already going to bake pies and cookies. Maybe cook chili. I'll feel guilty if I take up any more of your time. Didn't you mention a ranch? That's bound to be time intensive."

"It's a lot of work, but my mom and sister do their part, too. Plus, ranch hands carry the main load." He gave her an encouraging smile. "Anyway, I volunteered, didn't I?"

"Yes, but—"

"Look, we'll find a way to make the Hall work. Only thing, I've got a major commitment coming up."

"Not a wedding…I mean, a social event?" she said, sounding flustered and embarrassed at her words.

He grinned, feeling hope well up in his chest that she was wondering about his marital status. "Nothing social. I'm not engaged or going with anybody."

"Oh." She looked down at her hands. "I'm not either."

"That's good. Real good." Maybe he had a chance after all. He felt his spirits lift at the prospect of getting what he wanted, as well as what he needed—from her. "It's a cattle drive."

"Cattle drive? I didn't know cowboys did those anymore."

"Not too much, but they're still around. In this case, we recently bought Mr. Werner's ranch from his descendants.

Hated to lose him, but he'd gotten up there in years. He gave his pristine 1959 Cadillac to my sister, Sydney, and he wanted my family to take over his ranch. We were able to meet the price, so now we're in the process of getting it up and running after he let it dwindle down the last few years."

"That sounds like a lot of work."

"True, but worth it. We're calling the new ranch Steele Trap II, since it'll be in the family, but I'll be living there and running it."

She nodded but looked puzzled. "Congratulations on the new ranch, but what does it have to do with a cattle drive?"

"Oh yeah. We're going to move three hundred head of Angus cattle from our old ranch to our new one. Not far, like the old cattle drives, since it'll only be about five miles, but it'll still take the same stuff to get the job done."

"Do you have enough cowboys?"

He chuckled, glancing out a window as if he could see the situation. "No problem with that. Most every cowboy and cowgirl in the county wants to be part of it."

She joined his laughter. "You've got to admit it sounds like fun and once-in-a-lifetime opportunity."

"That's it. DJs Wildcat Jack and Eden are talking it into a big event on our local radio station."

"Why are they doing that?"

"It's smart because it helps promote our Christmas events. Wildcat Bluff hosts Christmas in the Country, while over in Sure-Shot they stage Christmas at the Sure-Shot Drive-In. Folks come in from out of town. We have a lot of family fun. And it's a boost to our economy." He gazed at her, thinking about the upcoming festivities. "Christmas is my favorite time of year."

"I like it, too. But why is it your favorite?"

"It's winter, so there's not quite as much ranch work. We get to spend more time with family and friends."

"Don't forget lots of good food like we'll serve at the Hall."

"And gifts." He smiled, liking her excitement about the season. "What do you want for Christmas?"

"I just want Wildcat Hall to do well."

"I don't doubt that it will. Did you know the Hall is on the old cattle trail we'll be taking, so Fern planned to serve snacks and drinks to the drovers? Wildcat Jack and Eden want livestreaming on KWCB from right here."

"Oh my." Ivy put fingertips to her lips. "I'm getting in way over my head. Fern is perfect for this type of event. Not me."

"I bet you've got more of your sister in you than you think."

"I'm a behind-the-camera type of person. Fern is the one who gets out there and makes people happy."

"Remember, I said I'd help you." He held out his hand to her, hoping she'd take it, hoping she'd trust him to get her through the coming days, hoping she'd come to see him as more than a strong shoulder to lean on.

She looked up, down, all around, then finally gazed steadily at him with determination in her green eyes. And clasped his hand.

Chapter 3

"I SAID I'D HELP YOU, AND I WILL, BUT THERE COULD BE A glitch in our plans," Slade said with narrowed eyes.

"Oh no." Ivy felt as if problems in Wildcat Bluff just piled upon problems. If she'd known she was going to end up here, she might have passed on the project. Still, she was as susceptible as everyone to Fern's great charm, meaning her sister usually snagged whatever she wanted in life. Besides, she'd liked the idea of Wildcat Hall Park and wanted to support it.

"We've got problems around here." He pushed off the bar, walked over to a window, and looked outside as if checking for incoming trouble.

"I hope they don't involve the Hall."

"Not directly, but it's possible."

"What's going on?"

"Rustlers."

"Do you mean cattle rustlers?" She felt as if she'd been dropped into the middle of an Old West movie. First, a cattle drive. Now, cattle rustlers. How could any of it be real? They were in the twenty-first century, not the nineteenth. Maybe she was so city that country made no sense.

"Yep."

"Are you making a joke? Do I need to worry outlaws are going to raid Wildcat Hall for snacks and drinks or make this a rendezvous point after their latest cow heist?"

"I'm not joking, but it sounds like you are."

"I don't know what to think. I lived in Houston until a few days ago. In that world, cattle drives and cattle rustlers are relegated to the dustbin of history."

"You're city," he said on a sigh. "And I'm country."

"And never the twain shall meet. Is that your point?" She was trying to keep her feet on the ground, but she'd been abruptly jerked out of a simple life and thrust into a world of escalating chaos.

"My point is that I'm trying to alert you to a situation that could affect you here at the Hall."

"I don't see how."

"That's what I'm trying to get across to you."

"Okay. I'd better listen." She gave up trying to make the problem go away and walked over to a table in front of a window, pulled out a chair, and sat down. She gestured for him to do the same before she placed her hands on top of the table. "I'm all ears."

He eased into the chair across from her but gave her a skeptical look with his blue eyes. "Are you sure?"

"I promise," she said, crossing her heart, "not to make any more jokes about cattle rustlers."

"We'll see." He gave her a wry smile. "I guess it does sound a bit far-fetched coming out of the blue like this."

She put her hand over her mouth so he could see she wasn't going to say a contrary word.

He chuckled—just a little sound at first, but it soon turned into a big guffaw as he grinned at her. "Thanks. I guess I needed somebody to put the whole thing in perspective."

She smiled at him, finding his ability to laugh at himself as big a turn-on as his hot body. "I guess you should start at the beginning and put cattle rustlers into my perspective, so it'll make sense to me."

"Might help me, too." He looked at the ceiling, as if for help, then back to her. "I told you we were in the process of taking over the new ranch."

"Yes. That's why you're having the cattle drive."

"Right. We moved the horses from those pastures over to the first Steele Trap, but we left the cattle in the pastures. No point moving cows just to bring them back again."

"Makes sense."

"Nobody's living in the ranch house right now." He placed his large hands on top of the table and clasped them.

"Did it get broken into?"

"Not yet. But cattle rustlers hit us."

"I'm sorry." She suddenly felt a lot of sympathy for him and wished she hadn't made light of his situation before she'd heard the details.

"Yeah. Sheriff Calhoun is looking into it, but so far he's had no luck catching the thieves."

"Did you set up guards or a security system?"

"Yeah, we set up a new system on the house and barns, but rustlers can be in and out before we get there. Here's how they do it. Nighttime. Two guys. A pickup. A one-ton truck with a thirty-two-foot gooseneck—that's a trailer—that'll haul eighteen thousand pounds. First rustler gets dropped off on foot with a bucket of feed near a gate. He either uses a ranch pen or brings a portable one. Once he has cows in the pen, he contacts his partner, who backs in the gooseneck. They load up the cows, leave the gate open so cattle will get loose and confuse the rancher until a count can be made in daylight. Two minutes tops."

"I had no idea it could be that easy or that it was still going on. What can you do about it?"

"For starters, keep our eyes and ears open. We'll just keep adjusting and figuring it out till we complete the move."

She didn't like seeing the worry and concern in his eyes, but it also revealed a depth to him that she hadn't noticed on first sight. He had a lot of fine character that was slipping under her defenses. A country cowboy like him shouldn't even be on her radar. And yet he was becoming more compelling to her the more time she spent with him.

"Even if they only round up a few cows, they're still ahead of the game. And we've still lost."

"That's a big problem."

"It's a mess, no doubt about it."

"Can't you go ahead and move into the house?"

"It's a mess, too." He shrugged, looking frustrated at the situation. "I'm renovating with updates and upgrades. Plus, I'm working so much at the café and ranch that I don't have time for guard duty. My family is the same way."

"I wish I could help out, but I'm already out of my depth here, so I doubt there's much I could do anyway."

He gave her a slow smile that reached clear to his eyes and crinkled the corners. "I'm not asking for help or sympathy. I'll get through this to the other side. But for now, I wanted to alert you that thieves are operating in the area. And if they create a diversion, I figure the cattle drive will be a prime time for them to strike the herd."

"Would they be so rash? Seems like that'd be an easy way to get caught—maybe even on camera."

"You'd think so, but I can't take a chance, so I have to plan for that possible scenario."

"I guess you do. And thanks for telling me about it. I needed to know even if I didn't want to." She reached out, clasped his hands in appreciation, and felt a sudden surge of heat spike between them. Surprised, she quickly pulled back her hand, but it did nothing to stop the blaze spreading through her. She took a deep breath, trying to regain her composure.

"I don't bite," he said in his deep, melodic voice. "At least, not unless you want me to."

She chuckled, doing her best to pretend he was teasing when she knew good and well that he meant those words. And that knowledge alone made her feel even hotter. She had to get the situation under control before it got completely out of hand, going fast from business to personal. "Look, I doubt you have time to take on the Hall right now, although I appreciate the offer. I don't even need to add to the menu, at least not right away."

"That wasn't my point." This time, he clasped her hand, holding her gently but firmly in place. "Wildcat Hall is important to the community. Fern's dream is a good one. I'm not the only one who'll help you. Christmas is only about a month away, so everyone wants the Hall to be extra ready for folks to enjoy when they come to Wildcat Bluff."

"I'd like that, too." She felt a shiver run up her spine as he rubbed his thumb across the back of her hand, almost absentmindedly, as if it was the most natural thing in the world.

"Then we're in agreement to make this the best Christmas ever at Wildcat Hall?"

"Why not?" She felt surprising happiness well up in her, partly from his touch but also from the prospect of doing something new. It'd be quite a challenge. She was comfortable creating illusions on a screen, but here, she'd be putting her skills to work creating physical reality. "If I fail, it won't be like anybody'll notice, will it?"

He laughed, squeezing her hand. "Right. If *we* fail, we'll just laugh at ourselves while—"

"They run us out of town?" She joined his laughter, feeling more lighthearted than she had since she had arrived and found so much responsibility on her shoulders.

"Not a chance. But you've reminded me that it's always better to laugh at trouble than to cry about it."

"I'd rather laugh than cry any day."

"Thank you." He raised her hand, turned it over, and placed a soft kiss on her palm. "You're good for me. I'm starting to think I may need a whole new perspective on life."

She smiled, feeling tender toward him as her heart began a steady beat to a drum that could only belong to him. "I'm glad to know I'm not alone on this journey. I've got a whole new life, so why shouldn't you get a whole new perspective, too?"

He returned her smile with a smoldering gleam in his eyes as he gave her palm another soft kiss. "We're definitely in this journey together."

"Let's just hope it ends well." She smiled and withdrew her hand before she wanted him to never let her go.

"It'll end the way we want it to end…or maybe it won't end at all." He leaned toward her with an expectant look in his blue eyes.

She swallowed hard, reminding herself not to fall too deeply into those azure depths that promised so much if she'd just take the plunge. She couldn't possibly stay in the country. She belonged to the city. "When Fern returns, I'll go back to Houston."

He shuttered his eyes with a quick blink. "Right. It all comes back to Fern."

"True." Ivy quickly shoved her chair back and stood up, feeling as if she'd just thrown away something precious. But it had to be done. She was in Wildcat Bluff for a job, not a love life. She couldn't let a too-hot cowboy turn her life upside down.

He rose to his feet, towering over her. "Guess we ought to get back to business."

"Yes." She glanced out the window and noticed white smoke curling upward from one of the cabins. That couldn't be right. She looked closer, but it was still there. "Is one of the cabins rented?"

"Not that I know about. Why?"

"I didn't think the cabins had fireplaces."

"They don't." He stared hard at her as his body stiffened in concern, going quickly from relaxed to alert.

"Smoke's coming out of that cabin." She pointed out the window.

He swiveled and looked outside. "I see it. Did you leave anything cooking on the stove?"

"That's not my cabin."

He whipped his phone out of his pocket and hit speed dial. "Hedy, I'm at the Hall. One of the cabins looks to be on fire. We may need a rig, but let me check it first. If I can put the blaze out with a can, I'll do it." He hesitated, listening. "Right. I'm always careful." He listened again. "I'll let you know the minute I know." He clicked off and slipped his cell back in his pocket.

"How could a fire get started in an empty cabin?"

"Good question." He glanced around the room, as if checking for a sudden blaze, then back at her. "Stay here while I get a fire extinguisher out of my truck and take a look at the cabin. You got a key?"

She felt shocked into inaction for a moment before she realized there was not a moment to lose. How would she ever explain to Fern if she let a cabin burn to the ground? "Over here."

"Good. I can bust in the door, but I don't want to damage property if I don't have to."

"Please don't." She slipped behind the bar and reached down to where a wooden board with hooks held several rows of keys with numbers under them. She selected a master key, hurried back, and handed it to him.

"Thanks." He put the key in his pocket, turned to go, and glanced back. "Stay here where it's safe. I'll let you know what's going on."

"Not on your life." She straightened her back in defiance. "Where you go on this property, I go."

He huffed in resigned reply. "No time to argue. If you're coming, come, but stay back where it's safe."

She walked up to him, looped her hand around his arm, and gave him a determined nod. "Let's go fight a fire."

Chapter 4

SLADE DIDN'T SAY IT, NOT AFTER IVY'S SKEPTICISM, BUT he had to wonder if the fire had anything to do with the cattle rustlers. On the face of it, no. Yet too many bad things coming together near the same time had to be more than coincidence. He didn't like it, not any more than he liked the problems cropping up since they'd bought the new ranch. But not liking something didn't mean not dealing with it.

He gave Ivy's fingers a squeeze when they reached his truck, then he opened the back door, grabbed a can, and looked toward the cabins. He could smell smoke now, as well as see it, but still no flames were in sight. Maybe he had time to catch the fire before it did much damage.

"Do you have another fire extinguisher?" Ivy asked, holding out her hand.

"Not with me."

"I don't know why I didn't think of it before, but I can get extinguishers from the Hall."

"First, let's see if we need them." He slung the canister by its strap over his shoulder.

"Okay, but I can run back and get them if we need them."

He was anxious to get to the fire, so he took long strides down the winding walkway that led toward the cowboy cabins nestled under live oaks that were green throughout the year. Rosebushes cut back for the winter and dormant flower beds were landscaped with neatly trimmed shrubs and leafless ornamental trees.

Bill and Ida Murphy had enjoyed restoration projects, so they'd built and decorated the cabins using recycled materials from deconstructed old houses and barns, as well as obscure items from junk stores and reclaimed materials.

They were currently enjoying an extended tour of the historic Old West, hauling a vintage trailer behind their pickup after leaving their legacy at Wildcat Hall Park. They'd built four rental units near their larger cowboy cabin that overlooked the dance hall, with rusty corrugated tin for roofs, weathered barn wood for siding, and natural stone for stairs leading up to the porches with rocking chairs. Each front window and door was reclaimed, so they were all different shapes and sizes and colors, adding an eccentric appearance to the buildings.

Slade always felt as if he'd stepped back in time here, walking original ranch land—and perennial cat land, because kitties usually lounged wherever they pleased after claiming the Park many generations ago. Most folks thought of them as guard cats. At the moment, he didn't see a feline in sight, and that alerted him to trouble.

As he walked fast with Ivy down the path, he kept a lookout for trouble or intruders, but everything appeared in order. Still, he stayed on high alert.

He followed the scent of smoke to a cabin on the far side of the Park, where he stopped at the edge of the stone walkway leading to the front door. The structure appeared orange from the rust roof and brown siding with turquoise window frames for bright accents. The house sat on vintage redbrick posts about two feet in diameter with brick posts holding up the front corners of the porch, leaving a crawl space underneath.

When he felt Ivy place a hand on his back in a gesture of warning as well as support, he glanced down at her, pleased she was comfortable touching him.

"What do you think?" she asked, nodding toward the cabin.

"If you'll stay here and keep an eye out for any movement around the cabins, I'll go closer."

"Do you think somebody's here?"

"I don't know, but let's don't take chances."

"Okay. Be careful." She gave him a quick pat on the back.

"If you see or hear anything wrong, holler at me."

He hurried up the path, smelling and seeing more smoke the closer he got to the rental unit. Suddenly a long-haired calico cat leaped out of the bushes, ran ahead of him, stopped in front of the cabin's stairs, and glanced back with narrowed eyes.

"Thanks. I'll take over from here," he said, smiling at the feline on the job, reminding him of Ash, the fire station cat.

The calico leaped away, sat down, and licked a paw while keeping an eye on the smoking cabin.

Slade hefted his canister as he walked up to the front porch. He examined the building with an eye to possible structural damage, but the fire appeared to be confined to the crawl space. He saw flames licking up from below, turning the dry wood black where it smoldered, ready to burst into flames and consume the entire structure. The old, dry wood would go up fast. He hated to think how fast if Ivy hadn't noticed the smoke and he hadn't been here.

He felt the heat, heard the crackle of flames, and smelled

the smoke as he dropped to his knees by the edge of the building. He aimed the nozzle and sprayed foam until the flames died down. He stopped, adjusted his position, and checked the results. He was shocked to see a scorched Santa's hat that had originally been red and white. Not an accident. He felt sick at his stomach knowing somebody had deliberately set the blaze. He sprayed again until the fire was completely out. He checked for any missed hot spots, but it looked good.

Satisfied, he stood up, walked up the stone steps, and used the last of the chemical in his can to coat the top of the porch and the runners of the two rocking chairs. He checked the area again and nodded in satisfaction before he turned to give Ivy a thumbs-up and also a gesture to stay back. He didn't want her closer until he'd completed his search of the area.

Somebody had trespassed and set this fire. That meant they had an entry and exit strategy. He wanted to find it and make sure nobody was still hanging around, although now he sincerely doubted that'd be a problem. Person or persons unknown had to be long gone, having completed their goal and not looking to get caught.

He slung the empty canister by its strap over his shoulder before he jogged down the steps. He glanced up and saw several iridescent-black grackles on the limb of a live oak, watching him. If the intruder had been near them, they'd have flown away, so that backed up his position that he was alone. Still, he wasn't done checking to make sure everything was okay.

He circled the cabin, searching for anything out of the ordinary or suspicious. He hoped he didn't discover a second fire. It didn't take him long to look, since the cabin was small, so he moved farther afield, checking the property. Nothing looked out of order till he came to the low hedge used as a fence line in back. He could easily see where somebody had pushed through the greenery, breaking and bending foliage. Made sense. It was a good place to enter without being seen from Wildcat Road. Leave your vehicle in the ditch not too close, then walk into the Park and disappear into the trees and shrubbery.

He immediately backed up, doing his best to retrace his own footsteps, so he didn't contaminate the scene. He needed to call Sheriff Calhoun to come out with deputies right away. Maybe they could find evidence that would lead them straight to the arsonist. First, he sent Hedy a text at the station to let her know he didn't need a rig. He'd debrief her on the fire later. For now, he'd done all he could do. It was time to get back to Ivy and reassure her.

He headed toward the cabin, feeling glad he'd caught the fire in time. And he'd also kept Ivy out of danger. They'd been lucky. But what if there was a next time? Somebody had intentionally set this fire. But who? And why? He had no more answers to those questions than he did to his own problems at the new ranch. But there he had help from family and cowboys. Ivy was alone here, except for the cats, and he didn't like that idea one bit.

When he rounded the side of the cabin, he saw the calico, tail held high, leading Ivy toward him. Funny thing— they looked like they belonged together, like old friends. And they were pretty as a picture. Maybe she had that way about her, like her sister, Fern, in that no one ever felt like a stranger around her. He figured she'd taken up where Fern had left off, setting out food and water for the polydactyl cats. If not, there were plenty of folks who'd gladly take over that duty. Folks in Wildcat Bluff County loved their cats as much as they loved their dogs, horses, and cattle—wildlife in general, for that matter.

"Is everything okay?" she asked, gesturing toward the cabin.

He stopped beside her, marveling at her impact on him. She made him feel young, even though he was still on the upswing of life at thirty-two, because she somehow stripped away the aches and pains and losses of a has-been bull rider and replaced them with the hopes and dreams and possibilities of youth. He felt a small blaze blossom in the center of his chest and spread outward to warm him all over, as if he'd landed back in the magical land of summertime, when school was over for the season. He gently clasped her hand, wanting to bring her to that special place and time with him, so they could share the sunrises together.

"Are you okay?" She glanced down at their joined hands, then back up at his face. "You're worrying me."

He smiled at her, feeling so tender that he couldn't help tugging her gently against his chest. She didn't resist, but she didn't nestle against him either. She waited for his reassurance, but he didn't give it to her, not yet, because he was struck by a sudden revelation. She was everything he hadn't known he needed but now knew he couldn't live without. He'd do almost anything to keep her. Anything.

"Slade?" she asked, trembling against him.

"It's okay." He said it gently as he placed a soft kiss on top of her head. "Everything's okay. I'll see to it."

She stepped back, dropping his hand. "I thought you saw something bad and needed to comfort me."

"I guess I was comforting us both. I've been dealing with problems, but now I'm concerned you have one, too."

"What do you mean?"

"I put out the fire. The structure is sound. Beyond that…you had an intruder in the Park."

She stared at him, eyes going wide, and clasped her arms around her waist as if reassuring herself or warding off a chill. The calico stretched up on Ivy's leg, silently asking to be picked up. When she lifted the cat into her arms, the kitty purred loudly and patted her chin with one huge paw.

"Let me make a call, then we can talk about it." Slade pulled his phone out of his pocket and hit speed dial. "Sheriff Calhoun, I just put out a fire under the porch of a cabin in Wildcat Hall Park." He listened a moment. "I'm afraid it's arson." He listened again. "Yes, I'd appreciate you sending out a deputy. Do you want to contact Hedy, so she can send out a firefighter with equipment to take samples?" He nodded, listening. "Okay. I'll be at the Hall with Ivy Bryant, Fern's sister. Thanks."

"Arson?" Ivy asked, appearing shocked. "Somebody deliberately started the fire?"

"Yep. No doubt about it."

"Why would someone want to hurt this wonderful place?" She shivered as she glanced around the Park, hugging the cat closer.

"I wish I knew. Sheriff Calhoun is good at his job. He'll get it sorted out."

"But when?"

"Wish I could answer that question. And I wish the cattle rustlers were already caught, but it takes time."

"Makes sense." She nodded, glancing up at the cabin. "Right now, please show me the damage."

"There's not much to see."

"It doesn't matter. I want to know exactly what happened to one of my lovely cowboy cabins. Wildcat Hall and these homes are my responsibility now. And I take it seriously."

"That's good."

She quickly kissed the cat between the ears, then set the calico down on the ground.

The cat gave them a satisfied, slit-eyed gaze before sauntering over to the nearest bush and disappearing from sight.

"Now, let's see the cabin." Ivy started down the path, beckoning him to follow her.

He watched her go with a hunger that would not quit. He had it bad. And he'd only been with her a few hours. What would it be like after he spent more time with her? From bad to worse to… He took a deep breath. Somehow he had to get a handle on the situation. He'd controlled thousand-pound-plus bulls, horses, cows, and never blinked twice. But let hundred-pounds-plus-change Ivy Bryant enter his life, and he was instantly out of control.

It wouldn't do. She needed him strong and supportive. Others depended on him to be his usual take-charge self and get done what needed to be done. Besides, danger had ridden into their county, and no way was he letting any of his loved ones get hurt.

He gritted his teeth. He'd do what he had to do, come hell or high water. But he'd pay a price in haunted days and sleepless nights—unless Ivy, by some miracle, came to regard him as he regarded her.

Chapter 5

IVY TOOK SEVERAL DEEP BREATHS AS SHE WALKED UP the gravel path, trying to steady her emotions. She felt like a Ping-Pong ball knocked back and forth across a net till she was almost dizzy. She was used to being in control. She certainly wasn't used to being rescued by a cowboy, but wisdom had prevailed, since he was the experienced firefighter and she needed someone to put out a fire. If she stayed here much longer, she might need to get training in that area. For now, she had to put aside preconceived notions and deal with the reality of country life.

Thinking of reality, had she really felt Slade place a soft kiss on top of her head? Surely not, but then again, it'd felt like it. He did seem to be a touchy-feely kind of guy, so that was probably just his way of comforting her. Still, there was that heat between them. She abruptly stopped those thoughts. She didn't need to be thinking about a hot cowboy. She needed to focus on taking care of business.

Sucking in her gut, she marched right up to the cowboy cabin and looked it over. She didn't see anything wrong except a chemical mess on the front porch that could be cleaned up later. She glanced back at Slade. "Is this the right one?"

He nodded as he joined her. "Look under the porch, but don't walk over there. I already tromped on any prints that could be useful, but the sheriff might still be able to come up with something."

"I hope so." She bent down but didn't see much except a blackened, crumpled Santa's hat. "That's it?"

"Yeah. And be glad of it."

"Oh, I am. It's just hard to believe that little bit of stuff could have burned down this entire cabin."

"And spread from there."

"Worse yet."

"You're lucky. Real lucky."

"Thanks. If you hadn't been here and known what to look for and what to do, I'd have been in trouble." She placed her hand on his arm, reaching out to him in appreciation. When she felt his muscles contract in response, her mind skittered sideways. He was built, really built—muscle upon muscle upon muscle. She quickly withdrew her hand, but her skin still tingled from touching him.

"Luck of the draw. You'd have called the fire station, but I'm glad I was here to catch it early."

"Me, too." She smiled at him. "I want to check inside the cabin for damage."

"Good idea. Why don't we check all the cabins and your house while we wait for the others to get here?" He pulled the master key out of his pocket.

"Wait." She held out her hand for the key. "I just realized I'm keeping you from all your other work."

"My work is right here today. I'm a volunteer for Wildcat Bluff Fire-Rescue." He shook the key ring, jingling the rowel on a dangling silver spur charm.

"But still—"

"There's no way I'm letting you go into any of those buildings alone."

"Do you think…really think I'm in danger?"

"What I think is that I want to check out the locks, security, sprinklers, and smoke alarms in every single structure."

"You're making a point I hadn't even thought about, but then I've only been here a couple of days."

"You'd have thought of it soon enough, once you had folks staying in the cabins and more folks hanging out in the Hall. I want you and everybody safe."

"Me, too."

"I'd guess Fern has all of that covered, but just in case, I want to make sure. And if you don't have outside motion-sensor lights, I'll install them for you."

"Thank you." She glanced around at the cowboy cabins, seeing them beyond their pretty setting and design for the first time. "I owe you dinner, beer, wine, or something more."

"I'll take something more." And he grinned, making it a hot one.

She simply shook her head, partly at his playfulness, partly at how he was getting to her without hardly trying. "I'll think of something special."

"I can handle special," he said, then bounded up the stairs and opened the front door. He glanced back. "Let me take a quick look around first."

She followed him up the stairs, appreciating again the beautiful rock work and the hand-carved wood railing on one side. She stepped up on the porch and past two comfy rockers—one orange and the other turquoise.

She stepped inside and was surrounded by the warm patina of old wood from floor to wall to ceiling. Turquoise was the dominant color in an open area that included a small kitchen with adjacent living area and bathroom. On either end of the room, stairs led up to sleeping lofts. Every bit of space was carefully designed for maximum use, since the cabin was so small in size.

In comparison, Slade appeared way too big. He moved carefully about the room, as if concerned he might break something or run into something. She liked his thoughtfulness.

"How does it look?" She walked over to the kitchen and admired the red-chili-pepper-on-yellow stoneware in a glass-fronted cabinet near the sink.

"Good. No problems. Far as I can tell, the Murphy family, and maybe Fern, added more security features."

"Do you think all the cabins are secured the same way?"

"I'd bet on it." He glanced around one more time, then walked over to her. "Bottom line, nobody's been in here."

"That's great."

"Why don't we check out the other cabins?"

She preceded him out the door, heard him secure the dead bolt, and walked down the path to another cabin. They followed the same procedure, checking and securing. Each unit was beautifully and rustically appointed with little luxury touches that were sure to please folks that came to stay for a night or a week or longer. By the time they stepped out onto the porch of the fourth cabin, they'd seen nothing amiss and plenty to be proud of in all the loving details.

Ivy set a rocking chair to rocking as she gazed out over the Park. "I love this place. It's not just Wildcat Hall, although that building alone is notable, but all these unique houses are wonderful."

"Folks around here set quite a store by it and like to come here just to relax or for special occasions."

She abruptly stopped the rocking chair. "Not everybody loves it, or... Could somebody have it in for me?"

He gave her a considering look. "Do you think the fire was personal?"

"I just got here and suddenly there's a fire."

"But nobody knows you. I wouldn't take it personal, not yet. There's something else in play. We just need to figure out what it is."

"Okay. Maybe it's not personal." She glanced around the Park, waiting for inspiration to strike, but it didn't. "Then again...do you know if anybody contested the Park's sale?"

"Nobody even knew about it till it was a done deal. Otherwise folks probably would've made offers."

"I guess speculation isn't going to get us anywhere." She rubbed the back of her neck in frustration. "Why don't we have a look at my new home?"

"Okay. I want to make sure you're as safe as possible there."

She quickly took the stairs down and headed to the larger cabin built with the same recycled materials as the smaller ones. She realized now that she hadn't been expecting so much responsibility in so many areas in so many ways. The fire brought home the fact that she was definitely out of her element. In Houston, she could call in professionals on a nonpersonal level to take care of anything and everything. Here, she was beginning to see that friends helped friends on a personal level to get things done. It must be like the old days, when most people lived in small towns or on farms and ranches and were neighborly. Even though she and her friends helped each other on occasion, this was still a major change for her. She wasn't sure she knew how to handle it. Country life was definitely shaping up to be more work than city life.

And that didn't begin to address the issue of Slade Steele. She was becoming more dependent on him every moment—and she wasn't sure she liked that fact. He was generous and helpful and oh so hot, but if she worked with him, how was she going to keep their relationship professional?

She didn't have answers to all the questions that suddenly loomed in her life, so she simply walked with her head down, counting the night-activated solar lights that lined the path. She knew that at dusk, soft illumination would stream along the winding path to give the Park a glowing, otherworldly appearance. Maybe that was part of why she was feeling so out of her depth. She felt as if she had stepped into an enchanted land that came with its very own knight in shining armor—or in this case, a knight in cowboy hat and boots.

"Look," Slade said behind her, "I didn't mean to discount a personal vendetta against you."

She stopped at the base of the stairs to her cabin and turned around to look at him. "That sounds ominous."

"I mean, do you have any enemies back home?"

"You think somebody followed me here to destroy my new life?"

"It happens."

"Not to me." She thrust her hands into her hair, wanting to pull answers out by the roots. "I live a very quiet life in Houston. I spend my days in front of a keyboard and my nights reading or seeing friends."

"You can make enemies online."

"I guess that's true, but I design websites, so I don't interact a lot with strangers."

"Okay. I just thought I ought to throw that possibility out there."

"Please take it back. Trust me, I'm probably the most innocuous person you'll ever meet."

He grinned, shaking his head. "That's the last thing you are, but I get your drift. What about Fern?"

"She's another story."

"Maybe somebody mistook you for her."

"We don't look much alike."

"From a distance, if somebody was expecting to see her."

"We're about the same height." She pushed long strands of hair back from her face. "I don't know. I just don't know."

"Bottom line, wild speculation gets us nowhere, but the sheriff will ask these questions and a whole lot more."

"I'll be as helpful as I can, but I'm clueless."

"Maybe something will come to you later."

"Maybe. For now, why don't we go inside and check out my cabin." She hurried up to the porch, then stopped and glanced back at him. She didn't have a key. He must have seen the frustration on her face because he tossed up the key ring. She grabbed it out of the air, unlocked the door, and stepped inside.

As in the other cabins, she appreciated all the wonderful, warm wood from floor to ceiling to walls. Ceiling fans with wooden paddles lazily stirred air scented by lavender and sage in dried bundles in a wicker basket on the kitchen counter. She hadn't had time to take in all the details of the decor, but nothing had been left to chance. Soft yellow and sage green were the dominant colors used to brighten the open floor plan of living, dining, and kitchen. A touch of cowboy had been added here and there, like the throw pillows in roping- and riding-cowboy designs on the leather sofa and armchair. A lamp in the shape of a cow with a green shade looked whimsical on a small table. She'd be days or weeks checking out all the little bits of vintage that had been collected for the cabin. And she looked forward to it.

"Great place," Slade said as he followed her inside, bootheels clicking against the hardwood floor. "I've always liked it."

"You've been here before?" She walked over to the green laminate-and-chrome dining table where she'd been working last night. She glanced at the website design on her laptop before closing the lid, knowing she wouldn't get back to work till later that evening.

"Sure. I'm friends with Bill and Ida, like most of the folks around here. Good people. Hard workers. They're having fun out West."

"Do you hear from them?"

"They text us with photos now and again."

"Please don't tell them about the fire. And I won't tell Fern. It'd just worry them all."

"I won't, at least not yet." He glanced around the room. "Everything looks fine from here, but I'd like to check closer. Okay?"

"Go ahead. Do you want something to drink? Maybe ice tea? I made a pitcher this morning and set it in the fridge."

"Sounds good."

As she opened the refrigerator, she glanced over at him walking around and looking at what was now her personal space. It felt way too intimate, as if they were sharing more than just checking out cabins for intruders and safety equipment. Maybe she was being fanciful, considering how the

Park affected her, but still, she couldn't shrug off the feeling that they were sharing so much more. She shook her head to dislodge the idea, suddenly remembering why she had the fridge door open. She quickly picked up the pitcher of tea and set it on the yellow-tile countertop. She selected two vintage yellow-and-white-striped glasses from the open cabinet above and filled them with ice and tea. Finally, she set yellow napkins beside them.

"Everything looks in order here." Slade walked into the kitchen and glanced down at the glasses and napkins. "Pretty."

"Thanks. Your friends have good taste, so I'm taking advantage of it."

"Might as well. That's what friends are for." He picked up a glass and a napkin, giving her a sly smile. "You know, taking advantage of."

She felt her breath catch in her throat at what he implied with his words and the look in his blue gaze. "I wish we had cowboy cookies to go with the tea, but somebody forgot to bring them." She teased to lighten the exchange and hoped he'd take her lead to back away from the intimacy of the moment.

He chuckled but the heat didn't leave his eyes. "Next time."

"Do you want to sit on the porch and wait for the professionals?"

"Good idea. They ought to be here soon."

She walked outside, sat down in a rocker, and set her glass on top of her napkin on the green metal table.

Slade sat down, took a big gulp of tea, and set his glass beside hers. "Like I said, I think it'd be a good idea to install motion-sensor lights over the doors of the cabins."

"Will it help?"

"Can't hurt. At the least it'll give you extra light around here."

"I hate to take up any more of your time."

"No problem." He leaned forward and put his elbows on his knees. "I want you and the property as safe as possible out here."

"Thanks. I'll pick up the expense."

"You may need to go bigger and better by placing motion-sensor cameras on the cabins and in the trees along the walkways. You'd have a live feed to your computer or cell phone that you could check."

"That seems so intrusive to guests and out of character for the Park."

"True. Electronics don't exactly go with retro, but still…"

"Maybe later. I'm not excited about adding to the expense and the learning curve of what I already need to do here."

"I understand. Let's keep that idea on a back burner for now."

"Okay. Thanks for all your help." She leaned back in her rocker.

"Happy to do it." He glanced toward Wildcat Road. "Sounds like a party is about to arrive."

"That does sound like a lot of traffic." She leaned forward to get a better view of the entry to Wildcat Hall. "I thought you said only the sheriff and a firefighter were coming here. That's only two vehicles."

He chuckled, standing up. "Hedy must have put out the word."

"What word?" She stood up, too.

"That the new lady of Wildcat Hall Park needs help."

"But I didn't ask for help."

"Too late now." He pointed toward Wildcat Road.

She was astonished to see a convoy of pickups, SUVs, a sheriff's vehicle, and a couple of ATVs turn off the road and make their way toward her. "Oh my." She felt her stomach turn over. "Didn't I tell you Fern is the one good with people? I'm a poor substitute."

He put an arm around her shoulders and tugged her close. "You're no substitute. You're the real deal."

And the parking lot filled with vehicles.

Chapter 6

IVY GLANCED BACK INTO THE CABIN AT HER LAPTOP, JUST waiting for her to resume work on her client's website. Comfortable, familiar, something she knew how to handle. She looked through gaps in the trees toward the vehicles arriving at Wildcat Hall—and felt a sinking sensation in the pit of her stomach. Uncomfortable, unfamiliar, something she didn't know how to handle.

She took a deep breath to steady her nerves and felt Slade's hand tighten around her shoulders in support and encouragement. She was glad of his presence, his strength, his commitment to the Park—even to her.

"They'll love you," he said with utter conviction.

"I'm not Fern."

"No question. She's gone. You're here to stay."

Ivy felt a chill run up her spine, as if he spoke prophetically. "Like I said, I'm just here long enough to take care of the place till she gets back."

"I know what you told me." He tugged her even closer. "But I'm not listening to your words. I'm listening to your body."

She shook her head in disbelief. "And my body is telling you I'm staying right here in Wildcat Bluff?"

He kissed the top of her head again. "Yeah."

"You don't know a thing about me." She shrugged his hand away and stepped forward as she watched the vehicles stop and park, and the doors open.

"I know enough." He spoke in a voice gone husky with emotion.

She turned to glance at him, feeling something in his words, his voice, his intent, strike deep—so very deep—that it unnerved her. She was city, not country, and she had no plans to change her lifestyle for a man. Any man.

He looked steadily at her, ignoring the growing noise from the parking lot of slamming doors, rising voices, and footfalls on asphalt. "You might as well know it upfront. I've waited a lifetime for you. I'm not waiting a second longer."

She put a hand to her chest, over her heart, feeling a resonance within her that echoed his words, as if she'd been waiting a lifetime for him. But it didn't make sense in her world, old or new. He was a stranger, and yet he didn't feel like a stranger. He felt like home. She caught her breath on a rising tide of emotion that made her want to fling herself into his arms. And stay there.

"Slade!" a tall man wearing a cowboy hat, red shirt, Wranglers, and boots called out as he walked briskly toward the cabin.

"Hey, Craig," Slade called before he stepped up beside Ivy. "Best go down and meet them."

She straightened her shoulders and moved to the edge of the porch.

"I'll be right beside you every step of the way." He clasped her hand, squeezed her fingers, and then let her go.

She pasted a smile on her face, walked down the stairs, and headed along the path, wishing she'd changed clothes because she was still in comfy yoga gear for cleaning and organizing the dance hall. No matter, she could handle the situation if she just viewed it as part of the job of owning and managing Wildcat Hall.

As she came face-to-face with the stranger, she could see the others were still arranging themselves into some type of order in the parking lot. She needed to establish herself in a position of strength from the get-go or chance getting into trouble later.

"I'd like you to meet Ivy Bryant, Fern's sister. Ivy, this is Craig Thorne," Slade said.

"Good to meet you." She shook Craig's hand, thinking she could see why Fern would've been reluctant to leave him. He was a good-looking, tall drink of water with a firm handshake, chestnut hair, hazel eyes, and a cowboy's strong body. He wore a windbreaker with the Wildcat Bluff Fire-Rescue emblem embroidered on the front and carried a bulging backpack.

"Likewise." He took a deep breath before he plunged forward. "Any news about Fern?"

Now she knew why he'd been first to greet her. He couldn't wait to hear about her sister. "She's fine and playing a gig."

"Did she...did she mention me? I mean, we're supposed to perform together at Wild West Days. I know that's a long ways off from Christmas, but still, I wondered if she'd be back by then at least."

Ivy felt sympathy for him, but she couldn't do anything about it or ease the situation. "I haven't heard much from her, and I don't know about her upcoming gigs."

He looked disappointed for a moment, then he shuttered his eyes. "If she asks, tell her I hope she's back by Labor Day."

"I hope she is, too." Ivy gave him a gentle smile. "In the meantime, I'm doing my best to fill in here at the Park."

"We've already had some ideas about changing the menu." Slade stepped up beside her as if staking first claim on her friendship. "But now we need to see if we can gather evidence from the fire."

"Right." Craig quickly turned take-charge. "Sheriff Calhoun is here. Hedy, too. And—"

"We saw the parade," Slade said, chuckling. "Did you bring all of Wildcat Bluff?"

Craig joined his laughter. "Pretty near. Folks want to meet Ivy."

"Tell you what," Ivy said. "You don't need me at the fire site, so why don't I take everyone who isn't needed there to the Hall and offer them something to drink?"

"Good idea," Slade said, agreeing. "Craig, are you taking samples?"

"Yes. I brought evidence bags."

"Okay. Let's introduce Ivy, then get on over there. I want to show you and the sheriff some stuff."

"Sounds good to me," Craig said.

Ivy walked on down the path with the two guys following her to the parking lot, where the group had assembled around a woman in a wheelchair and a tall man in a cowboy hat wearing a shiny badge.

Slade reached her side, then gestured at the group. "Folks, I'd like you to meet Ivy Bryant, Fern's sister."

She smiled and nodded at the friendly looking group as they chorused hey, hi, and hello.

"This is Sheriff Calhoun. He'll be leading the investigation into the fire and intruder."

"Howdy, Ms. Bryant." Sheriff Calhoun tipped his beige cowboy hat to her. He also wore a tan police uniform, black

50 KIM REDFORD

cowboy boots, and a holstered revolver on one hip. "After I
investigate the scene, I'd like a few words in private with you."

"Certainly," Ivy said. "I do appreciate you coming out
here so promptly. I needn't tell you how concerned I am
about the Park."

"We're all concerned," the woman in a power wheelchair
piped up. She had thick silver hair in a long plait dangling
over one shoulder and sharp brown eyes. She was wearing a
red shirt, Wranglers, and red boots.

"Ivy, meet Hedy Murray. She's the heart and soul of
Wildcat Bluff Fire-Rescue and owner of Adelia's Delights in
Old Town."

"Good to meet you," Ivy said.

Hedy chuckled as she smiled at Ivy. "I'm more like chief
cook and bottle washer."

"Thought that was my job," Slade said with a grin.

"Only at the Chuckwagon." Hedy teased right back
before she gave Ivy a sharp look. "Hope you're not going to
turn tail and run at the first sign of trouble."

Ivy took a deep breath, not knowing quite what to say in
response. "I'm still here so far."

"Hedy, what are you trying to do, run her off? Shame on
you." A tall, slim woman with long, curly ginger hair wearing an aqua blouse and a long, swirling skirt with turquoise
cowgirl boots and a dozen or so long necklaces walked up
and held out her hand. "I'm Morning Glory. Welcome to
the county. We love your sister and we're prepared to love
you, too."

"Thanks," Ivy said, shaking a hand with soft skin and
strong muscle. She felt glad for the warm welcome.

"That's MG if her full name is too big a mouthful," Slade

said. "Don't let her sweetness fool you. She's tough as nails and keeps us all in line. And she's the owner of Morning's Glory with all the handcrafted lotions, potions, and perfumes to set you up for life."

"Don't forget all the local artists I support, too," Morning Glory said. "Please come to visit me at my store. I bet you're in need of your own personal scent. I made one for Fern and she loved it."

"Thank you. I'd like that." Ivy smiled at the woman who could have been most any age, but she had eyes as mischievous as a teenager.

"And you must come to Adelia's Delights," Hedy added. "We'll all have tea in my tearoom. And you must meet Rosie."

Morning Glory chuckled as she put her hand on Hedy's shoulder. "Rosie is absolutely the queen of cats and certainly the queen of Adelia's."

"I'd like to meet Rosie, too." Ivy realized these delightful women were putting her at ease and reassuring her that all would be well, despite the fire, while she lived in Wildcat Bluff.

"Allow me to introduce Bert Holloway." Hedy glanced up at the tall, good-looking man with a hand on her shoulder. He wore a Western-cut suit with a bolo tie and expensive, ostrich cowboy boots. He had thick, dark hair streaked with silver and tanned skin that suggested a life spent mostly outdoors. "Pleased to make your acquaintance," Bert said in a deep voice. "If there's anything I or my son Bert Two can do for you, we'd be glad to help out."

Hedy patted Bert's hand, smiling with a glint in her eyes. "I have to admit he can be quite helpful."

Morning Glory laughed. "Nobody doubts it...not since you two got engaged."

"Thank you." Ivy liked this friendly group more all the time.

"Wildcat Jack, at your service." A tall man with kinetic energy stepped forward and thrust out a hand. He wore his long silver hair in two plaits wrapped with multicolored, beaded leather cords that dangled over his shoulders. He was dressed in a dark-blue shirt, Wranglers, and scuffed cowboy boots.

"Good to meet you." She shook his calloused hand, marveling that he was one of those rare people—like her sister—with a personal magnetism that couldn't help but draw you into his sphere.

"He's our DJ at KWCB, the Wildcat Den," Slade said. "But you better watch him. At seventy-nine years plus, he's pretty near stolen the heart of every woman in the county."

Morning Glory put her hand on her hip and grinned at Jack. "And he's heartless about it, too."

"No, ma'am," Jack said, disagreeing. "I'm simply a man who never wants to disappoint a lady."

Hedy laughed hard, shaking her head. "Now that's the truth. He's not known to disappoint."

"Better not go any farther down that road." Slade cut in, grinning, as he gestured toward another woman. "Meet Eden Rafferty. She's Jack's partner in crime at the Den."

"Now tell the truth," Jack said. "She's my boss and owner of our now-famous radio station, ever since we went after a global audience."

"And we found that cache of vintage recordings," Eden added before she smiled warmly at Ivy. "Welcome to

Wildcat Bluff. You'll have to forgive our teasing ways. We've known each other forever."

"Speak for yourself," Jack said, shaking a finger at her. "I never ask forgiveness."

Ivy joined the general laughter, feeling more at home with these folks the more she got to know them. For the first time, she could understand why Fern had been so charmed and so eager to be part of this community.

"Slade, thanks for the introductions," Sheriff Calhoun said, "but we best be about the matter at hand."

"True," Slade said. "If possible, we don't want any more fires around here."

"I certainly agree," Ivy said, turning from him to the group. "I'd like to invite all of you who aren't part of the investigation to join me in Wildcat Hall. I'm sure we can find something to drink there."

"If you can't find it yet," Hedy said, laughing, "I bet the rest of us know just where everything is kept."

"Right," Morning Glory said. "The Hall has been our home away from home forever."

"And I'd like to talk to you about live streaming from here during the cattle drive and the holidays," Eden said.

"I'll be happy to discuss it," Ivy said. "I suppose you talked about this with Fern before she left."

"Yes," Jack replied. "We made lots of plans. That's why we're still surprised she up and left so fast."

"She's a rolling stone," Ivy said, not wanting to go down that path anymore because there was no explanation that would satisfy them. Fern was as good as gold when she was with you, but when she was gone, she was simply gone.

"Craig, let's go with the sheriff," Slade said as he stepped closer to Ivy. "We might as well start over with all our plans. Ivy's in charge now and she's willing to work with us and the community to help make our upcoming events successful."

"Yes, that's right. Let's discuss what's possible and what's not." Ivy felt grateful to Slade for moving everyone past the Fern roadblock.

"Suits me," Hedy said, giving Ivy an understanding look with her sharp brown eyes.

"Right," Morning Glory said, agreeing. "I could use a glass of the Hall's famous sarsaparilla."

"I wouldn't mind trying it either." Ivy turned toward the dance hall, realizing they expected her to lead, wanted her to lead. One way or another, she'd do it. When she felt a touch on her shoulder, she glanced around to see who needed her attention.

Slade smiled at her with warmth in his blue eyes. "We won't be long. Save us a drink, okay?"

"I'm sure there's plenty for all."

"Good." He gave her a quick nod, then turned and walked away with Craig and Sheriff Calhoun.

She watched him a moment, still amazed at the impact he was having on her life. And then she turned back, squared her shoulders, and gestured for her guests to precede her into Wildcat Hall.

Chapter 7

"It's not just the fire," Slade said as he led Craig and the sheriff toward the cabin that had lucked out with no fire damage.

"What do you mean?" Sheriff Calhoun asked, looking around the area as they walked down the path.

"Somebody has targeted the cowboy cabins or the Hall…or, even worse, Ivy herself."

"Does she have enemies?" Sheriff Calhoun asked.

"I questioned her about that first thing."

"And she said?" Craig glanced over at Slade with a concerned look on his face.

"No. She's a website designer and mostly stays home."

"That means if somebody is after anybody, it's got to be Fern," Craig said. "She's the one who's out there with all the fans. I even warned her that she has to be careful, but she's so trusting that—"

"Don't go jumping off the deep end before we know what's what," Sheriff Calhoun said, interrupting.

"But Ivy just got here and Fern's been here, so it stands to reason the target would be Fern," Craig said.

"I'll say it again." Sheriff Calhoun gave Craig a stern look. "We don't jump to conclusions before we get the facts."

"You're right," Craig replied. "It's just that I'm worried about Fern. If she'd just told me her plans, I would've helped her. It's not knowing and wondering and figuring and probably getting it all wrong that's got me tied in knots."

"If it helps," Slade said, "Ivy doesn't seem to know much more than us. And she says it's not personal because Fern goes where the gigs lead at the drop of a hat."

"I believe it," Craig said. "Still, I'm worried about her."

"We all are." Slade stopped in front of the cabin. "Fern came to us out of the blue, but we came to see her as family."

"Still do," Craig said.

"We can't do anything about Fern right now, so let's focus on what we can do something about." Sheriff Calhoun pointed at the cabin. "Show me the problem."

Slade gestured under the porch, where the burnt Santa hat lay in a heap with the stench of smoke still lingering in the air. "I don't know if the arsonist meant to destroy the cabin or simply put a scare into Ivy."

"Or Fern," Craig said.

Slade nodded in agreement. "You can see it's not much material to torch under there, but it might've been enough to burn down the house because the wood is so old and dry."

Craig set down his backpack and pulled out booties, gloves, and an evidence bag. "It's probably as simple as flammable material and gasoline. Those are easy enough to get and easy enough to burn."

"But that's not the real problem, is it?" Sheriff Calhoun asked.

"No," Slade said. "It's the intent that matters."

"Right." Sheriff Calhoun studied the area. "If the arsonist didn't get what he wanted the first time, will he escalate until he gets the attention he wants or the reaction he wants or the final situation he wants?"

"That's what worries me," Slade said.

"Craig, check for footprints." Sheriff Calhoun pointed

at the ground as he looked closer at the front of the cabin. "Maybe we'll get a hit."

Craig examined the ground before he knelt down in front of the crawl space. "Ground's dry, so I'm not seeing anything other than what I'll bag up."

"I found where the arsonist entered the Park. Maybe you can find prints there." Slade pointed toward the side of the cabin. "It looks to me like he came in off Wildcat Road."

Sheriff Calhoun walked to the side of the building and looked behind it. "It'd be easy enough to get in here with nobody in residence, nobody on alert, and the Hall in transition from one manager to another."

"I don't think this fire was meant to take out all the cabins or maybe even this one structure," Craig said. "It's simply not enough material unless the wind had come up."

"Fortunately, it didn't." Slade was relieved to hear that news, but it didn't put him much more at ease.

"And it's fortunate you were here," Sheriff Calhoun said. "I'll go take a look at the entry point and maybe I'll see something that'll help."

As the sheriff walked away, Slade put his hands on his hips and kept watch for more trouble, although that horse had already left the barn.

He heard voices at the Hall and hoped all was going well. He wanted to be there for Ivy. More than that, he *needed* to be there for her. He shook his head at his own protective instincts coming into play. She was a grown woman with experience under her belt. Still, she was city, not country. He didn't want her getting into trouble before she even knew she was in it. And yet, if anybody could ease her from one life into another, it'd be the gentle attention of Morning

Glory and the firm determination of Hedy. Ivy was in good hands and he should let it go. Yet he couldn't and he knew why—he'd fallen hard.

While Craig finished up, Slade walked around the side of the cabin, searching for anything he might have missed the first time. The sheriff was out of sight, possibly following a trail down to the road. He hated the whole situation, but he had a similarly disastrous one on his hands, too, at the new ranch. Why couldn't folks—like most in Wildcat Bluff County—just live and let live?

But that was wishful thinking on his part. He simply had to keep putting one foot in front of the other to make everyone and everything in his county safe. Easier said than done, but still, it was the right goal.

As he continued to look around, he heard the sheriff return, pushing through the thick hedge. Slade walked over to meet his friend.

Sheriff Calhoun shook his head. "You're right about this being the entry and exit point. I couldn't find any footprints. I did see a few tire tracks on the side of the road down there, but those might not have been made by the arsonist. Still, I'll get somebody out to take casts. Hopefully, we'll get a chance later to compare it to somebody's tires. Right now, those look like about fifty percent of the tires on the pickups around here."

"But every tire wears different."

"That's our ace in the hole, if we get that far down the track."

"We will. It's just a matter of time."

"That's the attitude." Sheriff Calhoun glanced around at the ground another time, as if hoping he'd missed something the first time. "Looks like we've done all we can do here. I'll stop by later and talk with Ivy, but I doubt she can tell me much more than we already know."

"Thanks for the help." Slade walked with him back to the cabin.

"All finished here." Craig pulled off his gloves and booties, then stuffed them inside his backpack. "I'll go with the sheriff and write up my report."

"I'll stay here for a bit and—"

"What are you going to do?" Craig asked. "Camp out?"

"Wish I could make sure it's safe all the time," Slade said, "but I've got the new ranch, the old ranch, the café, and about a million other things to do."

"I'll send patrols by more frequently," Sheriff Calhoun said. "But I'd appreciate it if you'd keep an eye on Ivy and the Park, too."

"I'll be glad to do it." Slade glanced toward the honky-tonk, noticing that the party hadn't broken up yet. "Fern and I discussed enlarging the menu, particularly for the holidays. You know, Christmas treats. Ivy agreed it's a good idea. I can cook and bake at the Chuckwagon, then bring the food up here."

"It's a good idea, but do you have time with everything you've got going on?" Craig appeared skeptical.

"No, I don't, but I'll do it." Slade glanced from one man to the other, giving them a wry smile. "Those two sisters..."

"Yeah. Tell me about it." Craig looked toward the Hall. "At least yours is here, while mine is in the wind."

"What makes you say she's mine?" Slade asked, feeling defensive even though his friend had called it right.

"Take a look in the mirror when you get home," Craig

said. "I'm wearing the same expression on my face."

Sheriff Calhoun chuckled, adjusted his hat, and turned toward the vehicles. "Come on, Craig, let's get back to the station before you two start crying in your beers."

Craig gave Slade a sympathetic smile before he followed the sheriff down a path toward the parking lot.

Slade rubbed a hand across his jaw, felt slight stubble, and grimaced at Craig's words. Was he that obvious when he talked about Ivy? If so, the whole county would know in no time that Slade Steele had finally fallen to his knees—not after riding a bull, but after meeting a gal.

He thrust that thought from his mind. He wasn't going to get caught up in what others might think about him. He had too much on his mind to go there. Right now, he had to make sure Ivy was okay, then he needed to get out to the new ranch and check on things. Tonight he'd pull out his great-granny's cookbook written in spidery cursive, hardly legible in some places where the purple or blue or black ink from a fountain pen had faded over time. But it was the best cookbook in the world, with old-time recipes using old-time ingredients. Some stuff he couldn't even get anymore, so he found substitutes. Lard was one ingredient he could usually live without as could most of his customers, so he substituted what worked best depending on the recipe.

As he walked down the winding path between the cabins, he thought about cowboy cookies and what he could add to make them even more special for the Hall and Christmas. He needed some ingredient that went beyond the usual fare that had originally been quick, easy, and cheap for hardworking farm and ranch families. He wanted something unique to promote Wildcat Hall, as well as his own award-winning pies.

He gave the parking lot a glance, then a second look as he neared it. If he wasn't mistaken, even more vehicles were parked there now. Word must have spread that Wildcat Hall was holding an open house to meet the new owner, or at least that's what they'd all say just to cover everybody's itch to meet Ivy and find out about Fern.

He felt a sinking sensation in the pit of his stomach. Just what Ivy needed, more folks on her doorstep. He hoped he wouldn't find her locked in a bathroom. She'd had to endure a cabin fire, and now a horde of strangers had descended on her. He increased his pace, hurrying to get inside, assess the damage, and if necessary, take over as host.

When he pushed open the front door and stepped inside, he was almost knocked over by the wall of noise from patrons and Dolly Parton trilling from the camou-flaged speakers of a state-of-the-art sound system. All the tables were filled, and there was standing room only, with folks spilling outside into the beer garden. Beer, wine, and sarsaparilla were flowing by the look of the glasses in every-body's hands.

He hadn't seen the Hall this lively in many a long year. How was Ivy standing it? She'd said she wasn't used to a lot of people, particularly entertaining them. At least that's what he'd thought she'd told him. Maybe he'd gotten it all wrong. She didn't need to be rescued. She needed to be congratulated.

He smiled as he pushed through the crowd, using his height and size to cut a path for him. He said his hellos as he saw friends and neighbors, but he kept moving forward, looking for Ivy. Finally, he saw her. She stood behind the bar with Morning Glory and Nocona Jones, his favorite lawyer and cowgirl. They'd donned matching pink, rhinestone-studded aprons festooned with "Wildcat Hall" in Old West lettering. Fern must have ordered the fancy aprons before she left town because he'd never seen them before. They definitely suited the ladies and the place.

He bellied up to the bar, along with all the others who were ordering and being served drinks. Ivy was laughing and talking and filling beer mugs as if she'd been doing it all her life. She fit. There was no other word for it. City to country in one blazing moment.

And yet, he stood there, feeling like he'd lost her before he'd ever had her. She didn't need him anymore. She had all of Wildcat Bluff County at her beck and call—just like her sister, Fern. He'd wanted to keep her to himself, at least for a little while—or more likely a long while. And now…he turned to go.

"Slade!"

He looked back. She was smiling at him, beckoning him closer, giving him that look in her eyes that made the rest of the room fade away. He felt his heart beat faster. He leaned toward her.

"Thanks." She handed him a sarsaparilla in a frosty glass mug.

When their fingers touched, he felt that familiar zing between them. He was going nowhere fast. He'd fight the entire county for her if need be, because she was every bright color in his personal rainbow. "Are you doing okay?"

She grinned, white teeth flashing. "Impromptu party. Who'd have guessed I could handle it?"

"You look like a natural behind the bar." He returned her

smile as he felt his phone vibrate in his pocket. He pulled it out, glanced down at the text message, and felt his stomach clinch at the news. He set down his mug. "Gotta go."

"What is it?"

He leaned forward so only she could hear him. "Cattle rustlers struck the new ranch again."

"Oh no! Do you need help?"

"I'll get ahold of Sheriff Calhoun and take it from there."

"Will you let me know what's happening?"

"I'll text or come by later." He was glad she cared enough to be concerned about him.

She reached out and squeezed his hand. "Stay safe."

"Always."

And then he was out the door, on the run, and in his truck, hauling out of there as fast as he could go.

Chapter 8

"SHERIFF, HATE TO BOTHER YOU AGAIN SO SOON." SLADE cradled his cell phone between his shoulder and ear as he started his truck. "Rustlers hit my new ranch again."

"When?" Sheriff Calhoun asked.

"Not sure. Cowboys just found the gate open, cattle turned loose, and tire tracks."

"How many head did they get?"

"We won't be able to tell until morning, when we make a count. If the rustlers got scared off, probably not more than three or four, but that's still worth it to them. If they filled a trailer, we're looking at fifteen or more cows."

"Sorry to hear it. I'll meet you at the ranch house."

"Thanks. I'm headed there now."

Slade clicked off and dropped the phone on the seat beside him, trying not to get so mad he couldn't think straight. He pulled out of the parking lot and headed down Wildcat Road with his foot heavy on the gas. He forced himself to slow to a reasonable speed. No point in rushing to get there. The theft had already gone down and nothing could reverse the situation.

At this rate, there wouldn't be a cow left on the new ranch. If he didn't get the rustlers stopped, he risked losing even more head after the cattle drive. So far, they'd outsmarted him at every turn. He hoped the sheriff had some new ideas to stop the thieves because he was fresh out of them.

He turned onto the ranch under the brand-new sign that arched over the cattle guard in cut-out, black-painted steel that read "Steele Trap II." Looked good. A new and shiny barbwire fence of six strands made getting in or out of the pasture a lot harder than a four- or five-strand fence. It stretched beside the road in both directions. They were pouring money into the place and it'd pay off—if they got the rustlers out of their hair soon.

He drove up the narrow gravel road, looking right and left. Nothing appeared out of order here, but the spread was hundreds of acres with a lot of loose-wire fence that was just asking for trouble, so it needed to be replaced before the cattle drive. Fortunately, he had hardworking ranch hands who were on that job, but even so, he had to stay on top of that as well as everything else. And, as if he didn't have enough to do, he'd just added preparing holiday food for Wildcat Hall. But that notion simply made him smile because it brought him back to the fascinating and alluring Ivy Bryant. He'd do about anything to spend time with her. And he'd definitely carve out as much time as he possibly could for her.

Just the thought of Ivy made him feel better. He adjusted his weight on the seat, trying to ease the pain in his hip. Stress tightened the muscles that pressed on the nerves that… It was ancient news he didn't need to rethink. He'd healed as well as he was going to heal, and most of the time his old injury didn't bother him much. But right now, with arsonists and rustlers adding to the overall pressure of moving into the new ranch and staring at an upcoming cattle drive that was getting bigger by the moment, he was unable to exert his usual control over his limp. And of all the times for his injury to act up, it just had to be when he'd found a woman he hoped would see him as strong. Not weak. Sometimes life simply wasn't fair, and he knew that as well as anybody. He resisted a sigh. Ivy would just have to like him the way he was or not like him at all.

Amber lights on tall poles illuminated the area as he drove up to the sprawling, one-story ranch house that Mr. Werner had built with his own hands using large pieces of flat, red rock trimmed with natural cedar. He'd added dramatic, hand-carved double front doors made of cedar, too, with the same accent on the windows. All in all, it was a beautiful place, landscaped with dormant flower beds, green shrubs, and leafless trees and set on a rise overlooking acres of pretty pasture with blue ponds dotting the landscape here and there. In the future, there'd be plenty of grazing black and red Angus to see while watching horses kick up their heels in other pastures. He looked forward to getting it all set in place.

He wouldn't change the exterior for anything, but he was working on updating and upgrading the eighties-style interior because he planned to make this house his home and he wanted all the modern conveniences. He also needed new furniture, although it'd come completely furnished since Mr. Werner's children hadn't wanted many of the interior items beyond family keepsakes and a few mementos. He had made one major change. He'd traded the old furniture in the master bedroom suite for finely crafted red cedar pieces from a local artisan. On top of that, he'd added a big, new, king-size mattress. His hip thanked him every time he slept there.

Sheriff Calhoun hadn't arrived yet, so he glanced around, taking stock of the area. Again, nothing appeared out of place. He decided to check on the outbuildings, so he drove past the house, looked at the pastures, and stopped his pickup. More amber light illuminated the structures. Cattle barn. Horse barn. Storage buildings. Corrals. Several four-wheelers and two pickups were parked outside the barns. All looked normal, but something wasn't right.

He thought about it a moment, searching the area for what didn't fit. Finally, it struck him. Too quiet. No activity. He heard his truck engine idle, but that was it. Where was everybody? He honked his horn to see if he could get a rise out of somebody.

Tater, that rascal of an Aussie cow dog, ran out of the cattle barn followed by Oscar, the leathery-skinned, bald-headed, crotchety ranch foreman who'd most likely forgotten more than Slade would ever know about running a ranch. Tater wore a red bandanna around his neck, while Oscar wore hat, shirt, jeans, and boots. Both looked frayed around the edges, but he well knew it was just a guise to put you off their true, bred-in-the-bone toughness.

Slade lowered his window as Tater loped over and Oscar sauntered over. "Heard we had another visit from our new friends."

"Weren't from me." Oscar spit tobacco to one side. "I wouldn't use one of those cancer-causing, new-fangled devices if you paid me."

"I know." He quickly slid his cell phone out of sight before Oscar saw it and backed out of EMF range. "Sydney texted me. Owl called and let her know."

Oscar just shook his head. "That Sydney gets prettier all the time. And smarter. Can't wait to get this dad-nab-it cattle drive done and gone so I can get back to where I belong and see her every day."

"My sister misses you, too," he said.

"Sure she does. We're simpatico." Oscar gave a big tobacco-stained, toothy grin. "Not surprised it was Hoot-Owl done called her. He'd use any excuse. He's still smartin' that she up and got engaged to that Dune Barrett."

"You know you like Dune."

"Like him. Hate him. Don't matter. He's her choice, so that's that."

"Right." Slade twisted his mind back to business. Oscar could get you so far off track with his musings that you'd forget what you came for. "Sheriff Calhoun is on his way."

"And he'll find diddly-squat."

"Why do you say that?"

"These guys got brains. More's the pity."

"No argument. They have me running in circles."

"Hate to tell you, but this time those cows they rustled were a ruse."

"What do you mean?"

"They snatched Fernando."

"You've got to be kidding me." Slade felt his heart sink to the pit of his stomach, thinking of the value of artificial insemination. "That's our high-dollar Angus bull with the hottest sperm. He's an AI bull, not a cow bull. His straws go for big bucks."

"I know all that. Every rancher in Texas knows that. And I bet every one of them wishes they could afford even one Fernando bloodline calf."

"Are you sure he's gone?" Slade couldn't believe his ears. "He's massive—two thousand pounds easy. And he gets mad fast. Only Storm can soothe him."

"I know all that, too." Oscar spit to the side. "But he's one gone bull now."

"But Fernando was in the secure, climate-controlled barn Mr. Werner built for him. He has an EID button in his ear so he can be identified with a scanner. He's registered with the American Angus Association. He's got his own pasture and pond, but we don't let him out there at night."

"You're preaching to the choir here, even if I don't cotton to these new-fangled tag apps, computer downloads, and whatnots. Pencil and paper and brands work fine for me."

"Oscar, we're in the twenty-first century. Bigger herds mean we need faster methods for keeping track of them. I want matched pair tags, ear visual, and EID on the herds at Steele Trap II."

"I hear you, but count me out on spreadsheets." Oscar shook his head. "That EID button didn't save Fernando from getting snatched by rustlers."

"But it'll help get him back."

"Hope so. He should've been right as rain here, but nothing's normal and they took advantage."

"I won't believe it till I see he's gone with my own eyes."

"Let's go." Oscar headed toward Fernando's barn.

"Mr. Werner wouldn't have left anything to chance with Fernando's housing any more than he did with his 1959 Cadillac. Celeste was in pristine shape when he gave that car to Sydney." Slade caught up with Oscar and Tater.

"That's not the problem." Oscar reached the steel structure and nodded toward the oversized door. "Take a look."

Slade examined the door, the lock, the frame. He felt his heart sink because there was no sign of forced entry. "They had the lock combination number?"

"Remember that cowboy you hired a few weeks ago? You were shorthanded here."

"Yeah. Reggie Rogers. He wasn't from around this area, but he had good references."

"Maybe fake. He's gone, too."

Slade groaned as he slid open the door, stepped inside, and looked around the area. Nothing was much disturbed. "Drugged, you think?"

"Maybe. But if Reggie let him get hungry, he might've followed a bucket of feed into a trailer."

Slade took in the empty barn one more time, then stepped outside, shutting the door behind him. "I'll alert the sheriff and the American Angus Association. Sales barns will be notified about the theft, so the auctioneer brand inspectors will keep an eye out for him."

"I'm thinking they're selling our cattle in New Mexico. They'd cross the state line at El Paso. Least livestock checkpoints going west and less chance of getting caught at those sales barns than someplace close to home."

"I agree about the cows. But a bull like Fernando? It'd be chancy."

"Out of the country?"

"Mexico? Canada? I just don't know."

Oscar spit tobacco to the side. "Tough luck."

"It's bad all the way around. Storm will be crushed."

"Right. Your niece thinks that bull hung the moon."

"At least he's got good feet. At that weight, it's the first thing to go."

"No biggie right now. He's still young."

"You're right." Slade headed for his truck. "One way or another, we've got to get Fernando back."

Oscar nodded in agreement. "They're watching us like hawks somehow or the other. They know our every move, so they can sneak in and out with nobody the wiser."

"It's a mess."

"Look," Oscar said, "you got bigger fish to fry, so let me take the sheriff to the barn to bag his samples, take his photos, and get whatever else he thinks will make his fancy science whisper sweet nothings in his ear."

Slade chuckled at the image. "Sounds like you're still not too taken with modern science."

"Hah! The day I believe a bunch of machines can tell me more than a thinking-man's mind is the day you might as well cart me off to the glue factory."

"You can think circles around most everybody, so I see your point."

"Yeah. You may see it, but I'm not sure you get it."

"Let's save that for another day." Slade took a deep breath. "I've got other news."

"What now?" Oscar spit in the dirt again while Tater adjusted his haunches to a more comfortable position.

"I was at Wildcat Hall talking with Ivy, Fern's sister, about baking and cooking something special for the holidays when we discovered a fire at one of the cowboy cabins."

Oscar cocked his head. "When was this and what's the sister like?"

"Which answer do you want first?"

"Most important."

Slade just grinned, knowing Oscar had him. "Ivy's... well, she's real fine."

Oscar chuckled, looked down at Tater, and patted him

on the head. "Now here's something bears watching, don't you know?"

"I was able to put out the fire without damage. Sheriff Calhoun stopped by and checked it. Craig took samples."

"When?"

"Little while ago."

Oscar looked off into the distance, then down at Tater. "What do you think, old boy? Fire at the Park distracts Slade Steele, the new owner of this ranch, and Fernando goes missing about the same time. Think there's a connection?"

"Oh no," Slade groaned as he felt his stomach churn. "We thought somebody had it in for Fern or Ivy or the Park."

"Maybe. Maybe not."

"For sure it's something to discuss with the sheriff—and keep in mind."

"Yep." Oscar glanced toward the ranch house. "Here comes the law. You want me to take over or not?"

"I feel responsible to—"

"Think I can't handle it?"

"No, of course not." Slade watched Sheriff Calhoun pull up on the other side of Oscar and Tater.

"I'm guessing there's a lonely lady at Wildcat Hall in need of comforting after that fire fright. Home cooking always fits the bill. Maybe a slice of your famous pecan pie would perk her right up." Oscar gave a sidelong glance with a little smirk on his lips. "On the other hand, cowboys have always known how to perk up ladies with a song, a dance, or a—"

"Stop right there."

"Kiss." Oscar winked at Slade. "Better see to your lady friend while I see to the sheriff." He headed toward Sheriff Calhoun with Tater following him.

Slade just shook his head. You couldn't put anything over on Oscar because he was always one step ahead of everybody. But he didn't necessarily have to like it. He stepped down from his truck and walked over to the sheriff.

Sheriff Calhoun lowered his window. "Sorry about the bad news."

"Thanks." Slade gestured toward Oscar and Tater. "It's worse than we thought. They got Fernando."

"No! How'd they get him?"

"Reggie Rogers is missing, too."

"That new cowboy?"

"One and the same."

Sheriff Calhoun nodded thoughtfully. "If he's the rustler, I'd guess he used an alias, but maybe we can tie him into the system with fingerprints. I'll check for them."

"Appreciate it. Oscar can take you to the back pasture and the barn. I'm going to alert the AAA and we'll go from there."

"Good idea. I'll take care of things on my end." Sheriff Calhoun shook his head. "Storm is gonna have a fit."

"Don't I know it. We just have to get that bull back."

"We'll do our best."

"Right now I'm headed down to Wildcat Hall to check on things there."

"Okay," Sheriff Calhoun said. "I'll let you know what we find out."

Slade stepped back, gave Oscar a nod, and walked to his truck.

He started his pickup, backed up, and got out of there. Truth of the matter, he was glad to let them take over. If he could've helped, he would've, but they wouldn't find

anything like the other times. He was missing something...
something big and important. But he couldn't see it, not yet.

For now, he was better off making sure Ivy was safe.
That's where he wanted to be. And that's where he hoped
she wanted him to be. First, he'd best tell Sydney and let her
break the bad news to Storm.

Oscar was right about one thing, if not everything—
home cooking and lip-licking pie could be the way to Ivy's
heart. He'd just make a quick stop at the Chuckwagon Café
and pick up some good eats for her before he went back to
the Hall.

Chapter 9

IVY STOOD IN THE OPEN DOORWAY OF WILDCAT HALL as she watched the last pickup exit the parking lot. She felt a little numb, a little excited, and a little bewildered at the way she had been instantly accepted into the heart of this rural community. Suddenly she had more new friends than she could have accumulated in a year or more, if she'd been trying, in Houston. She wasn't quite sure how it had happened to her. Maybe Fern. Maybe Slade. Maybe Wildcat Hall. She was pretty sure it couldn't simply be her because she'd never had it happen before in her life. On the other hand, maybe it was country instead of city.

Everybody had even cleaned up after themselves, making sure she had nothing extra to do after they were gone. She was back to where she'd started when the day began, except now she had lots of new friends who had volunteered to help get Wildcat Hall ready for Christmas.

She stood still as she watched the quickly falling night, one hand holding open the door and the other stroking the soft lace on her fancy apron. Stars were appearing as the sky grew dark, all mysterious and evocative bright points. She didn't see them so clearly in the city, with all the ambient light sources. And she hadn't missed them—until this moment.

When she went back to Houston, she'd know they were up there, simply waiting for her to see their bright beauty again. She could almost touch the loss she'd feel when that time came for her. But the feeling didn't make sense, not when the city offered so much in shopping, eating, entertainment, work, friends, while the country offered wide-open spaces, beautiful skies, bighearted people.

She shook her head to remove the distraction. Spaces, skies, and people weren't a big enough trade-off. She was going back. It was just a matter of when she could get away.

As she cemented that thought in her mind, she saw another truck turn off Wildcat Road, pull into the parking lot, and stop near the front door. She recognized the solid black vehicle with silver trim sporting a big metal cowcatcher across the front grill—Slade Steele. She felt her heart speed up in anticipation.

He stepped down from his pickup, took off his cowboy hat, and tossed it onto the front seat. When he turned back, he saw her. And paused. He gave a slight nod in acknowledgment and started forward in his easy, ground-eating stride with his limp a bit more pronounced than usual.

She felt a little tug from him to her or her to him—or maybe both directions at once—that caused her to place a hand over her heart. She wasn't sure why she did it except that it seemed right as she became vitally aware of the softness and tenderness she felt toward him, the determined power he projected toward her, and the excitement that was building between them.

He stopped in front of her, tilted up her chin with one big hand, and placed a gentle kiss on her lips.

She was so astonished that she simply stood there, trying to get her mind to work again, but it had gone on hiatus, leaving only her body in charge. And her body demanded much more than the single kiss that had started a river of molten lava burning through her.

"Are you okay after all your guests?" He carefully tugged her hair loose, snagged her ponytail holder around his big wrist where the hot pink looked wildly out of place, and smoothed the hair around her face with the palms of both hands.

"You're touching me."

"I know."

"What makes you think that's okay?"

"This." And he cupped her face with both hands and pressed a longer, hotter kiss to her lips.

She shivered in response and took a step back. "I only met you today."

"I know."

"And...and I'm not sure it is okay."

"What can I do to make it okay?" He closed the space between them and kicked the door shut behind him.

She pressed her hand harder over her heart, as if to keep it in place. She felt almost light-headed from his hot kisses, his intense blue eyes, and his sage-and-citrus scent.

"Tell me." He leaned toward her, searching her face for an answer.

"I—I'm not sure." She held her ground this time, but it wasn't easy in his nearly overwhelming presence. "Today has been so much, and you—"

"I helped you."

"Yes, but—"

"I'm here to help you again. I brought supper. It's in the truck."

She smiled, feeling her eyes crinkle at the corners in plea- sure. "And you think the way to a woman's heart is through her stomach."

He grinned back. "Yeah."

"I suppose it's possible."

"I've got lots of food…and I know how to cook it."

She chuckled at his words.

"And I'm willing to share it."

"But still, you touched me."

"I know."

"And I suppose you plan to do it again."

"Yeah."

"And I suppose you think I'll let you."

"If you don't, I'll be in serious trouble."

If he hadn't looked so adorable, she might have been able to resist the kisses, the food, the banter, but those big blue eyes were burning a hole in her heart and she was falling deep into them—and she didn't want to climb out. She put her hands flat on his chest, feeling the muscles tighten in response, went up on her toes, and placed the softest of gentle kisses on his firm lips.

He sighed in relief and pleasure. "That's the answer I've been waiting for since the moment I laid eyes on you."

"I didn't know you asked me a question."

"Not in so many words, but it's been there between us from the first."

"Maybe I was too distracted to notice."

"Maybe…or you didn't want to notice." He lifted a hand toward her, then dropped it to his side. "You answered my question now. That's all that counts."

She nodded, feeling once again that this endless day-in-to-night was propelling her down a racetrack so fast that she could hardly catch her breath.

"It's been a long day for you." He raised his hand and this time tenderly cupped her jaw before letting her go. "I'm not helping matters, am I?"

"You mentioned food. I could use it."

"Your wish is my command." He glanced around the front bar. "Do you want to eat here or—"

"My place, please…or at least Fern's home."

"It's yours."

"For now."

"No, not for now. Like everything else in Wildcat Bluff, it's yours for the asking and for as long as you want it."

"Thanks." She knew he meant much more than the cowboy cabin and that he was putting himself on the line. Only a truly self-confident man could do that with a woman he'd just met. She didn't understand why he was doing it except that there was this *thing* between them that didn't appear to be going away anytime soon. And she was becoming more infected by it as each transformative moment ticked toward midnight.

"Let's lock up here and go to your place."

"I'll get my purse and keys."

"Take all the keys, will you?"

"Do you think somebody might break in here?" She took off her pretty apron and hung it up behind the bar as the importance of his words sank in deeper. She picked up her purse.

"I think we want to be extra careful."

"You're right." She grabbed all the keys from behind the bar and stuffed them inside her purse. As she walked back to him, she remembered she wasn't the only one who'd had trouble that day. "I'm sorry I didn't ask sooner, but what about the theft at your ranch? I hope it wasn't too bad."

He shrugged his broad shoulders, shaking his head. "It's

about as bad as it can get."

"Oh no." She reached out and squeezed his arm in sympathy. "Is there anything I can do?"

"Have supper with me tonight, and I'll tell you about it."

"That's easy. We're already on our way." She flipped off the main lights and then glanced up at him. "Do you think I should leave on more lights than usual?"

"Yes." He adjusted the light settings before he nodded in satisfaction. "If you like, I'll install extra motion-sensor and night lights tomorrow."

"I'd like that very much."

"Good. We're out of here, then."

After they stepped outside, she carefully locked up the Hall, hoping nothing would happen to it during the night. "Will your pickup be okay out here?"

He clasped her hand and threaded their fingers together. "After today, I'm not counting on anything staying safe, but it's got a loud alarm if somebody tries to break into it."

"My SUV is the same way, but at least it's parked near my cabin."

"Glad to hear it." He led her over to his truck, opened the door, pulled out a white paper sack, and handed it to her.

"Thanks. Smells delicious."

"House specialty." He locked his pickup, then clasped her hand again.

As they walked along the illuminated path with stars brightening the sky, she felt content—no, much more than that. She felt bubbly in a kind of way that she hadn't known was possible anymore. Even though they were dealing with an arsonist and cattle rustlers, Slade made her feel safe. And happy.

When they reached her cabin, it was dark inside and

outside, with only the lights along the path to help see the stairs.

"I'm glad I'm with you," he said. "You've got no business coming home to a dark house, even if you hadn't had that fire earlier."

"I didn't know I'd be out so late. I agree it is way too dark here, particularly in the shadow of the porch."

"If you'll give me your keys, I'll unlock the door and turn on the lights."

"That's okay. I need to get used to doing this for myself."

"Not tonight. I'd be more comfortable checking out the cabin before you go inside."

"Do you think—"

"Let's don't take chances."

She handed him the key. "I think I'd better put timers on the inside and outside lights."

"Smart idea."

She grasped the railing and walked up to the porch, letting him unlock the door and go inside. In a bit, lights came on outside, so she quickly looked around but didn't see anything to give her pause.

"Come on in," he called. "Everything is fine."

She quickly stepped into the cabin, shut the door, and locked it behind her. "Thanks. I need to get used to living differently in the country."

"You just need to take a few precautions."

"I will." She walked over, set the sack on the countertop, and pulled out two deep containers and two foil-covered plates. "Smells wonderful. What did you bring us?"

"Hearty beef stew. It's always good on a cool night."

"Sounds wonderful."

"And pecan pie."

"Be still my heart."

He chuckled as he stepped into the kitchen area. "Why don't you wash up while I set the food on the table?"

"Why don't we both wash up and get our dinner ready?"

He glanced at her with a big smile. "Togetherness. I like it."

As they fixed their easy meal, she was surprised at how well they worked together. They didn't bump into each other. They didn't get into each other's way. They didn't even question who got glasses out of the cabinet or who set the table. It was as if they'd already established the pattern long ago.

When she sat down across the table from him and spooned stew into her mouth, she moaned in delight. "This is delicious."

"Thanks. We only use the best ingredients and best sources to get the best taste for our customers."

"It's definitely worth it."

As a companionable silence settled over them while they ate, she realized how easily they were sharing a meal without any awkward moments. Comfortable in the kitchen. Comfortable at the table. Comfortable together.

"How's your heart doing?" he asked in a teasing tone.

She chuckled as she got his meaning about winning her heart through food. "It's too early to tell."

"Wait till you try the pie."

"Is that your secret to success?"

"I'm not an award winner for nothing."

"In that case, maybe my heart isn't too safe."

"Just try your pie and let me know."

She rolled her eyes at him, picked up her fork, and took a bite. "Oh my. Absolutely delicious." She licked her lower lip to get every little bit of the heavenly taste.

He grinned as he leaned forward. "Keep doing that and you'll taste more than my pie."

She gave him a mischievous look, then took another bite, licked her lip, set down her fork, slid her chair back, and patted her stomach in contentment. "I somehow doubt you can possibly match your pie."

"Really?" He stood up. "I think that's a challenge."

"I was kidding, honestly."

"Too late now." He stalked over, picked her up in his arms, and carried her to the sofa, where he sat down with her in his lap.

"Slade!" She wriggled in his arms, but he held her firmly against him.

"I'm going to kiss you properly now. That way you can compare me to my pie."

"What?" She couldn't believe he was serious, so she made a joke. "Is this a scientific experiment?"

"That…and a taste test."

"I can already tell you I prefer pie."

"No fair. You didn't give me a chance to prove my point."

Just to tease him, she puckered up and squeezed her eyes tightly shut.

He laughed at her antics as he rubbed her lower lip with his thumb. "We're going to do this right or we aren't going to do it at all."

She opened her eyes to see his expression. Surprisingly, he still looked serious. "Well, how long will it take?" She continued to tease. "Remember, I'm not finished with my pecan pie."

"If I do it right, all night would be about right."

And then he lowered his head and gently captured her lower lip with his teeth, running his tongue over the inside of her lip as he eased her head back to rest against his arm, while he thrust his fingers into her hair to hold her tighter.

She felt her entire being melt like ice cream left too long in the sun as he nibbled and licked and sucked until her lips felt hot and swollen and sensitive, her body throbbing and burning and aching for more of his touch. And when he finally delved deep into her mouth, she moaned and clasped his shoulders, pulling him closer to her.

He kissed like heaven on earth. He kissed like she was the most delectable of sweet treats. He kissed with such slow deliberateness it felt like he might really kiss her all night long. And she wanted his kiss to go on forever. And she wanted him to ease the ache deep inside her. And she wanted him to slake the thirst, the hunger, the need he'd created in her with every word, every look, every touch.

But she also wanted to give back...to make him crave her as much as he made her crave him, and so she kissed him, thrusting into his mouth, tasting the sweetness of pie, nibbling his full lips to sensitize them, licking his swollen mouth, teasing and tormenting while she felt the heat building between them as she ran her hands through his thick hair.

And then he swiftly turned the tables as he groaned deep in his throat and gently lifted her, set her back on the sofa, and leaned down until his hard chest pressed against her soft breasts.

Reality hit home as she was pinned beneath the hot, muscled strength poised to give her everything her body craved—and she knew he could take her there, over and over and over again.

But he didn't. He grew still. He raised his head. He looked into her eyes. "Me or pecan pie?"

Chapter 10

"OH! YOU'RE GOADING ME." IVY PUSHED AGAINST HIS chest in frustration to get up now that he had changed the dynamic and was teasing her. "Pie. I definitely want pecan pie."

"Are you sure?" He raised his body slightly and lifted her hand to his lips to kiss each fingertip while watching her with a smile in his blue eyes that crinkled the corners. "Don't I tempt you just a little bit?"

"You're tempting me to toss you off this sofa." She felt cross, caught between wanting him to satisfy her and not wanting him to complicate her life. Pie definitely seemed the safer of the two options.

"Think you could do it?"

"Not fair." She felt even more cross because she couldn't move him if her life depended on it.

"When is life fair?"

She sighed, knowing he was right in too many ways. He'd been right from the first, there for her from the first. And now he was tempting her and teasing her and trying to get a rise out of her. He didn't just want her physically connected to him. That was now the rub. He wanted her emotionally connected to him. And that bit of reality put her on high alert. Fun was one thing. Serious was quite another. She knew better than to endanger her heart. It'd been broken before and she never wanted to go there again.

Besides, even if he was playing for keeps, she was only in Wildcat Bluff for a short time. Houston was her home.

He leaned down and nuzzled her neck, tracing the swirl of her ear with the tip of his tongue.

She shivered in response. "Life can be fair, but you're definitely not playing fair. Food. Kisses. Help."

"There's plenty more where that came from."

She moaned as he nibbled along the curve of her jaw to her lips.

He stopped and looked down at her. "Where you're concerned, I wouldn't dare play fair."

"And why not?"

He softly kissed her. "I'd never chance losing you."

She bit her lower lip, feeling desperate to stop her fast slide into his endless charm. What was it about this man that made her so vulnerable to him?

"Let me do that." And he nibbled her lower lip, coaxing another moan from her as he tenderly plied her sensitive skin.

"Please," she finally said in a husky tone, needing him to be the strong one because she was fast on the road to losing the ability to resist him, along with any vexation she'd felt earlier. "Let's just finish our pie."

He gave her a tender smile as he gently stroked strands of hair back from her face. "I like hearing 'please' on your lips. I want to hear it again."

"Will I get my pie then?"

"If you're sure that's what you really want."

"Please...pie." She barely managed to get the words out, because she definitely was sure that pie was the last thing she wanted when she had the tastiest treat in the state kissing her. Sometimes life really wasn't fair, and this was one of those times. She'd just met Slade earlier that day. She wasn't the kind of woman who fell into bed with a hot guy simply because he was there—and she was in no position to further complicate her life or risk her heart.

"When I hear you say 'please' again, it's going to be for something a lot more satisfying—to us both." He started to stand up but groaned in pain and quickly slumped down on the far end of the sofa.

Startled, she looked at him in concern as she sat up. "What is it?"

He just shook his head with his jaw clenched shut.

"What can I do to help?"

"Nothing." He took several deep, controlling breaths. "Old injury acting up."

"I'm sorry."

"Yeah. Bad timing." He glanced around the room. "I'd better go."

"You can't drive in pain."

"Sure I can."

"It'd be too dangerous."

"I'm not helpless."

"I know." She stood up, feeling empowered and energized in her need to help the man who'd assisted her that day. "It's my turn to help you."

"How?"

"You can sleep on the sofa and go home in the morning."

"I thought you wanted pie—and me gone."

She slid down until she was almost touching him. She picked up his big, strong hand and held it between her own small ones. "I want you safe."

"Folks might talk." He hesitated, looking at their joined hands. "I never meant to stay tonight. It's just—"

"I know." She squeezed his fingers and felt his strong grip in return. "It's just that things got a little out of hand."

"More than a little." He gave a small huff of frustration. "I was in an awkward position too long. I know better."

"Did I make you forget?"

He glanced at her then, wariness in his eyes as he gave a slight nod.

"I forgot about everything, too—except you."

A small smile touched his lips. "I'll be better in a bit."

"Would heat help? I'm sure there must be a pad I can heat in the microwave."

"Don't bother. I'll just—"

"Lie down. Will that help?"

"Yes."

"Okay." She stood up. "I'll get a pillow and blanket."

"I wish you wouldn't go to the trouble."

"I'd be a poor host if I didn't help you." She looked down at Slade, feeling him get to her in a whole new way that was just as powerful as all the other little ways that had been building since she first met him. He was so strong, so powerful, so in control, and yet he had a small vulnerability that opened him up to her in a way that she would never have expected to experience. She liked him—probably too much for her own good.

She left him leaning against the sofa while she went to the linen closet in the hall. She slipped a fresh pillowcase on an extra pillow, then selected a multicolor, multi-fabric quilt for him. She hurried back. He sat with his head against the sofa, eyes closed. In that relaxed position, he looked surprisingly young—and vulnerable. She knew he wouldn't want her to see him or think of him that way, so she made noise as she reentered the room.

He snapped his head up, defenses falling back into place as he warily watched her.

She wondered if the pain was chronic, so that he had to stoically work past it all the time. If so, he was even stronger than she could possibly imagine. She wanted to ask about his injury, but she didn't want to appear intrusive, particularly not right now.

He gave a little smile, just a quirk of one corner of his sexy mouth. "Are you babying me?"

She hesitated, not quite sure what to say—agree or disagree. Neither seemed right, because there was already too much tension in the room. She needed to lighten this up, so his injury didn't come between them and cause problems now or later. "Maybe that's what it seems like, but in fact, I hoped to settle you so comfortably you wouldn't want to get up and keep me from stealing the last of your pie."

He grinned, chuckling. "So that's your final choice?"

"Didn't you know pie—and, of course, chocolate—always wins with women?"

"I'd suspected that was the case, considering my pie admirers, but I'd sincerely hoped it wasn't true."

She laughed, greatly relieved as she felt tension drain from the room. "I regret I must confirm what may very well be women's favorite choices."

He sighed as he put a hand on his chest in mock heartache. "Here I am in need of tender loving care and I get mocked by a pie lover."

"I'm sure there are plenty of Slade lovers out there."

He gave a rueful smile, dropping his hand back to the

sofa. "But what if the only one I care about is in here, not out there?"

She felt that zinger go straight to her heart—and pierce deep. If she wasn't careful, she was going to be the biggest Slade lover in town. Again, she didn't know how to respond to him. He was being so disarmingly straightforward. Even when he teased her, he continually closed the distance she kept trying to put between them.

"Is that pillow and quilt for me, or are you going to hog it?" he said with a knowing look in his eyes, as if he was letting her off the hook and they both knew it.

She realized she hadn't moved since she'd entered the room, so entranced by him that she still held what she'd brought him. "I'd offer you the bed, but it's so old and low and small that it sags in the center. The sofa is newer and will give you more support."

"Is that your way of saying the bed is off-limits?"

She tossed the blanket and pillow on the sofa beside him. "You do realize you have a one-track mind."

"That's not my fault." He grinned at her, blue eyes lighting up like a sun-washed sky. "It's yours."

"You are so full of malarkey." She rolled her eyes at him, then marched over to the table, sat down, and picked up her fork. "Still, you seem to be feeling better."

"Yeah…but I might have a relapse any moment."

She just shook her head, then forked a piece of pie, stuck it in her mouth, and smiled in contentment. "Delicious."

"Are you really going to take my piece, too?"

"Yes." She pulled his plate to her side of the table.

"Cruel." He lay down, propped the pillow under his head, and tossed the quilt haphazardly across his hips.

"Not at all. Realistic."

"I'm still hungry."

She glanced over at him as she finished off her piece of pie and took a drink of water. He was trying to look pathetic, but it only came off as comical. Well, and totally cute, but she'd never tell him that and chance bruising his ego. "If you felt up to driving, you could go back to the Chuckwagon for more food."

"No can do. My arms aren't feeling too strong. Maybe you'd better come over and feed me the last of my pie."

"What?" She couldn't believe his nerve. She was beginning to think there wasn't anything wrong with him at all. Was he playing her?

"I thought you were going to baby me."

"I thought you didn't want me to."

"Changed my mind." He gave her a sly look. "What if I said 'please'?"

She sighed, wondering how she had gotten into this situation. She thought back to the first moment she'd met him. The day had started out simply enough. She'd been trying to put up a few Christmas decorations. He'd arrived like a whirlwind with a big grin on his handsome face and turned her life upside down until she was sliding down a slippery slope toward his open arms.

"Please."

She glanced over at him. "Really, Slade, are you in pain?"

"Yeah, but you're making it all better."

"Be serious."

"I am." He gave a sincere smile.

"I don't know what to believe." She picked up his plate and fork. "I probably should just send you home."

"Please?"

She walked over and knelt beside the sofa, mentally shaking her head at her own susceptibility to him. "Open up." She cut off a piece of pie and gently eased the tip of the fork into his mouth.

He closed his lips around it and sucked off the piece, eyeing her the entire time as if he was tasting her and not the pie.

She licked her own bottom lip in response, hardly realizing she'd done it until he looked at her mouth—and gave a satisfied smile. She gently pulled back the fork and picked up another piece of pie. Two could play at this game. She put that piece into her own mouth and slowly chewed, never taking her eyes from his blue gaze that grew increasingly hot. She tucked the last piece onto the fork and held it out to him. When he took the pie into his mouth, he continued to watch her until she couldn't take the heat anymore. He was making her want so much more than food or laughter.

After he swallowed, he held out his hand, beckoning her closer. "That's the sweetest piece of pie I ever ate."

"It was good." She set down the plate and fork, then leaned toward him, letting him enclose her fingers in the warmth of his hand.

"Want to know why?"

She shrugged, not sure if she wanted to know what was on his mind now that they were getting past teasing each other.

"You're sweet."

She simply sat there, not sure what to say, because "sweet" was a fine, old Texas endearment.

"You ate from the fork first." He pushed his explanation.

She nodded, feeling warm all over from his words.

"You made the pie sweeter than anything I could ever make."

"You're sweet, too."

"Really?"

"You ate from the fork first."

He chuckled, grinning at her.

"That means you made it sweetest of all."

He laughed harder. "You're not going to let me get away with anything, are you?"

"Somebody's got to keep you in line, right?" She squeezed his hand, picked up the plate, and stood.

"They keep trying, but you may be the only one who can do it." He threw off the blanket and sat up.

"I was kidding." She quickly turned away and set the plate and fork on the table.

"I'm not."

She glanced back. He was serious again.

He limped over to her, took her face in his hands, and pressed a soft kiss to her lips. "I'm going now."

"But I thought—"

"I thought so, too, but trust me, it's best if I go."

"Will you be okay to drive?"

He nodded as he took a step back. "Yeah. It's eased up now. I've been worse."

"But you didn't tell me about the trouble on your ranch."

"Look, it's bad. I've been trying to forget it, but I can't."

"Let me help…at least I can listen."

He hesitated, then gave a sharp nod in agreement. "Here's the deal. There's this pedigreed Angus bull named Fernando."

"Fernando?"

"Yeah." He winced as if in more pain. "My niece, Storm, named him. He's massive. She's tiny. But they're friends."

"What happened?" Ivy tensed, fearing the worst.

"Cattle rustlers got him today."

She put a hand over her heart, this time feeling pain for a little girl's loss. "How do you get him back?"

Slade gave a harsh exhale. "Don't know. Sheriff Calhoun is on it. But I have to admit the chances aren't good."

"I'm so sorry." She reached up and hugged him, feeling his sorrow in the tenseness of his body, then stepped back so she could watch his face.

"I told Sydney, her mother. She'll tell Storm, but tomorrow I'll still need to explain and give my niece hope. I dread it."

"You'll do fine."

"There are a lot of things in life I'm ready to handle, but to see the sadness in a little girl's eyes is almost too much."

"She's your niece, so she's strong and resilient. Don't doubt her ability to handle this loss."

"Do you really think so?"

"Yes. I'm sure."

He glanced toward the door, as if needing to get away after sharing his vulnerability about his family.

"You'll do fine. If I can help, let me know."

He shuttered his eyes, took a deep breath, and when he looked at her again, his normal emotional defenses were firmly back in place.

She understood and didn't blame him one bit. He'd need all his strength to help his niece and everyone else.

"Thanks. I'll handle it." He backed up a step, glanced

down at his wrist, and snapped her hot-pink ponytail holder against his skin. "I like your hair better down, so I'll keep this for you."

"Plenty more here."

"Maybe I ought to confiscate them, too."

"Just try." She was grinning when she said it, because they needed to lighten the moment. Besides, she knew he wanted to take something of hers with him, and it touched her as deeply as everything else he'd done and said since they'd met.

He grinned, too, as he took another step back.

"I'll walk you to your truck."

"Stay here, where I know you're safe."

She realized she didn't want him to go. She put her arms around his neck and pulled his head down so she could kiss him—too little, too late, but with oh so much promise. He returned her kiss with a fire of his own before he stepped out of her embrace.

"I'll be back." And he was out the door, down the stairs, and lost in the Park's darkness.

And she was left in a house that felt way too empty without him.

Chapter 11

WHEN SLADE GOT TO HIS PICKUP, HE LEANED AGAINST IT to ease the pressure on his hip as he looked up at the dark sky and the sliver of new moon. He was definitely starting something new, so the moon was in the right phase, but still…this something new stood every chance of blowing up in his face if he didn't slow down or at least practice a little patience and caution. But where Ivy Bryant was concerned, he seemed to have only one speed—full throttle.

He'd like nothing better than to sleep on her sofa, because he didn't want to be apart from her. But if he hadn't left, it would've been difficult to resist her bed, even with a saggy mattress. And that was way too fast for her, no matter how she was responding to him, because she was uneasy and off-kilter from being thrust into a new business and location. He needed to give her time to get her feet under her, but that required patience he didn't know if he could muster.

Anyway, he had plenty of his own irons in the fire that needed to be addressed in addition to the little detail of his old injury flaring up. Storm and Fernando were at the top of that long to-do list. He'd do his best for them, but he feared the worst. With everything going on, he wouldn't have been at his best tonight, so he'd made the right decision in leaving. He looked back to where he could see the light on her house glowing yellow. He'd make sure she had more outdoor illumination tomorrow. He'd do whatever it took to keep Ivy safe.

He glanced around the Park to check the perimeter. All looked fine, but he hesitated to leave because he still had an uneasy feeling about the area. He gave the wisp of hot pink on his wrist a snap for motivation. At the same time, he felt a little movement of air over his head, as if a bird had flown by unusually low. He looked up, but he didn't see anything. Maybe a bat…a bug…a night bird. Nature at its finest.

He started to open his truck, but instead, he walked down the length of it, letting his hand trail over the smooth finish till he reached the long bed that carried a toolbox and a sack of feed. He glanced around again. A single amber light on a tall pole shed muted light over the front of the parking lot near the dance hall, but the asphalt was as empty as it had been earlier.

Something felt off, but he couldn't put his finger on it. He always trusted his instincts, but it'd been such an unusual day that maybe he was too tired and off-center to trust them now. He just needed to get home, get in bed, and get some sleep before he had to hit the ground running tomorrow.

As he clicked open his door, he heard an engine start up nearby out on Wildcat Road. He jerked around in that direction, listening and watching but staying still to be less visible. He waited for the truck, because it sounded like a pickup, to drive by the honky-tonk, but it went the other direction so he didn't get a look at it. Still, he waited until he couldn't hear the engine anymore.

He'd been right. All was not as it should be here. Of course, anybody could've stopped for any reason out on the road and then started up again and driven to their destination. But anybody could also have been parked out there, watching from the vehicle or sending someone in on foot to reconnoiter. If there'd been no cabin fire or cattle rustling earlier, he might've shrugged off the vehicle, but they'd had too much trouble to discount something that raised his hackles.

He glanced toward Ivy's cabin, then back at his pickup. He clicked the lock, sure of one thing—he wasn't leaving her alone tonight.

He took the long way around to get there, walking the parking lot, past the Hall, between the cabins, stopping and listening every few feet, but he heard nothing and saw nothing out of the ordinary. Suited him fine. By the time he reached Ivy's cabin, he was limping worse and wishing he was at home in his own comfortable bed.

"Ivy! It's Slade." He rang the doorbell, but he wanted her to know who was at her door before she even thought about opening it.

After a bit, she slowly pulled it ajar and peeked out, blinking at him as if she was already half-asleep. "I thought you went home."

"I…decided you weren't safe here alone." He didn't know how much to tell her because there wasn't much to tell her, and he didn't want to worry her. "Mind if I borrow your sofa for the night?"

"But I'm fine," she said, looking puzzled before she stopped and stared at him. "Something happened, didn't it?"

He nodded, suddenly feeling the day crashing down on him.

"You'd better come inside." She backed up toward the kitchen.

He stepped over the threshold and locked the door

behind him. He needed to sit—and fast. He limped over to the sofa, where she'd left the pillow and quilt, then eased down until he felt the cushion give under him as he let it take his weight. Finally, the pain eased up, and he breathed a sigh of relief.

"You're hurting again, aren't you?"

He glanced up, instantly forgetting about pain and danger in the wonder of Ivy. She must've taken a shower and gotten ready for bed, because she was wearing nothing more than an oversized, crimson T-shirt with Wildcat Hall's logo emblazoned across the front. Underneath, she was braless, since he could see the taut tips of her full breasts, and her long, bare, shapely legs seemed to go on forever—or down to her high-arched feet with tangerine toenail polish.

He forgot about sleep. He was so hot and hard that he didn't even feel any pain…or at least none that she couldn't make better.

"It's not even midnight," she said. "I think this may be the longest day of my life. It just will not end."

"Sorry."

"Not your fault. You're trying to help." She walked over to the sink. "I'm going to make tea."

He groaned at the idea. "See if there's any of my muscadine wine in the cabinet. That'd help a lot more than tea."

She glanced over her shoulder at him, grinning. "I see your point." She went up on tiptoe, lifted both arms, and reached up, causing her T-shirt to ride up all the way to her bottom.

He groaned again. She was wearing something else all right, but the tap pants didn't conceal the little half-moons of her firm, round butt. If possible, he got even harder at the sight. He needed to be home, or he needed to be at the new ranch house, or he needed to be anywhere except staring at Ivy's nearly naked body. He grabbed the quilt, tossed it over his lap to conceal his condition, and thought about ice and snow—but he didn't stop looking, because he couldn't tear his eyes away from her luscious beauty.

"We're in luck!" She grabbed a bottle, dropped back on her heels, and down went the T-shirt.

He should have felt relief, but instead, he felt a sense of loss. "Need me to open the bottle?"

"Just stay where you are. I've got it."

"Good." He was in no condition to move, so he adjusted the pillow, leaned against it, and tried to relax.

She poured wine into a couple of heavy glass mugs with Wildcat Bluff logos emblazed in red and gold before she came back. She handed him one, then sat down on the other end of the sofa, tucked her legs under her, and pulled her T-shirt down to cover most of her legs.

He took a big gulp of wine and enjoyed the taste of something familiar as well as good. This wasn't his latest batch, but it was a fine one. He was getting better at it all the time.

She sipped from her mug, then nodded at him. "This is great."

"Thanks. I try."

"More than try, I'd say."

"It's a learning curve, but I enjoy making wine."

She sniffed the liquid, then took another sip. "I can see why."

"Listen, there's not much to tell you." Now that he

was here, he felt a little foolish at his concern, but he still wouldn't be anywhere else. "A pickup was parked out beside Wildcat Road near the dance hall."

"Did you recognize it?"

"I didn't see it because it drove off in the other direction."

"Folks don't usually park beside the road, since there's plenty of room in the parking lot, do they?" she asked.

"Right. And the Hall's closed this week."

"Maybe not everybody heard about that."

"Maybe. But still, why park on the side of the road?"

"I guess there could be lots of reasons."

"True." He sipped wine, felt the warmth ease his aches and pains, and grew more relaxed. "I checked the grounds again. Everything looks okay."

"That's good."

"I just didn't want to leave you alone, not after the fire... and the theft."

"Thanks." She smiled at him, then sipped her wine.

He turned his mug around and around in his hands. "Cattle rustlers struck about the same time as the fire."

"That's odd."

"Or intentional."

"You think they're related?"

"Maybe. We can't rule it out."

She leaned toward him. "If so, that'd mean it didn't have anything to do with me or Wildcat Hall Park."

He wanted to reassure her, but he had to be realistic, too. "And yet, there's a connection because of the fire."

She sighed, pushing back a strand of hair. "No way to know, is there?"

"Not yet. We just need to take precautions."

"Okay. I'll just make it one more thing in my long list of things to do for the Park."

"I'll help."

"Thanks. You've been so good to help me. But you've got troubles, too. How may I help you?"

He just smiled at her, thinking about all the ways she could help him right on the sofa, but he didn't go there. He wasn't in any shape to do more than admire her tonight. When they got to the place he wanted to go, he'd make sure it was an unforgettable experience for them both.

"What are you thinking?" She chuckled as she cocked her head. "You look decidedly mischievous. I offered to help."

"I'll let you know if there's anything you can do. I just wish we were on the other side of this mess."

"Yeah. Me, too." She stood up abruptly.

He got another flash of long legs that set him on fire again, so he downed the rest of his wine to ease the blaze.

"Do you want more wine or do you want to go to sleep?"

"Let's finish the bottle, then sleep."

"Okay." She walked into the kitchen, picked up the bottle, and came back. "But I'm warning you that I'm so tired I may fall asleep in the middle of a conversation."

"That's fine." He held up his mug for a refill. "I'll just tuck you in."

She poured wine into both their mugs, then put the empty bottle in the sink.

"Come sit beside me." He patted the sofa near him.

"Are you still in pain?"

"A little." He patted the cushion again. "Distract me. Tell me about yourself."

She sat down and eased back, cradling her mug in both hands. "Not much to tell. I'm pretty boring most of the time. I create websites."

"Do you like doing it?"

"Yes. It's creative and it helps people build businesses."

He put his arm on the back of the sofa, then down around her shoulders and tugged her to his side. When she snuggled against him, he spread the quilt over their legs. "What kind of food do you like?"

"Barbecue. Tex-Mex. Hamburgers. Most anything, really."

"And pecan pie."

She grinned at him. "You know I'm partial to pie—your pie in particular."

"Glad to hear it." He rubbed a hand up and down her shoulder, enjoying the simple companionship. "Wait till you taste my barbecue. I swear it's the best in the state."

"I believe it." She sighed, took a sip of wine, and snuggled a little closer.

He kissed the top of her head, inhaling a fruity fragrance. "I could get used to this."

"To what?"

"You. Me."

"Wine?" She finished her drink, then set the empty mug by her feet.

"Yeah. Tonight it's just the two of us...and the world is locked away outside."

"I like it." She glanced up at him. "What's your favorite food?"

"Everything I cook."

She chuckled, then put one hand over her mouth as she yawned. "My eyes aren't going to stay open much longer."

"Rest them a moment."

"May I? You won't get bored sitting here."

"Never."

"Okay then…just a little while before I go to bed." And she softly exhaled as she relaxed against him.

He tossed back the last of his wine, set the mug on the floor, then gently eased them both into a prone position and covered them with the quilt.

She grumbled a little in her sleep at being moved, but she cuddled closer before growing still again.

He gently stroked her silky hair—and willed the sun never to rise.

Chapter 12

IVY AWAKENED TO THE SOUND OF HER SISTER'S ringtone—Trace Adkins with the insightful lyrics, deep drawl, and beguiling guitar. She struggled out of sleep, glanced around in confusion at the semidark room softly lit by a small night-light in the kitchen. Nothing looked right. And then reality hit. She was in a cowboy cabin in Wildcat Bluff County.

And then the second reality hit. Where was Slade? She didn't remember anything beyond going to sleep in his arms. What time was it? She struggled to a sitting position, hearing Trace continue his sensual croon to her. For that matter, where was her phone?

She felt completely disoriented as she stood up, swayed on her feet, and kicked over a glass mug. She reached down and fumbled with it before she got a good grip. That's when she noticed the other empty mug. She clutched that one, too, as she made her way to the sink and deposited them there.

Finally the ringtone stopped, allowing Trace to slip back into a dimly lit, line-dancing honky-tonk somewhere in the Lone Star State. She'd call Fern back when she got her mind in working order again. Yesterday had been mind-blowing in so many different ways—not the least of which was her slowly succumbing to Slade Steele's charms. At least she'd simply gone to sleep, instead of dragging him into her bed. If she'd done that, she couldn't have blamed the wine, because she hadn't had too much to drink unless she counted being drunk on Slade himself.

She focused on the microwave clock. Six in the morning. She'd been asleep all night. She guessed the previous day really had taken a toll if she'd been that knocked out by it. And Slade? She didn't hear him anywhere inside the cabin, so she could only assume he'd left in the night. How much earlier, she didn't know. Maybe he'd left for good sleep in a real bed. She felt disappointed that he hadn't held her all through the dark hours, but he was a practical man, so he would have made a practical decision. Funny how she'd slept so well that she felt as if she'd been safely cradled in his arms throughout the night.

She needed coffee to get revved up and going, because there was so much to do she couldn't lollygag while she got her feet under her. She fumbled in the cabinet until she had coffee makings, then she put it together with the coffee maker and sighed in relief when she heard liquid start to drip. While she waited for enough to fill a cup, she pulled a couple of cookies out of a cookie jar made in the shape of Santa's elf wearing a bright green and cocky cap. She picked a white mug with a pretty red snowflake pattern. She was getting her day started in just the right way. Christmas was coming up fast, and she needed to get in the right, happy frame of mind to do it justice.

That's when she noticed the bold handwriting on a yellow sticky note stuck to the table. She quickly read it. "Thanks for the night. Check in later." And then he'd drawn a heart. She felt that simple, little drawing touch her like a burst of hearts zinging across her life. So he had stayed the night, or at least until he was up by five like most working folks in the country.

She poured a cup of coffee, located her phone in her bedroom, and settled in a chair at the dining table. She ate the cookies, downed a slug of liquid energy, and hit speed dial for her sister.

"Ivy, I was getting worried about you," Fern said in her rich alto that always sounded as if she was about to lapse into song.

"It's early. You woke me."

"Hah. I'm just going to bed, so thought I'd check in." She hesitated a moment, as if giving what she wanted to say some thought. "How do you like it in Wildcat Bluff?"

"I've only been here a couple of days, but so far it's definitely the Wild West."

Fern chuckled in her trademark husky tone. "Do you like wild, or is it just me who developed a taste for it?"

"I thought maybe you developed a taste for a cowboy named Craig Thorne."

Fern hesitated again. "So you already met Craig?"

"Yep."

"What do you think?"

"He's a fine piece of male craftsmanship."

"Craig's a lot more than a pretty face."

Ivy went on alert, because her sister rarely defended a guy since they came to her in a disposable variety. "Is that so?"

"He's a fabulous guitar player. And he can sing."

"I only know him as a cowboy firefighter."

"He's that, too, but how do you know?"

Ivy sighed, realizing she'd let the cat out of the bag. "I

guess you ought to know there was a small fire in one of the cabins yesterday." She didn't mention arson so as not to worry her sister.

"Oh no!" Fern sounded horrified and heartbroken. "Is it gutted? How did it happen? Electrical wires or something?"

"No damage."

"That's a relief. I bet the new sprinkler system kicked into gear."

"We're looking into making sure it doesn't happen again." She didn't want to fib to Fern, but she didn't want to go into the details either.

"Okay. Wait…we? Did you already hook up with a cowboy?"

"Slade just stopped by to see if he could help get the Hall up and running, so he was here when we discovered the fire."

"Do you mean Slade Steele, the gorgeous but standoff-ish tall drink of water?"

"Far as I can tell, he's anything but standoffish."

"Oh, really?" Fern sounded very interested in the situation.

"It's nothing. I mean…well, he did spend the night."

"That was quick."

"I don't mean spend-the-night-in-my-bed type of thing."

"No?"

"He's been kind and concerned and helpful. In case of another fire, he wanted to be on the premises. He slept on the sofa." Ivy decided not to admit that she'd slept there, too, or she'd really stoke her sister's interest.

"Are you sure you're talking about Slade Steele, the cowboy firefighter who runs a ranch, cooks at the

Chuckwagon, bakes award-winning pies, and makes wine from his own vineyard?"

"Yes, I am."

"I'm surprised he took the time, because he hasn't had it for all the cowgirls that constantly troll him."

"He's concerned about the Park."

"Everybody in the county loves the place, so I can understand it. Is there anything else we need to do to protect our property?"

"Slade is going to install more outdoor lights today."

"He's taking quite an interest." Fern hesitated, then went on. "Will you recheck all the fire prevention, too?"

"We already did it. Everything looks okay."

"Good. And, Ivy...I don't want to see you hurt. Slade is—"

"He's a nice guy."

"Yes, but he's much more than that. He's a smart, tough cowboy with enough irons in the fire to brand an entire herd."

"I'm not exactly lacking in things to do either."

"I know. Still, Slade's a guy with a past and a guy on the move. I sincerely doubt he's looking to transition to a little love nest."

"Well, I'm not, either." She knew her sister was right, but she still felt hurt that Fern didn't think Slade could be seriously interested in her. "I'm here strictly to do your job."

"About that. I do appreciate you stepping up to the plate."

"Don't I always?"

"Yeah. I really had planned to stick this one out. It's just that...Craig was getting all serious and you know how that affects me."

"Was he the only one getting serious?"

"Well, I admit… No, I won't admit anything. Let's just say I always wanted to perform on a cruise line."

"How do you like it?"

"Captain's pretty hot, but I just can't seem to get interested in anything here except music."

"That's good, isn't it?"

"I guess." Fern sighed, then hummed a few bars of a lamenting song. "It's just not like me."

"Why don't you drop the gig and come home?"

"I signed a contract."

"Break it."

"I never break a contract. It'd be bad for my reputation."

"I'm not sure how long I can hold this together for you. I need to get back to Houston." She really did want Fern to take over before she lost all sense of perspective and succumbed not only to Slade's charm, but to the county's charm as well.

"What's going on for you there?"

"In case you've forgotten, it's my home."

"Not now."

"It's temporary here."

"Please give Wildcat Bluff County a chance. It'll grow on you. And I think it'll be good for you. You need a change in life."

"You're the one who likes change. I'm the one who likes to stay in one place."

"I put this deal together for both of us."

"Are you telling me that you took this new gig just so I'd have to leave Houston and move here?" Ivy suddenly felt manipulated and betrayed by the one person in her life she thought she could completely trust. "Tell me that's not so."

"I took this gig for a lot of reasons. Maybe that's one of them."

"Maybe? That there's any possibility it could be a reason is outrageous. You know I like my life in Houston and I have every intention of going back there."

"Give it some time. Think of life outside the box. Think of fun at the Hall. Think of hunky Slade Steele—he doesn't have to be a forever guy but a get-me-through-the-night guy."

"You sound like one of your country songs." There was so much more that she wanted to say, but she didn't go there—no way to change her sister's mind.

"Don't I always? And you know, it's all getting a little old, but I'm hanging in there."

"You might as well enjoy life on the high seas while you've got it. For me, I better be getting on down to the Hall."

"Thanks. And, Ivy...you know I love you and want only the best for you, don't you?"

"Yes, I know. I love you, too."

"Bye for now." And Fern was gone.

Ivy looked at her phone for a long moment, realizing that no matter Fern's good intentions, she couldn't let her sister run her life anymore. She needed to come up with an alternate plan. She was city, not country. Hot cowboys didn't matter. Historic dance halls didn't matter. Friendly folks didn't even matter. She needed out...and she knew one way to get there.

She hit speed dial again. She had a Realtor friend who was so good he could sell ice in Alaska. And he was always on the lookout for the big deal for his big-deal clients.

"Hey, Ivy darlin', how's life in the petrified countryside?" Peter Simpson answered in his deep Texas drawl.

"It's about as exciting as you can imagine."

"Please, I don't even want to go there. You missed opening night of the new opera season."

"How could that possibly compare to hearing a local country band in my very own dance hall?"

"That bad, huh?"

"You know the deal here. And you know Fern."

"Yep. I warned you not to sign on to her pipe dream, because she's a definite rolling stone."

"I know, but I did."

"That said and out of the way, how may I help you?"

"Peter, the Park is really charming in a precious country way. The cowboy cabins are adorable. And Wildcat Hall is a classic old-time dance hall. Surely somebody with money would be interested in either investing or building it up as a big tourist attraction."

"You want to sell?" He sounded shocked. "What would Fern say?"

"For now, she's gone and I'm not sure when she'll be back."

"But she might change her mind and return at any moment."

"Frankly, I don't think she'd object to selling the whole place if we got a great price that would leave us sitting pretty. She could travel the world. I could do whatever I decided to do."

"Sales-wise, I could always compare it to the wildly popular and lucrative Gruene Hall. There's nothing like that honky-tonk in North Texas."

"That's a plus."

"Buyers will want to see the books. Any good?"

"Profit—but limited."

"Can you get a better bottom line by the first of the year?"

"Christmas is coming up." She felt stronger and more in control by the moment.

"Good. Find a way to rev up the entertainment. Can you up the prices on beer, wine, and food by catering to the foodies—you know, small-batch stuff?"

"I already have that in mind. I've been talking with an award-winning chef in this county."

"Perfect." He hesitated before he sighed heavily into the phone. "Ivy, are you sure you want me to pursue this sale?"

"Yes, of course." She felt a sick feeling in the pit of her stomach that warred with her words, but she pushed it away.

"Remember, I'm good. If I pursue this, I'll probably find a buyer. And a great one. This property is unique. It's historic. It's back-to-the-good-old-days type of thing. People like that. Developers like that. I even like it."

"You're giving me hope I might be back in Houston right after the New Year."

"I wouldn't count on me coming up with a buyer that fast, but you never know."

"Remember, you're good." She glanced over at the happy-looking elf cookie jar, already feeling a little nostalgic for it. "I don't know how long I can last living among cows and horses."

"What about cowboys?"

"At least there's some eye candy up here."

"That always makes life bearable." He hesitated again.

"One thing—if anybody shows interest, we immediately contact Fern. I won't leave her hanging in the dark, as a friend or a client."

"Agreed. I'd do it anyway. And, Peter, you're the best. Otherwise, I'm afraid my sister is going to leave me stuck here forever."

"Would it be so bad? It's pretty country. Nice folks."

"It's all that. But you know I'm city, not country."

"Yeah. That's what all the city folks say before they desert us for the wide-open spaces."

"Not me."

"Okay. Send me all the info you have on the place. I'll research more on my end."

"I'll get right on it."

"Don't expect to hear from me right away."

"Fine. I'll be busy here, bringing in as much business as possible."

"Sounds like a plan." And he clicked off.

She felt almost light-headed at how fast that went. Had she done the right thing? Had she reacted more out of resentment and fear than anything else? Had Fern finally maneuvered Ivy into taking a stand that set her on a collision course with her past actions, which always put her sister first?

She set her phone down on the table and noticed Slade's note with the hand-drawn heart. She suddenly remembered his words that lots of folks in the county would've bought Wildcat Hall Park. Why hadn't she thought of them first? Why had she thought of Peter? But she knew. Locals would go straight to Fern and things would get complicated fast. They might even guilt her into staying...particularly one heartbreaker of a cowboy. For once, she was going to do things her way.

She picked up Slade's note, touched the heart with her fingertip, and felt a terrible sense of impending loss.

Chapter 13

LATER THAT DAY, IVY STOOD AT THE FRONT LONG BAR IN Wildcat Hall, contemplating what to do next, but she wasn't sure what to do first, second, or third, so it was hard to decide.

She'd already tacked red tinsel in a long line down the length of the bar. She'd hung a pretty silk wreath made of green boughs and red poinsettia on the front door. She'd set out cheerful red-and-green napkins. She wanted to hang strands of twinkling white lights in the tree limbs overhanging the beer garden, but that would require a ladder, and she doubted she was up to so much time and energy investment. Still, it was something to add onto her to-do list, so she leaned over her laptop, set up on a table near the bar, and typed "white lights" under the growing column of items for the Park.

She'd been keeping a lookout for Slade, but so far he was a no-show. She knew he had lots to do, so the Hall had to be far down on his personal to-do list, particularly when he needed to talk with his niece. But he had said in his note that he'd see her later. Much later was probably for the best, because she felt guilty about her talk with Peter and she feared it might show on her face. In any case, finding an outside buyer was probably a thousand-to-one shot, so she just needed to settle in and make the best of her situation until Fern's contract ran out.

If she was going to do something, she was going to do it right, so she'd already started on a fresh website for Wildcat Hall Park. She planned to build a narrative about the origins and the fact that the dance hall had been in the same family since its inception. Of course, she'd make the copy clever, find old photographs from past years up to present day. She'd also promote upcoming dates for the performers with photographs to show the Hall was a place to enjoy food, drink, and music, as well as see and be seen.

She quickly sat down at the table and made a few more notes for the website. She needed better visuals to promote not only the honky-tonk but the cowboy cabins, too. She could probably take the shots herself. A website was already online, but it was basic and outdated in design. She definitely had her work cut out for her since she needed to continue her regular business websites, too. Still, she was glad of the work, because she wanted her mind, body, and time filled completely, or she might go off on a tangent and think about nothing except one tall, strong, hot cowboy named Slade Steele.

As she sat in front of her laptop screen with her fingers on the keyboard, contemplating clever copy, the front door opened and three tall, muscular, blond, blue-eyed folks stepped inside. They were identically dressed in crimson, long-sleeve T-shirts with the Wildcat Hall logo emblazoned on the front, Wranglers, and black cowboy boots.

"And just when did you plan to call us?" The woman in front held the wreath that had been on the door out from her body as if in disgust, then dropped it with a plop on top of a nearby table.

"Uhhh...you don't like wreaths?" Ivy glanced from the object of scorn to the woman, then back again. How could a simple Christmas wreath manage to upset someone enough to be jerked off a door? And she'd thought folks in Wildcat Bluff were all friendly—obviously not so.

"Did you plan for us to keep going without a single word from you?" the man asked, sounding completely put out.

Ivy blinked several times, trying to bring the situation into some sort of focus, but it didn't help one bit. She had no idea who these people were or why they were here. She looked them over, trying to make sense of the intrusion. They were a good-looking group that must be a family. The older two appeared to be in their fifties, while the younger one was about thirty or so. They radiated strength and competence with a no-nonsense attitude. She admired all that, but why did they hate her wreath enough to jerk it down and confront her?

"You do know who we are, don't you?" the younger woman asked, putting her hands on her hips.

"No clue." Ivy finally stood up, so they weren't towering over her.

"No clue!" The man turned to look at the women, shaking his head. "She's never heard of us."

"But she needs us," the younger woman said to the others.

Ivy stepped toward them, gesturing at a table with four chairs. "Perhaps you'd like to take a seat and explain why you're here."

"It's not likely we have time to sit and chat, now is it?" the woman asked in a huff.

"Did Fern hire y'all for something?" When all reason failed, her sister was usually at the core of an issue, so Ivy would start there.

"We're the Settelmeyer family," the woman said. "I'm Lana. This is my husband, Claude. And that's our daughter, Alicia."

"Pleased to meet you." Ivy quickly walked over and shook their hands. "How may I help you?"

"Better question is how we can help you," Lana said matter-of-factly.

"It's not like I don't need help, but I'm not sure how you can do it." Ivy gave the group a smile in hopes it would ease the tension in the room.

"We maintain Wildcat Hall Park," Lana said, gesturing to her family.

"Inside and outside," Alicia added.

"From the get-go, our family has worked here with the original family to keep this place in top form." Claude gave a sharp nod of his head.

"Fern Bryant was mighty glad to continue our service," Lana said. "When you took over, we figured you'd be just as glad to have us, but we didn't hear from you."

"I regret if there are any hard feelings over the situation." Ivy tried another smile, but it appeared to fall as flat as the first one. "My sister didn't tell me about you. I haven't been here long enough to learn everything."

"And now?" Lana glanced around the front bar room, as if expecting to see accumulated dirt and dust that needed tackling with a firm hand.

"Oh, yes," Ivy said. "I'm delighted to meet you and to know that you're already in place. I've got so much else to do that—"

"Who put up those decorations?" Alicia asked, appearing horrified as she pointed at the tinsel swags.

"I did," Ivy said proudly, but she was careful not to look at the offending wreath. "I found them in a box in the storage room and thought they'd look festive out here."

"They're not in their proper places." Alicia pointed at the antlers. "A Santa Claus hat goes on the antlers."

"Always has," Claude said with a frown.

"Not only that, but you're three days early putting up Christmas decorations." Lana fisted her hands on her hips. "If you don't want things done right, we're not the family for you. We keep a strict schedule here for what needs doing when it needs doing."

"That way everything gets done properly without fuss or muss," Alicia said with a defiant nod of her head.

"You didn't tinker with the beer garden, did you?" Claude looked past Ivy toward the outside.

"No." She mentally backtracked, realizing she was stepping on toes right and left. She hadn't meant to insult them, particularly not since she needed them, but they came as a complete surprise—in a lot of ways. "I thought white lights in the trees would be pretty."

"Blue," Claude said. "That's what we've always used, so that's what we've got in storage."

"Blue is good, too." Ivy took a deep breath, wishing Fern had thought to tell her about the Settelmeyer family. With their attitude, they were obviously as much of an institution as Wildcat Hall itself.

"We don't order drinks or food or bar stuff," Lana said. "We don't pick bands or schedule them."

"That's fine. I'll take care of that." Ivy smiled, trying to make peace by being as conciliatory as possible.

"But we're pretty versatile," Alicia added, finally

returning a smile. "I mean, I can run into town on errands and pick up stuff if you need it."

"Thanks. I appreciate the offer."

"We're the maintenance crew," Claude said. "We know our jobs and we'll do them without any instructions."

"True." Lana cocked her head with a smile. "And like Alicia said, we're here to do whatever needs doing."

"That's good to know." Ivy was relieved she seemed to be making positive progress with this family she desperately needed to run the place. "Right now, I'm not sure what needs doing, so I'll be coming to all of you for advice."

"That's right smart of you," Claude said. "We'll help you any way we can. We treat Wildcat Hall Park like our own home."

"And that means you're one of ours, too." Lana's blue eyes twinkled as she smiled at Ivy. "We'll take care of you as best we can."

"Thanks. I may very well need it." Now that they were warming to her, she was warming to them. "By the way, Slade Steele was here yesterday to help out. He'd like to put up more outdoor lights."

"Good idea. I've been suggesting that for some time," Claude said. "I know Slade. I'll get with him about the lights."

"Thanks." Ivy was feeling better and better about the situation. This might actually work out. "Y'all are a big comfort to me. Fern pretty much dropped the Park in my lap with hardly a word about it."

"She did leave in a rush," Alicia said. "Is she okay? We're all worried about her."

"She got a new gig on a cruise line, but she'll be back later."

"Good to hear," Lana said. "She's an uplifting spirit for Wildcat Hall and everybody in the county."

"We miss her." Alicia gestured toward the dance hall. "She really livened up the place with her energy and glamour and music."

Ivy realized with a sinking sensation that they were looking to her for what Fern had brought to their beloved Wildcat Hall. She couldn't compete with energy, glamour, and music, but she did have a few skills of her own to offer. "I'm designing a new website for the Park. And I'm working with Slade to introduce new menu items for the holidays."

"That's good, real good," Lana said, smiling. "Nowadays, we know businesses need a strong online presence."

"And we haven't had one, so that's really good news." Alicia appeared excited at the idea.

"Slade's cooking is the best, so that works for me," Claude said, glancing behind the bar at the row of bottles. "Maybe you can persuade him to part with some of his wine."

"I'll definitely try."

"But let's keep it on the quiet, so it's all just for us." Claude gave a deep chuckle from the bottom of his broad chest.

Ivy smiled at the joke that probably wasn't a joke, feeling included in the inner circle of Wildcat Hall. It was a good feeling and that surprised her. Somehow, local folks kept drawing her deeper into their world, so much so that she wanted to do her best for them and make them happy. Maybe it was because everything was up close and personal here—nothing at arm's length, like was so often the case in the city or online. She just kept being astonished that they accepted her so readily and that she fit in so easily. Could

Fern have been right that she needed a change in life? Surely not...but then again, her sister had a way of seeing what others didn't, at least not at first. She suddenly had an uneasy feeling when she remembered that she'd requested Peter to find a buyer, but maybe he wouldn't be able to do it and that would get her off the hook.

"Anything special for us to do right now?" Lana asked, picking up the wreath and tucking it under one arm.

"Not that I know of," Ivy said, "but that might not last long."

"We've all got cell phones and we'll leave our numbers." Alicia walked behind the bar, pulled out a pad and pen, set them on the bar top, and wrote on the paper. She tapped her note with the tip of the pen. "Here you go. Night or day, if you need us, we're there for you."

"We don't live far away," Claude said. "We're in a log cabin on acreage off Wildcat Road."

"You'll have to come for a visit sometime." Lana gave a warm smile before she turned toward the front door.

"Yeah. Mom's a great cook." Alicia stripped the tinsel from the bar and wound it into a big loop. She glanced up at the antlers. "I'll get that tinsel later."

Ivy could only nod in agreement, not about to ever mention having had the nerve to put up unauthorized decorations.

"Never fear. We'll put it all back proper when the time is right," Claude said, turning toward the door.

"Got to get to work." Alicia tossed a quick smile, then followed her parents as they headed out.

"Thanks," Ivy called to their backs. "I look forward to working with y'all."

Chapter 14

BY THE TIME SLADE REACHED WILDCAT HALL THAT EVE-
ning, he was tired and disgruntled from his long day, but
he figured just being with Ivy would lift his spirits. Claude
had called him about installing more outdoor lighting, so
he'd gladly turned that job over to him. He didn't know why
he hadn't thought to mention the Settelmeyer family to Ivy
the day before, but he figured between the fire, Fernando,
and Ivy herself, it had simply slipped his mind. The family
was such a vital part of the Park that they were considered
almost one and the same entity. He was glad she'd met the
Settelmeyers and come to an agreement with them, because
they'd be a huge asset to her handling the place.

He parked his truck close to the front door under the
outside light. He was taking no more chances with possible intruders, so he was watching his back at all times. He
hoped Ivy was being just as cautious. If he had his way, the
Settelmeyer family would live in one of the cabins, but they
deserved their own place on their own land, with their own
cattle and horses, since otherwise they devoted their lives to
Wildcat Hall Park.

Lights were on inside the honky-tonk, so he figured
Ivy was there instead of in her cabin. He started to pick up
the box of food he'd set on the front passenger seat, then
stopped and decided to check with her first because what
he had in mind might not suit her. First, he'd see what kind

of day she'd had and what she felt like doing for the evening. He felt a spurt of pleasure at the thought of spending time with her, because she excited him and intrigued him and enticed him to want so much more from her.

After he locked the pickup door behind him, he hesitated, glancing around for anything out of place, sniffing the air for any hint of smoke, and tugging his jean jacket a little tighter since the nights had gotten cool. All appeared to be as it should, so he strode up to the front door and tried the handle. Fortunately, it was locked or he'd have fussed at her to be more careful. He smiled at the thought that he actually would chide her, even though they'd known each such a short time and it was something friends or family or lovers would do and accept as part of caring about each other.

With Ivy, time didn't matter. It hadn't mattered since that first moment they'd met and connected—time hadn't stood still, as the old saying went, but it had merged into one ongoing stream that bound them together. At least, that was the way he felt, and he hoped she felt the same way.

He looked in the front window and saw her sitting at a table beside the bar, totally absorbed in her computer. Maybe he should fuss at her after all. Anybody could see her there, and she looked vulnerable in her distraction and being all alone in the big, empty dance hall.

He rapped several times on the front door, not too loudly, since he didn't want to startle her, but enough to get her attention. He waited impatiently, anxious to hold her now that he was so close to her.

"Who's there?" she called from the other side of the closed door.

"It's me."

"Slade, you startled me."

"I tried not to, but you were distracted by your laptop." He grew more impatient. "Ivy, open the door."

She quickly turned the lock and threw open the door. She was bathed in soft light that illuminated her—long russet hair in a single plait trailing over one shoulder of a sage-green, long-sleeve T-shirt that she'd tucked into faded, ripped blue jeans. She wore soft, scuffed, leather moccasins.

She looked delectable, particularly when he caught the scent of lavender that she must have used in her bath or on her hair or maybe—the best thought of all—dabbed between her breasts. He inhaled, wanting to draw her completely inside him and never exhale or let her go. He smiled at the sheer pleasure of seeing her, smelling her, knowing her...and then he did take her in his arms, gently wrapping her up, against his chest, feeling her soft breasts, feeling her hair tickle his nose, feeling the unique essence of her.

"I missed you," he said, meaning it from the depth of his being.

"We haven't been apart that long."

"Any time apart is too long."

She chuckled softly, then leaned back and looked up at him, green eyes alight with mischief. "If you're not careful, you're going to completely spoil me."

"That's exactly what I have in mind."

"Really?"

"Are you done for the day?"

"I can be if you have something better in mind than a small screen."

"How would you like fresh-baked cookies?"

She grinned, eyes lighting up even more. "Texas tea cakes? Cowboy cookies?"

"Maybe." He decided to tease her a little bit just to watch the expression change on her pretty face. "I've got fixings in the truck."

"We're going to cook?"

"I'm going to cook. You're going to sample for the honky-tonk."

"You *are* going to spoil me."

"Every day." And he grinned, knowing it was absolutely true, because nothing would please him more than to see her happy.

"Hah!" She laughed as if she didn't believe him, but she still looked pleased by his words. "Let me grab my stuff."

"I'll get the lights and door."

"Thanks." And then she stopped and looked at him, suddenly serious. "How did it go with your niece?"

"Better than expected." He smiled, remembering Storm's reaction. "She's convinced Fernando will be home for Christmas."

"But how?"

"No idea. At least this gives her a chance to get used to the idea that he's gone—most likely for good."

"But when Christmas comes along and he's not back—"

"We'll cross that bridge when we get to it."

"And hope Fernando is a Christmas miracle." She picked up her stuff, smiling at him.

"Exactly."

He stepped outside right behind her, checking to make sure the door automatically locked behind them.

As she walked to his truck, she glanced back. "Do you need help carrying stuff to my place?"

He shook his head, thinking about the thousand-plus pounds of temperamental animal that he handled every day. He wasn't short on muscle, so he could easily carry a box of ingredients that might be too heavy for her. But he said none of that, because it'd sound like bragging and a cowboy just did his job, day in and day out, without flexing his muscles for a compliment or two. On second thought, he guessed cowboys were as susceptible as any other man to an appreciative glance from a gal, so they might be found to wear their shirts and jeans a little too tight, but only on the right occasions.

He opened his truck, pulled out the box, and locked up tight. He glanced around, but he didn't see anything unusual, so he followed Ivy up the path toward her cabin. The night was still, with not a breath of a breeze, while bright stars twinkled overhead in the dark sky. He was pleased to see Claude had already installed security lights, so that each cabin's porch blazed with yellow light as they followed the illuminated trail through the Park. Of course, night-lights wouldn't stop an intruder bent on mischief and mayhem, but it'd be harder to enter, exit, and cause problems without the concealment of darkness.

When they reached Ivy's home, she unlocked and opened the door, stepped inside, and waited for Slade to enter. As he set the box on the kitchen countertop, she locked up behind them.

"Home sweet home." She moved up beside him, sniffing the air. "What do I smell? Did you bring chili?"

"I surely did. Have you had our locally famous Chuckwagon chili?"

"No, not yet."

"Well, you're in for a treat." He pulled a tall, sealed container out of the box. "If you'll set the table, I'll spoon this up into bowls."

"I'm on it." She rubbed her stomach. "I haven't eaten much today, so I'm starved, particularly for something this great smelling."

"Perfect."

As she set the table, he pulled out rancher bowls with cattle brands connected by barbwire around the edges, black on white. He served up two bowls of rich, red, steaming chili and set them on the table. He found a cloverleaf serving dish in the same rancher pattern and filled it with grated cheddar cheese, chopped onions, and corn chips. He set that on the table, too.

"It looks wonderful." She gave him a warm smile. "I made sweet tea this morning and put it in the fridge."

"Good. I brought a bottle of wine. We can have it later." He quickly poured tea into green-frosted glasses and set them on the table. "Is there anything else we need?"

"I can't think of a single thing."

"Okay then. Let's eat." He pulled out a chair at the table and held it for her. When she was seated, he couldn't resist placing a quick kiss on the top of her head before he sat down across from her.

He put his cloth napkin in his lap while she did the same, then he waited for her to take a bite of his chili.

She dipped in her spoon as she smiled at him. "I'm not adding any of the toppings yet. I want to get the full taste first."

"Right choice." And he waited, watching as she put her

spoon in her mouth, closing her full lips over it, pulling it out, and then blinking as the impact of the chili hit her. "Oh my, it's hot."

"Yep."

"And flavorful."

"Yep."

She spooned up another mouthful. "Real chunks of beef."

"Sirloin."

"Oh my, it's wonderful." She blinked back tears. "Jalapeños or habaneros?"

He grinned, knowing she felt the burning on her tongue and in the back of her throat. "Both."

"You're wicked."

"Hope so."

She licked her lips. "I think I'm going numb." She took a quick drink of ice tea.

"Not permanently." He realized he could watch her drink and eat all day. He wasn't sure anything could be more sensuous. He was getting hot without taking a bite of his chili by just watching her.

"I bet you don't share the recipe."

"Never."

She chuckled, looking mischievous. "Carolyn Brown did in *The Red-Hot Chili Cook- Off*."

"Who? What?"

"She's a terrific author, and that's one of her novels."

"She put a chili recipe in her book?"

"Yes. I always thought it'd be fun to try." Ivy sprinkled cheese over the top of her chili.

"Just because she can write doesn't mean she can cook."

"What? You think she just made it up and stuck it in a book?"

"We'll never know unless we try it, will we?"

"Okay. You're on. We'll give it a try."

He'd been teasing her, but now he wouldn't mind seeing what an author concocted for chili. "You know Texans are big on chili cook-offs. Wildcat Bluff sponsors one now and again as a fund-raiser."

"Not a bad idea. We might try a different chili several weekends in a row leading up to Christmas and let folks vote on their favorite."

"Wildcat Jack at KWCB is famous for his chili recipe."

"Do you think he'd promote our chili cook-off on the radio?" she asked.

"No doubt about it, particularly since Jack will enter with every intention of winning."

"We could give out a trophy."

"I like it."

"I can promote our chili event on the new website I'm developing for the Park."

"You're getting into the swing of things here fast, aren't you?" He ate his own chili, noting that it was good as always. If they did the chili cook-off, it'd probably wind up coming down to a contest between Jack and him. Maybe he shouldn't enter, since he was a professional, but the author's recipe might be something interesting to enter.

"Well…let's just say I want to build the business as quickly as possible."

He hesitated with his spoon in the air, noticing that she suddenly looked away from him, almost as if she felt guilty about something. He couldn't imagine what, since she was coming up with great ideas, and that helped the entire community.

"What else did you bring in the box?" She pointed toward it.

He almost felt like it was a distraction or a way to turn him from where their conversation had been going, but that made no sense. Surely she wasn't hiding something from him. He shrugged off the thought, knowing he wouldn't get anywhere with it. Ivy had been up front with him from the first, so he couldn't imagine that she held any deep, dark secrets.

"Didn't you say you were going to bake for me?"

For some reason, he suddenly didn't feel so lighthearted or so much like baking cookies, and he didn't know why, except now he had this little niggling worry in the back of his mind that she wasn't being completely honest with him. He hated the idea.

"Cookies?" she prompted.

"Right. Texas tea cakes."

"Great."

"I brought what we need to cut them into holiday shapes and shake colorful sprinkles on top. You can see how festive they'll be for Christmas, besides being delicious with coffee."

"Sounds good."

"Let's start with the original recipe out of my great-granny's cookbook, then go from there. It's an easy recipe that allows lots of variations."

"I'm all in." She finished her chili, then leaned back in her chair. "Do you mind if I play some country music while you cook?"

"I'd like it." He finished his chili, too, and stacked their bowls.

"I need to listen to demos from country music groups that want to appear at the honky-tonk. They emailed me links to their websites that include videos and contact information. At this point, I'm not sure what we can afford or if they'll perform without charge for the promo opportunity. I guess it's another learning curve. You could help me make decisions."

"Didn't Fern leave you a list?"

"Yes. It helps, but I still want to check out these bands."

"I'm happy to assist, but Craig would be a good choice, too."

"Do you think he'd mind?"

"I think he'd be offended if you didn't ask him. Anyway, I'm sure he and his band are set to perform most weekends."

"That's good. I want local, but I want to attract up-and-comers from all over, too."

"What about big names?"

"I'd love to get big names to play here. Many of them are from Texas and Oklahoma. But how would I pull it off?"

"I guess you'd begin with their agents or representatives. Lots of country groups started out in Texas honky-tonks, so they're probably still supportive."

"You're right. I need to begin thinking about what is possible, not what I think is possible."

"Right. But you can't do it all in one day."

"One step at a time." She gave him a big, warm smile. "I really appreciate your help—and your support."

"Anything I can do…and wait till you taste my sugar cookies." He smiled as he said it, because he was really thinking about giving her a bit of his own personal sugar, as in lots of hot, hot kisses.

Chapter 15

IVY PICKED UP THEIR EMPTY BOWLS AND STOOD UP. "LET me clear the table and put these in the dishwasher while you start our cookies."

"No rush. I'll help." He picked up the serving dish, then walked over to the counter and started transferring leftovers to glass containers with tight lids. "I'll put these in the fridge, so you can have them tomorrow."

"Thanks. It's all delicious." She filled the dishwasher, once more noticing how easily they worked side by side. He was quite the cook, along with every other wonderful thing about him. She honestly didn't see how he could still be single. Fern said he was about thirty, perhaps a little older, but around their age. Maybe he just hadn't had time to pursue a relationship along with his many other interests.

She set their glasses of tea on the countertop, out of the way, in case they wanted them later. She plugged in her laptop and opened the Wildcat Hall Park website. Sure enough, a couple more country band queries popped up. She started to click on a link, then stopped and looked at Slade. Truth of the matter, she'd much rather watch him, or even help him, than look at music videos, because that was too much like work. She'd prefer to have fun with her own personal chef.

He turned on the oven, then looked at her. "Are you going to watch me or country bands?"

"I was just thinking I'd be happier watching you or even helping you."

"I'll share the kitchen with you any day." He grinned, blue eyes lighting up.

She joined him at the counter. "I should have brought aprons from the dance hall."

"How messy do think we can get? This is a simple recipe."

"If flour is involved..."

He chuckled as he set a glass mixing bowl in front of him. "You've got a point, but I think we can cook with little cleanup."

"Great." She watched as he pulled premeasured ingredients in glass containers out of the box and set them on the countertop. She quickly realized he didn't need her help because he was so well organized, but she stayed close anyway, so she could watch him.

"Texas tea cakes are quick, easy, and fun."

"I'm beginning to think you need your own TV show—something like *Country Cooking with Slade Steele*."

He laughed, glancing over at her. "Just what I need. Something else to do."

She joined his laughter. "You sound like me. I really needed to take over Wildcat Hall, as if I had nothing else to do either."

She watched as he quickly filled the bowl with the premeasured ingredients, then neatly cracked an egg on the edge and added it to the mix. He gently stirred the dough with a long-handled wooden spoon, using smooth, even motions with his large hand.

"See?" he said. "No muss. No fuss."

"You make it look easy."

"Experience makes all the difference—plus a grand-mother who believes everybody needs to know how to cook, particularly boys, so I learned at an early age."

"She sounds wonderful."

"She is that, but she's tough as nails, too."

"Just like a lot of sweet-faced Texas grannies."

He nodded in agreement as he continued to stir the cookie dough. "You'll get to meet her."

"Really?"

"Sure. She still cooks and runs the Chuckwagon Café with an iron fist. Nothing gets past her."

"I bet…if you were running around the café like a rascal when you were young."

He laughed harder. "That's pretty much it."

"I look forward to meeting her."

"I've no doubt she'll like you. And you'll like her."

"I'd like to eat at the Chuckwagon sometime soon."

"I'll set up a time to make sure Granny's there. She still works at the ranch and casts a long shadow over the cowboys."

"I bet they mind their manners around her."

He smiled at the idea. "They surely do—for that matter, we all do."

"Thanks for the heads-up."

"No problem for you."

She felt warm deep inside at the fact that he wanted her to meet his grandmother, who had to be the head of his family. Again, he was forging ahead, drawing her deeper and deeper into his life…and at the moment, she hadn't the heart or the will or even the desire to resist him.

As she watched him set the spoon aside, she realized she wouldn't have thought it possible, just how sensual he made the entire process of putting together a batch of cookies. Maybe it was the fact that such a large, strong man was creating food that she would nibble, taste, swallow—so intimate, just like his searing kisses. She felt engulfed by heat. She glanced at the oven, thinking maybe the warmth was coming from there, but she knew better. Slade was the hot point of the entire room.

"All done." He picked up the mixing bowl, walked over to the refrigerator, and set it inside. "I'll let the dough chill next." He turned back to her. "How about I open the bottle of wine I brought with me?"

"Sounds good. I'll clean up."

"No need. I'll just take these containers back to the café." He quickly put lids back on jars and returned them to his box.

"You did make this easy."

"Only one item needs a little work." He picked up the wooden spoon still coated with cream-colored batter. "With the ingredients I use, you can still eat cookie dough."

"Really?"

"Do you want to clean the spoon for me?" He held it out to her.

"I'm not sure there's anything that tastes better than cookie dough." She accepted the spoon and took a big lick, savoring the sweet taste.

"I disagree with you."

She looked at him in surprise. "Why?"

He moved in close, took the spoon from her hand, licked it clean, then smiled as he set it aside. "Want me to show you why I disagree?"

"I'm not sure... You look cagey."

He smiled again and leaned toward her. "Kiss?"

"Cookie-dough kiss." She chuckled at the idea, loving it. "Now that's an irresistible offer."

She turned her face up and felt the soft pressure of his mouth before he licked her lower lip, saying, "Yum," and then delved deep as they shared the sweet taste of cookie dough. As their kiss turned hotter, she wrapped her hands around his neck and he pulled her closer, devouring her as if she were the sweetest of sugar cookies.

When he finally raised his head, he smiled. "I was right, wasn't I?"

She smiled back. "Yeah."

"Why don't we take this someplace comfortable? I'll get us wine."

She simply nodded, still tasting him, feeling him, wanting him. She walked over to the sofa and sat down on one end, regretting being parted from him for even a single moment.

He opened the wine bottle, selected two long-stemmed wineglasses from the cabinet, poured crimson liquid into both, and carried them over to her. He held one out almost gallantly, as if presenting her with something that was very precious to him...something just for her alone.

And then she realized that she understood him in a way that was almost too intimate, too emotional—and placed too much responsibility for his happiness in her hands. He was a big, tough cowboy who connected to others with his cooking and his wine making, while at the same time allowing him to keep his deeper emotions safely locked away. If so—if she was right—why had he reached out to her from the first moment he saw her? And why had she responded in such a way that left her as vulnerable to him as he was to her?

She shivered as she took a glass from his hand, unwilling to meet his eyes for fear of what she'd see or what she'd reveal.

"It's my latest."

And she understood even more. He wanted her to like his wine, because it would also mean she liked and appreciated him. She took a sip, and it went down easy—too easy, just like him. "It's delicious." She cupped the bowl of the glass with both hands, avoiding his gaze as he stood before her because she didn't want to reveal her thoughts.

"What is it?"

Had he already come to know her so well, as she was coming to know him? Were they already so attuned to each other that they hardly needed words to communicate? It was too quick. Everything was moving too fast with them. She didn't get it. She'd never experienced anything like it. And yet, she was like him in one way. She connected with others through her website work. It allowed her to help others while keeping her deeper emotions safely hidden away, because she'd seen way too much of the heartache that flowed around her sister to ever want it for herself.

"You don't like the wine?" Slade sat down beside her.

Too close. He was simply too close. He was making her see things and acknowledge things that she preferred to leave in the dark. Maybe that was part of the reason she'd been so desperate to get back to Houston that she'd called Peter for help. In the city, there were plenty of bright lights and superficial encounters to make one feel as if they were

COWBOY FIREFIGHTER CHRISTMAS KISS 141

connected to the pulse of life. In the country, there was too much quiet, too many wide-open spaces, too much time to contemplate the reality of life.

"I'm coming on too strong, aren't I?" He moved down the sofa away from her. "If you want, I can slow down, but I can't quit."

She took a deep breath, knowing she couldn't hurt him or lose him, or give up what she was just beginning to glimpse. She had a feeling they were going to profoundly affect each other—even if she didn't yet understand it.

"Do you want me to leave?" He stood up.

"No." She got to her feet, feeling slightly light-headed, and took a sip of wine. "I want you to bake cookies."

He moved in front of her but kept his distance. "I'll do it, but tell me what's bothering you."

"It's just…I'm trying to *not* belong here." She sipped more wine, feeling the warmth give her courage.

"Why?"

"Everything is so…intense here. And so real." She tossed back the last of the wine, needing it.

"How so?"

"I'm not sure. I'm trying to find my way."

"Will cookies help the transition?" he asked, easing the moment with a bit of humor.

She smiled, feeling the mood lighten. "Your wine warmed me, so—"

"I wish you'd let me warm you."

"I'll take warm cookies."

"That I can do." He took her glass, then walked into the kitchen and set both wineglasses to one side on the countertop.

"Thanks." She meant for letting her off the hook, but she'd enjoy the cookies, too.

She followed him into the kitchen, but she moved aside because he really didn't need her help.

He washed his hands, opened the fridge, pulled out the mixing bowl, and went about molding the chilled dough into walnut-size balls. He placed them in rows on an ungreased cookie sheet, then dipped the bottom of a glass into a bowl of sugar and pressed the balls flat. He washed his hands again, then he finally slid the cookies into the pre-heated oven.

"How long until they're ready to eat?"

"About ten minutes."

"These cookies will be quick and easy for the Hall, won't they?"

"That's my plan. And like I said, we can fancy them up with red and green sprinkles along with holiday shapes."

"Perfect. I really do appreciate all you're doing for Wildcat Hall."

He stopped and looked at her, banked fire in his blue eyes. "Wildcat Bluff is my home, and the dance hall was created to be the center of our community. I treasure what my ancestors built here." He took a step forward, raising his hands at his side as if opening up to her. "And I treasure you, too."

"Oh, Slade…" Her voice broke as emotion overcame her, welling up from so deep inside that it came flooding out as if a dam had burst. She held out a hand to him, needing his touch, needing his comfort, needing him.

He clasped her hand, and then slowly, gently eased her against his chest until he hugged her. "I understand. I really do. I'm trying to hold back, but it's not easy. All day long, no matter what I did, I thought of you."

She shivered at his words and felt him hold her harder in response. "No, I don't think you do understand, not completely. I'm only here till Fern comes back from her gig."

"That's what you say now." He gently placed a hand on each side of her head and tilted up her face. "Give the Park a chance…give *me* a chance." He looked into her eyes as he slowly lowered his head to kiss her.

When he touched lips to lips, his fire ignited her fire. And any resistance she had went up in smoke.

Chapter 16

SLADE FELT LIKE HE WAS ON FIRE, BURNING UP INSIDE and outside. Ivy made him feel as if he'd lost every lick of sense he'd ever had...and he'd felt like that since the first moment he saw her. Sure, it was physical, but it was so much more that it scared him—or it ought to scare him. The fact that it didn't, that it just made him want her more, told him that she was the one—the only one for him.

He'd waited a lifetime and suddenly she was just there. He'd found her in Wildcat Hall, of all places, trying to do the impossible. It was obvious at one glance that she couldn't get the tinsel on the antlers, but that didn't keep her gutsy self from trying to make it so. And now, here he was trying to do the impossible. Somehow or other, he had to convince her that she was finally where she belonged, because her home was in no other place except his arms.

If he rushed her, he'd lose her, and if he didn't rush her, he'd lose himself. Caught between a rock and a hard place, he hadn't known which way to turn, so he'd given her what he knew she would accept of him—chili, wine, cookie dough. And a few kisses. But those kisses, no matter how hot, were like frosting on a cake—alluring on the outside but promised so much more on the inside.

He wanted inside her. He was desperate to sink deep into her. And make them one. He ached from his head to his toes, needing so much more than the kisses he was giving her. If he held back much longer, he felt as if he would explode. And yet, he had to show restraint, so she would know he could be tender and sensitive to her feelings and upended life. He was sure that's what she would want in a man, not some barely restrained wild animal that he was keeping on a tight leash, a leash that was fraying every single second he kissed and held her, feeling her warmth, her softness, her curves.

And then she bit him, just a little nip on his lower lip that was quickly followed by the soothing caress of her tongue on his sensitized skin...but it was more than enough to snap his leash.

He held back a growl as he reached down and grabbed her hips, lifting her off her feet. It was as if she'd broken free of her leash, too, because she wrapped her long legs around his waist as she thrust her fingers into his hair, never breaking the kiss that got deeper and hotter and stronger.

He pulled her tighter against him as he massaged her firm butt, finding a slight rip in the soft fabric beneath a back pocket. He quickly inserted a fingertip into the hole and discovered she was wearing a thong or nothing at all under her jeans, so he stroked soft, smooth flesh that heated under his touch. Fired up, he thrust another finger into the hole, hearing the fabric slightly rip to make way, but it wasn't nearly enough now that he had touched so close to the heart of her. He needed more. He had to have it. He stretched her jeans until he thrust his entire hand through the gap. He grasped her firm, round globe with his entire palm, and she wiggled against him, clutching him harder with her thighs and tugging harder on his hair, moaning all the while.

He thought he'd been unleashed before, but now he

growled low in his throat, looked around desperately for a good place to take this further, saw the sofa, rejected it as too small and confining, and finally focused on the door to her bedroom. He was all done with being patient, waiting for her to want him as much as he wanted her. No need, not now. She was with him all the way, because he'd let his fingers stray to the soft center of her—and she was hot and wet and ready for him.

Carrying her, he strode across the floor to the doorway into her inner sanctum. A soft light on the nightstand illuminated a sagging bed with too many cute pillows in all sizes, shapes, and colors with western themes on a rust-colored bedspread that had a black barbwire motif embroidered around the edge. Surely not Ivy's taste in decor, but then she hadn't been here long. Still, it didn't matter what the bed looked like. It was a bed, so it'd do. He hoped they didn't break it, but if they did, he'd be happy to buy her a king-size that would suit the size of his body and all the rigorous activity he had in mind for sharing with Ivy.

He gently laid her down among the pillows that scattered everywhere, but he never lost contact with her—not with his kisses, not with anything. And the heat built between them as he clasped her wrists, drew her hands from around his neck, and raised them over her head, causing her breasts to thrust upward toward him. He switched her wrists to one hand and let the knuckles of his other slowly stroke down her rosy cheek, sensitizing her as he went, to the hollow of her vulnerable throat, where he could feel her pulse beating fast.

He hesitated, not wanting to rush this pivotal moment for either of them. He looked into her eyes, the green now only a ring around the dark centers that focused completely on him, revealing that she waited, not patiently, not reluctantly, not easily…revealing that she wanted not only his kisses but everything…revealing that she burned for him and him alone.

"Please," she said on a whisper of breath, reminding them both of what he'd asked of her not so long ago.

"Again." He trailed his fingertips down her T-shirt, to the swell of one breast, where he circled but didn't touch the hard tip that revealed her neediness.

"Please." She arched her back, thrusting her breasts toward him.

"Again." He cupped her breast, feeling the soft, round fullness and the hard, beaded nipple that almost caused him to come undone, but he kept control, if only barely.

"Please." She tucked her lower lip between her teeth and tossed her head back and forth as she pleaded with her eyes.

He was satisfied that she was desperate for his touch. He didn't need to wait a moment longer to satisfy them. He lifted her T-shirt to reveal a silky, lacy, peach-tinted bra that covered just enough to make her appear even more delectable. And yet he still cautioned himself to go slow, to make this good for her, as well as for him. He eased one breast out of a cup and breathed a sigh of appreciation for the pale pink nipple. He leaned forward and kissed, licked, and sucked that center of sensitivity until she arched against him, moaning in growing agitation.

He moved lower, kissing down her flat stomach to her belly button and burying his tongue in that round depth before snapping open her jeans and zipping down till he saw that she wore a thong that matched her bra. He grew even harder at the sight and the thought of what awaited him—so close now.

As he moved his fingertips inside her thong, he suddenly froze. Did he smell something burning? He raised his head and saw smoke drifting from the kitchen into the bedroom, bringing the scent of burnt cookies.

"Oh no!" He jerked up, rising swiftly to his feet.

"We forgot the cookies." She straightened her clothes as she looked at him in wide-eyed horror.

He ran into the kitchen, turned off the oven, grabbed a potholder, and jerked open the oven door. At the hit of oxygen, smoke and flames leaped out at him. He quickly stepped back and looked around for a fire extinguisher. He had a can in his truck, but that was too far away.

Ivy ran into the room and stopped beside him, hand over her nose at the smoke and fumes filling the room.

"Where's the fire extinguisher?"

"I don't know."

"Let's find it!" He slammed the oven door shut, tossed the pot holder on the countertop, and glanced around for a can. It couldn't be far.

She opened several cabinet doors without success. "Surely there's one here someplace."

"Got to be." He jerked open the doors under the sink and was relieved to finally see the telltale red container of an extinguisher. He grabbed it and pulled the pin.

"What do you want me to do?"

"Stand back till I get this under control."

When he was sure she was safely out of the way, he opened the oven again and took a closer look. The cookies still burned but were now little black pieces of crisp dough.

He sprayed the entire inside of the oven, including the cookies, then quickly opened the front door to let in fresh air.

He walked back, set the canister on the countertop, picked up the pot holder, and opened the oven again. He eased the cookie sheet out, set it in the sink, and stared at the shriveled bits of black cookie covered in foam.

Ivy moved in close and looked around his shoulder. "You think we might have a little trouble selling those in the Hall?"

"Sell them?" He just shook his head, glancing at her. "They're a disaster. I'm a disaster. I swear I've never burned cookies before in my entire life."

She put fingers over her mouth, shoulders shaking, as she tried to keep from laughing at his mess. "What would your granny say?"

"Don't you dare tell her, or I'll never hear the end of it."

Finally, she did chuckle, pointing at what was left of the cookies. "I guess you aren't usually so distracted when you cook."

He smiled, picking up on her humor. "Can I place the blame on you?"

"Anytime. I have no reputation riding on my cookie-baking prowess."

"I hate to think of the ribbing I'd get if any of my firefighter friends found out I'd burned a batch of cookies."

She laughed harder. "Maybe you need to bribe me to keep this cookie mess a secret."

"What would it take to ensure your silence?"

She glanced from him to the cookies to him again. "Not cookies. After smelling these, I don't think I'll ever be able to eat another sugar cookie in my entire life."

He chuckled. "And there goes my grand plan to impress you."

"I think you better go another route."

"What would that be—maybe the same one that'd keep my secret safe?"

She looked him up and down. "I do believe we can come up with a way for you to compensate me."

"Name it."

"Its name is Slade Steele."

He took a deep breath, feeling her words go straight to his heart. "You've got it, but we're going to move to a better location."

"What do you mean?"

"You can't stay here, not when the whole place reeks of smoke and burnt food."

"It'll air out."

"Not anytime soon."

"If we clean the oven and the cookie sheet, it'll help."

"Somewhat, but not enough." He grinned, thinking that he could still turn this disaster to his benefit—and hers. "Why don't you pack an overnight bag and I'll take you to my place? There's a guest room, if you want it."

"Your home?" She appeared surprised, then she glanced out the front door, as if considering her options.

"Yeah."

"I could move into one of the empty cabins here."

"You could do that, but wouldn't you prefer to be with me, where you're safe…and warm?"

"As tempting as it sounds, I ought to stay here and clean up." She put her arms around her waist, as if hugging herself for comfort. "Besides, I can stand the stench."

"No." He put a fingertip under her chin and lifted her face so he could see her expression. "You've had more than enough stress since you moved in here. You need some tender loving care, and I'm going to give it to you."

"We can't leave the mess, and you know it."

"I'll toss the cookie sheet. There's no point in trying to save it."

"The stove?"

"Settelmeyers. No matter how good a job we do on the cleanup, it'd never be up to their standards. And I'd never intentionally upset them, particularly not on their turf. I'll let them know, and they'll be on it tomorrow."

"But that way, folks will find out about your cookie disaster."

"Our secret is safe with them. They never tell anything that goes on here. They protect Wildcat Hall Park like their own personal castle that needs defending against all harm."

"Are you saying they're our knights in shining armor?"

He nodded. "As close as we're going to get in this lifetime."

She chuckled. "You've got an answer for everything, don't you?"

"Wish I did, but tonight, I'm tired and I want to sleep in my own bed."

"Your injury?"

"I won't lie to you—I could use that comfort about now." He hoped that idea might persuade her to go with him, because he really didn't want to leave her alone with a mess she'd probably try to clean once he was gone. Besides, he just flat-out didn't want to leave her.

She hesitated, glancing around the room. "It won't be the same here without you. It'll feel so empty."

And he knew he had her just where he wanted her, so he slipped an arm around her waist. "I promise I have good food at home. And I'll even let you sleep alone…if you want."

She laid her head against his chest for just a moment, as if in agreement, then stepped back. "I'll go with you but just for tonight. And I'd better sleep in your guest room. Otherwise, what would your grandmother think?"

"She'd think I was a lucky man."

Ivy simply shook her head.

"Pack a bag…and let's get out of here."

Chapter 17

Ivy relaxed against the leather seat of Slade's pickup as he headed down Wildcat Road. She felt as if she rode in a cocoon toward an enchanted land where all her problems would melt away. She knew it wasn't true, of course. She didn't want to turn her life over to somebody else, even if, at the moment, it did seem like a delightful and blissful dream.

No, she just wanted a little break from the unending drama in her new environment. Even more, she wanted to be with Slade to pursue what had been building between them since the moment they met. She'd come to the point where she was even willing to chance her heart...as scary as that thought was to her. And yet, how could she resist a man who could be her dream guy if she'd only let him? For tonight, though, she didn't want to think that far down the line. She simply wanted to be in his arms to savor his caresses, his kisses...and so much more that only he could give her.

And then she realized that she had no idea where they were going. If she had fallen into a dream world, she had to wake up. She couldn't just let herself be taken off to who knew where. She shook her head to clear it.

"Slade, where are we going?"

"To my home."

"Yes, I understand. But where is it?"

He glanced at her with a grin. "I forgot you don't know all the ranches and their families. I'm still mostly at Steele

Trap I. I put a modular home there after my injury. It's all on one level."

"That sounds good."

"It's been fine, but I never intended to make it permanent. Now I'm fixing up the ranch house on Steele Trap II. I told you about it, didn't I?"

"Yes, you did."

"So, on the old ranch, there's the original house with Mom and Granny, then down from there in the next house is my sister, Sydney, with her daughter, Storm, and her fiancé, Dune. My house is closest to the Red River."

Ivy felt her breath catch in her throat as the implications of what he told her sank in. "Are you telling me that we're going to drive by your grandmother's house and your sister's house before we get to your house?"

"Right."

"I suppose there's only one road in and out."

"Right again." He glanced at her, appearing puzzled as he slowed down on the road. "Your point?"

"Are you trying to embarrass me in front of the whole county?"

He clenched the steering wheel with both hands. "I'd never do that. Surely you know it."

"Then why would you drive me by those houses? Anybody could see us and know I was spending the night."

"Why would they care…or you care?"

"As if you don't know—I'm now the face of Wildcat Hall. I'm rebuilding its reputation into a first-class establishment." She tossed a glare at him. "Its reputation is connected to my reputation."

"But I don't see how—"

"We're talking about entertainment and entertainers. They have a certain reputation. Fern has to deal with it all the time."

"I wouldn't do anything to hurt you."

"If I'd been here longer, it'd be different, but if I'm seen hooking up with you after I've barely landed in the county, I'm bound to be considered—no matter how old-fashioned it sounds—a loose woman."

He clenched the steering wheel again. "I thought maybe, if they even found out, that they'd see you as my girlfriend."

"Girlfriend?"

"Yeah." He glanced over at her. "I kind of hoped so."

"It's too soon. I believe that develops over time."

"Not in our case."

"Your grandmother is probably the straw-hat-and-white-gloves-in-the-summertime type of woman."

"She's not. She's a cowgirl and a cook." He gave Ivy a soft smile. "If I love you, she'll love you."

"Love?"

"We'll get to that." He grinned mischievously. "Right now I'm taking you home."

"No. You're taking me back to the cowboy cabins. I'll move into one of those for the duration."

"Haven't you been listening to me? I'd never do anything I thought would harm you in any way." He stomped on the brake, pulled to the side of the road, and turned to look at her. "I don't think you're safe there. I want you with me, where I can watch over you."

"I don't think you've been listening to me. I will not—absolutely not—be seen in your home so shortly after our acquaintance."

"You know this is the twenty-first century."

"I don't care what it is. Take me back to the cabins."

"No."

"No?" She stared at him in frustration. "What are you going to do, hold me captive?"

"I'm about to that point." He drummed his fingertips on the steering wheel. "Okay, let's compromise. I won't take you where it's warm and comfortable with plenty of good food. I'll take you to the new ranch house. Nobody is anywhere near there to see us."

"Except the cattle rustlers."

"Well, there's always that." And he grinned, chuckling under his breath. "On the plus side, it might give us a chance to catch them."

She just shook her head. "What kind of shape is this house in?"

"Not too bad."

"If it's not as good as the cabins…"

He chuckled again, easing back on the road. "Remember, I offered you the best."

She leaned back in her seat with an uneasy feeling that the night wasn't going to get any better.

"One good thing."

"What?"

"I think Granny left some sugar cookies there."

"Oh no. I told you I'll remember that burnt stench forever, and it'll make me queasy. Not even her cooking will tempt me."

"Might not be anything else to eat."

"I can wait." She glanced up at the night sky. "How far away can dawn and a good breakfast be?"

"Dawn, quite a while. Breakfast, just over at the Chuckwagon."

She glanced down at her clothes, remembering the big, new rip in the bottom of her jeans. "One thing's for sure—I'm going nowhere I can be seen in these jeans."

"Didn't you bring a change?"

"Just a top. I forgot you tore these. And, besides, I'm going home come first light."

He didn't say anything else. He just turned off the road, drove over a cattle guard, up a gravel road, and toward a spot-lit, single-story ranch house on a hill overlooking the pastures around it.

She liked the natural rock and cedar trim, double front doors, and big windows in front. She could easily see Slade living there in contentment as he watched over his land, created delicious recipes, and made wonderful wine. If things were different, she could even imagine living there with him, sharing love and family, hopes and dreams, happiness and sorrow...but she stopped those thoughts in their tracks. She wasn't even girlfriend material, because she was going back to Houston.

"I'm going to park in back, so my truck won't be visible from the entrance or the road."

"Thanks. If this works out like it should, nobody will ever know we spent the night together in your house."

"*Another* night together."

"Oh, that's right." She glanced over at him. "I don't know how that keeps happening to us."

He looked back at her, searching her face as if for an answer. "Do you want me to explain it?"

"No." She was beginning to feel testy about the whole

thing, even though she knew it wasn't really his fault, since she had to share some of the blame. "I just wanted a nice dinner."

"You had it."

"And sugar cookies."

"There're some in the house."

"That's not funny."

He chuckled, shaking his head. "Yes, it is. Later, maybe years from now, we'll sit on our back porch drinking my latest wine, and we'll laugh and laugh about my burnt cookies."

"*Our* porch?"

He just gave her a slow smile, then opened his door. "Come on. Let's get comfortable inside."

But she didn't move. She was stuck on "our porch" and the way it affected her—all warm and cozy and content. What was happening to her? Did she need to tattoo "Houston" on her forehead to remind her of what she truly wanted in life? At this rate, she could hardly even remember the city, much less think about spending the rest of her life there.

When Slade opened the passenger door and held out his hand to help her down, she cast all thoughts of city life out of her mind. She grabbed her purse with essentials, laptop in its padded bag, and a soft-sided overnight with a change of underwear, long-sleeve T-shirt, big sleep T-shirt, a button-up sweater, makeup bag, and toothbrush. It was plenty of stuff to get her through a few hours on a ranch.

Once she put her fingers in Slade's strong hand, she felt the now-familiar heat arc between them. He took her bags in one hand and wrapped the other around her waist. Her feet planted firmly on the ground, they walked together toward the spotlight over the entry to the ranch house.

He stopped at the back door, fished a key out of his pocket, and unlocked and pushed the door open wide. Only a faint night-light illuminated the interior, so she hesitated to enter.

"Better let me go first," he said, returning his key to his pocket. "I doubt the kitchen's in very good shape."

"Didn't you start renovating there first?"

"It's last on my list."

"But why?"

"I've got plenty of places to cook. Here I needed the bath and bed more than anything."

"Your hip?"

"Mostly I'm okay, but if I push too hard, too long, then…"

"I understand."

"Anyway, let me get the lights."

When the ceiling lights came on, she couldn't keep from gasping in horror. She was glad he'd prepared her for the destruction. He'd gutted the room. No cabinets. No countertop. No sink. No fridge. No stove. No nothing… Except walls with half-stripped floral wallpaper and a faded, stained, ripped vinyl floor. A round oak table with two mismatched chairs stood lonely in one corner. On top of it nestled a coffee maker, a cracked, red cookie jar, and two white mugs with "Merry Christmas" written on them in bright green.

"Home sweet home." Slade gestured around the room. "Hope you don't expect me to cook."

She finally laughed at the sight. "After our earlier experience, I'm not sure I ever want you near a stove again."

"Now that's flat-out cruel." He laughed with her. "I guess it'll take quite a feast for me to redeem my culinary reputation."

She laughed harder, suddenly feeling lighthearted about everything. "At least there's never a dull moment in Wildcat Bluff."

"Not since you arrived on the scene."

"What?" She walked carefully into the room. "I'm completely innocent."

"Yeah…just try convincing anybody. I never burned anything in my life till you showed up."

"Well, I have to admit I might have distracted you a bit while the cookies got a little overheated."

"Charred, you mean."

"Well, if you insist on being accurate."

"When it comes to food, I do." He patted her bags. "Come on, let's get you set up."

She followed him through a big room with early American furniture, all scratched wood and shiny upholstery that must have belonged to the original owners of the house. Large front windows would let in a lot of light during the day, for a picturesque view, but at night, with no drapes, they looked like big, dark, watchful eyes that would allow anyone to peer inside. She shivered and hurried through the room, into the hall, with Slade flipping on lights as they went.

When they came to the end of the hall, he opened the door and turned on a ceiling light with a fan that slowly rotated overhead. She stepped in front of him and smiled with pleasure. He'd surely outdone himself here. He'd painted the walls a pale-rust tint that echoed the warmth of the oak floor. The furniture—king bed, dresser, chest, and nightstands—appeared to be handmade of red cedar in a beautiful contemporary design.

"I made the furniture myself," Slade said, sounding proud of his accomplishment.

"It's absolutely gorgeous." She ran her hand over the rust-colored bedspread with brown suede throw pillows.

"Thanks. It's comfortable." He gestured toward a closed door.

When she opened it, she smiled at the welcome sight of the huge walk-in closet. "This is wonderful. Most of the older houses have small closets."

"I converted a bedroom to make the closet."

"Good choice."

"If you think the old closets are small, you should go further back in time, when there were no closets at all."

"That's why they had big wardrobes?"

"Right. Nobody built closets in houses because you had to pay a tax on each closet."

"You're kidding me."

"Nope. That's the truth, strange as it may be now."

"I'm glad I missed that era."

He just chuckled as he set her bags on top of the dresser with a large, square mirror behind it. "Come in here. You may like this room best of all."

She moaned in delight when she entered the final room of his suite, because it was the bathroom. He'd completely outdone himself from the black hexagon mosaic-tile floors to the white subway-tile walls to the jetted-tub to the glass shower to the enclosed toilet to the double square sinks in a vanity with a marble top to the large cone vanity lights above the bank of mirrors. Stainless steel accents and rust-colored towels added the finishing touches.

"You like?" he asked, leaning back against a wall of taupe tile.

"It's gorgeous. I could live in here."

"Wish you would." He shut the door to the bathroom. "Watch this." He touched a control panel that lowered the lights and turned on the shower, the sinks, and the tub. "I wanted the ultimate in luxury." He gestured toward the round and square baskets on top of the vanity. "Morning Glory stocked me with all sorts of lotions, shampoos, and soaps. They're probably the best luxury in the house."

"I love it. I really do."

He walked over to her, smiling. "I'm glad because I want you to try it all before you go."

"I'll take you up on that offer. In fact—" She stopped in midsentence when she heard a noise outside the door.

"Okay, you varmints," a deep male voice said, followed by the bark of a dog and the ratchet of a shotgun. "Put your hands in the air and come out easy or get a load of birdshot where the sun don't shine."

Ivy gasped and put a hand to her chest.

Slade simply rolled his eyes. "Oscar, don't you and Tater know when to mind your own business?"

Chapter 18

Ivy watched Slade push open the bathroom door, then she peered around him, hoping to remain mostly out of sight.

A tall, bald-headed, leathery-skinned man of indeterminate age in cowboy hat, shirt, jeans, and boots saw her. He quickly lowered his gun barrel, jerked off his hat, and held it over his heart. "Slade, do introduce me to this lovely lady."

Ivy stepped back out of sight, behind Slade, but it didn't help because a dog with short, tricolor fur, and upright ears darted around Slade, pink tongue hanging out, leaped up, put his front paws on her stomach, and tried to lick her face.

"Tater, get down!" Slade hollered, but the dog paid him no never mind.

"If you won't do the honors, I'll be happy to introduce myself. Name's Oscar Leathers and this is Tater, the best cow dog in the county."

"Call him off before I wrestle him off," Slade said, irritation lacing his voice as he glared at the dog.

"No need to get testy," Oscar said. "Tater is simply introducing himself to a lady so lovely he must pay homage in the best way he knows how."

"He's got a really long tongue." Ivy leaned back as far as she could, not about to touch the dog in hopes of avoiding germy saliva contact, in addition to leaving fleas or dirt or cow manure or whatever on her T-shirt.

"Tater, that's enough." Slade grabbed the dog's black leather collar and tugged him off. "He's got no manners."

"Not true." Oscar glanced at Tater, put his hat on his head, and patted his thigh. "Here. Sit."

Tater immediately sat down beside Oscar but continued to grin happily at Ivy with lolling tongue.

She brushed dusty paw prints off her T-shirt—at least she hoped it was just dust. Actually, she liked dogs, but small, trained, likeable ones were her preference. City dogs. This one had country written all over him. Even worse, he seemed to have taken a liking to her. And that had trouble written all over it, so she kept her position halfway behind Slade.

"Is your girlfriend shy, or are you keeping her hidden away from all the competition in Wildcat Bluff?" Oscar asked, grinning happily—a lot like the dog, minus the lolling tongue.

"I'm not his girlfriend," Ivy said before she realized the implications of that statement. "I mean...well, Slade burned the cookies and my cabin stinks, so he brought me here and..." She trailed off, realizing she was making the situation worse.

"Slade burned food?" Oscar threw back his head and guffawed before he glanced down and patted Tater, who appeared to think the news was just as funny, since he kept grinning at Ivy.

Slade gave her a narrow-eyed look before turning back to Oscar. "You didn't hear that. And you didn't see her."

"And who is this beautiful damsel in distress I don't see?"

Ivy just sort of gave up. Nothing about this evening was going as planned. Anyway, how much worse could it get?

Somehow or other, she figured Fern would know how to handle it all with aplomb, charming the cowboy and the dog. She'd just have to do her best. "I'm Ivy Bryant and—"

"*The* Ivy Bryant of Wildcat Hall?"

"I guess you could put it that way."

"Well, bless my stars." Oscar looked down at Tater again. "Now, isn't this just our lucky day? We thought we'd caught the rustlers, but lo and behold, we caught the pie baker with the most notorious woman in town. Don't that beat all!"

"Notorious woman?" Ivy asked, feeling a little faint. Was her reputation already in ruins?

"Notorious?" Slade echoed, pushing Ivy a little farther behind him as if for protection from the big, bad world.

"No other way to put it," Oscar replied. "Little lady comes to town and lickety-split snags the cowboy every single—and not so single—lady in the county has had her eye on for years. I'd say that's notorious, because they're all wondering what she's got that they don't."

Ivy leaned her forehead against Slade's back, feeling as if everything she'd tried to avoid was already a well-established fact in the county. And it made no sense. "He's not my boyfriend."

"Yes, I am."

"No, you're not."

"Whoa, doggies." Oscar held up one hand. "Settle down. I'm just relating gossip, not fact. But you've got to admit—"

"We're admitting nothing," Slade said.

Oscar gave a quick nod, agreeing with his head but not with his eyes. "That being the case, you'd both better be down at the Chuckwagon first thing for breakfast. Lula Mae will want an accounting. You can bet your bottom dollar on that."

Slade groaned. "There's nothing to tell Granny. I was baking sample cookies to serve at the Hall when I got distracted and they got a bit overdone."

"Distracted, huh?" Oscar said, chuckling under his breath.

"After that, I wanted Ivy where it was safe."

Oscar looked over his shoulder, then back again, but said nothing while implying that the half-restored house prone to rustlers wasn't his idea of safety.

"That's true," Ivy said, backing up Slade, not knowing why they were explaining themselves in the first place. "Anyway, I'm only here for a few hours before I go back to the Park. No time for breakfast anywhere. And Slade was just showing me his house renovations."

Oscar patted the top of Tater's head. "We better be on our way. Lula Mae will expect us early."

"Don't mention the burnt cookies," Slade said, "or I'll never hear the end of it."

"And don't mention the girlfriend thing either," Ivy added for good measure, although she had little hope of anything remaining secret for long in Wildcat Bluff.

Oscar's right eye twitched as he tried to keep a straight face. "Okeydoke. No cookies. No girlfriend."

"Yes, she *is* my girlfriend," Slade said, "and I want everybody to know it."

"If I'm your girlfriend, *you* burnt the cookies." Ivy gave his muscular shoulder a hard look since she couldn't see his face.

Oscar coughed, obviously trying to conceal laughter, as he backed up with Tater beside him. "I got no more to say on the matter...except I'll make sure all the critters get fed come dawn. See y'all at breakfast." He spun around and walked away.

Ivy didn't move, and Slade didn't either until they heard the front door open, close, and the lock snick into place.

"We don't really have to go to breakfast in a few hours, do we?" Ivy asked, thinking about her clothes back in the cabin in comparison to what she'd brought with her. "I don't have anything appropriate to wear."

"You wanted to meet Granny, didn't you?"

"Yes...at some time in the future when I had Wildcat Hall under control and my life back on track."

"How soon do you think that's going to happen?"

She gave a big sigh. "Not anytime soon."

"Granny's not a patient lady."

"Tell you what. You take me home. You go to your good home. In the morning, you go see your grandmother on your lonesome."

"No."

"What's wrong with my plan?"

"Everything."

She put her hands on her hips. "If I walk into that café with you first thing in the morning, all the gossip will be confirmed and that'll be that."

"Good. That's what I want."

"But I'm not your girlfriend."

He picked up her hand, turned it over, and kissed her palm. "By morning, you will be."

She shivered at his touch, while thoughts of Oscar, Tater, rustlers, and anything beyond Slade's kiss flew out the window. He grounded her in the here and now, taking her with him into his world as he pressed a hot kiss to her wrist. She felt her heart beat faster, knowing he felt it, too, as he lingered to trace her veins with the tip of his tongue. She shivered again.

He lifted his head, blue eyes blazing with intent as he stroked her palm with his thumb. "Cold?"

She just looked at him, knowing he knew how he was affecting her—and it wasn't a chilly night, although the house was cool, maybe not even heated throughout all the rooms.

"Why don't you try out my bath?"

"Really?" She tried to put disdain, disbelief, and denial in that one word, but it came out more as a question than a statement.

He grinned, eyes sparkling with mischief. "Well, yeah, I admit I am trying to get you out of your clothes, but it's for a good cause."

"And what cause is that?"

"Me. And you."

She couldn't help but laugh at his honesty. "I think you've been trying to do that since the moment we met."

He laughed with her. "I won't deny it."

She decided to be brutally honest before they went any further down this path. "I don't want us hurt."

"I'd never hurt you."

"But I might hurt you."

"Doubt it. Anyway, you don't think I'm man enough to take a little pain?"

"That's not it. I don't want to hurt you—or me."

"You're talking emotions, aren't you?"

"Yes." She straightened her shoulders, determined to get through this before she lost the courage. "I've told you from the beginning that I'm going back to Houston when Fern returns."

"I know. I've been hearing you. I just don't believe you."

"You don't want to believe me."

"There's that, too."

"So, to avoid the possibility of emotional pain, what do you say we leave this where it is and you take me back to the cowboy cabins right now?"

He lifted a hand and brushed loose hair back from her face, looking tenderly at her. "Do you think I've come this far and waited this long to let you go so easily? If you do, you don't know me at all."

"That's just it. I *don't* know you."

"I've been trying to remedy the situation, but you keep balking on me." He reached behind him to the control panel, lowered the lights, and started water filling the bathtub.

"What are you doing?"

"I'm doing what I should've done the moment we got here. You're tired. I'm tired. Let's take a bath and wash off the day."

"Together?"

He walked over to the vanity, pulled a bottle out of a basket, and poured liquid into the gushing water. The room filled with the scent of lavender as bubbles roiled and foamed in the tub.

"Are you trying to say we stink?"

"Burnt-cookie perfume isn't ever going to make it onto Morning Glory's list of favorite scents."

Ivy smiled, knowing it was true.

"I'm going to the kitchen and opening a bottle of wine." He took a step back toward the door. "When I get back, I want to find you in the tub underneath all those bubbles."

"And you?"

"I'll take a shower."

She nodded, feeling relieved he wasn't going to press the shared-bath point, because she really wanted a good soak, and she tended to get all weak-kneed and weak-willed around him.

After he left, she quickly stripped out of her clothes, noticing they reeked of smoke worse than she'd realized, but all she could do was fold and set them on top of the vanity. She pulled a fluffy, rust-colored washcloth and matching towel out of a cabinet and set them on the edge of the luxurious tub. She quickly stepped into the water and sank down to her chin under a massive amount of bubbles that covered her completely. She let out a long sigh of contentment and closed her eyes, feeling as if she could let go of all her concerns for the first time since setting foot in Wildcat Bluff County.

And yet, easing her body just set her mind adrift. To set the record straight, she did know Slade, partly through the eyes of those who'd known him forever. He was well respected and trusted in the community. And she knew him enough now to put her trust in him. Without a doubt, he'd keep her safe, watch over her, and respect her. Was there even a price that could be put on something that rare and valuable? They'd come together so fast that she kept discounting his feelings and her own, but did the length of time really matter? Is that what was important…or was the reality of how they'd meshed from the first moment they'd met more important? Maybe they'd made time stand still for just the two of them.

And then she had another thought. What if Peter received an offer for the Park? How would she ever explain to Slade that she had gone to a Realtor in the first place? Even if she didn't sell, he'd feel betrayed, as would everyone in Wildcat Bluff.

When he came back into the bathroom, carrying two mugs from the kitchen, she pushed down her uneasy thoughts, trying to convince herself that she might never get an offer, so there was no need yet to contact Peter about changing her mind. She accepted a mug and took a sip of his delicious wine. "Thanks."

"Anytime." He sat down on the edge of the tub and sipped his wine as he watched her. "You look perfect there—just like I knew you would from the first moment I saw you."

"Do you mean you thought of me in your bathtub?"

"Yeah. I admit it. It's as if I designed my suite with you in mind before I ever met you." He set his mug down on the vanity top, then jerked open his shirt, one snap after the other, until he pulled the tail out of his jeans. "I'm starting to sound like a sap, aren't I?"

She simply stared in wonder at his exposed chest, feeling her heart rate ratchet up a notch as she followed the trail of dark-blond hair across his sleek muscles down to his huge belt buckle.

"You're not saying anything. Are you agreeing with me?" he asked, sounding annoyed as he removed his shirt and tossed it beside his mug.

She swallowed hard to try to control the heat that had enveloped her at the sight of him nearly naked. "No. You sound like a strong man—"

"In love?" He stalked over, knelt beside her, and placed his forearms on the side of the tub.

"I didn't say... I didn't mean... I don't know."

"If you're allergic to the word *girlfriend*, how do you feel about *love*?"

She suddenly felt very exposed in the tub, even with the bubbles covering her. Maybe that was part of her reluctance to follow where he led—he made her feel more vulnerable all the time. And yet, could she let her fears dictate her life when Slade was offering his heart on a silver platter with whipped cream and a cherry on top? She was starting to adore everything about him.

"Are you going to answer me?"

"I feel as if... Are those tattoos?" She'd never seen him without his shirt, and she suddenly realized that a barb-wire tattoo circled his right bicep—which was about as big around as her waist—while a lasso twined around the other.

"Yep. I got them while on the circuit." He flexed his powerful muscles to make the tattoos move. "Hope you like them."

She reached out and traced the barbwire, leaving goose bumps in her wake, before she did the same to the rope. "Yes, I like."

"You got any?"

She smiled. "Not yet."

"Maybe you need a 'love' tattoo, then there'd be no doubt as to how you feel about me."

"When did we get from girlfriend to love?"

"Love is where we started. Girlfriend is simply a step in the right direction." He grinned like he was well on his way to winning a new belt buckle—one that read "Ivy Bryant" in big, bold letters.

And she couldn't deny that he might be right.

Chapter 19

IVY WAS SO TEMPTED BY SLADE, PARTICULARLY SINCE HE had enough muscle and testosterone to run a big city's power plant. She took a deep breath, trying to control her need to grab him and pull him into the tub...but that helped matters not at all, because she simply inhaled all that tantalizing, musky scent deep into her body. And that, of course, set her on fire.

"Need any help?" He picked up the washcloth on the tub's edge with a little quirk of his lips to let her know he knew she was looking at him and liking what she saw just as much as he liked what he saw in his bathtub.

She snatched the cloth out of his hands and dunked it underwater, out of his reach, not yet ready to give up her resistance. "Thanks, but no thanks."

He smiled, blue eyes crinkling at the corners as he teased her. "Need me to find that washcloth for you?"

"Do you mind? I'm trying to take a bath here." She was beyond grumpy, caught between wanting him and not wanting to succumb to him, because every step she took toward him felt like a step into the country and away from the city.

"I'm just trying to help." He chuckled, as if he knew exactly what she was feeling, swiped bubbles with the tip of one finger, and dabbed it on the tip of her nose. "There. You can't ever say I didn't help you take a bath."

Finally, she couldn't keep from smiling at his antics.

Somehow he always knew when to add a touch of levity to life...maybe because he knew when his attentions were getting too strong and she was getting too uncomfortable.

"Guess it's time for my shower." He stood up, suddenly serious as he looked down at her. "Want to help me?"

"Oh, Slade, you're such a temptation."

"I hope so." He smiled wistfully. "I'm doing my best."

"Your best is more than enough."

He grinned, then walked out of sight.

When she heard his jeans hit the floor and the shower come on, she grabbed the washcloth and began scrubbing all over, hardly appreciative of the wonderful, lavender-scented soap. It didn't matter. Nothing mattered now except Slade naked in the shower just a few feet away.

And that's what finally did it. She broke. Burnt cookies. Chili. Stew. Pie. Fire. Red tinsel. Images flashed through her mind of all he'd been to her since he stepped inside the Hall and found her trying to reach the antlers. He'd brought help, gifts, comfort...and most of all, he'd given her unconditional... She didn't want to think *love*, but it came close to that deep commitment. And on top of it all, there was the heat that arced between them every time they were together. Could she really pass up a man who offered her so much...and who was beginning to feel more like home than her real home?

She abruptly stood up, letting water cascade down her body to pool in the tub. She was clean. She'd washed away the stench of burnt cookies. She had no reason to stay in the bathroom. Except one.

She stepped out of the warm water, walked across the cool tile, and opened the door to the steamy shower.

Slade gave her a slow smile that gained in wattage as he stepped back to make room for her.

She caught her breath at his beauty, all shimmery with water and soap and sleek skin. If she'd been hot before, now she was positively incandescent. She probably cast a crimson glow as he took his time, his eyes feasting on every single inch of her body before returning to her face.

She feasted on him in return—male perfection, as in a ridiculous amount of musculature from head to toe after a lifetime of hard outdoor work gave his wide shoulders, broad chest, flat stomach, and long legs a chiseled appearance. She wanted to stroke him all over to feel the play of his muscles under her hands, watching what she could do to him with touch if just the sight of her had him so far over the edge that he jutted toward her.

"Coming in or staying out?" he asked in a husky tone.

"In." She moved forward, stepping into wet warmth, hearing him close the door behind her, enclosing them in a rainy mist of tropical fragrance.

She expected him to be eager, but he took his time, clasping her shoulders and holding her gently like she was the most precious gift in the world. He slowly stroked down her back with rough palms, finding every single dip and curve with his fingertips as if he was memorizing her. When he reached her hips, he paused, as if preparing for something so powerful, so life-altering that he had to be strong enough for them both to continue their passion.

She understood. She truly did—to trust or not to trust, to let in or to keep out, to take a chance or to turn back. Now was the pivotal moment. She cared about him, as much as she'd tried not to do it. She cared...and because she cared so much, she wouldn't put all the responsibility on him. They were in this together now. She reached up, gently cupping his cheek with one hand. He turned his head and pressed a gentle kiss into her palm.

Tenderness. She hadn't expected to feel so tender toward him. It almost overpowered the passion that had driven them toward each other from the first moment they met. Maybe he felt the same. Maybe it was also why he hesitated. Maybe he wanted to savor the feeling just a little bit longer.

As that tender feeling in her heart grew stronger, ratcheting up into a fast heartbeat, she smiled up into his radiant blue eyes and felt his hands grasp her hips harder, as if he was hanging on to control by his very fingertips. And yet she was the one who finally lost control, as the looks, the touches, the feelings ignited a hot, wild desire that drove her to throw her arms around his neck and kiss him with ferocious abandon.

And he returned her kiss with an equal ferocity, tugging her hard against his body so that they were touching from head to toe as water gently cascaded over them, enveloping them in their own private world.

She clasped his shoulders, straining against him, wanting more, needing more, getting desperate for more of what only he could give her.

Suddenly, he tore his mouth from hers and set her back, breathing hard. "Ivy, let's take this to the bed. I can't... It'd be easier for me if..."

"Oh, yes, of course." She was abruptly brought back to reality, remembering his injury. "Are you okay to—"

"Yes. I'm too big in here. And I want something soft for you."

She smiled, feeling tenderness well up again. "We're all wet."

"Like I care." He turned off the shower and thrust open the door. "You're all I care about." He stepped out, turned back, and held out his hand.

She put her fingers into his large, strong hand, feeling vulnerable but safe at the same time. Sometimes he engendered such conflicting emotions in her that she hardly knew how to handle them. She shivered a little at the intensity of her feelings and the cool air on her bare skin.

"You're cold."

"I'm okay."

"No, you're not."

"We're just going into the bedroom."

"Morning Glory said I'd need this someday. Guess she was right." He looked around, as if searching for something or trying to remember something, then he smiled in triumph. He quickly opened a cabinet under the vanity, pulled out a big, soft, fluffy, white robe, and draped it around her shoulders.

"Thank you. This is lovely."

"Once we're in bed, I'll keep you warm."

"Better yet."

He chuckled as he grasped her hand and led her into the bedroom, where he touched the wall control, turning off the overhead light and lowering the wattage of the lamps on the nightstands. He left her standing in the middle of the room while he tossed the throw pillows on the floor and pulled back the spread to reveal chocolate-colored sheets.

"I like that color."

"Thanks. Morning Glory again. I'd be lost without her

good taste…and her determination to see me properly
outfitted here. That's one lady who will not take no for an
answer."

Ivy sat down on the bed, running her palm over the
smooth, satiny sheets.

He stood over her, appearing perfectly comfortable in
his nudity, while he watched her all wrapped up in the robe.
"I want you to know…you're the only woman who has ever
slept in this bed."

She put her hand to her lips, trying to hold back all the
emotions that were cascading through her.

"Maybe it's not important to you, but it is to me." He
abruptly sat down beside her and picked up her hand, cradling it in both of his big ones.

"Yes, it's important, but you didn't need to tell me."

"Of course I did." He pressed a kiss to her palm. "I want
everything to be right, but so far tonight, everything has
gone wrong."

"Not everything." She felt her breath catch in her throat
as the tenderness in her heart swelled outward, threatening
to completely engulf her. She honestly wanted the passion
back, because it seemed so much safer, gliding across the
surface of it, than this deep tenderness that threatened her
entire world.

"Ivy, I'm going to make love to you in this bed. It's our
bed…in our bedroom…in our home."

She actually felt slightly faint, as blood rushed from her
head to her heart. He was going to be her undoing. And she
had no way to resist him—no longer even wanted to resist him.

"I'm moving too fast with you. I know it, but I can't stop.
I'm not going to stop. We're meant for each other."

"Slade, would you please just make love to me." She'd begun to shiver all over. "If you say one more word, you may scare me to death."

He placed another kiss on the palm of her hand. "I sure wouldn't want that...not when I'm finally about to do something right tonight."

"That was several more words, but you're forgiven since you're about to do something right." She teased, smiling as he laughed with her.

"I better, or all the words in the world won't impress you."

"You've already impressed me."

"Not like I'm about to."

She appreciated his self-confidence. And then all the words were driven from her head as he nudged her back, so she was flat against the bed, and opened her robe, revealing her sensuous curves perfectly etched in pale light and dark shadow.

"You're so beautiful." He exhaled quietly as he simply looked at her before he leaned down and pressed kisses to the tips of her breasts.

She felt her nipples go instantly hard, blazing a trail straight to her hot center and causing her to tremble all over. He didn't give her a chance to catch her breath as he continued his onslaught, sucking, licking, nibbling as he fondled her breasts with both hands. He kissed downward to her navel, where he stopped and teased with his tongue until she was damp—no, more than damp. She felt as if she were covered in sweet frosting and he was licking down to her rich, moist center.

And that is exactly what he did next—he parted her

legs and tasted her, stroked her, delved into her like he was devouring the tastiest of ice cream on a hot summer day... and she melted, lick by lick, into him.

She moaned, grasping his hair to hold him in place, demanding more, demanding satisfaction, demanding... And then she caught the wave, held on, rode it, clasping him as her only line of safety, until she shuddered to shore on the powerful crest that he created just for her.

But he wasn't nearly done. He said he'd salvage the night, and he was doing it. She wasn't just weak-kneed—she was languid with desire, feeling so feminine to his masculine that when he lifted her up, stripped the robe from her, and positioned her so her head was near the cedar headboard with the row of vertical copper bars, she simply sighed in pleasure.

"Ivy," he said in a voice gone rough from reined-in emotion. "I can't wait. I'm trying, but—"

"Please."

She didn't need to say more, because he opened his nightstand, pulled out a condom, and slipped it on.

"I know what this looks like, but it's not." He sat down on the bed.

"What does it look like?"

"That you aren't the first here." He grasped her ankles and gently spread her legs apart. "I swear I bought enough for both houses the day after I met you."

"You were that sure of yourself?"

"Nope...on a wing and a prayer."

"How do you feel now?"

"Like I just won that last bull ride." And he knelt between her knees.

"Speaking of ride…" She gave him a coy smile to beckon him closer.

"Grasp the bars above your head. I don't intend to be easy—can't even if I had the desire. I don't want to hit your head on the headboard or shove you off the bed."

"Thanks…so considerate." She couldn't keep from smiling as she curled her fingers around the bars, because it sounded like he was going to give her the ride of her life. And she was all in.

When he raised her legs and positioned them over his shoulders, she trembled with suppressed emotion. He grasped her butt with both hands, squeezed, and she shuddered with eager anticipation. When he leaned forward and gave her a hot, wet kiss, she turned into a pool of molten lava.

He nudged inside her slowly, carefully, cautiously, because he was so big and she was so small. She moaned, clutching the bars harder as she felt him fill her, stretch her—little by little—going so agonizingly slowly that she felt chills race up and down her spine. With one final push, he was buried deep inside her.

He started to move, slowly at first, then gathering steam as he pounded harder and deeper and stronger. She clung to the bars, feeling him wind her up tighter and tighter as his thrusts grew ever more intense, pushing them both toward the same goal of shared euphoria.

What was it about this man? She'd never felt like this before, not in her entire life. What was it that he did to her? She glowed. She gasped. She moaned. What was it that he meant to her? She dropped the bars and grasped his shoulders, desperately needing to hold him.

He paused—sweat beading his forehead, breath coming fast—and leaned down to gently kiss her swollen lips. "I love you."

That's when she knew he was right. It'd been love all along.

And he thrust hard, sending them right over the edge into a kaleidoscope world that belonged only to them.

Chapter 20

As light filtered in through the east window early the next morning, Slade lay with one arm crossed behind his head and the other snuggled around Ivy's shoulders, while she nestled against his side, breathing softly in her sleep. He felt satisfied, content, relaxed in a way he hadn't since his last rodeo win. He realized now that he'd been living in houses, helping family and friends, doing jobs, coming up with more jobs—anything to fill the empty place in his heart. But that was over now.

Ivy filled his heart. She completed him. She was home. He'd never let her go. And he'd make sure she never wanted to go.

As if she could feel him thinking about her, she mumbled and moved her hand across his chest, resting it over his heart. He smiled as he covered her small hand with his much larger one. She had such soft, smooth skin that he couldn't get enough of touching her, stroking her...wanting to be buried deep inside her.

If not for Oscar's parting words, he'd already have been up, gone, and making sure all the animals were fed before starting his long workday. The old coot had understood only too well why Slade had brought Ivy to his home. He'd find some way later to repay Oscar for the gift of a few hours of leisure. For now, he had no intention of squandering that extra time.

"I'd like to cook you a big breakfast," he said softly as he stroked long hair away from her face. He found it interesting that he'd chosen the exact right colors for his bedroom to complement her hair. Maybe some part of him had known she was coming and had been preparing for her. But that didn't really matter. All that mattered was that she was here now.

"Pancakes or waffles?" He continued to play with her hair. "Butter. Maple syrup. Strawberries. Whipped cream."

"Yum," she mumbled against his chest.

"You might want something more stick-to-your-ribs. Bacon or ham or steak? Eggs—over easy or scrambled? Biscuits? Redeye gravy? Blackberry jam?"

She groaned and opened her eyes. "If you're trying to wake me through my stomach, you're doing a good job of it. Still, I'm not moving an inch." She kissed his chest, then grew quiet again.

"If none of that suits you, we could skip it and go straight to pie. Pecan? Lemon? Boysenberry? Your choice. Ice cream topping?"

"I believe your larder is empty, so this is all truly pie in the sky."

"Or...I could give you a little sugar this morning."

"Sugar?" She traced circles around his nipples with one fingertip, turning them hard as rocks. "Now that sounds like something I wouldn't mind waking up to. And I suspect *your* sugar could build up a mighty fine appetite for *your* cooking."

He chuckled deep in his throat, feeling his entire body harden under her teasing touch and taunting words. "Why don't we find out?"

She rose up on one elbow and smiled contentedly at him, much like the cat that ate the cream, before she planted a quick kiss on his lips. "Now, where's my sugar?"

He quickly tipped her back and leaned over her, feeling such tenderness well up in his chest that for a moment he couldn't catch his breath. And then he gave her sugar, kissing her with slow intent as he traced her lips with his tongue, nibbling and stroking, until he delved deep into her mouth. He kissed her with such depth of feeling that he lost himself in her, feeling her kiss him back with the same wild abandon, knowing they bridged the gap from two separate lives to one pulsating life together.

He'd waited a long time for her. He hoped she'd been waiting for him, but she just hadn't realized it. Didn't matter—they were together now. He'd come on strong to get them this far, and he realized it. That fact could weigh on a woman like Ivy, who was used to being in charge of her own life. He could give her exactly what she expected of him right this minute, and it'd make them both happy, but he wanted to give her something she didn't expect— something she needed but might not know she needed yet. He could give her more control and power in their relationship...and he was happy to do it.

"Ivy," he said, lying down on his back, "when I took that bad tumble off the bull, I broke my pelvis in two places."

She sat up and looked down at him in horror. "That's terrible. It must have hurt... I can't even imagine how it hurt."

"I got through it."

"Of course you did, but—"

"I healed okay, but you know how old injuries can come back to haunt you?"

"Yes. I sprained my right ankle really bad, and it's always been weak since that time."

"Regret to hear it."

"I got through it." She gave him a tender smile. "Like you."

"Fact is…we gave me a workout last night." He threw back the covers to reveal his readiness. "Straddle me?"

"Can I?" She gave him a big grin, green eyes alight with mischief as she ran her hand down his torso to grasp the hot, hard, erect length of him. "Or will I?"

"If you don't, I'm going to be in real pain." He grinned back at her, enjoying the banter that prolonged their pleasure. "You wouldn't torment me, would you?"

"Could I or would I?"

"Show me."

She just gave him a lazy smile as she threw a long leg over him and knelt to straddle him. "I do believe I could… and I would."

He lost all reason when she came down on him so hard and fast, so hot and wet that he slid easily into her, filling her completely. She clenched around him, tightening so much that he almost came off the bed. He had to restrain himself if he was going to let her do this her way, but he could see she wasn't going to make it easy on him. She was going to tease him until he was out of his mind. He quickly raised his arms and grasped the bars of the bed to force himself to stay put and not grab her, throw her over, and pound into her.

She moved slowly, easily, up and down, smiling lazily at him as she leaned forward and let the hard tips of her breasts graze his chest.

He broke out in sweat all over. He was fast losing it. He

clenched the bars harder, hoping he didn't wrench them out of place. Why had he ever thought letting Ivy take control was a good idea? And yet, he didn't know when he'd ever seen a more erotic sight. She tossed back her head as if glorying in the feel of being impaled on him, hair hanging around her face like a curtain, full breasts bouncing as she picked up the pace.

He felt the bars move in his hands. He was going to do it. He was going to break his bed over her. And he didn't care. All he cared about was watching her, feeling her, knowing her...and joining with her.

"Oh," she moaned on a sigh, moving harder and faster, up and down, driving them both toward completion.

He groaned in response and felt one of the bars snap free. He grabbed another, determined to hold his position, no matter the cost to him. She was looking more delectable every moment, because she was flushed rosy all over, she panted in small gasps, and she licked her lips with her pink tongue.

He snapped another bar...and gave up. He grasped her hips with both hands and pounded into her. She bucked against him and fell forward, planting both hands on his chest as he brought them both to the edge...and then they toppled over together in a frenzy of passion.

She didn't move for a long moment as they both gasped for breath, waiting for their heart rates to slow, waiting to return to normal.

He didn't think there would ever be normal again. There was before Ivy and after Ivy. He only ever wanted to live in the land of after Ivy.

A little later, she eased off him, cuddled against his side, and kissed his cheek. "That was the best breakfast ever."

"Yeah."

"But don't you ever think about taking it to market."

He chuckled, twining their fingers together. "You think it might sell?"

"Better than chocolate."

He laughed harder. "I suppose you're going to keep me on a leash."

"Absolutely."

"I'll buy you the leash."

She chuckled this time. "You're on."

"Oh, Ivy," he said, squeezing her hand. "What am I going to do with you?"

"Feed me?"

"I did promise to cook you breakfast, didn't I?"

"I can make do with coffee and sugar cookies." She sat up and looked down at him regretfully. "Work calls, doesn't it?"

"Always." He sat up, too. "I need to bake pies today."

"For the café?"

"No." He ran a hand over his stubble, feeling frustrated about his business. "I'm trying to get my pie company off the ground, but it's just not getting there."

"I thought you only baked pies for the Chuckwagon."

"Foodies and other folks like small-batch items that can be shipped anywhere. It's a growing market, but I can't seem to tap into it the way I need to, even with glowing reviews and winning awards."

"What's your hook?"

He glanced at her, wondering if she was really interested in hearing about his business. "I don't want to bore you."

"You could never bore me. Besides, it's kind of my thing."

"What?"

"Websites. I like to help folks grow their online businesses."

"Like custom, homemade pies?"

"Sure. It's tricky but doable." She smiled at him, squeezing his hand. "Want me to take a look at your website?"

"It should be okay. I hired a local professional to do it."

"There's okay...and then there's great."

"Yeah. I can see that. But still—"

"I've got a lot to do, but I'll take a look later. I want to see what narrative you're presenting, as well as how easy the site is to use to understand the product as well as order it."

"I'd appreciate you taking a look, but I don't want to put you out."

"I'm happy to do it. You've already helped me so much I want to return the favor."

"You don't owe me anything."

She pressed a quick kiss to his lips. "But maybe I'd like you to owe me."

He grinned, feeling glad they could share something else. "I'll make payment anytime you want...right here in this bed."

"Don't tempt me or we may never get out of here today."

"Just say the word." He could live on cookies, coffee, and wine for a day. Everything else could go hang.

"You know we can't get away with disappearing for an entire day. Who knows how many folks would come looking for us?"

"True." He sighed, running a hand through his hair. "I guess we'd better get up, get a shower, and get dressed."

"I don't know what I'm going to wear, but since you're taking me straight back to the cabin, I guess it doesn't much matter."

"Did you forget about..." he started to say, but he was interrupted by his cell with a familiar ringtone. "Uh-oh."

"What is it?"

"Granny."

"Oh."

"Got to take it." He pulled his phone out of his nightstand and punched it live with speakerphone.

"Slade," a strong, sweet voice said. "Time's a wasting. Bring your new girlfriend. Be here in five." And the voice was gone.

He clicked off, gave Ivy a regretful look, and stood up.

"Do we really have to go to the Chuckwagon?"

"No. But I'd like you to meet my family on good terms, not after they're irritated that I've kept you secret and away from them."

"You're close to them?"

"Yeah."

"I guess I'd feel that way about Fern, except she's always on the move and friends are transitory with her."

"Will you do this for me? I want them to love and accept you."

"And this is the best way?"

"After last night, it definitely is."

"You're presenting me as your girlfriend?"

He smiled, feeling warm all over at her words. "Yes. And that makes me your boyfriend."

"I guess that's where we are, isn't it?"

"It is, if that's what you want, too. I'm not pushing you." He was, of course, but he wasn't about to say it.

She sighed, looking thoughtful. "It's just so sudden and not what I was expecting when I got here."

"I know, but—"

"I'm not about to share you, so you're definitely my boyfriend."

"Good." He grinned, finally hearing the words he wanted from her.

She found the robe and pulled it around her shoulders. "But what am I going to wear?"

"We'll think of something."

"I need to go back to the cabin."

"No time."

He walked over, pulled a crimson jacket out of a dresser drawer, and tossed it to her. "That'll cover up your ripped jeans."

"It's huge. And if I wear those jeans, I'll smell like burnt cookies."

"We can douse you with some of Morning Glory's smelly stuff."

"That'll be just great. I'll be a walking, talking odor machine."

"What do you want me to do?" He threw up his hands, feeling helpless to please everybody.

"First impressions are lasting impressions."

"I know."

"Do you have a washer and dryer here?"

"No."

"Needle and thread?"

"What?" He knew he looked as confused as he felt, but even if he had sewing stuff, he wouldn't know how to use it.

"Never mind. I'm going to get a shower, then figure out something."

"I'll join you."

She gave him a hard stare.

He took her meaning. "If there is time—"

"There's not." She cocked her head to one side. "Oh, come on. How bad can meeting your granny and family be?"

He didn't answer that, because...well, it was just better not to go there. And yet, it had to be better than a tumble off a bad bull.

Chapter 21

IVY SAT STIFFLY IN THE PASSENGER SEAT OF SLADE'S pickup. He was quiet. She was quiet. It felt as if they were going to their doom. And that was ridiculous. His family had to be equally as friendly and generous as all the other people she'd met in Wildcat Bluff. Of course, she hadn't been a girlfriend at the time, but that fact ought to make everything better. It was the unknown that worried her, like it had since she'd set foot in the country.

She just wished she looked better. Fern could walk out of a shower, throw on cutoffs and T-shirt, and look like she was ready for the red carpet. Maybe it was her attitude that always carried her across the finish line first. Whatever it was, Ivy had missed that critical gene in the family pool.

She glanced down. At least she mostly wore her own clothes. Dirty, ripped jeans. Long sleeve, sage green tee. But that was the end of *her* before *he* began. Slade had loaned her a big, red satin jacket with promo logos from some rodeo he'd entered back in the day. She liked the fact that it hung down almost to her knees, so it covered up the rip in the seat of her pants, but it also covered up her hands, so she had to keep pushing the sleeves up. Nothing could fault her moccasins except they were stay-at-home wear, not gadding-about-town wear. She could live with all that, but he'd insisted on something else that she still couldn't wrap her head around.

"I don't see why I have to wear your old scratched, beat-up buckle and this belt of yours that you cut down to fit me."

He glanced over at her, smiling. "I told you. It's a gift— from me to you."

"You're wearing a nice, new, shiny one. I'd prefer that buckle, if I have to wear one of these giant things that is cutting me in half."

"I told you. You're wearing the last buckle I won. It's the one I've worn all these years because it's the most important one."

She pointed at the multicolored stones and raised lettering on a gold-and-crimson background of the rodeo buckle he wore. "But that one is prettier."

"It's the next-to-last one I won."

"I'll happily take it."

"Won't do."

"And just why not?"

"My best buckle shows my commitment to you."

"What if you gave me your second best?"

"Then you'd be second best. I'd never do it."

"Will people, like your family, know what it means?"

"Yes."

"That I'm your girlfriend?"

"Well…it means a bit more than girlfriend."

She turned to look at him, but he kept his eyes steady on the road. "What's after that? Going steady? If it gets any more archaic here, I really will have to go home just to get a reality check."

"You are home. And it's sort of like…well, on our way to engagement."

"Engagement?" She felt shocked to the bone. "What next? I guess we could just skip all the in-between, catch a flight to Vegas, and find Elvis to marry us."

"I'm ready when you are."

"That is not funny."

"Are you getting cold feet?"

"More like the flu."

He chuckled as he reached over and squeezed her hand. "I didn't know you were going to be so grumpy in the mornings."

"And this belt!"

"You know I didn't have anything smaller, so I had to cut down one of mine."

"You used a knife. It looks strange."

"At least I had a hole punch."

"But it's for horse and cow stuff, not people stuff!"

"Best I could do."

She glanced down at the too-large holes and wondered how long before the whole contraption fell off her—naturally, if it happened, it'd be right in front of the entire Steele clan.

"You could dress in a feed sack and you'd still look beautiful."

"Thanks. If that's the comparison, I feel so much better." She knew she was being ungrateful and griping about little things, but she was feeling more out of control by the moment. She wanted to rewind the clock or opt out of the entire situation. Pouting, she looked over at Slade, but the sight of him made all her doubts fly out the window. It was just...what if his family that was so important to him didn't like her?

"I wish one of my hats fit you, but any one of them would be down on your ears."

"It's okay. I washed my hair."

"Your hair always looks beautiful. I just meant you'd look good in a cowgirl hat."

"Thanks. Maybe I'll get one." She felt a little better at his words. She just needed to hold her head high and carry on. That's what Fern would do, but she'd make a joke out of it and everyone would laugh with her, not at her. Maybe she could be Fern for a day and all would be well.

"Trust me, it'll be okay."

"I'll give you back your buckle when it's all over."

"Why would you do that?"

"It's your best buckle."

"I gave it to you. I want you to have it. For keeps."

"Thank you. I do appreciate the sentiment, but—"

"No buts. We're in this together." He glanced over at her again, blue eyes warm, then nodded ahead of them. "We're almost to Old Town."

"And the Chuckwagon Café." She adjusted the big, heavy buckle, hoping once more that it wouldn't fall off and take her jeans down with it. Still, she felt warm and tender at the thought of him giving her something so important to him, something that he wanted her to keep forever.

"I'll get you a new belt and a hat at Gene's Boot Hospital after breakfast." He glanced down at her feet. "Maybe a pair of boots, too."

"Jeans are first on my list."

"Oh yeah." He tossed a grin her way. "You can have new jeans with my blessing, but I get the old ones."

"Whatever for?"

"I've got real fond memories of those particular jeans."

When what he meant filtered through her worries, she chuckled at the memory of his hand on her bare butt. They'd come a long way since that moment. Suddenly everything seemed okay, or at least good enough. Slade was with her. She wore his prize belt buckle. With that thought, she really felt better, but anything to do with Slade always made her feel better.

"Have you been in Old Town before now?"

"No. I've pretty much stayed at the Park. This is lovely," she said, glancing at the street coming into view.

"I'll slow down so you can take a closer look. We're proud of all we've done to maintain the original structures."

She lowered her window so she could get a better look at Main Street's row of one- and two-story buildings built of stone and brick and nestled behind a white portico that covered a long boardwalk. Sunlight glinted off store windows. She felt as if she'd stepped back in time—just like at Wildcat Hall—into an Old West town like the ones she'd seen in tintype photographs. Yet everything appeared as fresh as if it'd been constructed yesterday.

The Wildcat Bluff Hotel anchored one end of the street. It was an impressive, two-story structure of red brick with a grand entrance of cream keystones and brass planters with Christmas-tree-shaped rosemary bushes. Fresh fir wreaths with huge, red bows decorated each window of a second-floor balcony enclosed with a stone balustrade supported by five columns.

On the other end of Main Street, the Chuckwagon Café held the place of honor, with Morning's Glory, Adelia's Delights, Gene's Boot Hospital, Thingamajigs, and other popular shops in between. Pickups were nosed in all along the front of the café.

Slade found an empty place, pulled in, parked between two other trucks, and turned off the engine.

In front of her, Ivy saw strings of blinking Christmas lights and star-shaped ornaments on a row of plate-glass windows with the words "Lone Star Saloon" painted in gold in old-fashioned curlicue script. A painted-wood cigar store Indian that stood sentinel on one side of the batwing-style doors had been irreverently adorned with a bright-red Santa hat.

"Looks like Christmas has already come to Old Town," she said. "I hope the Hall gets festive pretty soon."

"It will."

"Is that really an original saloon?"

"Like Wildcat Hall, Old Town hasn't changed much since the 1880s. This honky-tonk still serves the same function—food, drinks, dance hall, live country bands on weekends."

"Is it competition for the Hall?"

"Somewhat. The Lone Star gets more tourist trade, but there's enough business for both locations."

"Good."

"We get a lot of tourists looking for a taste of the Old West like they do in Tombstone, Arizona."

"I've been to Tombstone. It's fascinating."

"We'll have lots of folks in town during Wild West Days. They like to experience our reenactment of the shoot-out between the Hellions and the Ruffians for control of the town."

"Sounds like the shoot-out at the O.K. Corral."

"Right. Back then, outlaws fought the law, but they also fought each other for turf."

"Where does the shoot-out take place?" She was stalling

and knew it, but she still wanted to learn more about the town that was fast finding a place in her heart.

"Right here in front of the Lone Star." He pointed at the batwing doors. "When Wild West Days rolls around, you could play a part in the reenactment. Dance hall darlings in their white pinafores turned the tide."

"It does sound like fun."

He glanced over at her, smiling. "You'd look really good dressed up like that."

"Thanks." She smiled back at him, catching a hint of the heat that always smoldered between them. "With all the clothes women wore back then, it might take a while to remove them."

He grinned, blue eyes lighting up. "You'll need help. I'll be happy to get you in and out of a corset...stockings...and everything else."

She chuckled, shaking her head at him. "I sincerely suspect you don't care if I'm in the reenactment at all. You just want me dressed up for fun."

"Not true...well, somewhat true. I'd like you on my arm so we can promenade on the boardwalk while the other guys eat their hearts out since you belong to me."

"Oh Slade, sometimes I'm not sure what century you belong in. Let's just make sure there's no shoot-out involved with our promenade."

"You never know. I'll do my best to control my itchy trigger finger, but if some guy comes on to you, all bets are off."

She laughed, once more enjoying the banter that kept drawing them closer and closer.

"Fern is supposed to perform with Craig here in the saloon, but I guess we can't count on her making it."

"I'm sure she'd love to, but she hasn't mentioned it. Hopefully, she'll be back soon."

"Hope so."

"Me too."

"Come on." He opened his door. "They'll be waiting for us."

She took a deep breath, repositioning the belt buckle as if girding up for an upcoming battle. When he opened her door and held out his hand, she gave him a big smile as she let him help her down. She stepped up on the boardwalk with him at her side, almost as if they were beginning an old-fashioned promenade.

And then she remembered Peter and the fact that he was looking for a buyer for the Park. She felt sick to her stomach, as if she'd betrayed not only Slade but herself as well. She needed to call her friend and cancel the contract, although since she hadn't heard anything, maybe it was all just fine. She took a deep breath, forcing those thoughts away. She had plenty on her plate at the moment. She didn't need to borrow trouble. Right now she was going to enjoy being with Slade and starting off a brand-new day.

She glanced at Adelia's Delights, and saw a life-size Santa Claus dressed in bright-red velvet with a wide black belt and matching black cowboy hat waving back and forth in the display window. A pretty tortoiseshell cat snuggled up to Santa's cowboy boot. The kitty looked so perfect she might have been a stuffed animal until she turned her head to look in their direction.

"What a pretty cat," she said.

"You met Hedy, didn't you? That's her store and that's Rosie, Queen of Adelia's. She's one of the best Hemingway mousers in town."

"Do you mean she's a polydactyl?"

"Right. Extra dewclaws like the descendants of Hemingway's cats at his former home in Key West."

"Somebody must have brought cats out west over a hundred years ago," she said thoughtfully.

"They were worth their weight in gold in lots of places. They kept out vermin." He chuckled. "Plenty of fights over cat stealing."

"Hard to imagine now."

"Not so hard around here. Folks still prize their cats."

As they continued onward, she caught the scent of lavender, rose, and frankincense, so she stopped in front of a store with "Morning's Glory" painted in purples and greens on a front display window. Red and green Christmas lights twinkled around the front window. Inside, she saw bath products, framed paintings, and other items produced by local artisans.

"Morning Glory really supports the community with her store," he said, looking in the window.

"I can't wait to shop here."

"Everyone works hard to provide the best merchandise possible."

"Like your pies?"

"Yeah. That's what we do." He tucked her hand into the crook of his arm.

She walked slower, but there was nothing now between her and fate—also known as the Chuckwagon Café. She glanced up at the carved wooden café sign painted in red and white that hung from hooks above the boardwalk. Red-and-white-checked curtains filled the lower half of the windows. Someone had hand-painted colorful Christmas scenes on the upper half of the windows. Santa Claus and his gift-laden sleigh were pulled by brown-and-white paint ponies. Boisterous children wearing earmuffs and mittens tugged a green Christmas tree home from the forest.

"I wonder who painted these windows." She pointed at the artwork. "It's wonderful."

"Morning Glory would be my guess. She's talented enough to do about anything creative."

"There's lots of talent here, isn't there?"

"You bet. You fit right in." He opened the door to the café, setting off sleigh bells that jingled against the front door's glass window. "Ready or not, here we go."

She decided it was time to pull a Fern move to set the scene in her favor. She turned back, put a hand on Slade's chest, raised up on tiptoes, and gave him a quick kiss for all the world—but particularly the patrons of the Chuckwagon Café—to see.

"Hold that thought till after breakfast." He smiled as he held out his hand toward the interior.

She nodded in total agreement, then turned and stepped into the café.

Chapter 22

Ivy stepped inside the café to the sound of applause. She took a deep breath, feeling her heart thud hard in her chest. She wanted to back out, but Slade was right behind her and she couldn't let him—or herself—down. What would Fern do? No doubt about it—she'd *own* this room. Ivy could do no less. She pressed the fingertips of both hands to her lips, hesitated as she looked around and made sure everyone had stopped eating and was watching her, then flung wide both arms as if showering everyone in the room with kisses.

As if that wasn't enough of a reveal, she dramatically pulled open the jacket of Slade's that she wore to show his belt buckle around her waist.

He chuckled as he snagged her close with a strong arm, and all the while the clapping grew louder, boots stomped the floor, and whistles filled the air.

Oscar got up from a table and sauntered up to them. He made a slight bow, then turned to the crowd. "Looks like our pie-baking bull rider finally done gone and got himself roped, tied, and tagged by the latest lovely lady in Wildcat Bluff County."

Catcalls filled the air.

"Let me present Ivy Bryant of Wildcat Hall Park fame."

Ivy gave a slight curtsy, felt the buckle head south, and quickly grabbed and held it in place.

While she waited for what came next, she took a moment to look at the long room with its smooth oak floors and high ceilings covered in pressed tin squares. Wagon-wheel chandeliers—old lantern-type globes attached to the outer spokes of horizontally hanging wooden wheels—cast soft light over round tables covered in red-and-white-checked tablecloths. The spindle, barrel-back captain's chairs pulled up to the tables were full of folks. A tiger oak bar with enough dings and scratches to look original stretched across the back of the room with battered oak barstools in front and a cash register on one end. A window behind the bar revealed a kitchen updated with stainless steel appliances.

In one corner, a large cedar Christmas tree reached almost to the ceiling. Red-and-white candy canes, red-and-white-plaid bows, and twinkling red and white lights decorated the deep-green boughs. The scent of cedar battled with the tantalizing aroma of food for dominance.

"What are all these shenanigans about in my café?" A sweet, musical voice laced with steel cut through the raucous noise.

Silence quickly descended as everyone turned to look in the direction of the kitchen.

A small, silver-haired woman wearing a frilly, pink apron stood in the open doorway with her hands on her hips. She wore a red-and-white-striped, pearl-snap shirt with jeans and red boots. Two tall, strawberry-blond cowgirls dressed in similar attire stood beside her. A slim little girl about eight years of age with wild, ginger hair and big hazel eyes stepped in front of them. She wore a rhinestone-studded, long-sleeve T-shirt in bright green, jeans, and turquoise boots.

Slade cleared his throat, giving Ivy's waist a squeeze.

"Granny, you invited us to breakfast, so here we are. Ivy, I'd like you to meet my grandmother, mother, sister, and niece. Lula Mae. Maybelline. Sydney, and her daughter, Storm."

"Good to meet you," Ivy said.

"Not their fault we made a big to-do out of breakfast," Oscar said. "It's sort of a…well, heck, an unofficial Old Town get-to-know party for Ivy."

When nobody else said anything, Ivy could feel her nerve start to break. How long could she maintain Fern's stance in the face of what was not a warm welcome from Slade's family? Maybe they were in shock or simply too busy to take time with introductions. Anyhow, she wanted to slink out the door, but she was made of sterner stuff. At the very least, she wanted food before she left, because by now she was starving.

"Are you the one who made Uncle Slade burn the cookies?" Storm asked as she moved forward with a defiant step. "He's never done something dumb like that before—at least, nothing *that* dumb."

"Storm, be polite. You know better." Sydney reached out to snag her daughter, but she was too late. "Anybody can burn anything at any time. It happens."

Slade groaned, glancing around at the diners as they joined together in laughter. "Guess that cat's out of the bag."

Oscar shrugged, holding out his hands to each side. "It might've slipped out when I wasn't watching my tongue."

"I want a closer look at her." Storm stomped over and stopped in front of Ivy, looking her up and down with a calculating eye. "Guess that's a fashion statement, seeing as how you're a rock star. They say that's how you landed him, being fancy and all."

"Not polite," Slade said, echoing his sister. "If you can't say something nice, don't say anything at all."

Storm ignored him. "You better be good to him. He's my *favorite* uncle."

"I'm your *only* uncle," Slade said with a touch of humor, obviously replaying an old joke.

Storm pointed at Ivy's belt buckle. "Can't think why he'd give you that, but you better not lose it."

Ivy was getting her back up until she realized Storm, as well as her family—and maybe most of the county—was afraid of Slade getting hurt by the newcomer who hadn't been in town long enough for them to get to know her. They needed to be reassured, but she wasn't sure how to do it.

"All the fuss going on, you'd think a guy never got a gal before." Oscar gave Storm a sympathetic look.

"But Uncle Slade's never—"

"It was before your time." Slade pulled Ivy a little closer. "If you can't be nice…if none of my family can be nice, then we're going someplace else for breakfast."

"That'd be dumb," Storm said. "We got it all fixed for y'all in the party room."

"Ivy, I'm sorry. We don't have to stay." Slade stepped back, tugging her with him.

She felt bad for all of them. She guessed they didn't know what to do or how to react, since they'd been caught by surprise. Well, they weren't the only ones. Slade had come on so strong she was still reeling from that and how she'd reacted so quickly to him.

"Don't go." Storm held up a small hand, then dropped it to her side. "Don't be mad at me. It's just…he's my *favorite* uncle."

Ivy couldn't stand to see a little girl in pain, afraid she was losing the man who'd always been a father figure to her. "Isn't he your *only* uncle?"

Storm cocked her head to one side, not sure if Ivy was joking or not, but still looking a bit hopeful.

Ivy knelt down so they were eye to eye. "I suppose you know your uncle is a very strong, determined man."

Storm nodded in agreement.

"Trust me. What I'm wearing is *not* a fashion statement. It's an Uncle Slade statement. He actually *likes* this jacket and belt buckle. Can you imagine?" She rolled her eyes to show her disdain for Slade's bad taste in clothes.

Storm glanced up at Slade, checking to see how he was reacting to Ivy's words.

He grinned, rubbing a hand up and down Ivy's shoulder with the too-big sleeve hanging below her fingertips.

Storm giggled at the sight. "Don't rock stars wear anything they want? I can't, but I'm a kid."

"My sister's the star—and yes, she wears whatever she wants. But I'm not on that level."

Storm bunched up her eyebrows, looking up at Slade, then back at Ivy. "You're *not* a rock star?"

"I hate to disappoint you, but I just design websites."

"Uncle Slade, do you *like* websites?"

He laughed, ruffling Storm's hair. "I like anything about Ivy, so she can do whatever she wants and it'll make me happy."

Storm nodded sagely, as if he'd just proven a point she'd been hearing from the adults around her. "So she's got you on a leash, huh?"

"Yeah," he said, grinning. "After breakfast, we're going to Gene's to buy one."

"Forget the leash. He's just funning you," Ivy said. "We're going to get me new clothes. Do you want to shop with us?"

"Really? May I?" Storm looked excited as she glanced up at Slade.

"Sure."

"Can we dress him, too?" Storm turned to Ivy.

"Guess so. Barbie's got her Ken."

"Not so fast," Slade said. "I'm fine. This is all about Ivy."

"And Storm," Ivy said. "I bet she could use something new to wear, too."

"Yay!" Storm clapped her hands together.

Slade groaned even as he smiled at them. "I can see it's going to be a long morning."

"Best get some food under your belt." Storm grabbed Slade's hand, then shyly held out her other hand to Ivy.

Ivy felt warmth spread outward from her heart as small fingers slipped into her hand and squeezed her. This must be how Slade had felt when he won a belt buckle.

Storm tugged on their hands, urging them forward toward the rest of the family.

Still, Ivy had another hurdle before that one. She glanced around the room at the folks still watching with avid interest. She nodded at Oscar, then gave a thumbs-up...and received the same gesture in reply.

"Okay, folks," Oscar called out as he headed back to his seat. "Show's over. Let's chow down."

Ivy squared her shoulders and stepped toward the back of the café, where Slade's family had disappeared through an open doorway.

Storm tugged her inside a room decorated much as the main café. A long table was covered in a red-and-white-checked tablecloth set with white stoneware, silverware, and cloth napkins. A red-white-and-green holiday floral arrangement added a festive touch to the center of the table. Spindle, barrel-back captain's chairs were ready for use. An antique oak sideboard groaned under the weight of a variety of dishes covered to keep them warm.

As Slade shut the door behind them, Sydney hurried forward and enveloped Ivy in a big hug, which was followed by hugs from Lula Mae and Maybelline.

"Sorry we weren't more welcoming," Sydney said. "But we've been shocked to the core."

"And worried about Slade," Maybelline said. "This isn't like him…not like him at all."

"It's not like me either." Ivy glanced around the group. "I'm a cautious person, not like my sister, Fern."

"Everybody adores her," Lula Mae said.

"That's true," Ivy replied.

"We're glad you're here to take her place," Sydney said. "Wildcat Hall needs a steady hand."

Ivy chuckled at that idea. "Fern is a rolling stone, not a steady hand."

"Exactly," Lula Mae said, smiling. "Just what our boy needs."

"I'm not a boy," Slade grumbled. "Haven't y'all done enough to undermine me since we got here? Now I'm just a *boy*."

Storm giggled, squeezing Ivy's hand. "He's grumpy. Better feed him."

"Food is always this family's answer to everything." Slade looked eagerly toward the sideboard. "But we're hungry, so I won't complain."

"You've never complained about food a day in your life," Lula Mae said with a smile.

"What makes you so hungry?" Sydney asked with a twinkle in her eyes.

"If I mention Dune Barrett, that hot fiancé of yours, would you know what I mean?" He grinned, giving back as good as he got.

"No idea," she said innocently, but grinning big as can be.

"Welcome to the family." Lula Mae grasped both Ivy's hands and gave a good squeeze. "But you really don't want to let him dress you anymore."

Ivy joined the women in laughing, nodding as she pushed up the long sleeves again. "It's just that—"

"Let me take that huge jacket." Sydney started to slide it down Ivy's shoulders.

"Wait!" Ivy clutched it to her. "I've had a slight wardrobe malfunction, so the jacket is necessary to—"

"Might as well give it up." Slade sidled toward the sideboard. "Ivy's got a rip in the seat of her pants."

"Really?" Sydney laughed as she removed the jacket and draped it over the back of a chair. "One can only wonder how that happened."

"Don't wonder." Slade growled as he plucked up a cover and sniffed at the food underneath. "Steak. Great."

Ivy felt herself go pink at Sydney's obvious guess at what had happened to her jeans. She was beginning to see that Slade's family was just as straightforward and to the point as he was. The apple hadn't fallen far from the tree.

"You'd think they'd been raised in a barn," Maybelline said. "I swear they all have better manners than they've shown today."

"You raised us, so what does that say?" Sydney laughed as she started to uncover the food.

"Hey, you got a starving kid here." Storm sidled up to Slade.

He glanced down at her, chuckling. "Still too short to reach the food?"

"Still my favorite uncle?"

"Always." He kissed the top of her head, picked up a plate, and started to dish up goodies for her.

Ivy stood back, looking at the beautifully presented food that was much as Slade had described it in bed—waffles, eggs, steak, hash browns, biscuits, and all the trimmings. She felt a little intimidated not only by the food, but by the family, because they were obviously so close-knit, and she was the outsider.

Sydney moved up to her. "It's okay. Dune felt the same way at first. But we don't bite—at least not much. And we want Slade to be happy."

Ivy took a deep breath. She had to say this now and she had to say it fast, so she lowered her voice. "He's a great guy."

"But?"

"I just got here. I'm from Houston. And this is all so—"

"Overwhelming?"

"That, and—"

"Sudden?"

"Yes. I'm just not sure—"

"You're sure," Sydney said softly. "I can see it. Your mind just hasn't caught up to that fact yet. I should know. Dune had his work cut out for him, but now..."

"How did you know?" Ivy rubbed the belt buckle, feeling the scratches that had been put there by Slade over years of wear and tear.

"Like I said, you already know. Just give it a bit of time. Trust me, Slade's worth it."

"Thanks."

"If y'all are talking about me, you can just stop." Slade glanced over his shoulder. "Come and get it."

Sydney laughed, then gave Ivy a wink. "Why don't you chow down? We cook a mean breakfast. And everything looks doable on a full stomach."

Ivy couldn't argue the point. She was famished, so she quickly filled a plate and joined the others sitting around the table. She almost felt part of the Steele family—and even more surprising, she felt as if she wanted to be.

"Uncle Slade," Storm said, picking up her fork before setting it down again. "Do you think Fernando's hungry?"

Ivy watched everyone at the table freeze at those words. She hated to think what the little girl must be feeling about the lost bull.

Slade set down his glass of orange juice before he looked at his niece. "He's a valuable bull. They'll take good care of him."

"But they don't know his favorite food. And he can't tell them." Storm's high, sweet voice broke on those words.

Slade got up, walked over to his niece, knelt beside her, and put an arm around her small shoulders. "Fernando's a big, smart, tough bull. He'll make it. But he needs you to stay strong for him, so you should eat."

"I'm not hungry."

"When is a Steele not hungry?"

"I keep thinking about Fernando all alone and lost and hungry. It makes my tummy hurt."

Slade hugged her closer and kissed the top of her head. "Do you believe in Christmas miracles?"

"Yes...I guess."

"Remember what you told me?"

"Fernando will be home for Christmas." She picked up her fork. "He's never missed his special holiday feed."

"That's right."

"And he won't this time. He thinks I'm kinda scrawny. Maybe I better eat or he'll worry about me." She raised a forkful of scrambled eggs.

"That's our girl."

Storm glanced up at Slade, tears shimmering in her big eyes. "You'll see. Fernando's on his way. He'll be home for Christmas."

Chapter 23

A WEEK LATER, IVY STOOD BEHIND THE FRONT BAR OF Wildcat Hall, working with Alicia. She wore a teal-colored, pearl-snap shirt, Wranglers, a black leather belt with Slade's buckle, and black boots with teal stitching. She'd become accustomed to the new clothes she'd bought with Storm's approval. She'd even come to enjoy wearing them as she fit into the community. She'd also become more accustomed to living in the country and sharing meals with the Steele family, but most often she ate with Slade, because they really just wanted to be alone with each other whenever possible.

She'd never tell him, but she'd wondered if their sudden, inexplicable passion for each other might dissipate over time. It hadn't so far. If anything, it had grown stronger the more they were together. They usually didn't have much time for each other during their busy days until late at night, after she got off work. Fortunately, the burnt-cookie scent had dissipated or been eradicated by the determined efforts of the Settelmeyer family, so they could enjoy her place again. When the lights were out and the folks were gone, they'd walk hand-in-hand to her cabin, where they would share news of their busy days and their red-hot passion, and then cuddle in sleep.

Christmas had come to Wildcat Hall. The Settelmeyers had installed beautiful holiday decorations in the Hall, the beer garden, the cowboy cabins, and in the trees of the Park. They'd even put up a small evergreen tree with bright-gold bows and shiny silver balls in her new home. She hadn't added any packages under the tree yet, but she wanted to get something special for everyone in Slade's family, as well as the Settelmeyer family. She thought Morning's Glory and Adelia's Delights would be the perfect places to shop for everyone when she had time. As far as Slade went, he would be much harder to buy for, but she could probably find something great at Gene's Boot Hospital.

All in all, she was feeling better about her situation. Houston seemed almost like a distant dream, although she knew her old life still awaited her there. Fern kept in touch by text, and she seemed to be doing well, or at least pretended to be happy in her current situation. It was hard to tell what was real and what was not with her sister, but performing always suited her, so surely she was doing okay. Primarily, Slade filled her thoughts and dreams, as did Wildcat Hall and all she wanted to accomplish there.

With those thoughts, Peter Simpson came to mind. She hadn't heard from her friend and she was glad, but she wanted to get the situation settled while it was on her mind. She picked up her phone from behind the bar, nodded to Alicia, and stepped outside. She could hear the band playing, and it would drown out what she was about to say for anyone inside. She hit speed dial.

"Ivy, you still hanging out in the wilds of Texas?" Peter asked with a chuckle.

"Still here. And liking it better all the time."

"Knew it. Hunky cowboy firefighters, isn't it?"

"Maybe one in particular." She smiled at just the thought of Slade.

"Do tell."

"Not now. I'm working."

"Okay. But I'll hold you to it."

"Later, then. Right now, I'm calling to ask you to take Wildcat Hall Park off the market. I just can't see selling it."

"You are hooked, aren't you?"

"I'm getting there." She rubbed fingers across the scratched belt buckle that said it all.

"Look, don't worry about it. If you get an offer, you can decide how you and Fern want to handle it. Besides, you haven't been there long enough to know what you may want to do later."

"But, Peter—"

"Have I ever steered you wrong?"

"No."

"I won't pursue a sale hard. If a buyer turns up, let's leave that option open."

"I simply don't feel right about it anymore."

"I hear you. But your emotions may be talking instead of your head. Let's just let it be for now."

"Okay, I guess." She sighed, knowing he was being practical, but she wasn't feeling practical.

"Now go out there and enjoy your guy. Leave this to me." And he was gone.

She stood there a moment, feeling like she'd made a wrong decision, but Peter was always right, and he was practical, too. City had come crashing into country, and she'd been drawn back into her old city world after talking with him. Where did she really belong? Slade Steele. That's where she belonged…and she knew it. After Christmas, she'd be firm with Peter, take the Park off the market, and no one would be the wiser.

She glanced around, returning to the reality of her new life. It was a Friday night, so she could hear Craig and his country band playing in the dance hall. Folks were back there, listening, dancing, drinking, while more had spilled out into the beer garden with its twinkling blue lights in the trees. Tonight was a night for sweaters, needing little more to keep warm, particularly when folks heated up on the dance floor.

She walked back inside, still feeling uneasy. Things were winding down in the front bar with only a few customers still nursing beer, wine, or coffee and cookies. Fortunately, folks had taken a shine to the new addition to the menu, so she was encouraged to begin the other ideas she and Slade had discussed early on. Until now, they hadn't had the time to implement more, but she was anxious to get there.

She glanced over at Alicia, still looking fresh after a long day as she wiped down the bar and chatted with a customer sitting on a stool. She wore her family's traditional crimson, long-sleeve T-shirt with the Wildcat Hall logo emblazoned on the front, Wranglers, and black cowboy boots. She'd pulled her long, blond hair into a single plait down her back.

When she caught Alicia's eye, she beckoned her to come down to the end of the bar.

"What is it?" Alicia asked, joining her. "Are you tired? Do you want to knock off early?"

"It's not that. I wanted to ask you about coffee and cookie sales."

"They're good…maybe great even closer to Christmas, if Slade will cut the cookies into holiday shapes like trees, elves, reindeer, that type of thing, then sprinkle them with red or green tinted sugar. Customers want festive and happy and familiar. Do you know what I mean?"

"Yes indeed. Slade and I are already there. When do you think we should start?"

"Next week won't be too early." Alicia glanced down the bar to make certain she wasn't needed by a customer, then looked back at Ivy.

"Slade's so busy with the upcoming cattle drive, the café, and his pie business during the holidays that I'm reluctant to put any more on his plate. And yet, this is important, too."

Alicia nodded in understanding as she tapped a fingernail on the scarred wood of the bar top. "It's just sugar cookies, isn't it?"

"Yes. I'd like to sell cowboy cookies, too, but for now I'm focused on Texas tea cakes."

"And we're busy, too. This time of year and all," Alicia said. "But, like you say, it's important to offer new items, so we bring in more customers to grow the business."

"True. Maybe I need to bake—"

"Please, no. You really don't have the time. You're building out the website, and it's looking good with every improvement you make to it."

"Thanks. I wish I had more time."

"I hear you." Alicia took a deep breath as she squared her shoulders. "Here's what I suggest."

"What?"

"Mom is a good cook, even great by most standards. I'm not bad myself. We have a big country kitchen with a six-burner stove and two ovens at home. We're frequently asked to bake cakes and cookies for local fund-raisers. Folks will even pay extra if it's a Settelmeyer. We're not professional, mind you, like Slade and the Steele family. But I don't see why Mom and I couldn't make cookies in small batches for the Hall, if you like the idea."

"It'd be a real blessing." She gave Alicia a warm hug. "If you'll work out the cost, I'll be happy to pay extra."

"Thanks." Alicia grinned in approval. "There's this pair of red boots at Gene's that I've been drooling over."

Ivy chuckled, understanding perfectly. "Go get them, because you're on for cookies."

Alicia joined her laughter, looking pleased as punch. "I'll tell you something else. If Slade had time to bake pies for us, they wouldn't go amiss here. He's really got a fabulous rep as a pie baker."

"He already suggested it. Pie would be great with coffee. But we'd need to cut, plate, and serve, so I'm concerned that's too much extra work."

Alicia shook her head. "I don't think so. We cut the pies ahead of time, buy paper plates and plastic ware, then watch the customers chow down."

Ivy laughed at that positive image. "Okay. If you think it's possible, I'm not about to hang back. Let's see if we can clear an area to make space for it behind the bar."

"Let me talk with Mom and Dad. They're good at that type of thing. We might need to set up a separate table."

"Sounds great."

"Do you think Slade could have pies to us by next week?"

"I hope so. I'll ask him."

As if their discussion conjured him, the front door opened, revealing its beautiful Christmas wreath, and Slade stepped inside.

Ivy felt her heart speed up at the sight of him. He never failed to enliven her world simply with his presence, and that was before he spoke or touched or helped or gave her that special look that meant she was always foremost in his thoughts, just as he had become in her life.

"You're done early tonight," she said, smiling at him.

"I needed an Ivy fix." He smiled back, eyes lighting up.

"Not coffee or wine?" Alicia teased him with a big grin.

"Nope. I need Ivy—nothing else will do." He walked up to the bar, put both elbows on it, and leaned in for a kiss.

She quickly obliged, not minding one bit being a fix for Slade.

"I just finished up several orders. Sydney's going to mail them out for me in the morning."

"And you didn't bring us pie?" Alicia asked, shaking her head in disappointment. "We could sure use a slice right about now."

"I would've if I could've, but I barely got those orders done as it was. Nothing left over, not even a crumb."

"I hope you can make time for us," Ivy said. "Alicia says we can serve pie with little muss or fuss."

Slade groaned, running a hand through his hair in agitation. "It'd be great exposure for my pie business and to entice more customers into the Hall, but the orders are coming in steady now, particularly after Ivy upgraded my website." He stopped on that excuse. "I can't let y'all down, can I?"

"You can probably let me down," Alicia said, "but Ivy is another matter."

"I guess I better let you off the hook. After all, I did make your website irresistible." Ivy chuckled, reaching out and patting Slade's shoulder.

"It's made a big difference."

"I was just hoping—"

"You're right. I need to make time for local businesses. And especially you. Pecan pies sell best. Let me get hold of Gillette's. They run the best pecan farm in East Texas. I'm a rancher, but I appreciate farmers."

"We wouldn't have much to eat without them, would we?" Ivy said.

"Amen," Alicia said. "Anyway, ranchers are farmers, too, even if we do it on a small scale."

"True enough. We always have home gardens."

"Nothing is better than fresh veggies in the summertime and canned ones in the winter," Alicia said.

"I don't have that experience," Ivy said, "but I'm sure it's a good one."

"We'll get you hooked on country food in no time." Slade smiled as he leaned in closer, as if unable to resist her, like iron filings drawn to a magnet.

"I appreciate your help with the pies. It's great," Ivy said. "I hate to bring up something else since you're being so generous, but we discussed offering weekend specials, like beef stew or chili, in the winter."

Slade groaned, shaking his head as if it was all too much for him. "I remember. If we weren't in the middle of the new ranch and the upcoming cattle drive, I wouldn't hesitate to throw in on the project."

"It's okay," Ivy said. "I just needed to know if it was on or off the table."

"No, it's not okay." He straightened up. "Tell you what. Granny might be up for it. She'd view it as good promotion for the Chuckwagon with the tourists, as well as helping another local business. And you."

"I'm just making a lot of extra work for you and your family," Ivy said. "Y'all have already been so good to me that I hate to push for more."

"You've helped me, too, with the website."

"I can do more with it. And I will."

"Thanks. It's enough for now," he said. "Anyway, I already discussed adding to the menu with Fern, so you aren't the only one suggesting we expand our business. It's good...for the Chuckwagon and the Hall. It's just that—"

"Time." Alicia looked from one to the other. "And it's the holidays."

"Let me talk with Granny. If she can't take it on, I'll find another way. I've already thought it'd be good if we served old-fashioned corn fritters with the stew and chili."

"That'd be delicious," Ivy said.

"Yum." Alicia rubbed her stomach as she glanced down at the end of the bar to check on patrons.

"Let me see if I can get that show on the road in the next week," Slade said.

"Thanks." Ivy gave him a big smile. "But please don't push beyond what is reasonably doable."

"I won't." He glanced down the bar.

A customer looked their way with a nod, then got up, set down a tip, waved goodbye, and walked outside.

"Hope I'm not driving off business," Slade said.

"You're not." Alicia walked down, put the tip in the tip jar, and picked up the empty beer bottle. "He comes here every evening after work and now is about the time he usually leaves."

"That's a good customer," Slade said.

"The best," Alicia said, agreeing. "Can I get you anything now?"

"Not a thing." He looked at Ivy. "But Ivy can give me a dance."

"You want to dance?" she asked in surprise.

"I've been listening to Craig's band, and it's got me hankering to toss you around the dance floor."

Ivy laughed at the image. "You might get me out on the dance floor, but there'll be no tossing about. I'm only up to something slow and steady."

"Slow is exactly what I have in mind."

"I don't want to leave Alicia holding the bag here."

"Go on, you two. Enjoy yourselves." Alicia pointed toward the dance floor. "We're winding down, and I can handle it on my own."

Slade held out his hand to Ivy. "Join me?"

"Thanks, Alicia." She took off her apron, hung it on a hook, and walked around the bar. When she clasped Slade's hand, she felt the familiar zing of awareness arc between.

He leaned down close to whisper. "I couldn't get a country song out of my head all day."

"Really?"

"Yeah. I think you'll recognize the refrain." He grinned down at her. "You're always on my mind."

And she knew just what he meant.

Chapter 24

SLADE WALKED HAND IN HAND WITH IVY INTO THE DANCE hall, feeling like it was their first date. They'd gone from zero to one hundred in the first moment they'd met. Now they needed time to get to know each other better. With the intense schedules they both kept, it was almost impossible to take time out just for fun. And he'd meant it—she was always on his mind.

Christmas lights in blue and white had been strung in the rafters, echoing the blue lights in the beer garden. A few families sat at tables, enjoying the music and the dance, chatting together…grandparents and parents introducing their young ones to the community that'd been gathering there for generations and would, hopefully, continue for generations to come.

He wanted Ivy to experience the dance hall as a community center, not just a place that had been dumped on her, forcing her to work long hours every day till her sister returned to take over. He'd like her to appreciate Wildcat Bluff County in all its variety, so she'd come to love it like he did. Possible? The verdict was still out, but he lived in hope she'd come through just like she had on every other thing set before her since she'd arrived on his doorstep. But most of all, he just wanted her to love him. They could work out everything else.

For tonight, he simply planned to enjoy the evening.

He was tired, but in a good way. The work she'd done on his website still amazed him because it was really generating more social media interest and bringing in more sales for the holidays. If he got his pie-baking business off the ground, then he could branch out into other small-batch products, because he absolutely believed in providing the best unique products to folks across the country.

One good thing had come amid all the work—the cattle rustlers hadn't struck again. Maybe they'd done all the damage they were going to do and were gone from the area. He'd like to catch them and stop their nefarious schemes, but if they were really out of his hair, that'd suit him, too, particularly if there were no more fires. Unfortunately, there'd been no news on Fernando, but Slade wasn't giving up hope. And Storm still believed her beloved bull would be home for Christmas. He'd hate to see her disappointed, but he'd done all he could do for now, so he simply had to let it be.

As he stood there with Ivy, waiting for a slow song, Wildcat Jack came waltzing up squiring a pretty gal in a full skirt that swirled around her knees. Jack was lithe and lean, wearing his trademark pearl-snap shirt, jeans, and boots, with his silver hair in a single braid hanging over one shoulder. He said he was seventy-nine and holding, but nobody knew his real age—or cared. He was as strong a DJ on KWCB as he'd always been, and the women still loved him as much, if not more, as ever.

"Hey, Ivy. Good to see you again," Jack said, casting a warm and gentle smile on her as he came to a stop. "And Slade."

"Hi, Jack." Slade knew he was an afterthought, because Wildcat Jack was well-known for having an eye for the ladies.

"Like y'all to meet Miss Betsy here."

"Bitsy."

"Right." Jack gave his honey a big smile, then turned back. "Glad to see y'all taking advantage of the Hall instead of working all the time." Jack kept an arm around his dance partner, as she smiled adoringly at him.

"Plenty to do," Slade said.

"Don't I know it." Jack watched Ivy as he answered Slade. "Eden and I are getting all set up for live streaming during the cattle drive. Ought to be spectacular."

"Should be," Slade said.

Jack turned the wattage up as he smiled at Ivy. "You'll be serving grub and drinks at Wildcat Hall during the drive, won't you?"

"That's the plan." She returned Jack's smile with a little wattage of her own.

Slade stiffened beside her and squeezed her hand. Every guy in the county knew you couldn't trust Jack with the ladies, because he just had that way about him that would've earned him a fortune if it could have been bottled and sold.

"Are you up for live streaming from the Hall, too?"

"Why not?" She smiled even warmer. "You'll be here, won't you?"

"I wouldn't miss a minute of interviewing such a lovely lady as you."

"Thank you. I'll look forward to it."

Slade held back his temper. Jack was a bred-in-the-bone flirt. If he hadn't been so disarming with his charm, he'd probably have been decked by a guy six days out of seven.

"Oh, yeah," Jack said, "I heard there've been a couple sightings of that big, black Angus bull of yours that got stolen."

"Sightings?" Slade asked, hardly able to believe his ears. "Who? When? Where?"

"No facts. You know how folks call into the station with crazy ideas."

Slade rubbed a hand across his jaw thoughtfully. "Do you think it could possibly be true?"

"No way to know. Do you want me to announce it on the radio? I could just ask for anybody that sees your bull to give you a call."

"No," Slade said. "Folks would laugh their heads off if you announced to the world that I imagine my bull is so massive, strong, and smart that he broke loose, knocked out the rustlers, and is on the run."

"It'd definitely be grist for the gossip mill."

"Just in case, I'll ask the cowboys to keep a lookout for Fernando."

"Fernando?" Jack laughed, shaking his head. "Where'd you get that name?"

"Storm named him, like he's a lover not a fighter."

Ivy chuckled, too.

"It's going to be hard to resist talking about Fernando the bull outsmarting rustlers," Jack said. "This sounds like something right up the alley of the Ranch Radio Rowdies. They could investigate Fernando's capture and escape on their program. I mean, something like, 'Call in and share your Fernando sighting.' I bet we could come up with some dynamite songs to up the suspense, maybe from the Highwaymen. Now that I think of it, Fernando is important enough to have his own theme song. Craig could probably write and sing one for us. After all, he is Cactus Craig on the show."

"Don't breathe a word of it, or I'll never hear the last of Fernando." As it was, he'd probably never live down letting the big-bucks bull get stolen in the first place. If this kept up, Fernando could become a country legend and even end up with his own radio show with Jack impersonating a sharp-as-a-tack bull who saw all and knew all.

"Worse things than encouraging folks to laugh and have a good time." Jack grinned, excitement shinning in his dark eyes.

Slade groaned in disbelief. Jack looked too mischievous and happy for comfort. Why had he ever mentioned the bull's name? If Storm heard about Jack's idea, she'd be itching to get on the air and explain how she'd recognized unique qualities in the big bull and given him a suitable name...or something from her fertile mind. It didn't bear thinking on.

"Sounds like fun," Ivy said. "Maybe Fernando needs his own Instagram page. It might help find him. The entire state of Texas, or even beyond our borders, could get into looking for the kidnapped bull that broke free because he couldn't bear to be parted from his lady love. What's her name?"

"There are no lady loves," Slade said, doing his best to stop the momentum. "He's not a cow bull."

"Lack of love is enough to make any male break free. It's a powerful incentive. Bet Fernando is looking for a pasture full of hot honeys. Those AI bulls get no fun out of life." Jack chuckled, nodding as if agreeing with himself. "I'll talk to Eden. Maybe we could make Fernando's story part of the cattle drive."

"He's not part of the cattle drive. He's gone," Slade said with as much force as possible. He didn't want Storm given false hope by this fantasy.

"Got you." Jack winked at Ivy. "I'd better get back on the dance floor before this lovely lady on my arm deserts me." And he whirled Bitsy away in a swirl of full skirt and tapping boots.

"What an absolutely charming and clever man," Ivy said with admiration lacing her voice.

"That's Wildcat Jack all right."

"And he never married?"

"Too many times to count."

"Really? And now?"

"I think he's still on the loose."

"You know, Wildcat Bluff just gets more and more interesting."

"Maybe too interesting."

He didn't want her thinking another second about Jack or Fernando or anything except him. He led her out onto the dance floor as Craig started in on a slow two-step, singing all about lost love, found love, and the power of love. Slade could totally agree, except for the lost love part—and he had no intention of ever going there, not with Ivy.

As he held her close, moving in a slow circle to the crooning of Craig's deep voice, he pulled her closer, so there was little distance between them. She was warm and soft and everything he could ever want.

After a bit, she stroked his shoulder, sniffing his shirt. "You smell sweet."

He chuckled at her words. "That's what I baked for the orders—pumpkin and pecan. I wore an apron, but I guess I was messier than I realized when I cooked those pies."

She reached up, stroked his earlobe, and put her fingertip in her mouth. "And you taste even more delicious."

"Don't tell me I'm wearing batter."

"If you don't want to hear it, I won't tell you, but you do taste like pumpkin pie."

He chuckled. "That's what happens when I come straight from the kitchen to the dance hall."

"You can do it anytime." She reached up and stroked his cheek, smiling happily. "I'll lick you clean."

"If you keep that up, we won't last here long." He grinned down at her. "I'll be hauling you up to the cabin in no time."

"Yum. That sounds good, too."

He whirled her around faster. If she kept teasing him, making him want to go someplace private so she could lick him to her heart's content, he was more than ready to go there, plans or no plans. Still, he wanted them to have a sort-of date, so he'd stick it out a bit longer, because he savored having her in his arms, feeling her sway to the music, knowing she was thinking about him and wanting to be with him and willing to take him home.

After a bit, Craig's voice trailed away and the song came to a close, Slade stopped dancing, but he kept holding Ivy in his arms—close and tight and just right. He heard the other dancers leave the floor, but he didn't care. He didn't move. She didn't move. Neither of them wanted the dance to end, so they didn't let it. She laid her head on his chest, as if she could still hear the music or maybe she heard the beat of his heart.

"Okay, folks, I called last dance," Craig hollered, getting their attention. "Slade and Ivy, maybe you didn't hear me or maybe you don't care. Dancing for the night is officially over."

Ivy raised her head and looked at Slade with tenderness. "One dance with you isn't nearly enough."

"I know. It's not for me, either." He gently kissed her forehead. "I want to dance with you for the rest of my life."

She smiled just as gently as he had kissed her.

"Hey, you two," Craig hollered again as he stepped down from the raised platform while the band packed up. "I called last dance."

Slade finally looked up as Craig stopped beside them. "You couldn't have sung one more?"

"You don't need another song. You need to get a room."

Slade grinned at the old joke, shaking his head at the truth of his friend's words.

"We've got a room," Ivy said with a smile. "We just wanted to dance."

"Next time, come earlier." Craig returned her smile. "We'll play something special for the two of you."

"'Always on My Mind.'" Slade looked at Ivy.

"Willie Nelson," Craig said. "You got it."

"Thanks."

"You and the band were great tonight," Ivy said. "Y'all are a huge boon to the Hall, and I appreciate it."

"We're glad for the venue." Craig glanced away, hesitated, then focused on Ivy. "Fern? Is she okay? She doesn't return my texts."

"I'm sorry," Ivy said. "As far as I know, she's enjoying singing on the cruise. Yet I think she's a bit lonely, too."

"That's hard to imagine, but I know I am." He hesitated again. "Do you think she'll be home anytime soon?"

"I doubt it. Christmas is a big season for cruises."

"Yeah. I guess so—like it is for Wildcat Bluff."

"I meant to ask you before, but I've just been so busy," Ivy said. "If you have time, I'd like your help with planning gigs. You're much more knowledgeable about bands than I am."

"I'm happy to help. Fern and I...well, we'd made some plans about how to up our presence online and draw in more talent and tourists."

"Great. I want to hear it all. Maybe we can add to your list."

"Let's get together soon," Craig said. "I'm swamped with the ranch, the firefighting, the radio, and—"

"Reminds me." Slade cut him off. "If Jack comes to you with some cockamamy story about a big bull, don't listen to a word of it."

Craig appeared puzzled a moment, then he started to laugh. Finally, he took a deep breath before he started to tease. "This doesn't have something to do with that fancy bull you had snatched out from under your nose, does it?"

"Fernando does get around," Ivy said sweetly.

"Fernando?" Craig laughed even harder. "That's the bull's name?"

"Storm named him." Slade could see he wasn't going to get any backup for his position on the missing bull, at least not this night. "Apparently, he reminds her of some cartoon character that caught her fancy."

"Fernando's a lover, not a fighter," Ivy said even more sweetly, as if being nothing but helpful. "And there have been Fernando sightings."

"Sightings?" Craig chuckled as he looked from one to the other as if he couldn't believe his ears.

"Whatever you do, don't let Jack talk you into composing Fernando a theme song." Slade sincerely hoped this would be the end of the matter, but he had a sneaking sensation that he'd just made matters worse. "And for the record, I had that bull in a secure location."

"Right," Craig said quickly. "Everybody in the county knows it's not your fault. Those cattle rustlers are...are—"

"Not smart enough to hang on to a big, bad bull named Fernando," Ivy finished for him with a grin.

Craig started to laugh again. "Sightings? Theme song? Wait till the Ranch Radio Rowdies hear about Fernando."

"We don't know those sightings are a fact," Slade said. "And he does not need his own song."

"It's Christmas," Craig said. "Fernando may well be our miracle this year. Remember when Misty Reynolds came to town, and everything started to go right? We called her our Christmas angel."

"I remember." Slade gave up. Somehow or other, Fernando was capturing hearts in his supposed bid for freedom. He really hoped it was true, but how could it be?

"Wouldn't it be great if Fernando actually did come home in time for Christmas?" Ivy smiled hopefully.

"Yeah, it'd definitely be a miracle," Slade said, wishing it were possible.

"I'm all for miracles." Craig's eyes lit up with enthusiasm. "Maybe Fern will even be home for Christmas."

"I guess anything's possible." Slade didn't want to see anybody hurt by too much hope and too little reality. Then again, he was no one to talk. He'd been walking around with his heart on his sleeve since the moment he'd met Ivy.

"We'll just have to wait and see, won't we?" Ivy clasped Slade's hand. "For now, Craig, why don't you get some rest while Slade and I—"

"Get a room." And he said it with a great deal of relish.

Chapter 25

WHEN IVY WALKED INTO HER COWBOY CABIN WITH
Slade right behind her, she felt like she was coming home.
Everything was beginning to seem more familiar and com-
fortable now...and she liked it.

"Smells delicious." She glanced at the sack Slade carried
over to the countertop and set down. "I love the way you
feed me."

"I hope that's not all you love about me."

She just smiled as she put an arm around his waist and
hugged him while she peered around to see what he was
taking out of the sack.

He chuckled as he set out several closed containers. "Are
you sure Wildcat Jack didn't steal your heart tonight?"

"Ha! He doesn't feed me. But he is a funny guy, particularly the way he went on about Fernando."

"You didn't have to encourage him." He snagged a couple
of bowls out of the cabinet.

"I couldn't resist. It got too funny."

"Not for me."

"Folks know your bull was stolen. You didn't just lose him."

"Guess you're right. Still..."

"Tell you what. We lingered at the Hall to close up. Jack
might be on the air by now if he went straight from the
Hall to the station. If so, let's hear what he's saying. I bet he
doesn't even mention Fernando." She walked to the end of

the countertop and turned on the vintage radio shaped like a stagecoach.

Slade filled the bowls with thick, rich stew, then set them on the table. "Cornbread, too."

"Thanks." She set napkins, spoons, and glasses of water on the table and then turned up the volume on the radio. Wildcat Jack came in loud and clear.

"Did you miss me while I was boot scooting at Wildcat Hall to the renowned Craig Thorne? Hope so. I sure missed y'all. And as if you didn't know, this is Wildcat Jack coming to you from KWCB, the Wildcat Den, serving North Texas and Southern Oklahoma since 1946. Our ranch radio is located on the beauteous Hogtrot Ranch for your listenin' pleasure."

Slade snorted, chuckling. "Jack's gotten a lot of mileage out of that old joke over the years. In case you didn't know, it's the Rocky T Ranch, but he does like to tease."

Ivy smiled as she sat down. She could easily imagine Jack keeping a joke going for a long time. He was just a naturally comical guy.

Slade sat down across from her. "Hope you like the stew."

She took a bite, sighing in contentment. "It's wonderful. And it's really good after a long day."

"Folks," Jack said in a serious tone. "I've got a BOLO—be on the lookout—for you tonight."

"Oh no." Slade set down his spoon and stared hard at the radio.

"That's right. BOLO. I just received word that the big Angus bull that cattle rustlers swiped from Steele Trap II may have escaped his captors."

Slade groaned, shaking his head.

Ivy felt sympathy for him. She hadn't thought Jack—or

Craig—would actually go forward with the funny scenario. But here it was, right in their faces.

"Now we can't say for sure." Jack lowered his voice to a conspiratorial tone. "But we're sure hoping the sightings of this special bull are true. What I'm asking of you, my sharp-eyed listeners, is to keep a lookout for him."

Ivy reached over and patted Slade's hand as he continued to watch the radio like he wanted to smash it.

"If you see that bull, don't stop him or try to capture him. That'd be foolhardy. He's a massive critter. Two thousand pounds on his lean days. I know that means nothing to strong-hearted cowboys who can rope and ride like the wind. But if this bull got free, that means he's one big, bad bull on a mission. Don't get in his way. Make sure he's got an open gate or he'll plow through your fences, because he's making his way across pastures coming from who knows how far away, determined to get home to Steele Trap II in time for Christmas."

Slade groaned. "If anybody takes Jack seriously and leaves their gates open, we could have Angus bulls roaming all over the county. I don't know how long it'd take to get them sorted out and back to their ranches."

"It's just hyperbole, isn't it?"

"I can only hope. At least they'll be tagged or branded or tattooed. Jack's just playing this for all it's worth, and it could cause trouble."

"I'm sure the ranchers will know not to follow Jack's instructions."

"Normally, I'd agree. But if they decide it's a fun game, they might decide it's worth playing."

She hadn't thought about how wrong this could go. It

was one thing to think about a funny situation. It was quite another for it to become real life.

"Now here's something else for you." Jack chuckled low into the mic, luring listeners to come in a little closer for his next bit of news. "This big bull has a name…and not just any name, but a name bestowed on him by a little girl called Storm. She named him…Fernando. Let me say that again to make sure you got it. That's right. Fernando."

"Well, that did it," Slade said. "There's not a cowboy or cowgirl in the county who won't want to be part of Jack's growing bull legend."

"Fernando," Jack said again. "Now, folks, don't be sitting at home on your hands. Give me a call and tell me about your Fernando sightings…and rest assured Cactus Craig and the rest of the Ranch Radio Rowdies will be all over this story to bring you the latest news on Fernando."

"I guess I might as well give in and get in on the joke," Slade said. "It's always better to laugh than to cry."

"It could turn out to be fun for everyone…if they don't let their cattle escape, and ranchers are too smart for that to happen," Ivy said. "Best of all, this attention could make Fernando's sale difficult or somebody might recognize him."

"Guess that's an upside to this sideshow," Slade said, looking down at his cooling stew and shaking his head.

Wildcat Jack gave a growl into his mic. "To get y'all in the mood for your Fernando hunt, I cued up a song from way back when in the seventies, and I mean way back to the era of over-the-top glitter balls and rhinestones and leisure suits. Disco has never been my thing, but in honor of our missing bull, here's the Swedish rock band ABBA's 'Fernando.' Dig it."

Ivy waited until the song was over, then got up, walked over, and turned off the radio. "Well, I guess that's that. Cat's out of the bag."

When Slade's phone played Storm's ringtone, he picked it up, hit speakerphone, and held it toward Ivy.

"Uncle Slade!" Storm hollered. "Did you hear Jack? Fernando's on his way home. He'll be back in time for Christmas."

"We're not too sure of the facts yet," Slade said, sounding patient.

"I'm gonna get him a Santa Claus hat. He'll look good in red."

"I doubt he'll wear it."

"He'll be so glad to be home, he might even let me ride him."

"You're not riding any bulls." Slade sounded a lot less patient. "None of us are anymore."

"Yeah. Well…I'll give him a special treat."

"That'll work."

"I'm going on the Wildcat Den tomorrow and telling everybody exactly how I named Fernando." She dropped her voice conspiratorially. "You know, he was the handsomest and smartest and biggest bull I ever met, so I knew right away he needed a special name."

"Sounds good."

"I think so, too."

"Isn't it past your bedtime?"

"I'm too excited to sleep."

"You better get some shut-eye. You want to be fresh for your radio interview, don't you?"

"Yes! I'm going right now. Nighty night." And she was gone.

Slade looked at Ivy. "You know, by the time everybody gets through embellishing the personality of this bull, they'll probably interview him on television."

"Live stream, for sure."

"He's just a bull, even if he is top-breed bloodline. But the thing I remember most about him is that he likes water."

"What do you mean?"

"Well, all cattle like water. But Fernando has a favorite pond on the ranch. He's so massive he can take out a gate. He just puts his head under it and pops it off its hinges."

"I had no idea. Where's his favorite pond?"

"Right in front of my new ranch house. The pond is small and more ornamental than anything with lily pads in the water and flowers on the bank and an overhanging willow tree. In summer, it's really pretty. Anyhow, I'd find him just standing in it with water up to his stomach and... well, it looked like he was meditating on the meaning of life or something."

"Storm did say Fernando was smart." Ivy teased him in a low voice.

"If this wasn't happening to me, maybe it'd be funny."

"I thought Fernando had his own barn and pasture where you kept him safe."

"Right...but he has a thing for that one pond. He was safe enough meandering down there now and again till those rustlers showed up."

"You must admit, Fernando is getting more interesting all the time."

"Don't tell anybody I told you about the pond. It'll just add to his mystique." Slade rubbed his jaw. "When we found him there, Storm was the one to lure him back to his barn."

"Sounds like he has a mind of his own."

"I feel kind of bad about making him get out of that pond now, seeing as how he'll probably never run free or stand in that water again."

"How can you say that? Isn't he coming home for the holidays?"

"I wish." Slade just shook his head. "If it gets to the point where it'll disappoint kids at Christmas, I may have to haul out another Angus bull and call him Fernando."

"That'd be a real disappointment. I want him to come home."

"Don't we all." Slade got up, walked over, and took her in his arms. "But we can't count on it. We need an alternate plan."

"You're right. I suppose Angus bulls have a similar look."

"Yeah…but Fernando is bigger than most."

She reached up and kissed Slade's cheek. "You did your best to stop the legend before it reached critical mass. Now I know you'll do your best to see it through to the end for the best possible result."

"I just don't know what else I can do."

"Why don't you make this work for you? I could put up an Instagram account for Fernando. Do you have photographs of him? A few of him with Storm would be wonderful. If people are watching and looking for him, it could make him safer."

"What about a reward for his capture and return to Steele Trap II? That'd probably set every cowboy and cowgirl in our neck of the woods looking for him."

"Great idea! I can put that message up on Instagram with the photos. Do you have one of him standing in his favorite pond?"

"Storm probably has one."

"That'd help build his image, too."

"I can see this might help. With so much attention, the rustlers could actually let him go so they don't risk getting caught."

"True. But Fernando is smart and strong. Keep in mind, Jack said there have already been sightings. Our favorite bull might have escaped and be headed our way for Christmas."

"You're starting to believe the legend, aren't you?"

"Legends are born because we want to believe them."

"Yeah." He sighed, tugging her closer. "Do you suppose we could forget about Fernando for now and finish our dance in bed?"

"I suppose that means you don't want me to sing you a private rendition of ABBA's 'Fernando'?"

"If I never hear the name again, it'll be too soon."

She chuckled as she took his hand and led him into her bedroom. "I bet we can make everything right—together."

"I'm happy to help." And he started shucking his clothes.

She admired him as he stripped down, revealing sleek skin stretched tight over hard muscles. He was just so beautiful—inside and out—that sometimes her heart hurt when she looked at him.

He sat down on the bed, and it creaked, groaned, and sagged under him. "I've got to get you a new bed. This one is going to ruin me."

"Should we move that item up on our priority lists?"

"Either that or move into my good house."

"This is convenient for me."

"Yeah. And I don't want you out on the road late at night."

"I can handle it."

"I know. Still, I'll order a bed tomorrow and get it delivered here."

"Thanks. I won't complain. It needs to be upgraded anyway, along with other items. Send the bill here, will you?"

"Not on your life. I'm buying you—us—a new bed. It's not going on the Hall's expense account."

"But, Slade—"

"Call it a Christmas present if you want, but that's the way it is."

"Okay. Christmas. Now I'll need to think of something special for you."

He grinned, looking her up and down. "You're all the special I need or want."

"Fortunately, I'm all yours."

"Yeah."

She wanted to make this a night to remember, so she turned and lit several candles Morning Glory had been kind enough to give her as a welcome-to-your-new-home gift. She'd arranged them on the corner of her dresser, where they looked pretty in lavender, pink, and yellow. Soon the scent of lavender, rose, and frankincense wafted across the room. Last, she turned off the overhead light, so they were enclosed in soft light and sweet scent.

"Are you trying to cover up the smell of pies or entice me to greater exertion?" Slade teased her as he jerked off his boots and socks, then tossed them in a corner. He threw back the bedspread, bunched up a pillow, and lay down flat on his back completely nude, completely exposed, completely ready.

"I love the smell of pie on you…and I'm always ready for you to exert yourself."

"Glad to know I can please you." He sighed in pleasure. "It feels really good to lie down."

"If that feels good, I bet we can do something to make you feel even better." She grasped her belt buckle, then started her own stripping, although unlike him, she made hers slow and seductive, watching him watch her.

"That buckle never looked half as good on me as it does on you." He gave her a lazy smile as he crossed his arms behind his head, all ready for his show.

"I take it you still don't want it back." She pulled the belt free and dropped it to the floor before she ever so slowly pulled her shirttail out, then snapped open one button after the other to reveal the lacy, red bra she wore underneath. As she slipped off the shirt, his eyes grew dark.

"Never…but if you don't hurry up, I may have to get up and help you."

"Would it make you grumpy?"

"No, that's not what it would make me."

She grinned, liking his impatience as she sat down on a rocker in the corner. She leaned forward, knowing he was watching her every move, and heard him groan in response. She tugged off her boots and socks before she glanced up at him.

He rubbed his bare chest before slowly moving his hands downward. "How long do you expect me to wait for you?"

She just smiled in response, then wriggled out of her jeans and tossed them on top of the boots. She stood up wearing nothing but a bra and thong—in other words, just scraps of red lace.

"Get over here," he growled, patting the bed.

She was more than ready to join him, hot and wet and needy. She walked over, knelt on the bed, then slowly crawled up it on her hands and knees till she crouched beside his chest. "Is here good?"

"Here is perfect." He sat up, clasped her shoulders, kissed her, and eased her onto her back in the middle of the bed. "I don't think I can be slow and gentle tonight."

"I want you fast, hard, and now."

"That's what you'll get." He opened the nightstand drawer, pulled out a foil packet, and slipped on a condom.

She waited, shivering in anticipation as she raised her arms above her head and spread her legs.

When he turned back, he looked at her for a long moment, as if drinking her in deep and deeper. And then he knelt between her legs, casting her in the shadow of his body, and placed both palms flat on her stomach. She shivered harder as he clasped her waist, fitting his hands around her as he'd done the very first time they'd met. He squeezed possessively, then leaned forward and softly kissed her lips. He smiled a secret sort of smile before he nuzzled down her neck until he reached the swell of her breasts. He pushed down her bra, exposing her to his hot gaze, and then he kissed, nibbled, and licked until her nipples were hard points.

She ached all over, more and more desperate as he drove their passion higher and higher. She writhed up against him, straining for what only he could give her. She grasped his hips, tugging him toward her, beseeching him without words.

And he understood, because he raised her legs and

placed them over his shoulders. In one strong motion, he drove in deep, filling her completely and causing her to cry out his name. When he started to thrust, he leaned down, pressed a soft kiss to her lips, and whispered her name. She held on to him as all that was real in her world while he pumped harder and faster, longer and stronger—breath rasping, sweat beading—as she grew hotter and brighter in the fire that he was stoking between them.

Just when she thought she couldn't take another moment of the red-hot blaze that was burning her inside out, he sent her over the edge into a frenzy of unrestrained, rainbow-tinted ecstasy.

And he went with her...scorching her, scorching him.

Chapter 26

A WEEK LATER, SLADE SAT ON HORSEBACK IN FRONT OF Steele Trap II's ranch house. He felt as if he had a target on his back as he gazed at the pastures around him, even though there'd been no more rustled cattle. Nothing appeared out of place, but then it'd looked normal before Fernando went missing, too. He didn't trust much of anything at the moment, except Ivy and his family and friends. He wasn't even too sure about his cooking, since he'd burned the cookies, but that'd been unusual circumstances to say the least. Ivy. She had been making everything bearable and life so much better since she came into his world.

He decided to check Fernando's pond for hoofprints or any sign that the big bull had been around there. He wasn't the only one keeping an eye out for Fernando. Ivy's Instagram with Fernando and Storm photos had been an instant success and gained followers daily. After she'd posted the reward, cowboys and cowgirls all over North Texas had started the hunt. Slade wasn't sure if it was hurting or helping to get Fernando home, but it sure was causing a ruckus.

As he rode down the hill, he heard the creak of saddle leather and glanced up at a brilliant blue sky with fluffy, white clouds. A red-tailed hawk wheeled overhead before silently gliding away. Pretty day. Great time of year. If

Fernando was back, the rustlers were caught, and the cattle drive over, all would be perfect.

He let his horse nose past lily pads and drink from the water. He doubted if he'd ever find Fernando basking in the pond on a hot summer day or even taking a drink on a cool winter day again. But hope was still alive, and he wasn't one to stand in its way.

As he sat there thinking about what needed to be done, he realized he didn't want to do anything except be with Ivy. They had Christmas plans to make for the Hall, so he had a good excuse to call her. He plucked his phone out of his pocket just as he heard Storm's ringtone.

"What's up?" He clicked on speakerphone, hoping she hadn't come up with some new, unrealistic plan for getting Fernando back to the ranch.

"Uncle Slade," Storm said breathlessly. "There's been a big break in the case."

"Case?" He figured she must have been talking with Sheriff Calhoun.

"You know. Fernando's case."

"Right." He felt his stomach clench in anticipation of her next words, since good or bad, he had to be prepared for the news. He'd gladly pay the reward if some cowboy would just bring the bull home.

"Fernando's going to have babies."

"Babies?" He frowned at the phone, wondering if it was working right.

"Yes! I'm so excited. He's a cow bull now. And his babies will be here in time for fall calving."

"Storm, he's been gone a couple of weeks, so he's either—"

"Don't take my word for it! Get the Den on your phone. Wildcat Jack is talking to a rancher near Honey Grove right now."

"Fernando escaped and he's been caught?" Slade felt a huge surge of relief wash over him. Maybe miracles did happen. If the rustlers had taken U.S. 82 east toward Texarkana, where they could quickly slip into Arkansas or Louisiana, Honey Grove made sense, since it was on the west side of Paris. And if he'd escaped against all odds, he could have made it back there. Still, why would rustlers go east when west made more sense?

"Quick! Get the Den," Storm said. "I gotta get back to Jack to find out more." And she clicked off.

Slade couldn't understand why the rancher didn't call him about the reward if he'd caught Fernando. No way to know, so he used the Wildcat Den's new app, and soon, Wildcat Jack came in loud and clear.

"Mr. Reynolds, when did you figure out the bull covering your cows was the legendary Fernando?" Jack asked in a serious tone.

"What a big brute of a beauty! He went right through my fence—and it's not loose, no way, no how—like it was made of butter." Mr. Reynolds chuckled. "I had three cows in that pasture all ready for a bull, but I had no way to afford an Angus of Fernando's pedigree."

"He's high on the food chain, that's for sure," Jack said.

"I didn't see him till this morning. He was probably there a couple of nights…and believe you me, that's plenty of time for a bull like that to take care of business."

Wildcat Jack chuckled in a low, knowing tone. "I'm a cowboy myself, so I get just what you mean."

"I can't tell you how grateful I am that Fernando came calling on my cows. Maybe he brought candy and flowers."

"More likely oats." Jack laughed harder. "You're a lucky man to get that kind of sire for free."

"That I am. And Fernando's quite the lover, not the fighter...unless you make him mad."

"I take it you made him mad."

"When I got there, Fernando and my cows were licking each other, affectionate like they do."

"Sounds like Fernando," Jack replied. "So all was going well at that point."

"Yep. And he chowed down in the feed trough with the cows."

"Bet he was hungry after a couple nights' work."

"Yeah. Bulls can get real skinny, but he looked strong." Mr. Reynolds gave a heartfelt sigh. "Right then, I didn't know he was Fernando, but I'd heard about him and the reward and the little girl."

"Did Fernando cooperate with you?"

"What do you think? He didn't have an ear tag, but I had a scanner and that told the tale."

"Good thing you had a scanner."

"Early Christmas present from the wife."

"Guess you'll be thanking her for a long time."

"You bet. And I'll be thanking Steele Trap Ranch II forever."

"No doubt. Please tell our listeners that you roped Fernando and you'll have him back at his ranch later today."

"I roped him all right." Mr. Reynolds laughed as if at his own folly. "I knew better. I wasn't even on a horse. A bull like that can take a horse and rider down easy. For him, I was like swatting a fly."

"Did you get bruised up?"

"I could've been, but I'm not so stupid I'd hold on to that rope. Mad don't begin to describe him. He gave me a look that froze me into a solid block of ice, then he took off. I doubt if he even saw the fence he plowed through."

"So he's in the wind?"

"Afraid so. And I lost my best red Lone Star rope with him."

"How do you feel about finding and losing him?" Jack asked in a deep, sympathetic voice.

"Good and bad. I've got Little Fernandos on the way. But I wish I'd been the one to get him home safely for that girl."

"And the reward."

"Yeah. That, too. Still, I'm worried about him. He's big, smart, and strong, but there are dangers out there for a bull on the loose."

"How do you think he got away from the kidnappers?"

"No idea…but it can happen."

"What do you mean?" Jack asked, sounding intense. "I've got an idea or two, but I'd like to get your take."

"I had it happen once. I was transferring a bull from one truck to another. You know, you back them up, end to end, and the bull is supposed to go from one truck bed to the other. But this particular bull squeezed his big bulk out of a tiny spot between the trucks, making one truck roll, and plowed out of there, mad as hell. The cowboy standing on the bumper got knocked down and stepped on before we could get that bull back under control."

"Sounds serious."

"Sure was."

"Do you think that's how Fernando got away?"

"Don't know. But a bull that size and strength can do plenty of damage to trucks, horses, and cowboys."

"I'm with you on that assessment. I do appreciate your story, Mr. Reynolds. You've been real helpful," Jack said. "I don't want to take up too much time from your busy day, but do you have anything else you'd like to share with our listeners?"

"I'd like to thank Steele Trap Ranch II for the donation to my herd. I'm mighty appreciative. And I just hope somebody out there catches Fernando before something happens to him."

"We've all got our fingers crossed for his safe return. And thank you so much for joining us today to share your Fernando sighting."

"Anytime."

Slade clicked off and just sat there in stunned silence. Little Fernandos? He wouldn't have believed it if the cowboy hadn't had a scanner. Of course, he could be making the whole thing up for attention or whatever. Still, it had the ring of truth.

He turned back toward the house. Honey Grove. That meant Fernando was close to Bonham, if the rancher spoke the truth. Lots of ranches and farms along that route. Fernando wouldn't be following the road. He'd be going cross-country. That was about eighty miles away. A bull could make five miles a day...if he was motivated by food. And home.

He heard Storm's ringtone again, so he clicked Answer.

"Fernando will be home by Christmas," Storm said in a happy voice. "I just knew it."

"Hope so. But even if that rancher spoke the truth and

Fernando did escape the rustlers, he's still a long way from here." He didn't want to worry her by mentioning coyote packs or rifles or injured hooves or rustlers. It wouldn't be far in a truck, but for a lone bull, it was treacherous country.

"But he's Fernando, the biggest, baddest, bravest bull in the whole wide world. He'll be home for Christmas." And once more, she was gone.

Slade just sat there a moment, thinking. He hoped she was right. He knew some ranchers in that area, so he'd contact them and find out if Mr. Reynolds had a solid reputation. If so, he'd contact the rancher and see if there was any more to learn from him. He didn't care about the loss of revenue. He just wanted Fernando safely home.

When his horse had enough to drink, he turned the roan toward his cattle barn. Oscar and Tater were probably there by now. As far as he knew, he was pretty much on top of chores. Cowboys were busy on both ranches. He'd baked and sent off several orders of pies. Muscadine grapes were in vats turning into wine since the end of last summer. He'd ordered a new bed for the cowboy cabin. He wasn't due at the café to cook lunch till later, so Granny could take a break and whip up something special.

All in all, things were in about as much control as they ever got, particularly with Christmas coming up fast. He started to call Ivy again, then stopped. She was probably in the midst of designing websites or getting on top of something at the Park. Still, he wanted to hear her voice, so he hit speed dial to connect to her.

"Slade, the bed is wonderful. The Settelmeyers just installed it in the cabin. I'm so glad you ordered a queen."

"I wanted a king, but there just isn't room."

"True." She chuckled. "I feel a little naughty."

"Tell me about it." He hoped this was really good, because he could use hearing an erotic fantasy that featured her right now.

"I bounced on the bed several times."

"How did it feel?"

"Lonely."

"I'm here at the ranch. My bed is lonely, too."

"I think I'm getting addicted to you."

"Glad to hear it."

"Are you sure you don't mind?"

"Not in a million years."

She chuckled in a low, suggestive tone.

He felt the sound vibrate up and down his spine, causing him to miss her all the more. "Maybe I better come over, so we can try out the bed."

"See if we can break it, is that what you mean?"

He laughed so hard that his horse shied, jingling the metal on the reins. "I hope it's a better bed than that."

She hesitated for a moment, breathing into the phone. "Can you come over soon?"

"Pretty quick. I've got a couple of hours before I need to be at the café."

"Perfect."

As he neared the barn, he saw Oscar motioning urgently for him to come closer. Tater paced in agitation by his side. Something wasn't right. "Ivy, I've got to go. Looks like there's a ranch problem. We better wait to test the bed."

"Okay. I'll hold you to it. And, Slade, stay safe."

"Always." He put his phone in his pocket and urged his horse into a lope to get to Oscar faster.

When he got there, he slid off the roan and approached Oscar with trepidation. He'd known things had been going too well to last.

"We got trouble." Oscar took off his hat and scratched his bald head.

"What kind? Which ranch? Anybody hurt?" Slade took several steps toward the barn.

"Hold your horses." Oscar replaced his hat and spit to one side. "No rush. Fire rescue is on its way to the old ranch."

Slade felt his heart sink at the news. "Tell me it's not Granny...or Storm...or Sydney."

"They're fine. We're all okay." Oscar patted Tater's head. "But I think we're gonna lose a barn."

Slade shook his head at the bad news, but he felt galvanized at the same time. "I'd better get there and help contain it."

"I hate to tell you, but it's the old barn."

Slade felt sick at his stomach. No way to replace it, not a barn made by his ancestors of hand-hewn logs at a barn-raising well over one-hundred-fifty years ago. "Granny. It'll break her heart."

"Not to mention her bank account. She was pouring her heart, soul, and money into restoring that relic."

"Is she there?"

"By now, most likely. Sydney's taking over the café."

"Storm?"

"She's with Sydney."

"Good."

"They want you over there. We can go together."

Slade started for the barn, then stopped and glanced around the area. "Fire again."

"Yeah."

"You'd better stay here and keep an eye out...if it isn't already too late."

"What?"

"How likely was that barn to catch fire?"

"About as likely as any empty, dry-wood, under-construction barn."

"In other words, it's not too likely unless it had a little help." Slade felt even sicker at where his mind had gone.

Oscar spit hard to the side. "You think the rustlers struck again?"

"Fits the pattern, doesn't it?"

"Distract and hit. Works for them, but against us."

"Right. I'd hoped they'd left the county."

"If they were gone, all that Fernando brouhaha could've brought them back, put their rustler egos on the line."

"Something to prove?"

Oscar shrugged as he patted Tater's head again. "I'll get the cowboys to checking the far pastures."

"I'll make sure more cowboys come over from the other ranch. Damage is done there, but maybe we can still save something here."

"Right."

"I'll take care of stuff, then get back here as quick as I can."

"I hear you."

"Listen, I just caught Jack interviewing a cowboy from over Honey Grove way. He says Fernando covered three of his cows."

"How'd he know it was Fernando and not some other black bull?"

"He had a scanner."

"Fernando escaped the rustlers? Bull's got guts. When's the rancher bringing him here?"

"He isn't. Fernando got away."

"That's a right shame."

"Yeah. If the rancher's telling the truth, it means we have a chance of getting Fernando back. I'm going to make some calls. Guy's name is Reynolds."

"I'll ask the cowboys around here about him, too."

"Thanks."

Slade tossed the reins to Oscar, then jogged over to his pickup. He got in, backed up, and tore out of the barnyard. He did his best to hold down his speed as he pulled onto Wildcat Road, because he couldn't turn back time and save the barn to stop his grandmother's anguish. All he could do was get there, make sure the fire didn't spread, and comfort Granny...but it all seemed like too little too late.

From a distance, he could see smoke spiraling up from the ranch. He figured Wildcat Bluff volunteer firefighters were already there, but if not, he carried a limited amount of equipment in his truck at all times. He'd haul it out and get started at containment.

He turned off the road, drove under the black metal cutout that read "Steele Trap Ranch," with clear blue sky shining through the open letters and a red-suited, white-bearded Santa Claus perched on one corner slowly waving at passersby with his battery-operated, animated arm. Santa looked way too cheerful against the backdrop of rising smoke—and of Slade's own feelings.

He rattled over the cattle guard and headed up the single lane till he came to the sprawling redbrick ranch house with a red metal roof where his mother and grandmother lived together. Arches enclosed a portico where he often sat on the bright-yellow cushions of the cedar chairs. For Christmas, they'd outlined the arches with long ropes of red and green lights to match the bright wreaths in every window. Again, it looked way too cheerful for the occasion.

He turned left, instead of right toward Sydney's house and his own beyond it. He wanted to get to the barn, maintenance, and garage area on a hill overlooking the Red River. No, he didn't want it. He wanted to be anywhere else. But he followed the smoke that was growing thicker all the time.

When he got to the old barn, it was totally engulfed in a huge, red-orange blaze, shooting flames and smoke into the sky. Two Wildcat Bluff boosters had been backed up toward the barn. Firefighters had pulled out hoses and now sent streams of water out of nozzles onto the roaring fire. The whole area was hot and smoky with black soot caught by a breeze and tossed over everything. Even though it looked bad, Slade felt a surge of relief. So far so good. The fire appeared close to containment, so it wouldn't spread to the other buildings or nearby pasture. They were lucky.

Still, the blaze wasn't his main concern. Granny stood safely to one side with her arms wrapped around her middle, in comfort or protection. She still wore her pink, frilly Chuckwagon apron with her hair captured by a net over her thick bun on the back of her head. No tears scored her cheeks, but she had an iron will—all her tears would be inside.

He parked out of the way, stepped down, and hurried over to her.

She glanced up at him and gave a shake of her head.

He took her in his arms, so small, so frail, and yet so

strong. He loved her with a fierceness that sometimes surprised him. But that was family for you. They were the linchpin of life.

"And it was looking so beautiful." She stepped back from him, appearing sad and a little lost.

"I'm sorry, Granny." He didn't know what else to say, so he simply held her hand.

"Sorry won't cut it." She sounded decisive. "We've had enough of these shenanigans on our ranches."

"Are you thinking what I'm thinking?"

"Absolutely. How many head went missing this time?"

"Oscar is looking into it."

"Good." She turned back to the burning barn, black soot dotting the pink of her apron. "Sheriff Calhoun is a good man. He'll find arson here, just like at the other fires. He'll find cattle missing just like before. But he won't find the rustlers."

"Why not?"

"They've been one step ahead of us all the way."

"That's true."

"Why is it?"

"I've been trying to figure it out."

"We've got to try harder." She squeezed his hand. "Next time somebody might get hurt."

"We can't let that happen."

"No, we can't." She raised her face and stared at the destruction in progress. "The cattle drive is coming up."

"Do you think they'll pull an old-timey cattle heist by picking off stragglers?"

She squeezed his hand harder. "I suspect so, but that's not my fear."

"What is?"

"Our cattle drive is turning into quite the event of the year. Everybody wants to be involved in it. We're talking about ranchers and neighbors. That's okay. We're probably also going to get tenderfoot, weekend riders just out for fun. KWCB will be there live streaming, but we may get media from nearby towns or even Dallas and Fort Worth. We can't control it all…and somebody could easily get hurt by the rustlers, accidentally or not."

Slade groaned, watching the fire that didn't seem quite so bad now that he thought about cattle drive dangers.

"I talked with the sheriff," she said. "We'll have mounted patrol. Hedy will have EMTs, water, and first-aid available."

"That's all good."

"But will it be enough?"

"There's something else to add to the mix." He hated to bring it up, but he might as well get it over with.

"What?"

"Fernando."

She leaned into him. "How in the world did that ever get started?"

"It's a long story. If I mention Wildcat Jack, will you understand?"

"Oh yes. He's a showman, no doubt about it."

"Who knows how many people, some on foot, may show up trying to have a Fernando sighting?"

"Do you think they'll come in from the cities?"

"No idea."

"Okay." She nodded as she looked up at him. "We add Fernando to the mix. I'll alert the sheriff, although he's probably already thought of it."

"And something else—a rancher in Honey Grove just called into the Den and claimed Fernando covered his cows the last couple of days."

"I heard." She grinned, looking happy. "Update me. When is he bringing our bull home?"

"He can't. Fernando ran away, but if his story is true—"

"Fernando escaped his kidnappers."

"Right."

"That's good news, because those cowboys out there looking for him will find him."

"I hope so."

"Count on it."

"Granny." Slade put an arm around her shoulders and pulled her close. "I think this is going to be a Christmas to remember—if we survive it."

She chuckled, nodding in agreement. "We better hope Fernando is our miracle of the season."

"If he's not, I'd better pull a rabbit out of a hat."

"You never know about blessings in disguise." Granny held out her hand, palm up, and caught a few black ashes. "Maybe this fire is our wake-up call."

"You bet. We'll catch these rustlers." He kissed her cheek. "I'm really sorry about the barn."

"Me, too."

"Right now, I'd better see what I can do to help put out the fire, then I'll get back to the other ranch."

She straightened her shoulders and raised her chin. "I'll send cowboys over there to help, and I'll talk with the sheriff."

"Now, we just need to up our game."

Chapter 27

"WHICH PASTURE?" SLADE FELT A RED-HOT CURRENT run through him, but he tried to hang on to his anger.

"Southeast." Oscar rubbed his jaw, then spit to one side. "Sidewinders."

"How many?"

"A dozen or so, but no final head count yet."

"All cows?"

"Yep. But it could've been worse."

"I don't see how."

"Could've been two dozen," Oscar said.

Tater whined, lay down, and put his head on his paws.

Slade just shook his head. When even Tater was down about the whole deal, you knew it was bad.

"I don't get it," Oscar said. "Tater doesn't either."

"Rustlers seem to know where we are every single minute of every single day."

"Except the past couple of weeks."

"Why did they lay off, then suddenly come back?"

"You'd think after they made the big catch of Fernando, they'd have lit out for good."

"I thought they had," Slade said.

"It's almost like it's personal now."

"The barn." Slade thought a moment. "Maybe what's driving them now is revenge for all the publicity about Fernando and then losing him."

"Hope he bunged them up pretty good when he got away."

Tater raised his head and whined as if in agreement.

"Let's ride out there," Slade said. "I want to take a look at the scene."

"Sheriff Calhoun already checked it."

"I know. And he found where they parked a cattle trailer on that back access road, cut the fence, lured the cattle into a temporary pen, loaded them up, and took off."

"He took impressions of the tire tracks."

"Just like before, for all the good it did," Slade said.

Oscar nodded.

"I've got to do something. Let's go."

"Okay. Maybe Tater'll pick up what nobody else did."

"If there's anything with a wrong scent, he'll find it," Slade said.

Tater put his nose in the air, got up, and turned toward the southeast pasture, obviously ready to go.

It didn't take long to mount up and head out, with Slade leading the way. He was anxious to get to the far pasture. He was missing something about the whole situation. It didn't make sense, but if he thought about it in the right way, it'd make perfect sense. He just needed to twist his mind around to the way the thieves were thinking, acting, doing. So far, he'd been thinking like a rancher. He needed to think like a rustler. Could he do it? So far, he'd been clueless…and it hurt his pride, as well as his family and ranches. Something had to give. If it didn't, he was going to break it, bend it, twist it till he got the answers he needed to bring it all to a grinding halt. He knew how to win, and he was going to do it—just as soon as he got the key to this particular lock.

He looked out across the ranch, mostly bedded down

for winter. He always enjoyed a ride over the land, particularly with a friend and dog by his side. It was a beautiful winter afternoon with the sun casting long shadows across the land from the west. They wore lightweight jean jackets, but it was all they needed for warmth even with a cool breeze stirring leaves in the live oaks. They scared up cottontail rabbits and crunched across golden, dry grass. He also watched the fence lines, noting that they all looked straight and solid and strong. Still, they were no match for wire cutters...or an enraged bull like Fernando.

When they arrived at the southeast pasture, he stopped, looking around to see the damage. Everything looked okay, but it wasn't even close to it.

"Cut fence is on the backside," Oscar said, heading that way. "From here, everything looks fine."

"I guess that's why it took a while to find the problem."

"That...and it's a big ranch."

"I need to be living here full time."

"After the cattle drive, everything should settle down."

"If we haven't caught the rustlers by then, I hate to even think of the added problems."

"No point getting ahead of ourselves."

"You're right." He kept watch as they rode onward, looking for something—anything—that might give him a clue to solving the problem.

Tater ran out ahead of them, chasing a rabbit or two, sniffing the ground here and there, acting perfectly normal.

Slade sighed. Nothing appeared out of the ordinary. Still, he looked at everything with suspicion in the back of his mind as they came up to the fence that had been cut near the road.

"Rustlers used wire cutters over here." Oscar rode up to the fence, tossed a leg over the saddle horn, and slid down from his horse. "Cowboys already repaired it, but here's the break."

Slade dismounted, ground tied the roan, and walked over for a closer look. "They removed an entire section, didn't they?"

"Those rustlers don't do nothing by half," Oscar said.

Slade could easily see where the cattle had trampled dry grass and left hoofprints in the dirt road where they'd been loaded onto a trailer. The entire operation had required cowboy skills. The rustlers weren't amateurs. Nothing else looked out of place. It was almost as if the thieves had snatched the cattle and disappeared into thin air. Still, he kept searching the ground, hoping against hope he'd spot something to help.

Tater suddenly raced past them, went under the fence, and stopped on the edge of the road. He sniffed the ground, then started pawing, digging, and spraying dirt out behind him. He came up with a crumpled piece of white paper between his teeth. He turned, trotted back, and laid the paper at Slade's feet before he sat down in front of Oscar, pink tongue hanging out.

"What's that?" Oscar asked, leaning closer to get a look.

Slade picked it up. "Looks like it was trampled into the dirt by sharp hooves. Whatever it is, it doesn't belong. It can't have been out here long. If it'd been in the rain, it'd be a mess. This is clean."

"Something's printed on it."

Slade gently pulled open the crumpled piece of paper—as if somebody had crushed it with a fist. "You've got to be kidding me."

"What is it?" Oscar leaned closer.

Slade grinned, smoothing out the flier that had been printed in full color. "I hadn't seen one of these, but I'd heard about them. Nathan at Thingamajigs printed these up and posted them across the county like you do for missing dogs and cats." He pointed at the flier. "Look, it's got a photo of Fernando and a map of the area with a big X on Steele Trap Ranch II."

"Don't that beat all," Oscar said. "Good idea."

"Now think about this flier being all over the place. Somebody with a vested interest saw it. Somebody got mad enough to crush it in a fist. Somebody threw it down at the very site of the latest cattle heist."

"Temper tantrum?"

"Yep. I wasn't completely sure, even after I heard that rancher's story. Now I'm pretty well convinced—Fernando got away."

Oscar patted Tater on the head. "Good dog. You found proof for us."

Tater looked up, tongue hanging out in a big smile.

"Best dog," Slade said with a grin. "And when Fernando got away, he didn't go easy. He fought. He injured. He escaped."

"And the rustlers were laid up to heal?"

"Reckon so." Slade poked the flier with a fingertip. "If what we're thinking is right, all the Fernando sightings in the past couple of weeks are real."

"And Fernando is the smartest, toughest bull I ever knew."

"He sure is." Slade carefully folded the flier and tucked it in his pocket, wishing he'd worn gloves because it was most likely a piece of evidence.

"What are we going to do?"

"Right now, we don't know who the rustlers are, so the next move is up to them. But I truly believe now that it's personal for them."

"Mad as wet setting hens."

"Mad...and embarrassed, too. Think about it— Fernando has made them look like fools. If they're mad, it means they're going off half-cocked and that means they're not thinking straight. Our edge."

Oscar chuckled, nodding in agreement. "They're not only fools—they're damn fools. They should've gotten out while the getting was good."

"That's right." Slade walked over to the roan, picked up the reins, and eased into the saddle. "We may not know who they are yet, but they'll show their hand one way or another. Fernando—bless his stout heart—is our ace in the hole."

"If we're right, and I hope we are," Oscar said, "they'll turn mean."

"They already did." Slade glared at the place where the rustlers had taken his cattle. "Granny's barn."

"Yeah. I saw her face. They got payback coming, don't they?" Oscar mounted up.

"They'll get it. With Fernando on the loose, there's no way they're leaving the county till they get him back...or give it a good try."

"And in Wildcat Bluff, they're on our turf."

"Right. Home team advantage," Slade said.

"Feels right in my bones." Oscar turned toward the barn.

"I'd never go against your bones. They've been right too many times to count."

"Smart cowboy."

"Let's just make sure we get Fernando home for Christmas."

Tater barked once, as if in agreement, then barreled out in front as Slade and Oscar followed him toward home.

Companionable silence descended as they rode, like they had many a time before, across the pasture. Slade's thoughts ran in circles even as he appreciated the natural beauty around him. All appeared peaceful, like winter evenings tended to be with chores done and cattle fed and folks headed to families. But that was only on the surface. Like the surface of a lake, below the calm stillness, life teemed, seethed, and roiled in the dark depths. He needed to dive below the surface to get at the truth. And soon.

When they arrived at the barn, Slade dismounted and looked around to see if anything had been damaged while he was gone. Place looked okay. Still, he no longer felt as if anything or anyone on his family's property was safe. It was an infuriating feeling, since he'd worked long and hard to make a happy, safe place for his nearest and dearest. And that now included Ivy.

He patted his pocket with the flier. At least he had a beginning to the ending to his problem. He just didn't know how, where, or when the end would come. Sooner than later, he hoped with all his being.

Oscar stood beside Tater, holding the reins to his horse. He appeared thoughtful as he glanced around the area.

"We need to up security," Slade said. "I'm not comfortable leaving the house and outbuildings unprotected at any time."

"I hear you."

"Electronic surveillance only gets us so far. I want feet on the ground."

"I'll see to it. Both ranches."

"Best arm the cowboys. We don't know how far the rustlers will escalate their attacks."

"You got it." Oscar patted Tater's head. "We leave the dogs out both places. Any intruders, they'll alert us."

"Okay. Security makes rounds with dogs at their sides."

"Right."

"And let's bring the cattle in from the far pastures."

"You got it."

"What else?" Slade glanced around again, wishing he could do more and hoping he hadn't forgotten anything.

"We can only do what we can do," Oscar said. "I'm about ready to trust Fernando to be our Christmas miracle."

Slade chuckled, appreciating his friend lightening the moment. "If he gets our problem tied up with a big red ribbon, he deserves the best feed money can buy."

"I'll go ahead and get it."

"Why not?" Slade glanced toward the road, thinking about Ivy and the new bed. He wished that was all he had on his mind. "Why don't you wrap it up and go home? I can finish here."

"Let's do it together. I'll put up the horses. You need to call Sheriff Calhoun and check on your grandmother."

"I won't complain. I'll lock up the house."

"Don't you have a gal waiting for you at the Park?" Oscar gave him a calculating look.

"Yeah. But—"

"Slade, we've known each other a long time. Don't mess up a good thing. Women need attention or they're apt to get a wandering eye."

"You'll get no argument from me."

"I got nobody waiting for me. Tater will help me lock up and set up schedules with the cowboys. You make your calls and go to Ivy. Not that I'm saying you're good enough for her, but she's a special lady, so don't let her get away."

"I won't...but sometimes I think Tater may not have all the intelligence in your duo."

Oscar laughed, patting Tater's head. "Don't believe it. He's the brains of the outfit."

Slade joined his laughter, then headed for his pickup. He'd make his calls, but after that, nothing could keep him away from Ivy. And the new bed.

Chapter 28

IVY PUT THE FINISHING TOUCHES ON HER NEW BED, smiling in pleasure. She'd transformed the cowboy rope-n-ride decor to cowgirl chic that better suited her own taste. After all, she had a new bed, so she needed a new look to go with it. Once the Settelmeyers installed the bed, she realized she needed queen-size sheets and a bedspread. She had the day off, since Wildcat Hall was closed one night a week, so she'd run into town. She'd struck retail gold almost immediately at Morning Glory's unique store.

A luxurious, rose-colored quilt embroidered with a pale-pink rose-blossom design now covered the bed. She'd arranged colorful throw pillows in the shapes of wildflowers on top of the new pillows. She still needed a queen headboard, but there'd be time to find that later. She'd even discovered a knitted, cotton throw in a deep purple that she'd tossed on the foot of the bed. All of it was handmade by local artisans, so she felt especially fortunate to be able to support them and enjoy their work at the same time.

In the midst of her happiness, she'd learned about the Steele Trap barn fire and cattle theft from Morning Glory. They'd both been horrified at the news but also confident the Steele family was strong enough to handle it. Still, she was now anxious for Slade to get to her, so she could comfort him and give him whatever he needed from her to feel better.

She wondered if he'd even spend the night. He might want to be with his family or at the ranches to take care of business. She'd support him in whatever he needed to do. That thought made her realize how far along the path she was to meshing her life with his in Wildcat Bluff.

She'd been running so hard and fast since she'd landed in the country that she hadn't really had time to think about just how easily she was fitting into the community and how much she was enjoying it. Country life was nothing like she'd expected when she'd lived in the city—beautiful scenery, supportive people, fascinating events, and a hot cowboy who offered her everything she could possibly want in a man. All in all, she was getting hooked and she knew it.

Maybe Fern had felt the same way. What she still didn't understand was why her sister had taken off so suddenly. If it hadn't been normal for her sister, she might have questioned it more. She'd just figured Fern had simply moved on with her life. Now she wondered about Craig—he wasn't a guy to throw away, not when it was obvious he was hurting from her sister's rejection. Something serious must have happened between them. Maybe someday Fern would tell her, but in the meantime, she'd just be supportive.

While her sister was on her mind, she picked up her phone and called her.

"I'm in between sets," Fern said, "so I've got a sec. What's up?"

"Just checking in to see how things are going."

"Same old, same old." Fern coughed, then cleared her throat. "I can't seem to shake this bug I picked up."

"Sorry. Lemon and honey water?"

"Helps some. No matter, I have to keep going."

"You could come here."

"Contract, remember?"

"Right," Ivy said.

"Tell me what's going on there. Do you like it?"

"It's starting to grow on me. I can see why you liked it."

"Good. I thought Wildcat Bluff would be great for you."

"We're gearing up for Christmas," Ivy said. "We're serving cookies and coffee in the front bar at the Hall now."

"Wonderful. How's it working out?"

"People love it."

"I'm so glad." Fern coughed again. "And the music?"

"Craig and his band are terrific, and folks love to dance to their sound."

"They're good, no doubt. And…and how's Craig doing?"

"I'm working with him on hiring bands."

"That's smart," Fern said. "Craig and I…well, we had lots of plans. I'm happy you're going forward with them."

"He's a terrific guy. I'm surprised—"

"Did he ask about me?"

"Yes. He hopes you're doing okay. He wishes you'd answer his texts."

"No new cowgirl in his life?"

"He's hung up on you—surely you know that."

"No. I don't know anything." Fern coughed harder. "Got to go. Duty calls." And she was gone.

Ivy sat there a moment, feeling a little concerned at the abrupt disconnection from her sister. Something had happened…something that made her sister run. If she had to guess, she'd think it had to do with Craig. Maybe when Fern came back, if she ever came back, she'd put the pieces of

Craig's heart back together. But Ivy wouldn't count on it, not yet. She just hoped Fern was truly okay.

For now, she was expecting Slade at any moment. While she'd waited for him, she'd taken a shower and slipped into a comfortable green yoga set and flip-flops, so she was all set to welcome him. He'd called to update her, but he hadn't said much about his day. She knew he wouldn't have had time to cook, and she thought he'd want comfort food, so she'd picked up a quart of chicken noodle soup and fresh rolls at the Chuckwagon. Plus two pieces of buttermilk pie. She hoped she'd chosen well. When she had time, she was going to cook for him...not that she was in his class, but she wasn't bad at it either. But that was for another time, when there was the leisure to relax and catch her breath.

She'd moved her laptop to the coffee table, so she could set the table. Now there was nothing to do but wait. She paced from the kitchen to the living area and back again. She stopped, picked up the Fernando flier she'd gotten in town, where they'd been available everywhere. She chuckled again at the way the legend of Fernando had captured everyone's imagination. Wildcat Jack was pushing the sightings, along with Storm and the Ranch Radio Rowdies. Folks were calling in with outrageous stories of Fernando's determination to get home for Christmas. People were posting about him and following him on Instagram. It was turning out to be fun for the holidays. She just hoped the bull was truly okay. Maybe Slade would have news when he got there. She set the flier back down so he would see it when he arrived, since she doubted he'd had a chance to get one.

She opened the front door and looked out again, hoping she'd see him walking up the path. She'd know him by his size alone, but if he was tired, she'd also know him by his slight limp. Everything about him had become so dear to her that she couldn't imagine how she'd lived without him. Sometime soon she'd have to make some hard decisions about her former life, but for now, she didn't want to think about it. She particularly didn't want to think about Peter having the Park on the market, so she shoved that thought away. No news was good news on that front. She just wanted to continue her amazing discovery of living in the country...with her very own personal cowboy firefighter.

She gave up, shut the door, and paced again. What if something had happened to Slade? No, she wouldn't think it. Anyway, surely someone in the Steele family would let her know if there'd been an accident, or... No, she wasn't going there. But it did make her realize that she had no claim as part of his life, at least none that was official. And he was in the same position with her. She felt uneasy at the idea. When it came to Fern, there was no question she'd be notified if something untoward happened to her. With Slade... No, she still wasn't going there. Everything between them was too new, too fresh, too unsettled to follow that line of thought. He was okay. He'd be with her soon.

She turned on the radio to fill the silence, wondering if there was updated news about Fernando.

"Remember...we're here for you at KWCB," Wildcat Jack growled over the airwaves. "We're rooting for you to be the next one to call in with a Fernando sighting. Never doubt he's on the move, making his way home in time for Christmas. And tune in to the five o'clock news on...pick your TV channel. Fernando is definitely making his mark."

Ivy just shook her head, wondering how that little bit

of an idea at the dance hall had turned into such a major event. She wished Fern were here, because she'd love the drama of it all and totally get involved in it. And now, how had Fernando's story become mega news? She'd definitely watch the news at five.

"And don't forget," Jack said, lowering his voice to a confidential tone, "to enter the contest that benefits Wildcat Bluff Fire-Rescue. Pay your bucks, guess the correct time to the closest second that Fernando gets home, and you'll win gift certificates from Old Town stores while helping our volunteer firefighters take care of us for another year. It's a win-win."

She switched off the radio as she felt her breath catch in her throat, a strong surge of emotion enveloping her. What an amazingly wonderful idea. Fernando was no longer just entertainment. Now he was helping support the county with donations in his honor. Her growing admiration for country folks ratcheted up another notch.

Maybe she should enter the contest. In fact, she would enter it. She'd be supporting not only the fire department, but also backing the idea that Fernando really was coming home. She wanted to believe in the big bull, even though she knew the possibility was slim for him ever coming back.

But for now, she just wanted Slade home, just like everybody was rooting for Fernando to come home. Tonight, for some reason, their lives were running parallel in her mind. Maybe Slade had learned something to give them hope.

She walked back to the front door and flung it open, needing Slade in her arms, needing to know he was safe, needing to comfort him. And there he was, walking with a slight limp up the path toward her. He was obviously tired, but he also walked with a little bounce in his step, as if he'd gotten good news, not bad. She didn't understand it, but she didn't care. He was home—that was all that mattered to her. She quickly stepped onto the porch, hurried down the stairs, and rushed toward him.

When he saw her, a big grin split his face, and he held out his arms.

She flung herself against him, holding him tight as he picked her up and she wrapped her legs around his waist.

"Miss me?"

"I thought you'd never get home."

"Worried?"

"Yes. Anything could've happened…and how would I have known? Who would have told me?"

"Good."

"What do you mean?"

He walked up the stairs with her wrapped around him, slammed the door shut behind them, and walked straight into the bedroom. He gently deposited her on top of the bed, then glanced around the room. "Looks fine. I like the colors."

"What did you mean?" Had she given away too much of how she felt about him with those few words? If so, did it matter anymore?

"I really like the bed. It's high enough I don't have to practically get down on my knees to sit on it."

"Slade, you're avoiding my question."

"Never." He sat down beside her and clasped her hand. "It's about time, you know."

"No, I don't know."

He stroked her wrist, raised her hand, and kissed her palm.

She shivered, feeling as if something had changed in the past few minutes. Was she ready for it? Could she ever be ready for the intensity of her feelings for him? Did he truly feel the same about her?

"If something happened to you, would Fern know to call me so I could take care of you?"

She felt dizzy, as if the room reeled around her. "But she's there and—"

"If you weren't here and something happened, how would I know? Would anybody contact me?"

"No, I guess not." He'd made his point, and it was a valid one.

"This is bigger than us," he said quietly. "We've been in our own little world, keeping everybody else out…except for a bit with my family."

She took a deep breath, realizing what she'd started with that question. "I'm sure your family would let me know."

"Yeah. But hospitals and—"

"Please, don't go there."

"I work a ranch. I fight fires. Accidents happen. If so, I'd want you with me…and I'd want you to walk into my room with the legal right to be there."

She flushed all over—rights came with responsibilities and permanency.

"Are you ready to go there?" He placed her palm against his cheek.

She felt the roughness of his beard after a long day.

"Are you?"

She set her hand down in her lap, withdrawing as she suddenly felt protective of herself.

"No?" He sighed as he glanced over at her. "I'm beginning

to think Fern isn't the only one in your family with commitment issues."

"It's not that."

"Isn't it?"

"It's just been so fast." She tried to defend her position, but she suspected he might very well be correct.

"When it's right, it's right."

"I know. It's just—"

"Look, I didn't mean to go here tonight. It's been a long day. Your question threw me. I thought… I hoped… Let's table this discussion for another time."

"Thank you." She just couldn't go there yet. "I really wanted to ask you if there was any news about Fernando."

He grinned, nodding his head. "Absolutely."

"Well, what? Don't hold out on me." She leaned toward him, wanting to know what was making him so happy.

"Come fall calving, there are going to be Little Fernandos running around a ranch near Honey Grove. At least, that's the story."

"You're kidding me." She stood up abruptly, unable to contain her energy.

"Jack had this rancher on the radio, describing Fernando's amorous attentions to several of his cows."

"How could he know it was Fernando?"

"He'd seen photos and heard the stories. Plus, he had a scanner."

"That's great news. When is he bringing Fernando home?"

"He's not. Fernando took off, so he's in the wind."

"Oh no. But at least we know he escaped the rustlers."

"I'm pretty sure of it now. And that's not the only reason."

He pulled a flier out of his pocket, unfolded it, showed it to her, then put it back.

"I wondered if you'd seen Nathan's flier."

"I found it wadded up and thrown down at the new cattle heist."

"That's odd." She sat down again, needing to be closer to him.

"Not if somebody got mad about losing Fernando."

"The barn... Revenge?"

"Maybe so."

"This escalation makes me uneasy."

"I'll keep you safe." He hugged her close.

"Thanks. But I'm concerned about more than me."

"I know. But we're all on higher alert now."

"Good. That reminds me. Jack said there's going to be a news report about Fernando on TV. It's almost five. Let's check a Dallas station on my laptop."

"Okay. It's probably about that Honey Grove rancher."

"But still...this Fernando story just keeps getting bigger."

"I never expected this kind of attention."

She stood up, clasping his hand. "Come on." She led him into the living room, where they sat down, side by side, on the sofa. She quickly pulled up a Dallas station on her laptop and leaned the screen back, so they could both watch.

"I know you've all been breathlessly waiting for a Fernando the bull update. And just how do I know that?" Jennifer Sales, the beloved news reporter with big hair and big smile, fluttered her eyelashes at the camera. "We're being overwhelmed here with your questions and comments about Fernando."

Ivy gasped, squeezing Slade's hand. "I had no idea."

"Me either."

"Today, horses broke loose in Fannin County west of Bonham," Jennifer said with a smile. "We're lucky a cowboy caught this shot of Fernando and sent it to us."

Ivy watched in amazement as a blurry video appeared on her screen of downed fences, fifty or more mustangs running loose, cowboys riding down on them, and out ahead of the mayhem a big, black bull trotted west, trailing a red rope and tail switching as he went as if it was all in a day's work of freeing other critters, and disappeared into a thick stand of cedar trees.

Slade laughed, pointing at the screen. "If that's Fernando, he's a lot smarter than I ever gave him credit for."

"What's he doing?"

"Fence probably got in his way. Looks like he's treating the countryside as if it's open range. And with his size and strength, he can do it."

"But won't the cowboys catch him?"

"I doubt they broke off corralling their horses for one lone bull. Besides, they know it's dangerous to take on a bull his size."

"Why is that?"

"If he's mad, he can put his head under a horse and toss the horse and rider into the air. There'd be serious damage."

"I had no idea."

"Most folks don't. But cowboys do."

"How will all those looking for him catch him?"

"It'd take a team of ropers working together with a portable pen and transport nearby. He'd be safer if he was caught."

"I don't want him hurt."

"So far he's doing fine on his own. Hopefully, that reward will keep him safe, if nothing else."

"Good." She closed her laptop, turning to Slade and taking his hand.

He smiled at her, nodding as if in answer to her unspoken question.

"I'm glad you're home."

"You can't imagine how glad I am to be here…and to know you were here waiting for me."

"Dinner's ready. I got chicken noodle soup from the Chuckwagon."

"Thanks. But I don't want soup."

"You're not hungry?"

"I'm starving…but only for you."

She just melted, leaning into him, feeling his arm go around her shoulders, knowing she was so lucky to have him in her life.

"I've been waiting all day to try out the bed." He slipped the green ponytail holder off her hair, letting the long strands fall free, and slipped the elastic onto his wrist. "Are you going to make me wait any longer?"

"I've been waiting for you all day long, too." She said it with a breathiness that belied every roadblock she'd ever thrown between them.

He smiled, gently tucking a strand of hair behind her ear as he leaned forward and kissed her earlobe, then slowly traced the whorls of her ear with the tip of his tongue. He pressed kisses with slow intent all the way to her mouth, where he licked and nibbled, tasting her as if she were the finest of sweet ingredients. When she moaned, returning his kiss as she felt hot embers build between them, he thrust deep with his tongue…and set her on fire.

She shuddered from head to toe at this sensual sensation,

feeling heat roil through her till it centered between her legs and made her burn with need for him. He kissed down the side of her neck until he reached the base of her throat, where he lingered, toying with the indentation as he slipped his hands under her top, lowered her bra, and cupped her breasts, massaging until he created taut tips, while he built—layer upon layer—a tower of blazing passion.

He led her into the bedroom, giving her hot looks with his blue eyes. "You ready to make the bed our own?"

She just gave him a smile before she grasped the front of his shirt and jerked, snapping open the buttons all the way down to his belt buckle.

"I guess that's a yes."

She chuckled as she pressed her palms flat against his chest, felt his nipples harden under her touch, and slowly moved upward, feeling the soft hair, the smooth skin, the rapid beat of his heart.

"Keep that up and the bed will get a fast initiation."

"Fast is good," she said in a voice gone husky with desire.

He stood up, jerked his shirttail out, tossed his shirt on the floor, and reached for his belt buckle.

She smiled in satisfaction at the sight and rose to her feet. She quickly set the throw pillows in the rocker, then pulled back the quilt to reveal smooth, pink sheets. She liked the color, partly because it'd be such a contrast to Slade's masculinity.

She let her gaze linger on him stripping down before she couldn't wait any longer and kicked off her flip-flops. She started to pull her top off, but he was naked before her and came to her side. He didn't say a word as he slipped the top up and over her head, then unhooked her bra, drew it down her arms, and tossed it aside. He cupped her breasts, tracing patterns over them till she was covered in goose bumps. He lowered her yoga pants, then slipped down her thong until she stood naked, shivering from his touch, his intent...her need.

"You're so beautiful." He clasped her hand and led her over to the bed.

She sat down and leaned back, letting her head rest against the new, plump pillow.

"Perfect." He opened a drawer of the nightstand, extracted a foil packet, and put on protection.

"Yes, perfect." She felt such a cascade of emotions that she didn't know where one ended and another began... until a powerful tapestry of all the ways to love and be loved merged into a single image—Slade Steele. And she knew she'd fallen hard.

When he leaned over her, she opened her arms, her legs, and pulled him down to her. She needed to be joined with him, burned to be completed by him...wanted it more than anything she'd ever wanted in her life. She trembled when he slipped inside her, and she clutched him with her legs, riding him as he thrust deeper and harder and faster. She cried out, gripping his shoulders as she spiraled higher and higher...and then she heard him groan in pleasure as they reached ecstasy and hung in midair for a long, exultant moment together.

He pressed a tender kiss to her lips. "I love you."

"You aren't alone." Tears of happiness filled her eyes. "I'm in this with you all the way."

Chapter 29

EARLY THE NEXT MORNING, IVY SAT ON THE SOFA LOOK-
ing at her glittery Christmas tree while Slade started coffee
in the kitchen. She had pretty presents under her tree in bags
and boxes she'd bought the day before at Morning's Glory
and Adelia's Delights. She'd be giving them all away, but for
now, she simply took pleasure in looking at them and knowing her new friends would enjoy them on Christmas.

New friends. She was still a little amazed at the idea of
having friends in Wildcat Bluff County. It'd happened so
fast. She'd always thought life in the city was fast, but so far,
life in the country was even faster. She glanced at Slade as
he poured coffee into two mugs. Fast, yes, but oh so right.

He sat down beside her and handed her a mug.

"Thanks."

"Not much to eat here."

"That's okay. I'll get coffee and cookies down at the Hall
later."

"Sugar cookies?" He chuckled as he took a sip of coffee.

"When did I ever not like sugar cookies?" She couldn't
resist teasing him. "But the cowboy cookies are good."

He laughed, leaned over, and kissed her. "I get it. You
like cookies. You just don't care for the charred ones."

"That's so true." She patted his jean-clad knee, then
stroked it, feeling the hard muscle contract under her touch.
"I do care a great deal for the new bed."

"The bed or the activity on the bed?"

She stroked the inside of his thigh, up and down, up and down. "What do you think?"

"It's a fine bed." He covered her hand with his own, urging her higher. "But it'd be nothing without you."

"We made it all our own, didn't we?"

"We created enough heat to brand it. That's for sure."

She leaned in close for another kiss.

He obliged, then stood up, cradling his mug in both hands. "If we don't stop now, we'll be right back in that bed."

"Quickie?"

He shook his head. "Not enough...not nearly enough for me."

She nodded, understanding as she sipped her coffee. "Guess we don't have that kind of time, do we?"

"I need to get to work, but I wanted to mention something before I left."

"Not much time to talk last night, was there?"

He chuckled, blue eyes alight. "Our focus was on the bed."

"And Fernando." She contemplated her coffee a moment, then looked at Slade. "I'm thinking of making a map of Fernando sightings and putting it up on his Instagram page. He's getting lots of likes and DMs...and not just from our state. I can add to the map to show everyone where he is in Texas as he makes his way home for Christmas."

"Great idea."

"Good. I'll get it put up today." She glanced at the kitchen. "We never did eat that soup. Are you sure you aren't hungry?"

"I'll get something later. And you can have the soup."

"Thanks. I'll eat it for lunch." She wrapped her hands around her mug, enjoying the warmth. "What did you want to tell me?"

"With everything going on with Fernando, the rustlers, and the fires, I want you to be more careful than ever."

"Do you think I'm in danger here?"

"I'm worried about you."

"We've done all we can about security."

"Right. Still, I don't want you walking home at night alone. Wait for me and I'll bring you here or to my place."

"That's not convenient for you."

"You're too important to take a chance. Besides, surely it'll all be over by Christmas."

"I'll be careful, but I want you to be cautious, too."

"I'll do my best."

She glanced around the room, no longer feeling quite so secure in her cozy nook of a cowboy cabin.

"You're safe in here. I'd never let anything happen to you."

"Thanks." She wrapped an arm around his waist and leaned into him. "But we can't let those rustlers ruin Christmas."

"No, we can't."

She straightened up, then stood and walked across the room. She picked up the Fernando flier, looked at it, and dropped it back on the countertop.

"What is it?"

"With so much going on this Christmas weekend, I'm concerned Wildcat Hall may get lost in the mix. We might even lose business."

"You mean Christmas in the Country in Old Town and Christmas at the Sure-Shot Drive-In in Sure-Shot?"

"Yes. They're such big, popular, well-known events. And now Fernando fever is taking up a lot of attention."

"We talked about a chili contest for a couple of weekends, so people could vote on their favorite."

"If I'm going to do it, I need to get started right away with promotion and invitations."

"Maybe you need to forego the contest this year and go straight to serving up good chili."

She nodded, thinking about it. "You may be right. There's just so much to do, and I'm still on a learning curve."

"What about something more unusual to draw tourists to the Hall for Christmas?"

"I've been thinking about it." She paced back to him, too agitated to stay settled anywhere. "Craig and I have been talking bands and dancing as a draw."

"But that's what's always there."

"I know." She looked out the front window, then turned back. "What about another event that can be promoted as special, too? I mean, could the area handle another one?"

"If it's at night, why not? What do you have in mind?"

"I thought some folks who didn't go to the traditional Christmas events might like something special at a honky-tonk. And like you say, it'd be a place to gather at night."

He nodded, smiling thoughtfully. "I see where you're going with this and I like it. But what makes it special?"

She shrugged, feeling as if she was groping toward something that she couldn't understand or see yet.

"Maybe the dance hall and beer garden are special in their own right."

"What do you mean?"

"Think back. Folks here originally would have met in

their community center, as well as their churches, to celebrate Christmas."

"Do you mean we dress up in period costumes and serve food and drink they would have had back then?"

"They dress like that in Old Town for Christmas in the Country."

"In that case, we'd fit right in with costumes. I believe it could work." She felt renewed energy at the idea. "I knew you'd be a big help with this worry of mine."

"Glad to help. I suggest you talk with Hedy and Morning Glory. Granny and Mom, too. They have access to old photographs and have participated in our Christmas events forever."

"I'm getting really excited about this, but it needs a name, like the other events, if we're going to make it distinctive."

"Right. What do you suggest?"

"Let me think." She paced across the room, then back again, thinking furiously. "Simple is usually best."

"I agree." He smiled at her with encouragement.

She stopped and looked at him, fixing him in her mind as her handsome, blond, tall, muscular cowboy. But that was simply his physical beauty. He was so much more…and that was what really drew her to him. He was kind and smart and strong. And still that didn't do him justice. He was just so much more of everything than she'd ever known before in her life. She really did adore him.

"What?" He looked at her in confusion, as if he'd caught the play of emotions across her face.

"I think you're a keeper." And she gave him a hot, hot look that promised a workout on their new bed later.

"Don't look at me like that or I'll never leave you."

She glanced away, teasing him, and just like that it struck her. "Wildcat Hall's Honky-Tonk Christmas."

"Simple. Direct. To the point. I like it."

"Thanks. I can design fliers and get them printed up."

"Local businesses will distribute them for you. Everyone is supportive of each other in Wildcat Bluff."

"That'd be perfect. And I can promote on the website."

"Talk to Hedy. She'll see that it gets listed on the town's website, even at this late day."

"Better yet." She hesitated, suddenly struck by the enormity of this new job. "But can I get it all done in time?"

"Don't worry. You can do it."

"But there's so much to do in such a short amount of time."

"I've got faith in you."

"Thanks. But—"

"No buts. Keep in mind, you have lots of support. Talk with the Settlemeyers. If anybody can help pull this together quickly, they're the ones to do it. They probably have costumes, for that matter."

"Good idea. I'll talk with them. I think I'll give Fern a call, too. She's always good with show-biz stuff and definitely this qualifies for that area of expertise." Another thought struck her. "What about a honky-tonk dance contest?"

"Great idea. How would it work?"

"It'd be like a dance off. We would have several different contests with a special name for each one. We could give out trophies to the winner of each contest. This fits with the dance hall, too."

He nodded, smiling as he stood up. "Ought to be a big draw."

"I hope so. I'll talk with Craig about putting together a

playlist to go with the contest names." She grinned, chuckling. "For sure we need a country version of 'Honky Tonk Women' made so famous by the Rolling Stones."

"I agree. Let me know if you want help coming up with contest names. That'll be fun to do."

"I absolutely want you involved every step of the way."

"That's what I want, too."

"Thanks." She slid her hands up his broad chest and rose on her tiptoes so she could kiss him.

"Call me or text me if you need anything else or just want to discuss something. I'm always there for you."

"I will." She stepped back to give him room. "You better go, hadn't you?"

"Yeah. I've got my own issues piling up, but I have good help, too."

She walked over and opened the front door. "I'm not going to keep you a moment longer, even if—"

"I don't want to go. You can be sure of that."

"I know. I'm just glad we stole an evening in our new bed."

"Those memories will keep me going all day long."

"Me, too."

He enfolded her in his arms, held her close for a long moment, then pressed a soft kiss to her lips before he quickly crossed the porch, jogged down the stairs, and walked away.

She watched him, feeling the loss even though she knew she'd talk to him and see him later. She couldn't turn away, not when he was still visible. When he was almost lost to view, he turned back and waved at her with a big grin. She returned his wave and felt her loss lift. They couldn't ever be separated, not by distance or work or anything else.

She stepped back inside, shutting and locking the door behind her. She had to turn her mind to work, but Slade would stay in her heart.

Chapter 30

NINE DAYS BEFORE CHRISTMAS, IVY SAT ON A STOOL IN the immaculate kitchen, updated and upgraded with stainless steel, of the Chuckwagon Café. She held a signed copy of Carolyn Brown's *The Red-Hot Chili Cook-Off* turned to the section with the crazy chili recipe that she was determined to serve at Wildcat Hall.

Slade stood in front of the commercial range. Lula Mae watched him from nearby with narrowed eyes. Storm was too excited to sit or stand still, so she kept flitting here and there. Sydney had left with Dune for a Christmas in the Country committee meeting. They'd commandeered the kitchen after hours, so there was no one to interrupt their "experiment," as Slade insisted on calling the chili recipe.

"I still don't see why you can't serve our regular chili." Slade glanced over his shoulder.

"It's a secret recipe," Lula Mae said, "and everybody loves it."

"But everybody in town, probably the entire county, eats it on a regular basis." Ivy wasn't sure she'd ever get her point across, although she kept trying to explain why she wanted her own special chili.

"That's the point," Lula Mae said. "They like it."

"I like new and different," Storm piped up. "So does Fernando."

Slade looked back again. "What does he have to do with chili?"

"Nothing, I guess." Storm shrugged, looking down at her ratty sneakers. "It's just that he's not home yet. I'm worried about him."

"We all are, but we're still getting sightings as he parallels eighty-two, moving west," Slade said.

"But will he be home in time for Christmas?" Storm asked, sounding sad. "It's a long way on foot."

"You're not losing faith, are you?" Slade asked.

Storm straightened her shoulders. "Never. I just wish he'd get here."

"We all do." Ivy felt her heart go out to the little girl who was worrying about Fernando, even as she tried to keep up spirits and interest by talking about him on the Den.

"I put good money on that bull's nose," Lula Mae said, smiling. "I could sure use those gift certificates for Christmas."

"Granny, we all guessed the time he'll arrive, so you have stiff competition. Anyway, didn't you finish your shopping yet?" Slade chuckled as he turned back to the big stainless pot set over blue flames on the gas stovetop.

"You know good and well I'm a last-minute kind of gal."

"Just don't lose the Christmas list I gave you," Storm said.

Lula Mae cocked her head, giving Storm a considering look. "Are you sure that's your complete list?"

"Yes! But don't forget Fernando. He's gonna have a growly tummy by the time he gets home."

"Oscar already bought him special feed," Slade said.

"A big bull like Fernando can never have too many oats." Storm gave them a stern look.

"True." Slade glanced at Lula Mae with a smile.

"I've never lost one of your lists yet, have I?" Lula Mae asked.

"No…but there's always a first time for everything," Storm said, tapping her toe on the tile floor.

"That's sure the truth of it." Slade glanced at Ivy, letting her know he was thinking about them.

She nodded in agreement.

"Wait! It's past news time. Maybe there's a Fernando update." Storm grabbed the remote control and turned on the flat screen on the wall.

Jennifer Sales smiled sadly at the camera. "In other news, there was a six-pickup pileup on the west side of 75, just north of Sherman. Fortunately, no one was hurt, but here is the chaotic scene from earlier today."

A visual popped up on the TV of an aerial view that showed mangled trucks, drivers standing around angrily jawing at each other, and frequently pointing west, as if that was the direction of their problem.

"We have an on-site interview to share with you," Jennifer said with a smile, as if suppressing a secret.

The camera focused on a cowboy in black felt hat, red shirt, Wranglers, and black boots. He looked mad as he leaned toward the mic pointed at his face. "I tell you a big, black Angus bull ran across the road like the hounds of hell were after him. He was dragging a long red rope. I can tell you right now a rope like that is dangerous for a bull if he steps on it or gets it caught on something. Anyway, I slammed on my brakes not to hit him…and it all went bad from there."

"Where did he go?" the interviewer asked.

"Don't know. Don't care. But the rancher that owns him ought to be liable for letting a fine bull like that roam free. It's dangerous for the bull…and us."

"Do you suppose that might have been Fernando trying to get home for Christmas?"

"Who?"

"Haven't you heard about the rustled bull that's trying to get back to his ranch?"

"You're kidding me."

"No. It's all over TV, radio, and the internet."

"Never heard of him. But if that's the case and that was the bull, then the rustlers are liable for the damage."

"Good point. I'm sure it will be taken under consideration by authorities. Thank you so much for your time and trouble." The interviewer turned to the camera. "Folks, I do believe we have another Fernando sighting. The Honey Grove rancher roped Fernando with a red rope, so that is the giveaway here. This means Fernando is in Grayson County now, heading for Wildcat Bluff County. If you feel called to do so, please leave out feed along his route north of 82 to help this big, brave bull make it home to Steele Trap II Ranch in time for Christmas."

"Thank you for that exciting news," Jennifer said as the camera focused on her face. "Fernando is so smart and strong, nobody can catch him. And he has one thing on his mind. He wants to get home to celebrate Christmas with a little girl named Storm who is anxiously awaiting him."

A photograph of Storm and Fernando flashed on the screen, showing the tow-headed Storm dressed in pink, standing close to the big Angus.

"And if you're so inclined," Jennifer continued, "Wildcat Bluff County celebrates Christmas in a big way with Christmas in the Country, Christmas at the Sure-Shot Drive-In, and Wildcat Hall's Honky-Tonk Christmas. You might want to check out the events...or throw your hat in the ring to guess the time that Fernando will arrive home at the ranch. Proceeds benefit the volunteer Wildcat Bluff Fire-Rescue."

Jennifer smiled at the camera. "And in other news…"

Storm clicked off the television before she turned around with a frown on her face. "That's not the best picture of Fernando. He's way more handsome."

"He looked very handsome," Ivy said. "It's a photo you gave me for Instagram."

"Maybe I could find a better one."

"I hope I'm not liable for that six-pickup pileup," Slade said with a big sigh. "But I'm glad to know Fernando is still safe and sound."

"If we catch the rustlers, liability may be their problem." Ivy did her best to soothe Slade.

"The pileup is a shame," Lula Mae said. "But nobody was hurt and truck dings can be fixed. The important thing is Fernando got across that big divided highway in one piece. He is a smart one."

"And fast." Storm smiled at everyone. "But I'm worried about that red rope."

"He'll lose it soon enough," Slade said. "It'll either come loose or he'll scrape it off on a tree branch or remove it some other way."

"I hope it's right away."

"Yeah. Me, too." Slade agreed. "Now I'm thinking we have another problem."

"What?" Ivy asked.

"After that kind of TV publicity, how many people do you think are going to descend on the county for our Christmas events? Can we even handle them?"

"We'll cross that bridge when we come to it," Lula Mae

COWBOY FIREFIGHTER CHRISTMAS KISS 297

said. "For now, it looks like your chili is boiling and that's our first order of business tonight."

"Right." Slade grabbed a large, long-handled, stainless spoon. "Let's start messing up the best chili in North Texas."

"We're not going to mess it up unless you've already done it," Ivy said, pointing at her open book. "It says right here that the ladies started making their chili with a gallon can of store-bought chili."

"And I told you there's no way I'll go near store bought. We use my chili or we don't do this at all."

"Okay." She tossed a frown at his back. "If that's the way you want it, I guess that's what we'll have to do."

"No point in trying to change his mind," Lula Mae said. "He's been hardheaded since he was born."

"I thought that was me." Storm pointed at her chest, giggling.

"You, too." Lula Mae grinned at her granddaughter. "Runs in the family."

"That's the truth of it," Slade replied. "Now, can we get on with this mess? I sincerely doubt it'll be edible by the time we're through with it. I mean, you ought to listen to a cook, not an author, when you want good chili."

"You might as well give it up and get on with it. You're not the only hard head in the room." Lula Mae laughed as she walked over and peered into the pot. "It looks about right to add the new ingredients."

"Let me help." Storm ran over to the countertop and started touching one item after another that had been set there.

"Best not get in between Ivy and her culinary creation," Slade said, glancing at the row of products.

"You can help." Ivy stepped up beside Storm and picked

up a can of beer. She pulled the tab and slowly poured it into the chili while he stirred the whole time.

"Waste of good beer," Slade said.

"Let's just wait and see." Ivy checked the next ingredient in the book, then set it on the countertop out of the way. She measured and added a half a cup of Worcestershire sauce and four tablespoons of liquid smoke to the chili.

Slade keep stirring the pot, looking interested but skeptical.

"Okay." Ivy picked up the book again and turned to the page marked with a sticky note. "Next comes two cans of chili beans and eight ounces of chopped jalapeño peppers."

"I've got those ready to go." Lula Mae picked up the ingredients from the countertop and dumped them into the pot with a chuckle.

Ivy checked her book again to make sure she put everything into the chili in the right order. She didn't know if it'd make a difference to go out of order, but she was taking no chances. She spooned six teaspoons each of chili powder and Cajun seasoning into the mix, feeling moist heat on her face from the chili. "Smells good."

"So far so good," Slade said as he returned to stirring the mixture.

"Okay, I'm putting in the last ingredient." Ivy closed the book and tucked it under her chin. She pulled open a gallon bag of cooked hamburger meat, leaned over, and dumped it in the pot. But as she did so, the book slipped from under her chin and headed for the pot.

Slade tried to catch it, but he was too slow.

The paperback hit the edge of the pot, slid down the side, and landed next to the flames where it promptly caught fire.

"Oh no!" Ivy cried out, reaching out to save her book.

Slade pushed her hand aside. "That book's not worth getting burned over."

"But it's my signed copy of *The Red-Hot Chili Cook-Off*."

"I don't care if it's gilded in gold." He used his spoon to knock the flaming paperback onto the floor.

"Don't put out the fire with water. It'll ruin the pages." She watched in horror as the pretty, colorful cover turned black while the edges curled up.

"It's burning to a crisp. What's a little water?" Slade said. "Besides, it's about to burn down the kitchen."

"Can't we save it?"

"What do you think?" He stomped on the book with his boot, breaking the spine and crushing the pages.

"That's one hot chili recipe," Lula Mae said with a chuckle.

"Not my fault." Slade looked at the mess, then glanced at Ivy. "Sorry about your book, but I had to put out the fire."

"You didn't have to stomp it to pieces." She bent down and reverently picked up the broken remains.

"I'll buy you a new one."

"Signed copies aren't easy to come by."

"Where does the author live? I'll go get her to sign a new book."

"I'm sure her address isn't public knowledge, or everybody would be at her door wanting signatures."

"Uncle Slade," Storm hollered. "Chili's about to boil over."

He wheeled around, grabbed a spoon, and started stirring fast as he turned off the flame. "That was close. At this rate, we're going to trash the whole kitchen."

"It's just one little accident," Ivy said, gently holding the remains of the book. "Could I get a baggie for it?"

Slade glanced at her. "Trash is over there."

"Never."

"Do you want to bury it on the ranch?" Storm asked. "We can all go to the funeral and you can say a few words about what a good book it was."

"Thanks," Ivy said, smiling. "For now, I think I'll just take it home."

"Here's a baggie." Lula Mae handed her a small zippered, transparent bag.

"I guess that size is all I need since there's not too much left of my book."

"That's what I thought."

"I'm not attending any funeral for a book." Slade stirred the chili harder. "It's bad enough I had to make the chili."

Ivy held the bag protectively to her chest as she walked over and looked into the big pot. "Wasn't there another ingredient?"

"Uh...uh, maybe," Storm mumbled as she backed away.

Ivy looked over and saw chocolate staining her mouth. "The chocolate bar! You're eating the secret ingredient."

"I got hungry," Storm said as she pushed what was left of the bar with a fingertip toward Ivy. "And it's a big bar—supersize. I only ate a little bit."

"I'll stuff your Christmas stocking with candy bars," Slade said, chuckling. "I doubt we need any chocolate in the chili."

"I told you, it said right in the book that chocolate is the secret ingredient. We've got to have it. Hopefully, this will be enough. If not, Slade, you'll have to raid Christmas stockings or presents."

"I think it'll do." He stepped back and motioned to the

pot. "Go ahead and add the secret ingredient that isn't so secret anymore."

"All our lips are sealed," she said.

"How can it be secret if it was printed in thousands of books?" Storm asked, appearing puzzled.

Ivy paused in the process of ripping off the candy wrapper. "Good point. It's a secret in the book, but not here." She walked up to the pot, looked down at the red mixture, and sniffed the pungent scent. "Smells good." She quickly broke off sections of chocolate, tossed them into the pot, and stirred the chili, watching dark swirls disappear as the chocolate blended into the red.

"Who's going to try it first?" Lula Mae asked. "Any volunteers?"

"Not me," Storm said. "I'm full of chocolate."

"It's Ivy's masterpiece." Slade glanced down at the chili, shaking his head. "She ought to do the honors."

"I'll be happy to be first," Ivy said. "After all, a book gave its life for this chili, so somebody ought to be appreciative."

"Do you want a bowl?" Lula Mae asked.

"She won't need a bowl," Slade said. "Get her a spoon. One bite will do it."

Storm opened a drawer, pulled out a teaspoon, and handed it to her. "Good luck."

"Thanks." Ivy set her book down well away from the stove, then walked over. Had she been foolish to insist on following a recipe out of a novel? No. She trusted the author. She dipped her spoon into the chili, filled it, raised it to her mouth, and hesitated, feeling eyes on her. She glanced over. Slade, Lula Mae, and Storm leaned forward, earnest expressions on their faces.

"You don't have to do it." Slade held up a hand as if to stop her. "We can throw out the whole mess."

"It's not that the added ingredients are bad," Lula Mae said. "It's just an odd combination."

"We know the chocolate's good." Storm gave an encouraging thumbs-up.

Ivy blew on the chili, started to just touch it with the tip of her tongue, then decided to go all the way. She plunged the spoon into her mouth and pulled it out completely clean. Taste hit her—hot, smoky, spicy with a back burn as it slid down her throat. She started to smile, then it turned into a full-out grin.

"What?" Slade asked. "Is it good or are you teasing us?"

Lula Mae set out a tray and put four bowls, three spoons, four napkins, and four bottles of water on it. "Let's retire to the dining room. From the look on Ivy's face, we may very well have a winner. I'll be the first to admit I'm wrong if that's the way it turns out."

"You've got to be kidding me," Slade said. "If that author is a better cook than me, I'll—"

"Eat your hat, Uncle Slade?" Storm giggled as she sniffed the big pot of chili. "I hope it's good, so we didn't waste the chocolate."

He quietly filled the bowls, then carried the tray into the dining room with everyone following him.

When they were seated around the table, Ivy dipped her spoon into her big bowl of chili, hesitating as she waited for their verdict. She watched as first Lula Mae took a bite. Slade followed her. Storm came last.

"It's great!" Storm dug into the chili in her bowl.

Lula Mae nodded in agreement. "You've got a winner."

"I agree," Slade said, grinning.

"Do you admit now that authors make good cooks?" Ivy smiled at him, enjoying her victory and teasing him.

"I wouldn't go quite that far, but this is a good chili recipe."

"It's so different than our recipe," Lula Mae said thoughtfully. "But that's the great thing about chili. There are about as many favorite recipes as there are people in the state of Texas."

"True," Slade said, agreeing.

"Does this mean y'all don't have any objections to making and serving this chili at Wildcat Hall?" Ivy looked around the group again.

"Not a one," Lula Mae said. "In fact, it's smart if we have one chili here at the Chuckwagon and you serve another at the Hall."

"As much as I hate to admit I was wrong, I was, so I'm on board, too." Slade tapped the edge of his bowl with his spoon. "I like cooking new recipes. It's fun, like tonight. I just may start coming up with new chili recipes for the Chuckwagon."

"Count me in," Lula Mae said. "New projects keep us young."

Storm frowned around the group. "Stay young all you want, but I'm telling you it's not all it's cracked up to be."

As everyone laughed, Ivy glanced around the group, feeling her heart grow warm as she sat in the midst of this family. They were special, like the chili recipe...with just the right amount of unique ingredients.

"Enjoy it while you can." Lula Mae reached over and squeezed her granddaughter's hand. "Growing up isn't all it's cracked up to be either, but it does have its compensations."

Ivy met Slade's gaze, and they silently communicated just how strong and wonderful that compensation could be in a couple's life.

Storm set down her spoon. "I've decided it's the secret ingredient that makes this chili special. And it's a good thing I ate those pieces of chocolate, or it would have thrown off the whole recipe."

"In that case," Ivy said, chuckling, "we'll need you to eat a few pieces of chocolate from every bar before we add it to the chili."

"Just what I had in mind." And Storm gave a big grin.

Chapter 31

SLADE SAT ON A STOOL AT THE END OF THE BAR IN Wildcat Hall. Christmas was only four days away. He was trying to think if he'd forgotten anything vital. Of course, Fernando wasn't back, so that was a worry, but if he was still on foot, he couldn't have made it yet—not at five miles a day. Slade was surprised the bull hadn't been caught by all the cowboys and cowgirls looking for him, but perhaps they'd tried and hadn't known how to handle him. Maybe that was his good bloodline, because he had to be super smart to get away from the kidnappers in the first place. In any case, Slade kept his phone with him at all times just in case somebody called him about Fernando.

He just hoped against hope Fernando somehow made it safely back by Christmas, or a little girl named Storm was going to be devastated in a way that no amount of gifts could fix. For that matter, thousands of folks rooting for Fernando, checking Ivy's map of sightings every day and leaving lots of hearts on Instagram as the big bull made his way across North Texas, would be deeply disappointed, too. They all needed—and wanted—a Christmas miracle.

He'd spoken with Mr. Reynolds and learned he was a straight-talking, no-nonsense rancher. Slade had turned down the generous offer of one of the calves come fall as a stud fee. He'd simply explained that it was Christmas come early and to enjoy the new cattle bloodline. They'd parted ways friends and vowed to keep in touch. Fernando was proving that he had a way of bringing folks together during this special time of year.

Ivy's book chili had been an instant success. Now it was a popular staple, along with the Settelmeyer corn fritters and Christmas cookies. They were great cooks, and Slade was glad they were picking up the slack, because he could only be in one place at a time. Everything was coming together just fine—so well, in fact, that it worried him. They hadn't even been plagued by cattle rustlers, so maybe the extra security made the difference. Still, he figured at some point, something had to break. He only hoped he was there when it happened so he could pick up the pieces.

He didn't want to go there tonight. All the long months of planning were coming together, and starting tomorrow he'd be up way before dawn to begin the cattle drive. They'd received permission, since mostly just dirt roads or ranch roads were allowed for cattle anymore, to drive three hundred head of cows, no calves or bulls, up Wildcat Road the five miles from Steele Trap to Steele Trap II. It'd take all day, but they could do it.

He needed to be at his best for the cattle drive. Everybody did. A lot was at stake and a lot was invested in it. People were coming from all over to watch and participate. Fernando had fired their imaginations, and they wanted to be part of the trail drive, along with the other Wildcat Bluff County Christmas events. If everything went well, they would all come out winners. Anything else was unacceptable. But for now, he just wanted to be with Ivy until he walked her home.

He watched her work the bar with Alicia, looking like

she'd always been there. She'd adapted so quickly that he was still a little surprised that she'd picked up the business and endeared herself to so many people so fast. Yet that was the way of his Ivy—*his* was the important word. And he belonged to her. He'd known it the first time he saw her and the feeling had only increased every day since that first moment.

He wanted to pop the question—the big one—to her. But was it too soon? Was she ready? Would it scare her clear back to Houston? He'd get no complaints from his family, because they adored her, along with their friends and the community at large. What he really wanted so badly that he ached from it was to build a life with her that stretched into an endless future filled with love, laughter, and bassinets.

Should he get a ring? He didn't know what to get, because she didn't wear much jewelry. He'd hate to get the wrong style. He could ask Sydney, since she was sporting a pretty, sparkly ring on her left hand—or maybe he should ask Dune, since he'd gotten it for Slade's sister. Still, he wanted this to be personal, something they did together. Maybe he ought to just get her a Christmas present, but again, he hadn't a clue what to get her. If she was a cowgirl, he'd know what to buy. Maybe he should consult with Morning Glory, since she was the de facto good-taste guru in Wildcat Bluff. Plus, she got people, so she understood their wants and needs in a way he'd never be able to do, not in the way he could handle horses and cattle or a good recipe. He guessed everybody had their special gifts, including Ivy, with her ability to create websites and draw people to her.

"More coffee?" Ivy stopped in front of him, smiling with warmth in her clear green eyes.

"I'm good. Thanks."

"Hey, y'all, let's catch the news," Alicia called as she turned on the wall-mounted television above the bar.

"Good evening." Jennifer Sales smiled at her viewers. "We know you're all watching and wondering and waiting for news about Fernando. I have good news for you. He was sighted north of Whitesboro at a golf course today. Golfers sent us videos shot on their cell phones and we're happy to share them with you now."

Slade laughed as he pointed at the screen, which showed Fernando belly deep in a pond at the golf course. As usual, he looked contemplative, even as the golfers gathered as close to him as they dared to get.

"He looks okay, doesn't he?" Ivy asked. "He's missing the red rope around his neck, isn't he?"

"Yes…and it's a relief." Slade checked the bull for any signs of problems or injuries, but he didn't notice anything overt. Still, he couldn't see Fernando's hooves, and that was his main concern because that much weight for that many miles could spell trouble. Still, the bull looked good, all things considered.

"After this message, we'll be right back with more about Fernando," Jennifer said, smiling happily into the camera.

"What more could there be?" Alicia asked. "Do you suppose they caught him?"

"That'd be big news," Slade said, "but nobody contacted me about the reward."

"Maybe there hasn't been time." Ivy arranged a pile of coasters as everyone waited for more news.

Jennifer reappeared on the screen. "We have more video of Fernando. Golf course officials called in a local search-and-rescue team to catch him. Mind you, these are strong, experienced cowboys with their equally well-trained horses. They know what they're doing with animals. But as you will soon see, Fernando is more than a match for any man or horse."

"Oh no," Slade groaned. "I hope the injuries aren't too bad."

"You don't think they caught him?" Ivy asked.

Alicia laughed. "Fernando? Ha! Not if they irritated him or made him angry. You've seen the size of him."

When the next video appeared on the screen, Fernando was out of the water and surrounded by six cowboys on horseback with coiled ropes in their gloved hands. He appeared unconcerned at their intrusion into his world. Golfers could be seen in the background recording the confrontation.

"I hope they don't make him mad," Slade said. "Surely they know better than to try to rope him."

As he watched, that was exactly what they attempted to do. One cowboy managed to get a rope around Fernando's neck, but the big bull simply stepped back and tugged, almost unseating the rider who at least had the sense to let go of the rope. Another cowboy came in close, trying to herd Fernando toward a temporary pen. The bull simply put a massive shoulder against the horse and gave a slight nudge. The horse almost went down, causing the rider to fall off right in the way of Fernando's hooves. The cowboy scrambled up, then quickly limped away. Another cowboy tried to grab the rope around Fernando's neck, but the bull lowered his head and bumped the horse, causing the rider to thrust out his leg for balance, catch the rope around

Fernando's neck with his spur, and drag off the rope as he fell, losing his hat as his head hit the ground.

"That cowboy probably got a broken foot. The other might have a concussion. They'd better go to the hospital," Slade said. "Still, Fernando is just toying with them. He could've knocked that horse and rider over or tossed them into the air."

Jennifer came back on the screen. "And that is the way it went until the cowboys finally gave up. An ambulance arrived to help the injured team. No one was badly hurt, but there was a lot of wounded pride. Fernando—obviously a lover not a fighter, or he'd have done a lot more damage—left the golf course to continue his journey home."

Alicia smiled as she muted the television. "Whitesboro is getting close to us."

"You're right," Slade replied. "If nothing happens to him, he just might make it home by Christmas."

"That'd be so wonderful," Ivy said. "I wish we could do more for him."

"Lots of folks are looking for Fernando. If they find him, they know to call me…if they don't get cocky and try to capture him first. Storm could help me get him loaded up." Slade felt encouraged by the news he'd just seen, but he still worried about the miles between Fernando and the ranch.

"That's good." Ivy poured a cup of coffee and looked over at him. "Alicia and I have been trying to come up with titles for dances in the dance contest."

He cocked his head to one side, turning his mind from Fernando to Wildcat Hall.

"We thought we'd focus on couples. Will you help us?"

"Maybe you'd do better discussing it with Craig."

"He's setting up the music." Ivy smiled at him. "Alicia thinks we should definitely use 'Couple Most in Need of a Room.'"

Slade laughed. "Are we going that direction?"

"It is a honky-tonk."

"But it is Christmas."

Ivy grinned, looking mischievous. "That's all the more reason to get every little thing our hearts desire."

"I won't argue with you on that one." He stretched out his hand to her and felt a deep satisfaction when she squeezed his fingers. "I don't know what to get you for Christmas."

"You're more than enough."

"Seriously?"

"I am serious. I want you for Christmas."

"You've already got that. I want to get you something special."

"You're special."

"You aren't going to tell me, are you?"

She traced a pattern in the palm of his hand. "I did tell you... Anyway, you already bought me the new bed."

"That's for both of us."

She smiled, eyes filled with sudden heat. "Yeah."

He felt that heat as if she'd sent it straight into him...and he burned like brush fire in a high wind.

"Surprise me."

"Okay." He'd go to Morning's Glory tomorrow. She'd have jewelry made by local artists. He'd get a ring. It wouldn't be *the* ring, but it'd be another step on the way to *that* ring.

"Now, are you going to help with the contest titles or not?"

"I'm happy to help." He gave her a big grin. "Couple Most in Need of a Honeymoon."

She laughed, shaking her head. "I want fun more than serious."

"That's fun and serious."

"True."

Alicia sidled up to them, grinning. "I've been thinking about those titles. 'Couple Burning up the Hall.' This is so much fun."

"Good one," Ivy agreed. "I've been thinking about it. No time to get trophies made, but we can give out a Wildcat Hall gift certificate with each award."

"I like it," Alicia said.

"Folks will appreciate it." Slade thought a moment. "And it'll bring them back here, too."

"Exactly." Ivy smiled like a contented cat. "Glad y'all like that idea. I'll cross it off my to-do list."

"I'm not sure about more winner titles," Slade said, noticing that the room had emptied out except for them, "but I can think about them."

"No rush…at least we don't need them till our very own honky-tonk Christmas."

"I'll think about them, too," Alicia said, then glanced up as the front door opened. "New customer."

Slade turned to see the stranger, feeling oddly uneasy. The guy was city, not country—styled, dark hair tinted with silver, middle-aged, and sleekly muscled. He'd tried for casual in a leather bomber jacket over a silk lapis tee tucked into designer jeans with brand-new cowboy boots. Expensive everything, from top to bottom. He didn't belong…not only that, but he reeked of trouble.

Slade'd been right—something was about to break. He felt it deep in his gut. He glanced at Ivy to get her reaction to the man. Her eyes had gone wide, as if she was seeing something or someone she hadn't expected and didn't want anywhere near Wildcat Hall.

The stranger looked all around the front bar, as if he was calculating the value of every stick of furniture in the place. He glanced at the floor, rubbed the sole of his boot against it, and nodded as if in approval. Finally, he perused the people, as if they were the least of his considerations.

"I'm here to see Ivy Bryant." He spoke in a carefully neutral voice with no accent at all. "Would you be so good as to tell me where I might find her?"

Slade slipped off the barstool, turned toward the guy, spread his feet wide for balance, and let his hands hang easy at his sides. He was bigger and stronger and younger than the stranger—probably more experienced in a fight. He could take him, if it came to it. Bottom line, he'd protect Ivy, Alicia, and the Hall any way he needed to do it.

"I'm Ivy Bryant," she said in a soft, hesitant tone.

Slade didn't like the sound because it was so far removed from her usual strong, confident voice.

"Emory Meadows." He pulled a business card from an inner pocket, crossed the room in a few strides, ignored Slade, and held out the card.

Ivy hesitated a long moment before she accepted the card, then she looked down at it. "You're from Houston."

"Yes. Your friend contacted me."

Every instinct in Slade was screaming to get this guy out of the county and never let him back. He stiffened, fists clinching instinctively.

"Ms. Bryant, I'd like to discuss the proposition with you," he said. "I believe you'll be very happy at what I'm prepared to offer you."

"Offer?"

"Yes. Otherwise, I wouldn't waste my time. Would you like to take this discussion into your office?"

Ivy looked from right to left, obviously in a quandary about what to do.

"I'm not leaving you alone with this guy," Slade said, making it a final statement.

"Me either," Alicia said, moving down to stand beside Ivy.

"I guess y'all will know soon enough." Ivy sounded resigned. "Please believe me that I never expected an offer. I just reached out to a friend right after I got here. Everything has changed since then."

Slade felt a chill run up his spine as his muscles hardened in anticipation of defending all he held dear. What the hell had Ivy done or planned to do? She was signaling that it was a mistake, so she knew she was in the wrong place at the wrong time with the wrong person.

And he remembered, with a sickening sensation in the pit of his stomach. This situation mirrored exactly what they'd discussed about having no legal or other rights in each other's lives. It'd worked okay...until now. He couldn't do anything except stand by and watch the disaster unfolding before him.

"Mr. Meadows, this is my office."

The stranger glanced around again, shrugged, and slipped a Montblanc pen out of his pocket along with another business card. He quickly wrote on it, then held out the card to Ivy.

Again, she reluctantly took it. She read his note, then gasped. "Is this real?"

"Absolutely." He smiled, showing bright white teeth. "I checked out Wildcat Bluff County. There is a lot of potential for development here. My investors and I are known for making very attractive offers."

"What are you talking about?" Slade had finally had enough of the guy's cryptic remarks. He had a good suspicion about where the guy was headed and he disliked everything he heard.

"Do you work here?" Meadows finally looked at Slade.

"No. I'm a friend."

Meadows turned back to Ivy, dismissing Slade with a single glance. "We believe Wildcat Hall Park could be turned into a profitable theme park."

"Theme park!" Alicia sounded horrified.

"Naturally, a substantial investment will be required for development, to purchase adjacent land to build rental units, and to enlarge the infrastructure to accommodate vehicles and tourists."

Slade felt sick to his stomach, hardly able to believe his ears. A theme park would not only ruin Wildcat Hall and its heritage, but it'd probably ruin the entire county for farms and ranches and country folk. Of all people, Ivy had brought this down on their heads. She'd intended to sell the Park to outsiders from the first. He felt absolutely and utterly betrayed by her.

His entire world tilted sideways. He gripped the edge of the bar as he felt a wave of dizziness wash over him. They were in the middle of holidays, cattle rustlers, cattle drive...and he'd been contemplating asking Ivy to marry him at Christmas. And the entire time, she'd had one foot out the door.

"This is a huge offer," Ivy said in a stilted voice. "I'd need to check with my sister before I made any decision. She owns the property with me."

"Understandable. We'd like to move on this project in the new year." He looked covetously around the room again. "How long before you can give us a final decision?"

"Not long." Ivy tapped his card with a fingernail. "Naturally, I'll need to discuss this offer with my friend in Houston."

"Of course. We'll negotiate through him." He stepped back. "Do you have any questions?"

"No. I can talk with Peter to get more details."

"Excellent. He's a fine Realtor, so he'll be able to guide you well."

"Yes, of course," she said, sounding slightly faint.

Slade wanted to snatch the business card, tear it into shreds, and throw the guy out the front door. He might have no rights to interfere in Ivy's life, but he had plenty of rights when it came to Wildcat Bluff. Folks should've listened to Nocona Jones, the best lawyer in town, that the Hall needed to be made a National Historic Landmark to protect it. Nobody had done it. Now, it might well be too late.

Suddenly he was galvanized. Wildcat Hall Park wasn't sold yet. Fortunately, he'd been here to hear the offer, so he could do something fast. He needed to contact Nocona and start the landmark process. Hedy, Morning Glory, Granny, and so many others needed to throw their support to fighting Ivy every step of the way. They wouldn't go down easy, and he wouldn't let emotions get in his way. He felt cold as ice, chilled to the bone at her deception.

"If you have any questions, please don't hesitate to call me or my assistant," Meadows said.

"Did you look over everything?" Ivy asked.

"Yes. I've been here a couple of days. Excellent work on your part, but we can bring this place up to the twenty-first century and still keep its roots in the 1800s. People want a taste of the Old West, but they want it with all the amenities of a first-class lifestyle."

"I understand," Ivy said faintly.

"I'm headed back to Houston right now." He walked over to the door and opened it. "If you need me, my cell number is on my card."

"Goodbye," Ivy said.

He gave a quick nod, then was out the door.

"You aren't actually thinking about taking the offer?" Alicia sounded close to tears.

"It's a substantial amount," Ivy said. "It'd set Fern and me up for life."

"If you want to sell, Craig is interested and other folks, too. You don't need to sell to an outsider. A Wild West theme park"—Slade growled out the last words—"is totally unacceptable."

"I agree." She turned haunted green eyes on him. "Trust me. I never expected this to happen. It's just that my friend is a Realtor."

"And you just happened to contact him about selling the place."

"Yes." She hung her head, then looked up. "But that was before I came to love the place and the people."

He clenched his fists, wanting to bust something, but it wouldn't help the pain she'd inflicted not only on him but the whole community.

"I need to discuss this with Fern before I do anything," Ivy said.

He shook his head in disgust, walked to the front door, and glanced back at Alicia. "Make sure she gets home safe, will you?"

"Sure…and I think we need to close early."

"Slade, can't we talk about it?" Ivy stepped around the side of the bar with a hand raised toward him.

He slammed the door shut behind him, thunderstruck.

Chapter 32

IVY SAT IN THE CENTER OF HER NEW BED, IMAGINING SHE could still feel Slade's body heat from the previous night. She desperately needed that warmth, because she felt so bone-chillingly cold. She shivered and pulled the quilt higher, trying to get warm, but it didn't help. She'd never felt so alone...or so cold.

Unbelievably, he was gone. He'd ripped her right out of his life and tossed her away with hardly a backward glance. Gone. Simply gone. And he'd taken her heart with him. Why had she been so resistant to his love? Why had she dodged and hedged his advances until finally she'd had to acknowledge that he was the one—the only one—for her. If they'd had more time together to solidify their feelings, maybe this intrusion into their world wouldn't have torn them apart. But everything was too fresh, too fragile to be sustained under pressure.

It'd all happened so fast and so out of the blue that she was still reeling from the impact of that row of numbers on a fancy business card. She picked the card up from her night-stand and flicked it with her fingernail. High quality. Emory Meadows appeared to be the real deal. He could back up his offer. Peter wouldn't have sent him otherwise. She needed to talk with Peter, but Fern came first. She couldn't just toss away an offer that would put them both on easy street. And yet, she couldn't imagine selling to a developer and being the most hated person in Wildcat Bluff County—or even worse, being the cause of losing the wonderful historic building.

She needed to talk with someone. She couldn't call Slade. The fact that she didn't feel she could reach out to him hurt. How many people had he told about the offer for Wildcat Hall Park? Or was he waiting until the next day, because it was too late and folks got up early? Of course, the Settelmeyer family knew about the offer, but they were tight-lipped with disapproval. She couldn't blame them. She was playing with their entire lives. She hated to even think what Slade's family would say to her, or more probably, not say.

First though, she needed to talk with Fern. She picked up her phone and hit speed dial, hoping her sister was in a position to answer.

"Ivy, what's up? Not your usual time to call."

"Do you have time to talk?"

"For a sec, sure."

"We've got a situation here." She was so relieved to hear her sister's voice that she almost felt like crying.

"Is it Craig?" Fern coughed. "He's okay, isn't he?"

"Far as I know, he's fine. But I'm not so good."

"What is it? I thought everything was going great."

"By morning, I'm going to be the most hated person in Wildcat Bluff County." She crumpled the business card in her fist.

"You're kidding me!"

"No, I'm not."

"What's going on?"

She sighed, knowing this wasn't going to be easy, but she wouldn't go easy on herself. "Peter Simpson."

"Right. Friend. Realtor. What's he got to do with the Park?"

"Well…"

"Tell me you didn't ask him to put our property on the market."

"It happened right after I moved here. And I never dreamed we'd get an offer."

"I'm hurt, truly hurt, you didn't consult me before you took such a big step."

"I'm sorry. Really, I am. It's just I was so unhappy about being uprooted from my life in Houston and stuck out here in the country that…well, it seemed like a good idea at the time."

"But Craig…or other folks there would snap up the Park in a second."

"I didn't know any of them. And I don't know why, but I just called Peter."

"Oh, Ivy." Fern coughed. "It wounds me to think you'd do that to such a special property, but tell me what's going on with it."

"Slade and Alicia were in the front bar with me when a stranger came inside."

"Buyer?"

"Yes." She swallowed hard, feeling worse but feeling better, too, just from talking with her sister.

"How much is the offer?"

"A lot. He wants to turn our property into a Wild West theme park."

"What? That's shocking!" Fern coughed several times, finally gasping. "I just can't seem to get rid of this bug. I try not to talk during the day."

"I'm sorry I'm straining your voice."

"It's okay."

"He wants to buy surrounding acreage and build it into something big."

"Oh, Ivy. That's terrible. It'd hurt so many people."

"But it'd bring in jobs."

"And traffic and pollution and who knows what else."

"I agree." She straightened out the business card. "You haven't heard the amount yet."

"I don't care. There's no way I'd sell and you know it."

"Listen to this." She read the long string of numbers on the card. "Can you still say no?"

"That's huge. It'd change our lives, wouldn't it?"

"Yes. But it'd also change the lives of the people here. I don't know about you, but I just can't do it."

"I agree." Fern coughed. "Let them build a Wild West theme park someplace that isn't already established."

"I'm relieved we're in agreement. I couldn't turn him down until I'd talked with you."

"How did Slade take the news?"

"He left me."

"Oh no. You've come to care about him, haven't you?"

"More than I thought possible, and now—"

"He'll understand once you explain the situation."

"He feels betrayed. And rightly so."

"You can't let it stand. Go to him. Tell him we're not going to sell."

"I can't. The cattle drive is tomorrow. He needs a good night's sleep so he can be up early."

"Do you think he'll sleep well? Will you?"

"No. And I'll be serving food to the cowboys and cowgirls. Plus, KWCB will interview me."

"What a mess. The timing couldn't be worse."

"Tell me about it."

"You must get some rest."

"I'll try."

"I wish I were there to help you. I feel guilty for dumping the Park in your lap and running off—again."

"Don't go there."

"But it's true. If I'd stayed there, you wouldn't be there, and this issue would never have come up."

"True." She crumpled the card again. "But I wouldn't have met Slade, and I wouldn't have found out how much I love living in the country."

"I don't feel so guilty now."

"Good. And you're right. I need to do something. I'll text Slade and see if he'll come over to talk."

"Call...but you'd better tell Peter the deal's off before you talk with Slade. Slade will need to know there's no chance of losing Wildcat Hall."

"You're right. I'll see if I can get Peter. He's probably asleep, but he'll pick up for me."

"Sure he will."

"He'll be disappointed to lose the big commission."

"Somehow I doubt it. He loves that place as much as we do."

"Okay." She took a deep breath, feeling as if she might come out of this in one piece after all. "Thanks. You've been a big help and eased my mind."

"That's what sisters are for."

"Thank you. I'd better let you go. Love you."

"Right back at you."

Ivy stared at her phone for a moment, missing Fern. She wished her sister were here right now. They'd hug and get this mess straightened out together. For now, she was on her own and that'd just have to be okay.

She hit speed dial for Peter...and waited and waited for him.

"Ivy," Peter mumbled. "What the hell are you doing calling at this hour of the day or night?"

"Emory Meadows paid me a visit."

"Hot for the property, is he?"

"Did you know he was going to make an offer?"

"No. I only knew he'd gone up there to take a look. He actually made an offer right then and there?"

"Yes. And, Peter, it's big."

"Well, don't tease me."

When she told him the amount, he whistled loud and long. "But there's a downside. He wants to turn it into a Wild West theme park."

"That's outrageous. He'd ruin it."

"Fern agrees."

"Besides, he'd never get those changes past a historical commission."

"It's not registered as a historic building."

"Why not?"

"I don't know."

"Well, get on it. You can't take chances with a structure like that. It needs to be protected."

"I'll contact an attorney to start the process soon."

"Good. And, Ivy, believe me, I'd never have sent him to you if I'd had any idea he wanted to make such drastic changes."

"It caught me by surprise, too. I think I was sort of in shock till I talked with Fern."

"I can imagine. How is she doing?"

"Singing away at her gig."

"Is she coming back soon?"

"I wish, but you know her."

"She may surprise you this time. She loves that place, that town, those people. If you two keep this up, I may have to move there myself."

"Somehow, I can't imagine it."

"Well, you never know," he said. "For now, do you want me to tell Meadows to ride off into the sunset without Wildcat Hall Park?"

"Yes, please."

"You got it." He hesitated again. "And, Ivy, do you really like it there?"

"I'm surprised every day, but I love it here. You need to come and visit. Stay in one of the cowboy cabins."

"Thanks. I may just take you up on that offer. For now, I'd better get some shut-eye."

"I really appreciate your help. Also, I apologize for getting you into this mess and then turning down the offer."

"I'll let you pay me back someday."

"Come up and stay a spell."

"Thanks. I'll let you know when. Bye for now."

And that was that. She'd tell the Settelmeyers first thing in the morning that there would be no sale. She'd contact Nocona Jones to start the historical registration process. Hopefully, no one else knew about the offer, so she wouldn't have to explain her actions.

She set her phone aside...and felt cold and alone all over again. She wondered if she would always feel lonely without Slade. He'd come into her life like a whirlwind and snatched her up in it. They'd come through a lot together. This was no different. Fern was right. She needed to reach out to him now.

She picked up her phone again. She trembled as she hit Slade's number, anxious to hear his voice. But she waited... and waited...and waited. When it clicked over to voicemail, she shivered as she felt his rejection go deep. Then again, maybe he was asleep. But if he wouldn't pick up or was too busy to do it, how could she reach him?

And then she knew. Tomorrow was the cattle drive. He'd be at Wildcat Hall with the other drovers and folks on the scene at some point during the day for food and drink. She'd see him and explain everything. He'd understand. And all would be just like it was before Emory Meadows waltzed into Wildcat Hall and handed her a business card.

She set her phone aside again and snuggled under the covers of the bed Slade had lovingly bought for them. But she didn't fall asleep—thoughts of him laughing, talking, cooking, kissing kept flitting through her mind.

He'd taken her heart, and he simply had to bring it back home.

Chapter 33

EARLY THE NEXT MORNING, SLADE WATCHED PALE LIGHT from the rising sun slowly spread across Steele Trap Ranch, pushing aside the darkness to welcome a new day. He sat on his favorite bay roan on a hill overlooking three hundred head of Angus cows, rounded up and ready to be headed out.

Cowboys and cowgirls kept watch over the herd from the backs of fine horses—palomino, chestnut, buckskin, gray, and other colors. They were well outfitted with bridles and saddles trimmed in silver, shotguns or rifles slipped into long holsters, and canteens filled with water or stronger drink.

They wore a wide variety of traditional clothes. Their boots ranged from scuffed leather to fancy snakeskin. Hats were Stetson, Charlie 1 Horse, Resistol, or other brands in a wide variety of styles, like rodeo, western, desperado, with hat bands from fancy to plain in silver, rattlesnake, or braided leather. Cowboys wore Wranglers, while many of the cowgirls wore Rockies with shirts in a variety of bright colors. For the cool weather, they wore long-sleeve, fleece-lined jean jackets or something warmer, like black wool, three-pocket, leather-trimmed, sleeveless rancher jackets.

Dust drifted upward from the restless herd, along with the sounds of mooing and snorting, as the animals anticipated something unusual happening to them. Leaders were on alert, swishing their tails. Cow dogs roamed the outer perimeter, checking for strays or stragglers that needed to be brought into line.

Slade adjusted his Stetson as he appreciated the sight that re-created the old-time cattle drives of the 1880s. They'd done it. Cattle and drovers were in place. Sheriff Calhoun and his deputies rode horses while some followed in vehicles, along with two fire-rescue rigs. Wildcat Jack and Eden would be live streaming with Nathan and Ken for the KWCB radio station, so they were in an SUV, but they would also be getting out and walking to capture video and share online with their worldwide audience. Families with elders and kids were already lined up here and there along Wildcat Road to see the historic trail drive.

Granny, Maybelline, Sydney, Dune, and Storm, along with other friends from around the county, were all on horseback with the herd. Nobody who wanted to be part of the event had been left out, even though they now had more riders per cow than would have ever been economically feasible in the old days. It suited him fine. He wanted everyone who wanted to be there to join in.

Amazingly enough, so far, all had gone as planned, but that could change at any moment once the cattle drive got underway. Everyone was on alert for cattle rustlers, but that fact just added extra excitement.

He had anticipated this moment for so long. He'd worked so long to get here. He should be able to enjoy it. Instead, he had a hole in his heart that was leaking out happiness with every beat. His thoughts kept turning back to Ivy...and the sharp-dressed stranger from Houston. Was he the kind of man she really wanted in her life? Was he, or somebody like him, the real reason she'd fought so hard not to like the country? Were men like him why she wanted to live in the city? Slade's gut clenched at the thought. It was bad enough she'd ever considered putting Wildcat Hall up for sale, but it was even worse that she had so little regard for their heritage…and him.

He couldn't compete. He didn't want to compete. He'd give her up before he'd compete. Yet how could he let her go without a fight? How could he go on without her? How could he walk away from the light that shimmered in her green eyes when she looked at him? And yet, even though thoughts of her haunted him, he had to go forward with the day—too many people and animals depended on him to do anything else.

He focused on the scene below him. Jack and Eden were interviewing cowboys and cowgirls with Nathan and Ken live streaming. Storm had joined the group on horseback, so she was probably telling her story about naming Fernando and updating the audience about his long trek home. Still, Slade didn't need to be thinking about Fernando…or Ivy. He had to focus on the cattle drive, particularly because everyone had turned to look up at him. He checked his watch. Yep, it was time.

He kneed his roan to start the trek down to the front. He noticed that Nathan was recording him as he reached the group, nodding, smiling, welcoming everyone to the cattle drive. He felt like he was starring in some old black-and-white movie or television show. He was dressed for the part in his crimson, pearl-snap shirt, black rancher jacket with brown leather lapels, pressed Wranglers, knee-high black boots, and a black felt hat. He also wore brown leather gloves.

It'd all be perfect if Ivy were riding beside him, although he doubted she'd ever been on a horse. When things settled down, he needed to remedy that oversight—but then he remembered there might not be a future for them, so he shelved the idea. He didn't have time to think about it right now anyway. It's just that she was always on his mind.

When he reached the road, he looked back and saw everyone waiting expectantly for his signal to go. Well, truth be told, the cattle didn't look expectant. They looked patient but skeptical in their typical bovine way. They were probably expecting extra hay or feed at the end of their journey, and they'd get it. He knew they'd like their new pastures.

He took off his hat and held it high, then he waved it in a circle over his head. "Round 'em up! Head 'em out!"

And he rode onto Wildcat Road with the trail drive coming alive behind him. He walked the roan, taking it slow and easy as he listened for the sounds that told him cattle and drovers were getting into position behind him.

As he led the trail drive, he saw folks lined up on both sides of the road. He wanted them to stay well back. If they were ranchers, they knew how to handle any troublesome cattle or horses, but if they were city folk, they might view the cows as pets and reach out to touch them. Hopefully, nobody would get hurt. When they waved, he waved back as he passed them.

Soon he started to see signs—hand-lettered, rough ones and professionally printed ones—that read "Fernando Home for Christmas."

He couldn't keep from laughing at the signs, giving a thumbs-up at the sight. Talk about capturing imaginations. Fernando had it all. Again, he wished Ivy rode beside him, but she waited at Wildcat Hall to feed and water riders as the cattle made their way past the honky-tonk, just like they had a hundred-fifty years ago—at least that was the plan.

He glanced back. All was going according to plan so far. Cowboys and cowgirls were joking, laughing, waving, and getting great responses from the audience. He sighed in relief, deciding that all their plans had turned the cattle drive into a rousing success.

He couldn't help but wonder what the original cowboys, driving a thousand head of wild, cantankerous longhorns up from South Texas, would think about the sight. Those brave drovers would have been covered in dust and dirt, boots thick with cow droppings, and hats stained dark with sweat. They'd have been armed with the best their meager money could buy in the way of knives and guns to protect not only themselves but also their precious cattle on the dangerous trip. By now—near the Red River—they'd have sat low in their saddles from the long, hard drive across Texas, knowing they still had to get safely through Indian Territory to the railhead in Kansas.

Even with Slade's experience, he couldn't imagine the guts and fortitude it would have taken to make that long, hard haul. But it would've been worth it to them, because it was good, honest, paying work. On the way back, they'd have celebrated at dance halls in Dodge City, Kansas. They'd have picked up their handmade boots at Gene's Boot Hospital that they'd have ordered on the way up. And they'd have danced some more in Wildcat Bluff. They'd have lived life to the fullest and wouldn't have asked for more than the freedom to follow the cattle trails north.

And now here he was, following in their wake so many

years later. He felt honored and humbled, stirring up dust from the past to settle into the present.

He kept a lookout for rustlers, but as they headed north, all was quiet except for the well-wishers camped out here and there along the trail. He saw more signs about Fernando, urging him home for Christmas. The drive was slow, passing the turnoff for one ranch after another until he saw Wildcat Hall up ahead. He'd soon be near Ivy…but did he want to talk with her? He didn't want to stir up anything, not on the trail drive. Still, his heart was hurting, even in the middle of his current success.

When he got close, he could see the Settelmeyers had outdone themselves. They'd placed an old-time chuck wagon with big, wooden wheels and white canvas stretched over the top out front. They'd set up food and drink provided by his family's Chuckwagon Café behind the wagon in the beer garden. He could smell the delicious aroma of barbecue and all the trimmings that had been placed in long, aluminum trays on top of picnic tables.

Cattle and drovers were spread out behind him on Wildcat Road. They'd be passing the Hall in waves, so there wouldn't be too many people in the beer garden at once. At least that was the plan. Now he saw that a lot of the spectators were already making their way to the Hall for a community gathering, like in the old days. He hadn't expected that aspect of the cattle drive, but he was happy to see that the tradition lived on.

He looked for Ivy and saw her right away. She was serving food in the beer garden and chatting with folks. She'd dressed in western wear and looked good—real good, if his body's response told him anything. Maybe he'd better keep his distance. He didn't want any type of emotional confrontation.

When he reached Wildcat Hall, he slipped off the roan and grabbed a bottle of water in a tub of ice out front. He'd stay near the road in case someone needed something, then he'd quickly head back out.

As he watched the cattle, he felt someone come up behind him. He glanced back, saw Ivy, and his heart picked up speed.

"Aren't you hungry?" She looked at him with veiled eyes as she held out a sandwich wrapped in paper.

"I can't stay long." He sounded stilted and knew it, but he couldn't stop his powerful reaction to her.

"Slade, I want to talk with you about last night."

"There's not time now." He grabbed the sandwich, careful not to touch her fingers.

"I don't want it coming between us."

"That happened the minute you called your Realtor friend."

"I didn't know anybody here. I wanted to go home. I didn't expect a buyer to show up."

"It's a historic site."

"I understand the importance now." She held out a hand, beseeching him. "I want to apologize for my thoughtless actions."

He shrugged and took a step back, squeezing the sandwich in his fist. He was getting angry all over again. She obviously thought a few words could make everything right, could put everything back, could heal the gulf between them.

"I talked with Fern last night, and she said—"

"I don't want to hear it." He tossed the water and the sandwich in a nearby trash barrel, then walked over and leaped into his saddle.

"But, Slade, please..."

He didn't look back as he rejoined the cattle drive, pushing his roan to the front of herd. Maybe later, he'd be ready to listen to what she had to say, but not now...not in the middle of the trail drive. He had to make sure the cattle got safely to Steele Trap II.

And his heart was just going to have to hurt.

Chapter 34

SLADE RODE IN FRONT OF THE CATTLE DRIVE, KEEPING watch, waving at spectators, reading "Fernando Home for Christmas" signs, enjoying the entire experience. He glanced back, taking in the colorful sight of cattle and drovers, horses and dogs. They were coming into the final stretch. The sun had moved from east to west during their long day. Now, a brilliant sunset of red and orange set the western horizon ablaze. And up ahead was the new Steele Trap II sign above the entry to the ranch.

Suddenly, he felt uneasy. Something wasn't right. But what? He thought back to Ivy. Was she okay? She'd been fine, at least physically, when he'd talked to her. She'd even apologized for her actions. He appreciated it, even felt the tightness in his chest ease a bit with her words. Maybe he should've let her continue, but he'd been impatient—too much was happening too fast and he didn't want a confrontation in the middle of the trail drive. Maybe he'd been wrong. Maybe it wouldn't have taken long, and he wouldn't be uneasy now.

Yet he didn't think it was Ivy. Something else was bothering him...something just under the surface like an irritating itch. Ranchers and farmers learned to watch for those signs, because they were at the mercy of nature so much of the time.

He focused on the ranch. Trouble. All of his senses came

on alert. They hadn't seen the rustlers all day. Could they be here? Had they decided to hit the ranch instead of the cattle drive? With everybody gone and concentrated on the event, they had plenty of time to get in and out with no one the wiser. He should've left guards on duty, but he hadn't wanted to deny any cowboy the opportunity to be part of the trail drive. He'd needed the sheriff and his deputies with him. And he'd hoped the thieves were long gone.

Hindsight was perfect, but it didn't help him now. He glanced back again. Sheriff Calhoun and two deputies on horseback weren't too far behind him. If the rustlers were at the ranch, he didn't want the cattle drive going in there. It'd be too dangerous. Somebody could get hurt. If the thieves weren't there, then his worry was for nothing.

He had to make a decision, and he had to make it fast. He wouldn't take a chance. He'd go in alone, check out the situation, and call the sheriff for backup if he needed it. Hopefully, his instincts were haywire because he wasn't thinking straight due to Ivy. But everything in him was screaming trouble.

He wasn't concerned about getting over the cattle guard on horseback, because at both ranches they'd opened up a line of fence so the cattle could easily be driven to pasture. He turned toward that open section now, urged his roan into a gallop, and thundered into his ranch. He saw nothing amiss, so he slowed down and turned onto the road leading up to the house. Surely the rustlers wouldn't be so bold as to come out the main gate.

As he headed up the lane, a big truck—two ton at least—with an attached gooseneck kicked up a cloud of dust as it barreled toward him. He realized the rustlers must have seen him. Not only had they seen him, but they were headed straight at him to run him down as they drove out the front gate of the ranch ahead of the cattle drive. One way or another, he had to stop them, even if he was a lone cowboy on horseback and way overmatched by the monster truck.

He rode off the road, jerked his trusty .44 Magnum Henry rifle out of its saddle sheath, levered a round into the chamber, and raised it to his shoulder. He thought about shooting the tires, but the big truck could roll a long way on the rims. So he aimed at the truck's front grill and fired to take out the engine, so they couldn't go anywhere with his cattle. He quickly cranked the lever for another round and fired again, then again and again, drilling holes in the grill every time. The truck had so much momentum it kept coming, but the engine died and the truck finally rolled to a stop.

He rode closer and aimed his rifle at the windshield. "I've got five rounds left," he shouted. "Don't make me use them." He aimed the rifle with one hand and pulled out his phone with the other. He called the sheriff.

"Heard the shots. What's going on?" Sheriff Calhoun asked, sounding calm and in control.

"You'd better get up here. I've got the rustlers pinned in their truck."

"What?"

"You heard me. I caught them on their way out hauling a load of my cattle."

"Bold as brass."

"I hear you." He kept an eye on the shadowy figures in the cab to see what they'd do next. "I'll call Oscar for help."

"Sounds good. We're on our way."

While Slade waited for the sheriff, he quickly phoned Oscar.

"Looks okay from here," Oscar said. "How's everything on your end?"

"You'll be hard-pressed to believe it, but I've got the rustlers pinned in their truck. We're waiting for the sheriff."

Oscar hooted and hollered. "Perfect end to a perfect day."

"They were headed out on the main road, if you can believe their nerve."

"I believe it...but it's odd they're just now leaving the ranch. They've had most of the day to get in and get gone."

"Odd, yeah. But okay by me. We've got them."

"That's the main thing."

"If you'll slow down the drive, we'll finish up here. I don't want anybody getting hurt."

"You got it."

Slade slipped his phone back into his pocket just as the sheriff and his deputies rode up to him.

"Good job," Sheriff Calhoun said. "Come on. Let's see what we got inside that truck."

Slade kept his rifle aimed at the cab as he rode closer with the sheriff and deputies.

"Come on out and put your hands on your heads," Sheriff Calhoun called, stepping down from his horse, followed by his two deputies. He motioned for one deputy to go to the passenger side of the truck.

Slade stayed on horseback, where he held a more strategic position in case the rustlers decided to make a run for it on foot.

After a moment, the driver's door opened and a man cautiously stepped down. He had shaggy, dark hair and yellow bruises on his face. He wore a shirt, jeans, and one boot. He also had a big, white cast on his left foot.

"Put your hands on your head," Sheriff Calhoun said.

The rustler complied, swaying slightly on his feet.

"You know you're in a lot of trouble." Sheriff Calhoun adjusted his belt with the big rodeo buckle.

The rustler didn't reply. He simply stared sullenly at the ground.

"Bring that other guy around here to join his partner," Sheriff Calhoun called to his deputy.

When the rustler walked around the front of the truck, he looked similar to his partner, wearing shirt, jeans, and boots. Instead of a cast on his foot, he had one on his right arm.

"Looks like you two were in a bit of a tussle," Sheriff Calhoun said. "Identification, please."

"You can call me Tom. He's Harry," the driver said. "And that's about all you'll get from us."

"Frisk them." Sheriff Calhoun motioned to his deputies. "Get their IDs. And cuff them."

Slade watched everything, ready to step in if things went south or he was needed by the sheriff and his deputies.

"No wallets. No nothing."

"That's not an accident," Sheriff Calhoun said. "Looks to me like we've got a couple of pros on our hands. Did you rustlers ever work North Texas before?"

"Don't know what you're talking about," Tom said.

"And we wish we'd never heard of Texas." Harry glared at everyone.

Sheriff Calhoun just shook his head as he looked at the two men. "You've caused a lot of trouble around here—time and expense, too, not to mention the loss of cattle."

"No walk in the park for us," Tom said. "One more time and you'd have seen the last of us."

"Right…one last time," Sheriff Calhoun said, disbelief coloring his voice. "Slade, would you check the cab and see if their IDs are in there?"

He nodded, holstered his rifle, dismounted, and walked around the front of the truck where the engine still steamed, hissed, and pinged. He stepped up to the cab, doing his best not to touch anything as he glanced around. It was a mess. Fast food wrappers. Empty pop and beer cans. If the IDs were there, it'd take a day to find them.

He started to back out, then stopped as something on the floorboard caught his attention. He saw an open box filled with electronic equipment…and everything fell into place.

He backed out and slammed the door behind him, feeling like he'd been way too slow since the heists had started on his ranch. He stalked over to the sheriff, seething inside.

"What'd you find?" Sheriff Calhoun asked.

"Big mess. Good luck finding any IDs, but I bet their fingerprints will do the trick."

"I wouldn't take that bet," Sheriff Calhoun said.

"But I did find out what's made us such easy targets."

Tom and Harry snickered, glancing at each other in amusement.

"What?" Sheriff Calhoun asked.

"Drones."

"Got to give us credit," Harry said in a proud voice. "We're twenty-first century all the way."

Sheriff Calhoun just shook his head. "If you're such smart cookies, how come you ended up getting caught? You had time to be on your way long ago."

COWBOY FIREFIGHTER CHRISTMAS KISS 341

Harry glared at Slade, adjusted his stance on his cast, and spit on the ground. "Look at us. We're slow as molasses due to… What the hell kind of bulls do you raise around here anyway?"

"Fernando! You two clowns snatched him?" Slade pointed at the casts, then started to laugh. "He took you both out?"

"Ha!" Harry said. "He took out three of us when we tried to transfer him from one trailer to another."

"Shut up," Tom hollered.

"Why? They got us." Harry frowned at his partner.

"We got us a bargaining chip," Tom said. "Don't blow it."

Slade exchanged a look with Sheriff Calhoun as they both realized at the same time that something was going on beyond cut-and-dried cattle rustling.

"What the hell kind of name is Fernando for an Angus bull anyway? That breed's Scottish." Harry sounded disgusted by the whole idea.

"Reggie Rogers." Slade glanced at the sheriff. "He must be the third rustler."

Sheriff Calhoun nodded at the thieves. "So you had an inside man help you take Fernando. Why'd you want that bull anyway? He wasn't easy, not compared to backing up a trailer, loading up cows, and heading out."

"That's our bargaining chip," Tom said.

"How so?" Sheriff Calhoun asked.

"You're right," Tom said. "Not our normal way of taking cattle, no way, no how, but the money was the best—or should've been if that bull hadn't fought his way out."

"We're sick of hearing how sweet-natured Fernando is from that little girl on the radio," Harry said.

"Storm is my niece." Slade clenched his fists. "You better be careful how you talk about her."

"We can't figure out how that bull came to be so popular," Tom said, shaking his head. "It was bad enough to lose him, but that's made it a hundred times worse."

"Yeah," Harry said, then spit on the road. "Saw his picture everywhere. Folks rooting for him to get home by Christmas. Crazy."

"That's what got us into this mess," Tom said, agreeing. "I guess a special bull is a special bull."

"What do you mean?" Sheriff Calhoun asked.

"That's our bargaining chip," Tom said.

"It'll go easier on you both and Reggie, or whatever his name is, if you come clean," Sheriff Calhoun said. "Sounds to me like somebody got you into this fix. Let me help you straighten it out."

"Lots of folks have been hurt by your actions," Slade said. "Cattle rustling, barn burning, pickups crashing. You have a lot to answer for."

Tom looked at Harry, then back at Sheriff Calhoun. "If you cut us some slack on the charges, we can give you the name of the man who hired us to snatch Fernando."

"I can't do that," Sheriff Calhoun said, "but I can ask for leniency on the charges. I'd be happy to do what I can if we nail this guy."

Tom consulted with Harry again, then nodded. "Name's Brux Brennan. He's got a big spread in East Texas."

"I've heard of him," Slade said. "He doesn't need Fernando. He's got some of the best bloodlines in the state, if not the country."

"Not the point," Tom said. "Some guy named Werner

bested him when Fernando was auctioned, and he's had a bee in his bonnet about it ever since."

"You're kidding." Slade just shook his head. "All this for revenge? Mr. Werner was a fine man...gone now and a big loss to our community."

"Don't know nothing about Werner. Just Brennan," Harry said.

"Are you willing to make statements and sign them attesting to these facts?" Sheriff Calhoun asked. "We'll need your other partner to do the same thing once we pick him up."

"Reggie won't be hard to nab," Tom said. "He's more bunged up than us, so he's still in bed."

Slade felt a surge of satisfaction at that news. At least a little justice had come out of all the injustice.

"Okay," Sheriff Calhoun said. "We'll get him and we'll get Mr. Brennan, too. Nobody's going to get off scot-free."

"Sounds good to me." Slade felt a vast sense of relief that his ranches were safe again. If Fernando were back, everything would be fine, but the big bull was still in the wind. He heard an engine so looked back to the ranch's entry and saw an SUV driving up fast. Doors opened and folks leaped out.

Wildcat Jack was followed by Eden, Nathan, and Ken. Jack stalked over with Nathan live streaming all the way.

Slade took a few steps back to make way for them. He wished Ivy was with him to share this moment—talk about history making history. It just didn't get any better than a trail drive and catching cattle rustlers all in the same day. He realized how much he missed her and all they could share with just a glance. Maybe he'd been way too hard on her earlier.

"Wildcat Jack coming to you live from KWCB, the

Wildcat Den, at Steele Trap Ranch II...final destination of today's trail drive. Folks, it looks to me like Sheriff Calhoun caught the cattle rustlers who've been plaguing our county." Jack turned toward the sheriff. "Sheriff Calhoun, would you care to say a few words to our listeners?"

"Thanks, Wildcat Jack," Sheriff Calhoun said. "As you can see, these two rustlers were caught in the act of stealing more Steele Trap Ranch cattle."

"Good for you. That's mighty fine police work." Jack looked at the rustlers. "I'm sure you didn't think you'd ever get caught because you're so clever. What tripped you up?"

"We are clever." Tom puffed out his chest in pride.

"Twenty-first century, too," Sheriff Calhoun said. "They used a drone to keep watch on the ranches."

"Well, knock me down with a feather." Jack gave the rustlers an appreciative look. "But here you are in handcuffs."

Tom and Harry glared at him.

"Would you care to tell our listeners what led to your downfall?" Jack lowered his voice intimately. "Is it Wildcat Bluff County? You didn't expect such fierce, determined folks? Maybe it's the Lone Star State. You didn't know not to mess with Texas?"

The rustlers glared harder.

"I know." Jack drew out the suspense. "You thought the Steele Trap Ranches were easy marks."

Wildcat Jack was interrupted by the thundering of hooves. Everyone turned to look toward the entry. Storm rode up fast, pulled her horse to a stop, and leaped down. She ran toward the rustlers, but Slade grabbed her and pulled her back against him, feeling her small body quiver with outrage.

"You miserable, rotten, thieving cowards!" She pointed her finger at the cattle rustlers. "We heard just now on the radio."

Slade glanced up and saw Nathan live streaming it all. He groaned silently, knowing everybody in the county and their dog were glued to the unfolding drama on his ranch.

"I know what did you in!" Storm shouted, struggling to get free.

"What do you mean?" Wildcat Jack asked, encouraging her to continue. "Somehow these two smart rustlers were brought down. Just look at them. Broken foot. Broken arm. Bumps and bruises. What could possibly have happened to them?"

Storm stuck out her chin. "I can tell you right quick. They got done in by one big, mad bull."

"That's right," Wildcat Jack agreed in his deep voice. "Fernando just as good as caught the rustlers."

Tom glanced at Sheriff Calhoun. "Get us out of here. We don't have to listen to these country folk bad-mouth us."

Storm wriggled out of Slade's arms and stood up straight. She pointed at the rustlers. "Nobody, and I mean nobody, messes with Fernando. He's our miracle...and he'll be home for Christmas."

Chapter 35

ON CHRISTMAS EVE, IVY STOOD PROUDLY AT WILDCAT Hall's Honky-Tonk Christmas. The dance floor was packed with folks while even more spilled out into the beer garden under the twinkling, blue lights. She'd never dreamed her idea would be such a success, but it was fueled by tourists in town for Christmas in the Country and Christmas at the Sure-Shot Drive-In. Even the cowboy cabins were full up.

Everyone working the floor had raided the town's costume storage that was used for their many Old West events. Women wore sweet, flowery, muslin dresses or crimson satin with black-lace trim dance hall gowns. They'd fashioned their hair in buns or piled on top of heads with ringlets dangling over their shoulders. Men dressed as cowboys in shirts, jeans, and boots with Colts tucked in gun belts riding low on their narrow hips or as gamblers in pinstripe, gray trousers with matching jackets, white shirts, and colorful brocade vests. As custom dictated, hats weren't allowed on the dance floor, so those had been set aside earlier.

She loved to see folks dance their hearts out, eager to win an award. She'd come up with a good list to match Craig's music choices, so they were ready to roll when the time was right. For now, it was still a little too early in the evening. She wanted everyone who wanted to come to have a chance to arrive, and she wanted those already there to get warmed up for the big event. Besides, Wildcat Jack, Eden,

Nathan, and Ken hadn't arrived yet to live stream the dance contest because they were busy recording the other events in the county.

She looked toward the entry of the front bar, sighing in disappointment once again. She wanted to see Slade walk into the honky-tonk, so she could at least talk with him. She hadn't seen or heard from him since their encounter during the cattle drive, and that hadn't gone very well. Still, he hadn't told anyone about the offer she'd received for Wildcat Hall, as far as she knew, so she viewed that as a good sign. Of course, he might be waiting until after Christmas to spring the bad news on everyone, but she hoped not.

She might appear to be floating on the calm surface of her emotions, but underneath, in the dark depths, lurked the pain of separation from him. She hadn't slept well without being held in his protective arms. She hadn't eaten well without his wonderful food. She hadn't laughed as much without his quirky humor. All in all, she'd taken a downward tumble…and she wanted him to help her get back on her feet.

She'd waited and watched for him when people had shown up to celebrate the trail drive and cattle rustler capture, but he had never darkened the door. If he had, he would have been the man of the hour. Folks had asked for him all evening long, so she knew it was unusual for him not to be there, particularly for such an important celebration. She hoped it wasn't because of her—not wanting to talk to or see or be with her. If so, she didn't know how she could stand the pain of his loss. And yet, no matter what, she still had to go on and help others enjoy the festivities.

Fernando was a bigger celebrity than ever, because he

was credited with catching the rustlers. Folks were still busy guessing his arrival time on Christmas Day. Wildcat Bluff Fire-Rescue would end up well funded for the upcoming year. If the big bull didn't make it home, there would be a lot of broken hearts in the county, but everyone was holding firm for his return.

She'd expected Slade to be at her side for the dance, since they'd planned it together, but he was still a no-show. She took a deep breath. So be it. She would rally without him— and she would enjoy herself. She smoothed the front of her lace-trimmed, deep-décolletage, red satin gown. She'd felt like a sassy dance hall darling since the moment she'd slipped into it with black stockings and soft ballet slippers. She'd even left her hair down so it trailed over her shoulders. She loved her old-time look because it was so unusual and so much fun.

When she felt her phone vibrate in the red satin reticule she'd attached by a ribbon around her left wrist, she slipped out her cell and checked the screen. She hoped to see Slade's name, but it was her sister. That was good, too.

"Hey, Fern, how are you doing?"

"I hear music in the background. Sounds terrific. Is that Craig and his band?"

"You know it."

"I honestly wish I were there. How is your event coming along?"

"Fabulous. We're wall-to-wall people and more are still arriving for the dance contest." She glanced toward the front as additional folks entered the front doors, laughing and talking.

"Congratulations. That dance contest is a brilliant touch."

"Thanks."

"Did you get enough titles for the awards?"

"Yes. Everybody chimed in to help. I'll send you a list later. I think they'll give you a chuckle."

"I'm sure they will." Fern coughed, then cleared her throat. "Are you entering the contest?"

"Oh, no. I'll be sitting it out."

"What about Slade? Won't he want to dance?"

"I haven't seen him since the cattle drive, and he barely talked to me there. Of course, he's been busy."

"Do you mean you haven't told him that we turned down the offer?"

"I haven't had a chance."

"Sister dear, you better make a chance and not let this fester between the two of you."

"I'd like nothing more than to talk with him and explain everything. He doesn't return my texts or calls. I guess I'll have to wait until after Christmas." Ivy felt renewed frustration.

"I understand. I just wish it was different for you now that you've found someone you really like."

"Me, too. Trust me, I'll waylay him somewhere soon and sort out what's between us."

"That's my sister."

"How is your Christmas Eve?"

"I'm working, too, so we're both making this a happy occasion for others."

"That's a good thing, isn't it?"

"A very good thing." Fern coughed again. "I'd better go. Enjoy your evening. Love you."

"Love you, too."

Ivy slipped her phone back in her bag, missing her sister. She wished Fern would come home soon. But for now, Ivy was determined to carry on alone and make this a night for others to remember.

"Ivy!" Wildcat Jack called as he sauntered into the dance hall wearing his trademark fringed leather jacket, jeans, and tall boots. Eden was just a step behind him in an emerald silk gown trimmed with white lace. Nathan and Ken were dressed like gamblers in all black with blue silk vests, and they carried recording equipment.

"Y'all are just in time." She gestured toward the packed dance hall. "It's about time to start the dance contest."

Eden glanced around the room. "This is so festive. I love the costumes. And of course, the music is terrific. This will all live stream really well, and sound good on the radio."

"Thanks," Ivy said. "We worked hard to reach this point. I do appreciate your help this evening. Did the other events go well?"

"Great, as usual," Jack said. "Looks like you've got enough folks here to establish Wildcat Hall's Honky-Tonk Christmas as an annual event."

"Looks like it. And I'm really happy about it, too."

"You done good." Jack gave her his trademark sassy grin.

"You should be walking tall and proud." Eden pointed toward the band. "Do you want us to set up near the stage?"

"That'd be perfect. Jack, if you like, you can step up beside the band to announce the categories," Ivy said. "Craig is expecting you."

"Okay. Let's get 'er done," Jack said, straightening his shoulders and assuming his radio persona as he prepared to go onstage.

Ivy watched them walk away with a sense of satisfaction, then glanced back at the entry and realized she was instinctively looking for Slade. She straightened her shoulders just like Jack. She wasn't going to spend her evening waiting for Slade. She was going to dance, if she could find a partner, and enjoy Christmas Eve just like everyone else.

She watched as Jack, Eden, Nathan, and Ken set up to announce and live stream, appreciative of their professionalism and willingness to help their community.

Wildcat Jack stepped up on the stage so he could be better seen from the dance floor. "Listen up, all you wild and crazy dancers. Grab your partners and be ready to get out there, shake a leg, and make it count in the first annual dance contest of Wildcat Hall's Honky-Tonk Christmas."

Everyone clapped and crowded the dance floor.

"There's only one judge tonight, so you better impress her with your fancy moves. Eden Rafferty, your next-to-favorite DJ at the Wildcat Den." He pointed to Eden as she gave a curtsy to the crowd.

She leaned in toward the mic. "I believe you mean I'm their *favorite* DJ, don't you, Wildcat Jack?"

He gave a mock horrified expression. "Slip of the tongue." And he winked at the audience to let them know he knew he was really their favorite.

Eden stepped back, smiling and nodding.

"You know 'em. You love 'em. You can't live without 'em." Wildcat Jack flung out an arm toward the band, long fringe swaying. "Craig Thorne and his cowboy band are playing for us tonight. Give them a big round of applause."

The audience clapped, whistled, and stomped their boots.

"We're starting off the contest with an award that you surely are going to want to win. It's a doozy." He pointed toward the drummer and got a drum roll and a rim shot cymbal crash. "Here it is, folks. 'Couple most likely to end up wearing each other's boots.' Go for it!"

As the band hit the dancers with an upbeat number, Willie Nelson's "Whiskey River," everyone laughed as they swung into a fast two-step. Song after song, they danced, kicking up their heels, throwing back their heads, whirling each other around the dance floor.

Ivy watched from the sidelines, enjoying the fact that everyone was having so much fun. She tapped her toe to the music, wishing she were dancing, too, but so far no one had invited her and she didn't know anyone to ask.

As the music faded away, Wildcat Jack held up an envelope and waved it back and forth. "The winner of that contest gets a gift certificate to none other than Wildcat Hall!"

That brought another round of loud applause from the dancers.

"Eden, point out the winning couple, will you please?" Jack said.

She walked into the crowd and beckoned to a couple who clapped their hands in delight and ran forward. She leaned toward them, smiling, then whispered to Jack.

"Okay, folks. This lovely lady and gentleman are here all the way from Waco, Texas. Lottie and Elmer Sampson. Folks, put your hands together for them. They're the first winners of the 'Couple most likely to end up wearing each other's boots.' And, honey"—Jack leaned down—"those are mighty fine cowgirl boots with rhinestones and everything that you're wearing tonight. I wouldn't let this guy near them."

Everyone laughed and clapped as Eden handed the envelope to the winners and they melted back into the crowd.

"Now don't rest on your laurels, folks. You've got another chance to win coming up right now." Wildcat Jack pointed at the band and got another long drum roll and rim shot. "Are you ready? Here it comes—'Couple that shows best how the West was won.' Go for it!"

And the band played, the people danced, and Wildcat Jack swayed to the magic of the music while Nathan and Ken performed their own electronic magic, sending out images of Wildcat Hall to the world.

After a time, the music stopped again. Jack called up another couple. Eden presented the award, and everyone went back to dancing their hearts out.

Ivy watched it all, glad it was going so well but feeling more and more alone.

And then she wasn't alone anymore—Slade stood beside her, smiling that little quirk of his lips that lit up his blue eyes.

He leaned in close, so that she caught the scent of him, the power of him, the specialness of him. And she felt happiness race through her.

"You wanted to tell me something," he said. "I'm sorry I didn't listen. I've been kicking myself every minute since that time."

She glanced up into his eyes to make sure she'd heard him right. He looked absolutely sincere, but she still hesitated in case he rejected her again.

"I can't lose you." He clasped her hand and lifted it to his lips. He kissed her palm slowly, lingeringly, lovingly. "You're everything to me."

She felt the love she'd tried so hard to hold deep inside expand outward toward Slade, enveloping him, pulling him toward her. "I'd never sell Wildcat Hall Park to an outsider… someone who didn't know and love it like we do."

He smiled, love lighting up his eyes. "I know…I was just so scared you were going to leave me that I couldn't think straight."

"I'm not going anywhere."

"Good." He tugged her toward the center of the room, joining the throng of people. "Let's enjoy this dance we planned together."

As the band played a slow number, he took her in his arms, and she laid her head against his chest. This is where she belonged…not in some faraway city like Houston. As they continued to dance, lost in each other, they let the world slip away until there were only the two of them, despite the crowd around them.

When Craig sung the Willie Nelson classic "Always on My Mind," Slade nestled her closer, curling their hands together against his chest. "You know it's true," he said. "You're always on my mind…and you always will be."

She raised her head and looked up at him, feeling love expand her heart until she trembled with emotion. "You're always on my mind, too."

"I want you to know that…" he started to say but was cut off by Wildcat Jack calling out that they had another winner.

Ivy realized the music had stopped, but Slade continued to hold her, moving slightly as if they were still dancing to what was fast becoming their song.

"That's right, folks." Jack held up another envelope. "Eden's made her choice. There can be no questions about this one. She's right on the money. This is one special couple."

Eden walked over to Ivy and Slade, grinning from ear to ear. She pointed at them. "Folks," she called out, "meet Ivy Bryant and Slade Steele."

Ivy gave Slade a startled look, then shook her head at Eden. "I'm not supposed to win," she whispered.

Eden nodded, still grinning. "Please give a big shout-out to the winners of 'Couple most likely to soon be dancin' down the aisle.'"

Chapter 36

Ivy teetered on the edge of midnight between Christmas Eve and Christmas Day, between city and country, between past and present. She wanted to tip over the edge and grasp the other side with both hands…but not alone.

She glanced over at Slade. No, not alone.

He drove out of Wildcat Hall's parking lot, which was packed with vehicles of all makes, models, and sizes. He hit Wildcat Road and headed toward Steele Trap Ranch II, moonlight turning the pavement into a silver ribbon as if gift-wrapped for this special occasion.

"I feel guilty we didn't stay to see our Honky-Tonk Christmas through to the end," she said.

"We didn't have much choice."

"But—"

"After we won 'Couple most likely to soon be dancin' down the aisle,' it was all going to be downhill from there."

She rolled her eyes. "They practically kicked us out."

"Everybody knew you needed a break, so give yourself one, too."

"It's just that I like to complete what I start."

"Alicia was happy to take over for you. Jack and Eden needed no help. Craig and his cowboy band know what they're doing." He reached over and squeezed her hand.

"Bottom line, you got the ball rolling, and that's what counts. Let the others do their jobs now."

She leaned her head back against the seat, sighing in relief. "You won't get an argument from me."

"Good."

"We won everything, didn't we? The trail drive. The cattle rustlers. The Honky-Tonk Christmas."

"Yeah...but we won the most important thing on the dance floor."

She glanced over at him. "What's that?"

He smiled at her, then looked back at the road. "How soon do you want to go 'dancin' down the aisle'?"

"What do you mean?"

"I'm asking you to marry me. I figure I've been asking you to marry me since the moment I met you."

"You're asking me here and now?"

"Should I pull off the road and get down on a knee?"

"Don't be silly."

"I'm not. I'm as serious as I can be."

She looked at him, realizing this was it. He'd popped the question in his pickup truck on Wildcat Road. On one hand, it wasn't at all romantic, but on the other hand, it was just perfect. He was country...and now, so was she.

"It needs a lot of thought?"

She chuckled, leaning over and planting a kiss on his cheek. "It needs no thought at all. I'll marry you. And if you want, we can dance down the aisle together."

"Tell you the truth, the dance is optional, but the marriage isn't."

"I wouldn't have it any other way."

"Good. I got you a ring."

"Really?"

"Morning Glory said if I was getting you jewelry for Christmas I better make it an important piece."

"How important?" She smiled, enjoying teasing him.

"It's the next step after the belt buckle."

"That's pretty important."

"Better be. It's a lifetime commitment." He glanced at her. "I'm serious. It's all or nothing."

"Do you think I can't commit to you?"

"Your family does appear to have a few commitment issues."

"That's all in the past…at least, for me." She smiled, feeling her words go deep and lodge inside her.

He glanced at her again. "In that case, you get the ring."

"When?"

"At the ranch house…our home now."

"It's sort of half a house."

"Now that I've got a good reason, I'll get right to work on it."

"I can go quite a while on that bedroom and bath alone."

"That's where I'm taking you the minute we get there."

"The bath?"

"No. The bed."

"I might need some help getting out of this outfit." She smiled to herself, imagining him taking his time undressing her. "There's a corset, stockings, layers of petticoats, and—"

"Stop. You had me at corset. Any more and we won't make it home."

"I guess you'll just have to find out the rest for yourself."

"Can we play dance hall darling and her daring gunslinger?"

She swatted his arm, laughing. "I can see you're deter-mined to torment me tonight."

"Trust me, I'm just getting started."

"That's just it. I do trust you." And she was suddenly serious, because she did trust him—with her life and with her heart.

He reached over and squeezed her hand again. "You won't regret trusting me. I'll never let you down."

"I've got your back, too."

"Let's go dancin' down the aisle soon." He turned off Wildcat Road and drove under the sign for Steele Trap Ranch II.

He slowed down across from Fernando's favorite pond and pointed at it. "Looks empty, doesn't it?"

"I'm sorry to say there's no big, black bull relaxing in it." She felt a deep loss at the sight. "Storm's going to be terribly disappointed because he didn't make it back to the ranch."

"It's not Christmas Day yet."

"I know, but it's too close for comfort now."

"Everything's gone so well," he said. "I guess we can't have it all."

"I guess not, but so many people are counting on him."

"We've done the best we can do. It's all up to Fernando now. He'll make it back in time for Christmas...or he won't." Slade drove on up the road, leaving the empty pond behind them.

"Home," she whispered, almost to herself. "I'm really finally home."

"That's right." Slade stopped in front of the ranch house, where lights illuminated the rock walls and big windows, giving the building a warm, cozy, inviting appearance.

"It's beautiful here."

He turned to her. "It's not the house, the land, the cattle, the horses…or even Fernando. What makes this place home is *us*. As long as we're together, we're home."

"Oh, Slade, I do love you so." She reached over, tugged him toward her, and kissed his lips.

He lifted his head, looking at her with a smile. "It's about time I heard those words from you. I love you, too."

"Let's get up there to that big bed of yours."

"*Our* bed now."

Chapter 37

CHRISTMAS MORNING, A PHONE RINGTONE WOKE IVY from a deep, satisfied slumber. She cuddled closer to Slade's warm body, feeling wonderfully happy. He'd been true to his word the previous evening in slowly, carefully unwrapping her as if she were the best Christmas present ever, and then he'd given her the best of all gifts—love. She held up her left hand to the early morning light slipping through a slight gap in the drapes. She was almost dazzled by the sparkle of an emerald and diamonds in the ring on her left finger.

Slade grumbled as he sat up and grabbed his phone.

"Look out your front window," Oscar said, chuckling as Tater barked excitedly in the background.

"This better be good," Slade growled back.

"It's the best. Now take a look, get dressed, and get out here. All hell's about to break loose." And Oscar was gone.

"What was that?" Ivy asked, yawning.

"Merry Christmas." Slade leaned over and gave her a lingering kiss. "Oscar. Something's up."

"What?"

"Don't know." He walked over to the front window, pulled open the drapes so sunlight brightened the room, and looked outside. He blinked hard, grinned big, and turned to her. "You better come here."

"I'd hoped to sleep in with you today."

"Come on. It's worth it."

She sat up, grabbed his big robe, slipped it on, and walked over to him. She leaned against his side as he put an arm around her.

"Take a look."

She sleepily peered out the window and gasped at the sight. A big, black bull strode determinedly up the lane. He turned toward the pond, walked across short, golden grass, and eased into the water up to his belly. He lowered his head, drank deeply, and when he lifted his head, a green lily pad sat rakishly over one ear.

"Fernando made it home for Christmas." Slade chuckled in pleasure. "Wait till Storm finds out."

"Nothing could make her happier. I'm so happy, too. Fernando looks like he's all dressed up for Christmas with that green lily pad hat." Ivy hugged Slade excitedly before she danced across the room. "Did Oscar get the exact time?"

"Let me see." He hit speed dial.

"Where are you?" Oscar growled.

"Did you get the time?"

"Yep. 09:23:18."

"Thanks. We'll be right down." He disconnected as he looked at Ivy. "We've got the exact time, thanks to Oscar."

"Great. Do you suppose he was up all night waiting for Fernando?"

"Wouldn't doubt it. Tater, too."

"They're the best."

"You bet." Slade called another number and engaged speakerphone.

"Merry Christmas!" Sydney said.

"Merry Christmas to you too. Is Storm awake?"

"It's Christmas morning. She's been up since before dawn."

"I've got good news."

"Really? Are you truly calling to tell us Fernando made it home?"

"He's relaxing in his favorite pond as we speak."

Sydney let out a cowgirl yell of excitement. "Let me get Storm."

"Uncle Slade," Storm said breathlessly, "you wouldn't be kidding me, would you?"

"Not about something as important as Fernando. Merry Christmas."

"I knew he'd make it." Storm gave a loud yell like her mother's. "Everybody's got to know. Did you get the time?"

"Oscar got it."

"I'll dress and come right over. Fernando needs me."

"I don't want to worry you, but after all this time, he may not be in the best shape. I haven't been down to check on him."

"I won't worry. He's Fernando, the biggest, strongest, smartest bull in the whole wide world."

"That's right."

Ivy gave Slade a thumbs-up as she listened to the touching exchange. Now this Christmas was absolutely perfect.

"I'll call Jack and let him spread the news." Slade gave Ivy a smile as he grabbed his jeans.

"He'll want to interview me and Fernando," Storm said, "so I'll wear my new pink hat and jacket."

"Sounds good."

"Gotta go." And she clicked off.

Ivy walked over and hugged Slade again. "This is going to get big, isn't it?"

"It's already big. Now it gets bigger."

"I'll put up photos on Instagram. I can't even imagine the number of likes we'll get."

"Plenty." He hit speed dial again.

"I'm awake," Jack growled, "and enjoying a cup of coffee with a lovely lady. This had better be good. Wait! Do you mean to tell me—"

"He's cooling his feet in the pond right now."

"Well, I'll be. And this started out to be nothing more than a publicity stunt. Goes to show you can teach an old dog new tricks."

"I'll let Hedy know the exact time, so she can announce the name of the winner. Some lucky person is going to be very happy."

"I bet."

"And just so you know, KWCB has the exclusive on Fernando."

"Thank you. That means a lot."

"Y'all have been on it from the get-go, so you deserve it."

"Let me get hold of the gang. We'll be there in two shakes of a lamb's tail."

"Another thing," Slade said. "What do think about contacting Jennifer Sales? She's been supportive of Fernando and Wildcat Bluff on her news reports from the beginning."

"I'll do it," Jack said. "I know her. She's not just a pretty lady. She's smart as a whip. If she can, I bet she'll step out of the studio long enough to make a trip up here for an interview. If not, she might send somebody. If none of that, I'll send her our video to use on her station."

"Great," Slade replied. "See you in a bit." He looked out the window again, and sure enough, Fernando was still in the pond.

"News will spread fast now." Ivy slipped on jeans and a red sweater she'd left there, then topped those clothes with one of Slade's flannel shirts and rolled up the long sleeves.

He quickly pulled on clothes, watching her the entire time. "As much as I'm glad to have Fernando home, I'd planned to spend our morning in bed."

She grinned, seeing the heat in his eyes and returning it with a hot look of her own. She raised her left hand and flashed her engagement ring. "We'll have plenty of time later."

"Good thing. I've had about as much as I can take of stuff coming between us."

"There'll always be stuff, but we'll have the rest of our lives together."

He walked over, enfolded her in his arms, and held her tight for a long moment. "That thought is all that's holding me together right now."

"Come on." She picked up her phone, so she could catch Storm and Fernando's reunion for Instagram. "Let's go welcome Fernando home."

As they walked out the front door hand in hand, she looked up at a beautiful blue sky with a few fluffy, white clouds on a mild winter day. It was the perfect weather for the perfect day...and a perfect walk on the ranch.

When they reached the pond, Oscar and Tater were patiently waiting a respectful distance from Fernando.

"How's he look?" Slade asked, also keeping his distance from the massive bull.

"Far as I can tell, good." Oscar spit to one side. "But he's edgy."

"No wonder." Slade stepped closer, but Fernando swung his big head and snorted in irritation.

"Don't make him mad," Oscar said in warning. "We'll never get him in his barn, or at least not without a lot of trouble."

"I bet he's waiting for Storm," Ivy said. "That'll put him in a better mood."

"Feed is more likely to do the trick." Oscar took off his hat and rubbed his bald head.

Slade agreed. "That, too."

And as if the mention of Storm's name brought her to them, a pickup pulled up, a door opened, and she jumped out. "Fernando, you're home!"

As Storm ran toward the bull, Slade caught her and brought her up short. "Go slow. He's had a rough time of it. Most likely he's not in the best of moods."

Lula Mae and Sydney stepped down from the pickup and walked over to the pond with big smiles on their faces.

"Merry Christmas," Lula Mae said. "Storm never doubted, and here he is right back in his favorite spot."

"He's all decked out for Christmas. Just like me." Storm pointed at Fernando. "Look at his green hat."

"Wonder how he got that lily pad on top of his head," Sydney said.

"He looks so handsome." Storm glanced up at Slade. "Are you sure I can't go close to him?"

"Wait a bit. Jack and Eden are coming. Once the news gets out, others, too. He might get testy."

"I bet he's hungry." Storm reached out toward Fernando. "I've got your Christmas oats in the truck."

Fernando turned his head and looked at her, patience in his dark eyes, then he went back to contemplating the horizon.

When a pickup came roaring up the road and pulled to a stop, Jack, Eden, Nathan, and Ken jumped out, carrying recording equipment.

"I almost can't believe it," Jack said. "But there he is, big as life."

"I'm so excited we're the ones who get to announce on air that Fernando is back on his ranch." Eden gave a big grin all around. "Storm, please come a little closer so we can get you in the visual with Fernando. And of course, we want you to say a few words."

As Wildcat Jack, Eden, and Storm moved closer to the pond, Fernando glanced toward them but made no move to leave the water. Nathan and Ken started recording and live streaming to the world.

Ivy raised her phone to capture this special moment, realizing that she was now part of this loving Steele Family, and she couldn't have been happier about it.

"I always knew Fernando would be home for Christmas," Storm said, looking into the camera with a sincere expression. "He's the biggest, smartest, handsomest bull in the whole wide world."

"How do you feel about him being back?" Eden asked.

"Happy." Storm glanced at Slade. "It's just that Fernando is all I wrote on my Christmas list this year."

Slade stepped into camera range. "You want Fernando for Christmas?"

Storm bobbed her head up and down, pink cowgirl hat catching the morning sunlight. "Uncle Slade, do you think he could come live with me? He needs me...and well, I need him, too."

Ivy felt Storm's words tug at her heart. Maybe the big

bull had been lonely in his own barn and pasture except when Storm came to visit him. She stopped recording, stepped up, and put a hand on Slade's arm. "I think it's a wonderful idea."

He glanced down at her, then looked over at Lula Mae and Sydney. "What do y'all think of this idea?"

"That's all she asked for this year," Lula Mae said. "That's how much he means to her."

"It'd just require moving him from one ranch to the other," Sydney added. "It's doable."

"We could fix up a barn and pasture for him," Lula Mae said in encouragement.

"I'll take really good care of him." Storm sent Slade a beseeching look with her big blue eyes.

"Okay." Slade smiled at his niece. "Merry Christmas, Storm. Fernando is all yours."

"Yay!" She threw herself into Slade's arms, hugged him hard, then hugged Ivy, too, before she raced back to Eden and Jack.

"Thanks," Lula Mae said, grinning.

"And that, cowgirls and cowboys everywhere, is how you make a little girl happy for Christmas." Wildcat Jack looked at the camera with a twinkle in his brown eyes.

"Fernando made his way home against great odds," Eden said. "And he gets his reward...not just oats but his friend, too."

"Once more, this is Wildcat Jack and Eden Rafferty coming to you live from Steele Trap Ranch II on Christmas morning. If you're just now tuning in, we know what's uppermost in your minds. Will Fernando get home for Christmas?" Jack gestured, fringe on his jacket swinging as he pointed to the pond and the black bull standing there. "Well, I'm here to tell you that Fernando made it home for Christmas."

"That's right, Fernando is home for Christmas," Eden chimed in. "And we have more good news for you. Storm, who you've all come to know and love, just had her Christmas wish come true. Fernando is going home with her.

"Storm, would you like to say something else to our viewers?" Eden asked.

"Fernando and I want to thank all of you out there for believing in him. He's home now for good." Storm gestured toward the big bull, who raised his head and looked at her. "Everybody wanted him to return home safely," Storm said. "And me most of all."

Ivy put her hand over her heart, almost overcome with the emotional impact of it all as she heard a pickup head up the lane. Behind it came more vehicles of all shapes and sizes. Obviously, Wildcat Bluff was descending on the ranch to share Christmas with Fernando.

Hedy exited her special van in her wheelchair accompanied by Bert and Bert II. She zoomed up to Wildcat Jack and Eden while they hung back with all the well-wishers who were slamming doors and descending on the pond.

Eden smiled at her friend and gestured her closer. "Hedy Murray has joined us with what I'd guess is a very special announcement."

"Indeed." Hedy smiled at the camera. "Wildcat Bluff Fire-Rescue is ready to reveal the name of the person who guessed to the closest second the time Fernando arrived home on Christmas Day."

"Please don't keep us in suspense." Wildcat Jack leaned forward as if in great anticipation.

Hedy gave him a quick nod. "Oscar and Tater clocked Fernando's entrance to Steele Trap II at 9:23 and eighteen seconds this morning."

"And who is our lucky winner?"

Hedy looked out over the big group that had gathered around her. They wore ranch clothes with colorful bits and pieces of Christmas finery, like red Santa hats, green sweaters, jingle bell pins, and even mistletoe tucked into cowboy hats.

"Please, Hedy, don't keep us in suspense any longer," Wildcat Jack said with a chuckle.

She smiled before she gestured toward the two men standing near her. "Bert Holloway Two."

Bert Two appeared completely surprised but took off his rancher hat to reveal his thick, dark hair as he gave her a smile. "Thank you so much, but I can't accept such a generous gift. I only intended to support Wildcat Bluff Fire-Rescue...and, of course, Fernando."

"In that case," Hedy said, continuing to smile, "what would you like us to do with your winnings?"

"I believe the creative arts department at Wildcat Bluff High could put those gift certificates to good use. I'm a strong supporter. Please give them to the department with my best wishes for Christmas."

Hedy gave him a big grin, then turned back to Jack and Eden. "There you have it, folks. The spirit of Christmas is alive and well in Wildcat Bluff."

"Thank you. I'm sure Wildcat Bluff High will be most appreciative." Wildcat Jack looked out over his audience. "And now, let's not keep Storm from her Christmas gift any longer."

Sydney walked over to her pickup, opened the back door, and pulled out a shiny silver bucket of oats. She handed the bucket to her daughter.

Storm held up the bucket to the camera and then she turned to Fernando with a big grin on her face. She shook the bucket so the oats rattled inside it.

Fernando's head snapped up.

"Come on, Fernando. Let's go home. It's time for you to celebrate Christmas with me."

Fernando sniffed the air, looked at Storm, and walked out of the pond, dripping water all the way with the lily pad still balanced on his head.

Storm shook the bucket again, then headed down the lane with Fernando following in her wake.

"Now that is truly a Christmas miracle," Wildcat Jack said in his deep voice. "The littlest cowgirl tames the biggest bull with nothing more than a heart of gold."

"That's right. Love conquers all...particularly at Christmas." Eden focused on the camera again. "From all of us here at KWCB, we wish you a very Merry Christmas. And please return to us for future updates about Fernando. For now, we return you to our regular programming."

Ivy sniffed, feeling tears of happiness gather in her eyes while she watched Storm lead Fernando to his new home.

"Is she going to take him all the way?" Slade asked, looking in concern at his niece.

"Let's give them a little time together," Lula Mae said. "Sydney will walk behind them. Oscar can help me get a trailer and pick them up in a bit."

"I'd better go, too."

"No." Lula Mae glanced at Ivy. "You're needed here."

Jack walked up to them. "Great stuff. Oats were a good touch. She'd never have gotten him to follow her otherwise."

"Maybe," Lula Mae said. "Maybe not. You know as well as I do that animals have their own minds…and they know their own."

"So true," Sydney replied. "Come on. Let's don't let them get too far ahead."

As Lula Mae and Sydney left to follow Storm, the crowd slowly started to disperse, laughing and talking happily among themselves.

Ivy slipped her hand into Slade's as she watched everyone load up and head out, finally leaving the lane empty. The pond was empty, too, almost as if Fernando had never been there.

"I guess I lost the bull after all," Slade said thoughtfully.

"But you made a little girl happy."

"Yeah. I couldn't ask for more." He snuggled Ivy close. "Let's get up to the house. It's time to make us happy."

She smiled at him. "It's truly been a Christmas of miracles."

Wildcat Hall Recipes

Texas Tea Cakes (sugar cookies)

- 1 cup butter
- 1 cup granulated sugar
- 2 ¼ cups flour
- 1 egg
- 1 teaspoon baking soda
- 1 teaspoon cream of tartar
- 1 teaspoon vanilla extract

In a large bowl, combine all ingredients using a handheld mixer. Chill dough thoroughly. Mold into walnut-size balls. Place on ungreased cookie sheet. Press with bottom of glass dipped in sugar. Bake about ten minutes at 350 degrees.

Cowboy Cookies

See Texas Tea Cakes recipe above.
Add whiskey to taste.

Book Chili from Carolyn Brown's
The Red-Hot Chili Cook-Off

- 1 gallon commercial chili
- ½ cup Worcestershire sauce
- 4 tablespoons liquid smoke
- 2 cans chili beans
- 8 ounces chopped jalapeño peppers
- 6 teaspoons chili powder
- 6 teaspoons Cajun seasoning
- 1 gallon bag of cooked hamburger meat
- 1 large milk chocolate candy bar

Mix all ingredients in large pot and bring to a boil.

Corn Fritters from Sabine Starr's
Belle Gone Bad

- 1 cup flour
- 1 cup cornmeal
- 1 teaspoon baking powder
- 1 pinch salt
- 1 tablespoon honey (or sugar/sugar substitute)
- 2 eggs, beaten
- 1 one-pound can creamed corn
- 1 cup milk
- 2 tablespoons butter

Mix the first four (dry) ingredients in one bowl. Mix the last five (wet) ingredients in another bowl. Add wet to dry and stir until moistened. Pour ¼ cup at a time onto oiled, sizzling hot griddle or skillet, and brown on both sides, turning once. Makes about fifteen fritters.

Texas Pecan Pie

- 1 cup Karo syrup (light or dark)
- 3 large eggs
- 1 cup pecans
- ¾ cup white sugar
- 2 tablespoons melted butter
- 1 teaspoon vanilla extract
- Dash of salt
- 8-inch unbaked piecrust

In a large bowl, beat eggs slightly. Add sugar, syrup, and salt. Stir in butter and vanilla. Add pecans. Pour in pie crust. Bake approximately 45 minutes in 350 degree oven.

Acknowledgments

Once upon a time, Carolyn Brown and I were eating ice cream and discussing books when I mentioned my upcoming novel about a bull-riding cowboy cook. We got excited talking about recipes that I might include in the book—and that got her thinking about a funny scene with a chili recipe in her *The Red-Hot Chili Cook-Off*. She offered that recipe for this book, so I took her up on it and had fun weaving her recipe into the storyline. Here's a big shout-out to Carolyn for her generosity.

Sabine Starr thought her old-timey, yummy corn fritters from *Belle Gone Bad* would fit right into this book, so lots of thanks to her for sharing her delicious recipe.

On a cool afternoon in East Texas, Shirley Praetor Whiteside and Wanda Barton Barber happily discussed recipes that might fit into this book. They came up with cowboy cookies and Texas tea cakes. Many thanks go to both of them.

For my Tater, I borrowed the name of Darmond Gee's blue heeler cow dog that always rides shotgun in his pickup. Christina Gee's Aussie cow dog named Sweetheart inspired me—he might be the runt of the litter, but he's big in spirit, just like my Tater.

Bull rider Milton Snow trained with champion Freckles Brown in Soper, Oklahoma, and gave me excellent advice. When I asked him about his bull-riding days, he said in his easygoing, modest way, "Well, I tried to ride bulls...and there are some tough ones you never forget."

Special thanks go to Sylvia McDaniel, bestselling and beloved author, for the suggestion of a contemporary trail drive during a fun lunch.

As always, I'm grateful to the cowboys and cowgirls of Gee Cattle Ranch—Brandon, Christina, Luke, Lank, Logan, and Laren. Not only did they feed me, but they were also instrumental in making Fernando a larger-than-life bull.

Oodles of thanks go to R. A. Jones, terrific comic and novel author, for the outstanding titles in my Wildcat Hall Dance Contest. At one time, R. A. and I judged dance contests together at conventions in Dallas, and he always came up with the absolute best titles...and still does.

About the Author

Kim Redford is the bestselling author of Western romance novels. She grew up in Texas with cowboys, cowgirls, horses, cattle, and rodeos. She divides her time between homes in Texas and Oklahoma, where she's a rescue cat wrangler and horseback rider—when she takes a break from her keyboard. Visit her at kimredford.com.

Also by Kim Redford

Smokin' Hot Cowboys
A Cowboy Firefighter for Christmas
Blazing Hot Cowboy
A Very Cowboy Christmas
Hot for a Cowboy